NO PLACE
LIKE HOME

Other Books by Ben Gilbert
The World Peace Journals
Mumbo Jumbo

NO PLACE LIKE HOME

BEN GILBERT

Other Books by Ben Gilbert
The World Peace Journals
Mumbo Jumbo

GARUDA BOOKS

Published by Garuda Books
First edition: September 2013
Second edition: August 2017

Cover Design by Paola Minelli
Interior Formatting by Paul Salvette

CONTENTS

My bones are black, all burnt and cracked
Beached upon a shore.
As birds pick at my tattered frame
My soul screams out for more.

1.

MAWJI'S PAY DAY

West Africa, 28th August 1968

'THIS YOURS?'

The girl nodded but didn't take the backpack. She just stood there, vacant and bewildered, as the first rays of sunlight caught her eyes. The noise of a vehicle broke the early morning silence and Mawji felt the need to move.

'Come on, my boat's over there.'

Taking her by the arm, he walked her to the end of the old pontoon where his dinghy took them out to Jaffa, bobbing in the early morning breeze.

He had started to anchor Jaffa away from the pontoons and quay since nervous soldiers had begun to fill the port – tough looking men had recently drifted in from the country looking for work or, more likely, trouble and money. He worried he'd wake up to a knife and some ugly face with that look in its eye. Better to sleep in peace and anchor further out.

ABOUT FORTY MINUTES before he met the girl, Mawji had woken to the familiar sounds of loose rigging flapping in the wind, the odd bark from a stray dog and the lapping tide against nearby empty boats, all indicating the start of another long and languid day. As light broke and gulls started their endless screeching, he stepped down to the dinghy and headed for the quay.

Stretching on the old wooden pontoon, Mawji yawned and started to cross the quayside towards his ramshackle bar that lay across the small square in front of him. Eyeing a solitary backpack by a stack of lobster pots, he stopped and purposefully glanced around. Something wasn't right, not just the backpack – something cut through him, some sense of what this place was capable of, and he instantly threw off his early morning fog.

Through the pot webbing, he could see the silhouette of a man.

Sensing trouble, Mawji casually took out a cigarette from the pack in his shirt pocket and lit it, taking a long inhalation before moving into the square and ducking out of sight behind a solitary parked car. He waited and listened. A few moments passed before he heard a muffled cry and the scrapping of feet on gravel. Probably another stray tourist being mugged, robbed of all, to be left broke, bruised and dejected after all the police stuff and dull paperwork.

He moved silently back to the quayside and along the water's edge under the shadow of some broken timber fishing sheds. Crossing the pontoon gangplank, he arrived behind the lobster pots where he had heard the noises. At a particular shrill squawking of the gulls, he made his move. The scene that unfolded wasn't what he had expected and Mawji momentarily froze.

Dark gnarled fingers clasped hard over the girl's mouth; the other hand held a knife and was pulling at her clothes. Down on the gravel, neither had seen Mawji, as he scoured the harbour junk for a handy weapon. On seeing a piece of rusty trawler chain, he grabbed it, noisily lifting it from the ground. The rattle and a chink instantly disturbed the man who was quick to his feet, crazed looking and heading for Mawji, knife in hand. One clout sent him back, reeling and crashing to the ground. Mawji had seen this one hanging around outside the bar. He had a nasty scar across one cheek that made him stand out, but they were all the same to him — bad news.

The girl, now sitting up, was silently sobbing, her frightened face half hidden by thick brown hair and suntanned hands. Her skirt was hitched up and Mawji stared. She looked up and he looked away embarrassed, focusing on the man who was getting to his feet, clasping his wounded face and eyeing Mawji for an exit. Mawji flicked his head to say get out of here and he stumbled across the square into the early morning shadows.

'Guess I got here in the nick of time.'

He looked straight into her blue eyes this time. He knew this girl. She was from the old Mission up on the hill. Her folks were still around bashing their bibles to whoever might listen, except the Mission had been burnt down like most things up there. The few people left, etched out their days struggling to survive, remembering a glory time when life was good and the sun always seemed to shine.

He had never spoken to her before.

Looking down and covering herself, she said:

'He nearly...'

She hesitated. Mawji, not wanting to hear the next word to be reminded of something bad, noisily dropped the chain and fetched the backpack, presenting it to the girl as she was standing up, smoothing down her long skirt. Her jacket was ripped and some buttons missing on her blouse.

OVER THE HILLS behind the port, at around the same time Mawji pulled the starter cord of the dinghy motor to take the girl to his boat, a man stumbled across a shallow stream and into a pitch-black forest. Darkness cocooned him and he stopped to take a gulp of air. The oppressive heavy air of the wet forest had him quickly panicking, dashing back towards the light, out of the trees and gasping for breath.

On the other side of the stream lay the reason for his flight. In the glimmer of dawn, he could make out the half-wrecked car, engine still running and standing inches away from a fall into the stream. Next to the car by the open driver's door was his friend, lying face up in the soft mud.

A moment of terrible realisation was broken by the sudden splutter of the dying engine as the ashen face, looking across the stream towards his dead friend, called out:

'Ralph?'

Only an eerie silence answered back.

Bewildered by the unforeseen, he stared questioningly at his friend's lifeless eyes, which not so long ago had been full of verve, daring and the foolish wisdom of those who think they know. He knew he was no different from his friend, seemingly invincible and dancing with angels on every hairpin bend during their perilous nighttime dash.

He looked up at the forest slope to where the car had left the road, slicing through the thick green undergrowth without hitting a tree. Acting with unnatural intensity, he crossed the stream, took the keys from the ignition and opened the trunk, taking out a backpack, rifle and spare magazine. He removed the fuel cap and stuffed an oily rag down the open pipe.

Grabbing Ralph by the shoulders, he sat him up against the running board by the open door. Anguish momentarily showed on his face as he searched through his dead friend's pockets to find a passport and an air ticket. By the time he had put these documents into his own pocket and was standing up, the distant hum of car engines broke the silence, telling him his pursuers had found their getaway and were closing fast.

Ferocity soon overtook sentiment and he roughly bundled his friend back into the driver's seat before slamming the door shut. Ralph stared out from behind the wheel as he lit the oily rag.

Like a man who had finally found god after many years of searching and disillusionment, he assuredly hurried up toward hazy crags along the edge of the shallow streambed. The absurd picture of a man formally dressed for dinner, carrying a heavy rifle and a backpack was soon lost as billows of smoke rose from the burning car.

BACK AT THE PORT on board Jaffa, the girl stood staring out to sea across the harbour entrance into the shimmering reflections of the turning tide. She had changed below, taken an age, and had then appeared on deck to watch Mawji prepare some tackle for a fishing charter. It had been difficult for her to move away from her shock, and focus on what had happened after he left her alone in the cabin. She had instinctively locked the door but was unable to remove her clothing until the realisation of being on a boat and away from the quay with some semblance of safety permeated her frightened body. She now watched this odd man not much older than herself, watched his careful movements, strong body in old smelly clothes, his handsome, strangely mixed exotic features with black hair, unkempt and crudely slicked back, and his nervous sharp eyes, constantly looking around so not to miss a thing. They hadn't exchanged a word since leaving the quay; she had simply followed him. As she was about to say something, he looked up and grinned, a smile that she would have normally found endearing. However, she felt the cold chill of evil run through her. She now remembered him. His rugged features had terrified half the town for the last year or so. She was on Mawji's boat and needing to get off.

Her stiff body and pensive thin face spoke of who he was, how he was judged and how he was bad news.

Instantly aware of what she was thinking, he stood up and put his hands in his pockets.

'Guess I'd better take you home,' he said calmly, trying to smile in a way he had long forgotten.

'Thank you...'

She fumbled with her words, with taboo names she had often heard and grown used to but knew she couldn't use.

'Freak! If that's what ya thinking...'

He instantly regretted his meanness and struggled with the rising tide of hate that had started to consume him.

She looked away, flushed with a mixture of confusion, embarrassment and fear.

Agitated, he took his hands out of his pockets and placed them on the boat rail. He stared far out to sea. Wanting the girl gone, he also felt some kind sympathy he dared not show.

Turning back, he caught her eye. She stared back, composed herself, and in a low voice, coldly said:

'I know who you are. Just drop me at the quay.'

Mawji faced her and let out his suppressed steam in one continuous barrage:

'Are you crazy? Scar Face is still out there. He'll be wanting some revenge, some kind of payback from one of us.

Maybe in a week, after he's done a whole slew of new bad stuff or maybe locked up or maybe dead will you be forgotten and it safe for you to walk the quay and town alone.'

'Then take me to the police station.'

He felt relief, knowing he'd soon be shot of her.

'If you think it will do you any good.'

She followed Mawji to the metal ladder and lowered her backpack to him in the dinghy. He looked up momentarily as he took the pack, dropping it onto the salt bleached seat before opening the choke and pulling the cord several times to start the motor. They were soon at the quay and heading across the now busy square into the narrow, dirty streets of the port. He pulled out a pack of cigarettes and a box of matches from his shirt pocket and paused for the light.

'Stay close to me. What were you doing at the quay so early?'

The noisy throngs of people bustling through the small port helped bring her confidence back and she raised her voice so he would hear her above the crowd.

'I had a row with my mother and wanted to catch the ferry to visit friends in the city.'

'At dawn! That must have been some row.'

She noticed that people avoided them, gave them a wide berth, and she soon found herself becoming angry with the man who had saved her.

'That's not your business.'

'That's for sure. Why don't you give your friends a call, get them to come up and fetch you.'

'There're not those kinds of friends.'

'What kind are they?'

The girl stayed silent and Mawji knew he wasn't going to get anymore out of her.

Having stopped outside the entrance of the grubby, ramshackle police building, they stood facing each other.

He gave an awkward smile, flattened his hair back and started to walk back the way they had come.

'Aren't you coming in with me?'

Mawji looked back and smirked.

'Nope.'

The girl was incensed.

'What kind of coward are you?'

'The kind who knows what's good for him,' he shouted, disappearing into the crowd.

HIS BAR OVERLOOKED the port from the east side of the square. As usual, it was empty. The lean, dark scrawny looking barman nonchalantly gazed at Mawji who took a seat at the long wooden bar, which had long lost its lustre along with everything else in the place.

'Black coffee Joey. What a morning!'

Mawji gave him a cursory glance before looking out across the square to Jaffa anchored near the harbour entrance.

'I heard, it's the talk around here. Scar Face is pretty pissed – you messed up his good side. Best let him cool down.'

'He had a good side?'

They both smiled.

'Never been too smart that Mission Girl.'

'Probably preaching to the inspector as we speak. Got him on his knees, singing alleluia.'

Both men laughed loudly at this absurdity and Mawji forgot the morning and his mixed up feelings.

'Did that fishing charter turn up yet? Said he'd be here today.'

'Not come nor called. Maybe he'll come tomorrow.'

'More likely to have got cold feet.'

Mawji slapped some cash on the counter.

'Better take some beer, in case he turns up.'

Mawji carried the crates across the square towards the floating pontoon. He eyed the thugs and layabouts who always gathered around the quay looking for work or some easy money. They didn't bother with him and Mawji felt the incident was probably already history.

MEANWHILE, in the police lobby, the grimy walls, once brilliantly whitewashed, were grey and greasy. The overhead fan whirred and turned at a slow hypnotic pace, casting annoying and flickering shadows throughout the small room. Dried blood specked the dirty concrete floor. A few well-worn wooden chairs lined one wall and a beat up counter, much like a well-used hotel check-in desk, ran along the back wall. Behind it was an office in semi darkness. A guard sat on the first chair near the front door. He was drunk and she could smell the alcohol on his breath as he silently watched her through bloodshot eyes. An old rifle lay across his lap and the shadows of the fan opened and closed his fey face. The room was lit and aired by a small glassless window, like the type you might find in an old brick barn, and through the hole, she saw the glisten of brilliant blue sea.

She felt oppressed and gasped.

'Hello?'

A moment passed.

'Hello?'

Another uncomfortable moment passed before she nervously turned to face the drunken cop for some semblance of law and order, but he just stared, saying nothing between the moving shadows.

She turned away from the disturbing image and back to the counter where an imposing figure now stood. Eyes of furious brown pierced into her.

Yet another moment of silence, a silence so thick she could feel it like sticky glue, clinging and transfixing her to this awful place.

She turned and fled into the street, leaving behind the nasty sounds of two men laughing.

IT WAS LATE MORNING when Mawji moored Jaffa to the fuel dock. Instinct told him to fill the tanks. He had collected supplies – food, fresh water, bait – checked the engines, pumps, tools, radio and anything else he could think of until he was satisfied he had all things sorted for a good few days' fishing or more. Hoping his charter would turn up so he could make some money, out at sea where no one could trouble him, he looked out across the small harbour with its rusty gantry and broken pontoons. Small boats dotted the water and, at the far end of the harbour where the square and bar lay, was the lopsided ferry puffing black fumes and slowly chugging out to sea. It was packed, overloaded with people and their chattel leaving the decay of this once pretty port to find a new beginning. The deep whistle of the ferry echoed across the vast seascape and Mawji looked up across the town to the hill with its silhouette of a burnt out church fiercely visible against the bright morning sky, and then to the long horseshoe ridge in the distance that effectively cut the port off from the rest of the country. He remembered a time when the church was surrounded by green and the bells always rang on Sunday – sounds of a time gone; and now, when he lay in his bunk at night, he only heard the noise of desperation that he was somehow part of.

He looked at the pump hand and then to the hill above the town.

'Fill her up, got a funny feeling about today.'

Mawji left Jaffa at the fuel dock and walked towards the square, heading for the bar.

'BEER JOEY.'

'Hear what happened on the hill?'

'Nope, and I don't rightly care.'

Mawji blanked his mind.

'You got company. She's been waiting a while now, asking questions.'

Mawji saw the girl standing at the end of the bar and his heart sank. He studied her for a moment, saw tired red eyes in a pretty face looking rough and right at him, but she still had that look of high and mighty indifference that left him cold.

'You left me at the station.'

'You're not my business. You said it yourself.'

He looked up at Joey.

'What ya tell her?'

'That you like the smell of fish.'

'You're not me, and if you was, you wouldn't mind the smell of fish. In fact I like the smell of fish.'

Mawji slammed his bottle down hard on the counter.

'Jesus!'

The girl focused on the two men. They seemed indifferent to her presence, her plight. They were men without others. Maybe they had each other in some way she could not understand, but they were men who had abandoned the world she knew. Even though she lived a short walk away from their world, she didn't understand anything about it. Her mother had warned her about such men.

These were men without souls.

'They laughed at me.'

Both men turned towards the girl. Mawji stared hard at her. This was the second time today he felt emotions well up from the deep and he started ranting:

'That police inspector is so mean, I'm surprised he even knows how to laugh anymore. There was a time he was full of liberty….'

'And freedom,' Joey added quickly.

'Ranting and raving.'

'This revolution.'

'That revolution.'

The two men stopped and looked at each other with memories in their eyes.

Mawji turned to the girl.

'He was a good guy once. I loathe him now.'

'He loathes you too,' Joey added, smiling.

'Things went bad. He's sure not gonna help me any more than I'm gonna help him…and he's sure not gonna help you.'

She stared back with tears and a fury that startled him.

'He had me and Joey running up and down the coast and creeks god knows how many times…'

He broke in mid sentence, eyeing the girl edgily.

'Never heard you complain on pay day,' Joey said nonchalantly.

'What is it with you?'

Mawji turned away from the girl, finished his beer and slammed it on the bar.

'Give me another.'

Joey opened and handed him a bottle, leaning over the bar while the girl looked on with disbelief.

Mawji grabbed the bottle and turned back to the girl.

'What the hell are you doing here anyway?'

'Police told Scar Face where to find her. Bust up her house.'

'How'd ya know that?'

'Inspector told me.'

'So he's a drinking buddy now?'

'Gives me no trouble. I gotta listen, right?'

'Jesus Joey.'

'I need somewhere safe to go,' the girl butted in.

'What has that got to do with me?'

'You helped me before.'

'So go to the city. There's a coaster leaving tonight. You couldn't get off my boat fast enough once the penny dropped.'

The girl looked despondently at the floor and then looked up.

'I lied. I don't know anyone there. We don't have money or friends since the uprising.'

Mawji took a drink.

'Join the club.'

'My mother said you would help.'

'The Preacher Woman?'

Mawji looked at Joey.

'There's a room upstairs.'

'I don't need that trouble.'

'So you agree…it's nothing but trouble.'

'You only know trouble and fish.'

'Trouble and fish don't mix.'

'And she said if you refused, to tell you – Maya.'

Mawji looked deep into his empty beer.

MUCH LATER, over the high ridge behind the port, the man pushed up along a narrow stony ledge set between the stream's steep bank and dense forest. The long afternoon shadows from tall trees and the constant hum of a helicopter told him the day was running out and his pursuers on his heels.

Late afternoon brought a clear still sky; the day had been hot and he was exhausted.

Taking the water bottle from the pack, he drank slowly whilst scouring the complicated landscape of his escape, in particular to the stream tumbling down from the shadows of the jagged crags above.

He booby trapped the backpack and left it by the stream. Opting to travel light, he only took the rifle, spare magazine and water bottle. Dropping into the streambed, he headed up towards imposing rock walls.

A little later, as the valley steepened under the rocky cliffs below the ridge, the forest petered out. Realising he would soon be in the open and totally exposed, he chose to follow a small overgrown gully, edging up towards a small gap he had noticed in the rocks.

An explosion made him stop. Breathing hard from fear and exertion, a bead of sweat rolled down his dirty brow. As a dog barked from the stream below, he felt the drawn out wait of the inevitable, exaggerated by a foul metallic taste in his dry mouth.

Scanning the darkening cliffs looming in the fading light, he heard the crackle of a walkie-talkie radio. A moment later, a shot rang out, the whine of the passing bullet sounding close before the whir of the helicopter made him push frantically from one sharp boulder to the next.

The guns of the helicopter strafed the craggy mountain-side, showering the fleeing man with rocky debris, before circling around to continue its barrage of destruction; but he had already made it through the gap, disappearing into tangles of undergrowth.

Listening to his furious heartbeat and wiping sweat from his stinging eyes, he moved on into the enveloping darkness and down towards the lights below.

MAWJI, HAVING HEARD the sounds of the helicopter somewhere over the imposing ridge and having seen a column of troops moving towards the port along the main highway, figured it safer to anchor the boat further out to sea. Jaffa now sat well outside the harbour entrance, away from any chance of being hit by stray gunfire.

The girl sat in the bridge looking far out to the horizon. She seemed serene. As Mawji eyed her thoughtfully, he again regretted his meanness but wanted out of the complications she had brought.

'We need to talk.'

She smiled knowingly, her candid features melding with something Mawji didn't understand anymore.

'Don't you want to know my name?'

'Hell no! Why make trouble? Let's keep this simple.'

Running his hand over his head to flatten his oily hair, Mawji said, thoughtfully:

'In a couple of days or so, when things have settled down a bit I'll take you back to the Mission.'

'Until then?'

'You can stay on board. I've got a charter, they should have come today, maybe tomorrow, so best you learn it if you're gonna work it.'

'Work it!'

The girl got up and stared at Mawji, her blue eyes horrified.

Mawji grinned. His meanness, although toned down somewhat, still blazed unabashed.

'Yeah work it. If I don't use you, I need to hire one of those layabouts on the quayside to run the chores, tie the baits, make the food. You can set a rig, right?'

'What about your friend Joey?'

'He hates fish. Likes money though,' Mawji laughed, eyeing the girl.

'I can tie a shoe lace.'

'Then you can tie a bait.'

He gestured to the boat.

'I'll show you round, not much to it. This is the bridge, below are the guest quarters. You take the berth at the back, same one you used this morning.'

The girl nodded as they strolled along the main deck with Mawji animatedly pointing and explaining different parts of the boat. She could see he loved the boat and now had an easy air about him, as if the problems of the day just stayed on shore.

She understood none of it.

Jaffa was a large refitted fishing boat, which currently looked like an old, small dirty passenger ferry. It had two powerful inboard motors, too large considering Mawji only steered the coastline and deeper creeks. The girl knew this boat had seen different days. Her parents had spoken a lot about the man whom the locals now called nasty names and loved to vilify, of his skills on the ocean and how he had had respect until the uprising. But the horror of this man's acts had erased any good that people might remember and she blanked her mind – she didn't want to think about that right now. This was temporary, and after all, he had pulled her from that ugly hyena's jaw.

'I'll leave you to it. Look around, make yourself at home.'

'Who's Maya?' She asked rashly, needing to know.

'My sister...'

Mawji gazed out to sea and leant against the rail.

She stood inside her cabin taking it all in slowly, trying to understand her new, albeit temporary, home. It was a large berth, enough to sleep four people, with one double and two single bunks, some closed cupboards, portholes on two sides and a large series of windows along the back. It was larger and cleaner than she imagined. She had visualised a filthy, squalid boat, rusty and neglected. However, she had met with something different and, if she had not known his history, she could have almost liked Mawji.

Stepping into the toilet, she met with her original vision. Slamming the door shut and gagging on the foul air, she instantly headed for the deck.

Mawji heard the door bang, flicked his cigarette into the wind and turned away from the rail, sardonically mouthing:

'Been meaning to clean it out for some time, you might as well do it now. You'll find the gear down there somewhere.'

The girl sighed. She would accept her lot for now.

'Don't take it so bad – you might even get to like Jaffa.'

'Jaffa's not the problem.'

Mawji's smile turned into the wide knowing grin.

'Why do you have such a large boat? It's not really a tourist charter.'

'Nope, it was my father's, we used to fish commercially.'

'So why not still fish?'

'You ask too many dumb questions. You try getting a crew in this lousy port. You try selling fish to people who have no money. You try getting a permit without bribes. It all sucks now.'

'Sorry, I didn't know.'

'Sure you know! You're dying to get out…desperate if you need my help. Your folks know the changes. It's different for each of us…you remember the big farms, the shoots, the parties, holidays in Europe, fancy people with no real worries. Now you have nothing, not even your church.'

'That wasn't my life, and they weren't my people! Mine was the Mission.'

'So why aren't you doing the Lord's work with your Mom, hanging on to the bitter end up on that cursed hill.'

'And why are you so mean, what gives you the right to judge others and why are you hanging on to your own bitter twisted end?'

She paused briefly.

'Is it true what they say about you? Did you do all those heinous things?'

Angry and upset, she looked at him furiously through tears.

Maybe she would go if he told the truth.

'Sure it's true, all of it true.'

She burst into tears.

'You bastard, how could you?'

'With ease,' he said, turning back to the empty ocean view.

A few minutes passed and the girl stopped crying. Mawji was looking at the setting sun. He felt twisted up inside, full of the hate he had tried to forget.

He heard her voice, a voice that reminded him of his sister.

'Why are you helping me?'

'I need a deckhand,' he lied.

'I don't have the right clothes.'

'I knew you were trouble.'

LATER THAT EVENING, Mawji and the girl sat in the bridge. The radio chattered softly in the background. He had fallen asleep in an old tattered armchair and the girl watched him sway with the gentle movements of the sea as his arms hung languidly by his sides. The tranquillity of his sea life was apparent, a long shot away from the stories she had heard. Behind him, through the rain that had started trickling down the windows, she could see the glisten of town lights. She had changed into an old pair of baggy khaki trousers and a grimy orange coloured oilskin jacket and was adjusting these ill-fitting clothes when the radio got slightly louder.

'The President is dead. Assassinated last night by two…'

Mawji sat bolt upright, staring into space before lunging out of the chair. He was a man possessed, the calm a moment ago giving way to an urgent storm.

'Get to the dinghy, quick!'

She was speechless and frightened as they both hurried to the metal ladder and motored to the old pontoons in the dark of a cloudy night. They were soaked within moments and drenched by the time they moored up against the boards. They had said nothing to each other and she followed him across the square into the bar.

As they entered, Joey stood behind the old bar staring at them. It was empty as usual. Mawji stopped near the door as it slammed shut with the increasing wind.

'Haven't you heard?'

Joey picked up a glass and started to polish it.

'I heard alright.'

'So what's wrong? We need to go.'

'It's not that simple.'

'Sure it is. It's not safe. Get the stuff Joey.'

A moment of silence allowed Mawji to notice a trail of wet footprints leading to the toilet.

He looked at Joey and then looked back at the open toilet door.

A man in a tuxedo, well what was left of it anyway, stood in the doorway pointing a rifle at him.

Mawji looked at Joey who shrugged.

'Like I said, it's not that simple.'

Mawji studied the man. Dark stubble, fresh scratches and specs of dry blood covered his sweaty grimy face, but it was the intense blue eyes, boring right into him that unnerved him. He knew these kind of eyes and knew this would end badly for someone.

A long moment of steely silence broke.

'That must have been some party.'

The man ignored Mawji's sarcasm.

'I'm your morning charter.'

'It's not morning and anyway you're a day late.'

The man, angry, raised his voice.

'Two hundred a day. We made a deal.'

'Screw your deal! You said fishing – not war!'

'A deal's a deal and I'm booked, so let's go. All of you.'

He indicated with the rifle towards the door and then seemed to change his mind. He gruffly spoke to Joey:

'What stuff?'

'Just stuff.'

The rifle rose.

'Tell him Joey. He don't look like fooling.'

'From the uprising we kept a few guns…in case.'

'Which side were you on?'

'No one's. Minding our own business, protecting my wife here,' Mawji snapped.

The man looked hard at him before looking at the girl, who was avoiding eye contact and despondently looking at Mawji.

The man knew it was a pack of lies.

'Alleluia,' he growled at the girl.

She said nothing, only flashing him a fearful glance that showed recognition.

Smirking, he seemed more determined and pointed the rifle to the door.

'Let's go.'

Before he could continue, the harsh sound of a car's brakes squealed outside. Doors opened and slammed shut.

The man instantly backed off into the shadow of the toilet, keeping his gun trained on Joey who was the only target visible from this position.

Mawji was in panic and hissed at the girl:

'Quick, get to the toilet and come out a moment after whoever it is comes in.'

She moved fast and was out of sight before the bar door opened.

The mean inspector entered. He stopped and eyed the scene, following the trail of wet footprints to the toilet. In his hand was a revolver and behind him, peering in through the open door, were two heavily armed policemen. The wind blew hard, bringing in the rain.

'Shut the god damned door will ya!' Mawji shouted.

The door banged shut.

The girl stood staring at the familiar face that only looked at Joey down the barrel of his gun. Having heard the bar door open and bang shut, she immediately flushed the toilet and turned on the tap to rinse her shaking hands before walking past the man, back into the bar.

The girl looked at Joey. Raising her hands slightly, her voice broke nervously.

'Do you have a towel?'

He handed her his cleaning towel.

Turning towards the room, she found the drenched inspector and his two fierce men looking right at her. She hesitated, and for a terrible moment, everyone stared at her.

Mawji, trying to break the tension, moved to the bar. He turned to the inspector.

'Drink?'

The inspector nodded, moving to the end of the bar near the door, his noisy footsteps breaking up the awful silence. The two policemen stayed where they were, nervously eyeing all.

Joey reached out and took the towel back to clean the inspector's glass. He uncapped a beer bottle, which made everybody jump.

The girl silently moved next to Mawji.

Slowly taking a drink, the inspector shifted his eyes from Mawji's face to the toilet door and back again.

'You heard?'

Mawji nodded. 'We heard.'

The inspector looked at Joey.

'Seen a man in a tuxedo, maybe wounded?'

'I've never seen a man in a tuxedo, inspector.'

He looked to Mawji.

'You?'

'Not since that time they made you inspector, Inspector.'

'Since when did you call me inspector?'

The inspector seemed irritated and took a quick swig from the glass.

'Don't be like that and don't tell me you're mourning that old Dictator?'

'We need your boat again.'

'That's one popular boat Mawji.'

'Sure is Joey. Things must be bad.'

Mawji looked at Joey who looked at the inspector who looked back and saw Joey's sweating brow. Keeping it firmly in his grip, the inspector placed the revolver on the bar and looked over towards the open toilet door.

The wind started rattling the bar room door.

Joey broke the tension.

'There's a squall coming over. Just what we need to break this damned heat.'

He mopped his wet brow with the cloth.

'Must be some sort of fever, get-me-outta here fever I'd say,' the inspector said slowly, still looking towards the toilet.

Turning to Mawji:

'Well?'

Mawji shrugged, 'Got a charter tomorrow. After that, it's all yours.'

The inspector looked at the girl and then back at Mawji before leaving the bar with his two men. The door slammed shut behind them with the wind.

Moments later, as the car drove off, the man moved back into the room and snapped at Mawji.

'How cosy.'

'It's a small place. We have to get on.'

'Shut up and get moving.'

'We're going nowhere. Anyway, where's your friend? The call said there'd be two of you,' Mawji seethed.

Incensed, the man moved with great speed and jabbed Mawji in the ribs with the barrel of the gun.

Collapsing off the bar stool, Mawji briefly crumpled to the floor before pulling himself up, clutching his side, gasping:

'You can kill me right here and now. One shot and that mean inspector will be over here. How do you know he's not waiting outside? Besides, the weather's kicked up and the dinghy won't make it through the swell. You gotta wait until it breaks.'

The man backed away a little. He knew he was in a tight corner and found it hard to keep his cool.

'When?'

'Twilight before dawn, and you gotta tell me where we're going. A boat needs to be supplied, rigged right for a journey. Your phone call said fishing…what you after?'

'Don't get funny. You don't need to know a thing.'

'Sandbars, fast currents, tides…you don't wanna risk getting grounded somewhere waiting for your boys to charge over the hill while that inspector does a little fishing of his own.'

'What does he want with your boat?'

'Same as you, a little fishing trip.'

'The Black Shells.'

'The boat'll never get in there. Just take the dinghy at first light.'

'Just get what you need.' He turned to Joey, 'where's the stuff?'

'Out back.'

Then to Mawji, 'don't even think of any tricks or your friend's dead,' and to the girl, 'get some food.'

Joey led the man to a back room.

The girl hesitated before asking:

'You ok?'

'Sure, the day's just getting better and better. You'll find two fishes and five loaves in that old freezer over there. We could do with a miracle.'

He indicated with a nod and clutched his side, as she whispered:

'Then pray hard. He lost everything in the troubles.'

'I guess he wants it all back now and not taking no for an answer.'

She seemed angry, and then shocked Mawji with blame.

'Where's your monster when we need him?'

'All twisted up and feeling sorry for itself,' he snarled back.

She grabbed Mawji by the arms and shook him.

'Fading fast you mean just like that fake storm you told him about. I don't want to die like this,' she gasped, holding back a sob.

The man looked into the bar from the back room doorway.

Mawji held her close and whispered softly:

'He's a pro. We gotta wait for him to make a mistake.'

'And if he doesn't?'

'Then pray hard, Preacher Girl.'

He roughly pulled her away and she went about the cooking.

Joey returned to the bar room, noisily pulling two large wooden boxes by short ropes, followed by the man and rifle.

Mawji, who had stayed aimlessly put in the middle of the bar room, eyed the big clock on the wall opposite the bar, which he and Joey had stolen from the old bus station one drunken night some years before. They had many hours before the dark night gave way to the grim reality of morning light where any chance of escape would become increasingly slim. Once on the boat, the man would no longer need restraint and there would be no measure for his temper. Mawji understood this well.

Joey stood next to the boxes and briefly shared a glance with Mawji. They both knew the man was unlikely to drop his guard and that only luck would now get them out of this.

The man indicated to the boxes.

'Looks like you were planning your own little war.'

'It's a rough neighbourhood,' Joey replied.

'Where are all your customers?'

The man looked around the empty bar as Joey indicated to Mawji.

'He's here.'

'Hey Joey, do ya remember the night we stole that big clock from the old station?'

Mawji pointed to the wall.

'Shut it!'

The man's nerves were beginning to fray. Pacing around like a caged beast, he too looked at the clock unable to stand the long wait until morning, its rhythmic ticking reminding him of the endless wait while sitting out the storm.

The tension broke, as plates loaded with steaming fish and chunks of bread clonked noisily on the counter,

The man moved to the bar, saying to the girl:

'Take them theirs. You two over there and keep your hands on the table.'

He indicated with his rifle to a gloomy corner at the far end of bar where a table and a few chairs sat under the unwelcoming yellow hue of a lamp hanging from the crumbling ceiling. As the two men sat down, he growled to the girl:

'You stay here.'

She stood along the bar with her food. In the strung out tension, they ate in silence.

The man quickly finished his food. He had not taken his eyes off anyone as he ate, leaning on the bar with one elbow and scooping up the food whilst pointing the rifle at the two men with his other arm.

'Let's go, now!'

'We can't! The swell will overturn the dinghy.'

'Then we'll have to swim. Get moving, grab those boxes.'

He was up and animated, unable to bear another moment's wait.

Mawji's ploy had failed; the man was desperate and prepared to risk the make believe storm.

A wail arose from the bar. The girl was on her knees praying loudly, asking God to save them all.

'Dear Lord please deliver us from the evil of men and give us…'

'What the hell? Hey, shut it you!'

Enraged, the man immediately turned his rifle around so he could smash the girl's head with the butt at the other end. As he turned to land the blow, Mawji and Joey saw their chance and were on their feet, rushing him. The butt cracked against the girl's forehead sending her reeling into the room. As she lay sprawled on the floor, blood pouring down her face still wailing prayers, the first blow struck the man.

It wasn't much of a fight. The man took the first blows without crumpling. All seemed lost for him, but his deft skill in turning the rifle around in a flash allowed him to squeeze the trigger. A loud bang rang out, sending the other two men diving for cover.

The clock glass smashed and time stopped.

The man came to his senses. He knew he had made a huge mistake and that in moments the police would arrive; but if he made a dash, he just might have a chance.

Mawji and Joey still lay on the floor looking up at him.

There was a second of unbearable tension before he turned and ran to the door, throwing it open and disappearing into the night rain. The door banged shut behind him.

The girl was mumbling unintelligibly.

A moment later, a barrage of shots rang out and then nothing. All was silent.

Mawji and Joey were both on their feet, agitated and urgent.

'Hey, Preacher…'

Mawji shook the girl. She was conscious but out of it.

'Mawji, we need to go, back way through the cellar into the alley.'

'Give me a hand.'

'Leave her, she's crazy trouble and will slow us down.'

Grabbing the girl by the feet, Mawji dragged her across the floor to the back of the bar followed by Joey.

Joey indicated to the heavy boxes.

'What about the stuff?'

'It's too late for that now and besides, they're much too heavy to sneak around with.'

Joey stood at the girl's head and glanced down and across her body to Mawji still holding a foot in each hand.

'Depends what your priorities are.'

'Just grab a gun.'

THE WIND HAD EASED and the night rain soft and warm. The harbour lights glistened in the fine drizzle of the dark tranquil sky as the man lay motionless amongst the crates and disused junk that littered the sprawling quayside. Miraculously, he had survived his mad dash from the bar into the waiting night. From where he lay, tucked between crates, he watched the boots and searchlights of the men still looking for him and listened to their urgent shouts. Still far from safety, he regretted the jubilant singing and high spirits that led to the car spinning off the road and for losing his cool with that bunch of freaks in the bar just now. He had been careless, and with the way things had gone, should be dead.

THE TWO MEN were in the small alley behind the bar, both standing with their backs against the wall, smoking. The girl now lay unconscious on the wet paving slabs, dried blood caking her pale face. The rain had stopped and the clouds had cleared, the waxing moon casting eerie shadows across the trio. As they smoked, they listened to the sound of distant gunfire and shouting from the quayside, a stone's throw from the bar.

'Reckon they got him?'

'He's got nine lives that one. She probably saved us with that crazy stunt of hers.'

'Watch it Mawji, she'll have you on your knees.'

Mawji flicked his cigarette away.

'Bah.'

The gunfire got closer and the two men knowingly looked at one another.

Mawji said it first: 'Tuxedo Man's friends will be charging down the hill soon. We'd better move.'

They lifted the girl on to a small handcart, the kind used to ferry goods around the port and one that Joey used to collect crates of beer from the coasters at the dock. Mawji pulled and Joey pushed, but they soon stopped where the walls formed a large dark arch at the end of the alley just before it joined a small street that led onto the square. In the shadows, Joey whispered:

'Not worth risking the square, especially with your precious cargo here slowing us down. Let's go across to the fuel dock.'

Mawji looked down at his cargo, then up and down the empty cobbled street and nodded. They crossed the bumpy street into another dark alley.

MEANWHILE, the man crouched low behind some lobster pots by the water's edge on the quayside. He looked out to sea at the small motor boats tied to the coloured buoys bobbing with the changing tide near the harbour entrance, then at the silhouettes of the soldiers patrolling the square nearby. The gentle lapping of the sea against the quayside told him that the strange freak had tricked him – there was no storm or swell to thwart his plan.

THE WHEELS OF the cart squeaked and rumbled on the cobblestones as the two men pushed it through the darkness. They stopped and eyed the inky water, rippling and shimmering under the silver moonlight. The dock seemed empty, although they could clearly hear the shouts of troops getting ready to protect the town. They didn't see the figures hiding in the shadows behind the fuel pumps.

'We gotta get to Jaffa before light. Once they move their heavy guns to Mission Hill, we'll be sitting ducks.'

Mawji stripped to the waist, removed his deck shoes and lowered himself into the murky water of the harbour. He looked up at Joey.

'I'll get the dinghy.'

He swam, disappearing into darkness.

Joey waited in the shadows. He was nervous. It had been a long time since they had needed to act with such daring.

The girl stirred, woke up, her body tensing as she jumped up.

She clutched her head and looked at the dried blood on her hand in the soft moonlight.

'Lord…'

Joey instantly put a finger to his mouth and came close to the girl.

She stared at him.

'What happened?'

'Mawji's getting the dinghy. We'll be safe soon.'

'Safe from whom? What's that noise?'

'Guns, they'll be at the Mission soon, might destroy the port.'

'Why would they hurt us?'

'It's not them, I'm worried about.'

He eyed the girl nursing her wound.

'You better leave. There's still time for you to get back to the bar, fix up that cut and hide out until it's over – maybe a day or two, then join your Ma up on the hill.'

'It's not as bad as it seems, and anyway, I don't want to join her and hang out for salvation day anymore.'

'Just go before Mawji gets back, I don't want you slowing us down. This will only get worse.'

'He saved my life.'

'And you saved ours right back there in the bar with that spectacle of yours. So let's call it quits.'

'He asked me to pray,' she said defensively.

'Alleluia!'

'Why are we running?'

'Not you, just go before it's too late.'

She stared, defiantly.

Resigned to her stubbornness and needing to take his mind off things, Joey told her a story:

'Once upon a time…'

'During the troubles?'

'No, long before that, that mean old inspector and Mawji were pals, not that he was so mean or even an inspector back then. They were the sort of pals that would do anything for each other…well almost, but even back then they were both stubborn mules. Mawji and me got taken in by that inspector's self-deluded righteousness. He was one charming man, if you can believe that, thought he owned the revolution, that it was all his idea to run those arrogant pigs out of town. It wasn't long before he had a band of men causing trouble, shooting and blowing things up. Well, we ran his gang of bandits, pirates and wannabe revolutionaries up and down this coast, in and out the creeks in Mawji's old man's boat…'

'Jaffa?'

Joey nodded.

'Used to drop them off, pick them up, supply them with whatever money we and the inspector managed to steal from passing coasters. It was a real revolution back then. That inspector even used to read us Marx like prayers in the morning. Can you believe it, early morning Marx as the sun came up over the swamps, all fired up like a preacher man – you'd know all about that, not that we could have cared less, we was drunk mostly, having a hoot. Then he got the taste for power, got it bad, and things went from bad to worse until one day those pigs were running and it was all for the taking. It became really messy after your lot ransacked all the loot and fled into the swamps...'

'They're not my lot...and Mawji?' She interrupted.

'After all that trouble there was no law and only more trouble, different trouble, the kind of trouble that only happens after a whole lotta trouble like that trouble I just said. That inspector was too busy basking in the glory to give damn. Then one day a bunch of thugs, people just like us, murdered Mawji's folks, chased Maya into your church, but she weren't safe there, raped her and burnt it to the ground....'

Joey paused.

'...that's why it's all black and broken...but you know all that...'

'No one told me – that!'

'Mawji and me couldn't see the wood for the trees, went looking for them, not that we ever knew who them was. Had to do a load of bad things before I got sick of it, except Mawji kept on looking and the inspector kept giving him false leads so Mawji could rub out anyone the inspector didn't like. No one stopped him – it was chaos then – the inspector protected us but not for much longer. We need to leave before those who remember come looking.'

'So it's true, you did do all those terrible things.'

Joey shrugged.

'What made Mawji stop?'

'Ran out of steam. And now, without the inspector, we have to run.'

'Why do they loathe each other?'

'They don't…just see each other in each other if you get my drift. Now don't you start getting any smart ideas that you can save us – save yourself.'

'I am.'

After a minute's silence, Joey looked up and caught the imposing figure of the inspector looming over them from behind the cart.

MAWJI SMELLED AND tasted the familiar murky warm water of the harbour, full of diesel fuel and rotting fish. Keeping low, behind the buoys and small vessels moored away from the pontoons to stop them being stolen, it had been a few hundred yards of easy swimming to arrive at the seaward end of the broken pontoon. He untied his old black dinghy and started the slow swim back to the fuel dock whist holding onto the tie ropes, dragging it behind. He calculated that there was just enough time to get to Jaffa before light broke. Eying the port and the dark shadows of the approaching fuel dock where Joey and the girl waited, something flickered in the moonlight, splashing in the water. At first, he thought it was a shark, but then clearly saw the man swimming awkwardly out towards the motor launches, both shoes held high out of the water with one hand. Wedged into one of them was a handgun.

'Those must be some shoes.'

After glancing into each other's loathing eyes, the noise of an exploding shell made both continue on their separate ways.

MAWJI WAS SOON pulling himself out of the water by the fuel dock. Although he had noticed the inspector and his two hench men, he started to dress without saying a word.

'I need your boat.'

'What is it with you Jona? Can't you talk about anything else?' It was the first time he had used the inspector's name.

'What is it with you? Can't you see it's all over for us here?'

Shells exploded near the port and all six of them hurriedly got in the dinghy; it was overloaded and low in the water. As Mawji pulled the starter, he heard the distant hum of an outboard motor.

'Tuxedo Man…something out there's waiting for him, and I don't like it.'

Shots rang out and the wiz of bullets cut through the night air across the harbour.

All of them looked back at the port and town full of smoke and fire and the shouts of those in the throngs of madness.

In the twilight, Mawji stared at the girl. The dry blood still caked on her head and face was moist and beginning to trickle from the spray; her hair was a mess and she looked washed out and grey. Facing him, as he steered towards the dark outline of Jaffa a few hundred yards away, she stared hard back.

They reached the boat as dawn cracked open the fading night, the cold light exposing the boat to the shore. Minutes later, as Jaffa motored away from the harbour, shells exploded in the sea nearby.

As Mawji aimed the boat towards the green swampy coast-line to the north, he turned to the girl.

'Pray hard, Preacher Girl. We could do with another one of your miracles, except we got no bread this time.'

The girl prayed aloud on the bridge. The noise of explod-ing shells and crashing waves against the boat drained out the songs of war that Jona and his two men had started singing.

They all fell silent as a radio bulletin filled the bridge with the expected news.

'Welcome to the new government broadcast station. Our troops continue to...'

Mawji turned the radio down as the boat moved around the headland, out of view and reach of the big guns.

'It's official – we're fugitives.'

Jona was fired up.

'We'll get men like last time...'

'Sure you will, one week, one year – ten?' Mawji cut in.

'He's right. Whose gonna help you now?'

The hum of a distant plane cut Joey's conversation and he glanced up, then down to the water, before exclaiming:

'Tide's running, Mawji.'

'Let's run with it, run the boat aground in the swamp.'

The boat hugged the desolate coastline with its grey sandy beaches, tightly hemmed by dense green jungle swamp. The girl, sitting upright in the large tattered chair, trying to steady herself as the fast moving boat hit some swell, asked:

'Where are we going?'

'It's a bit late for that!'

Taking the pack of cigarettes from his shirt pocket, Mawji pulled out a cigarette and, whilst putting it into his mouth and turning to the girl, said:

'Pass a light on the table there.'

She rose, grabbed the matchbox and stood next to Mawji, fumbling to strike a light.

It lit and she raised the flame to the end of the cigarette. Her hand was shaking and Mawji grabbed her wrist to steady it. Looking straight at her, he dragged in deep before blowing out to extinguish the flame, sending smoke into the girl's eyes. She coughed, pulled her wrist free and backed away.

'You're mean like that inspector.'

Mawji didn't reply.

'Joey told me everything.'

'Told you what?'

Joey stood in the door smiling.

'That you like the smell of fish!'

'She already knows that, what else you tell her?' Turning to the girl, 'Have you any idea what you got yourself into here?'

'It's no good praying and hoping unless you know what you are praying and hoping for,' she parried back.

'For the hopeless!' Joey shouted over the wind and engines.

One of the Jona's men pushed passed Joey.

'Spotter plane. Not seen us but it's circling the swamp.'

'Are they looking for us?'

Joey answered the girl: 'They'll look along the coast and the creeks for months, mopping up, clearing out anyone they find.'

'Like us?'

'Just like us,' Mawji drily answered. 'Take the helm Joey and turn into the first deep creek you find.'

'Black Shell, mighty shallow up there.'

'Perfect.'

Joey changed places with Mawji, who skilfully flicked his cigarette out of the open door into the wind and spray, before turning to the girl.

'We need to fix you up. Let's go below.'

'I'm fine.'

'Do you always look like that?'

'Only on a day out with you.'

Mawji had grabbed the first aid box and stood waiting by the open stairway that led below.

'Go ahead, he's all show these days,' Joey said without turning around.

'What is it with you, Joey?'

She said nothing and followed Mawji down the stairs.

The berth at the back of the boat had great sea views through a series of reinforced windows that had replaced the old portholes. The room was decked out with hardwoods and the girl felt strangely comfortable as she swayed with the swell, looking out at the foamy wake and listening to the hum of engines. She sat on a bunk as Mawji cleaned and plastered her wound. Her backpack was open and her clothes sprawled across the covers from where she had changed, yesterday. Normally such a mess would have embarrassed her, but now she felt indifferent.

'Lucky you don't need stitches, my sewing skills are best left to fishing nets.'

She touched the plaster, looked up at him and smiled.

'I heard that trouble and fish don't mix. Don't blame Joey, I made him tell me about it.'

Mawji packed the first aid kit back into the box.

'It's like a bad dream I don't want to remember.'

'What's going to happen now? Are you going to fight?'

'For what? Anyway, I'm through with all that stuff.'

The girl felt relieved and showed it visibly as her face relaxed.

'I'll run the boat deep into the swamp. It'll ground when the tide turns, we'll be stuck of course, but for sure no one's gonna follow. Gives us a breather, time to think, and we can leave anytime the tide floods back in again.'

The girl nodded knowingly, suggesting that she seemed to understand the seriousness of their predicament.

'Are we really in such a fix? Can't we do something to make it right?'

Mawji, realising she had no clue to the door of no return they had entered with their early morning flight, said, rather meanly:

'Don't kid yourself that we can go back and say sorry, plead and ask forgiveness. Both me and Joey will be on the town's most wanted list by now. As for Jona – everyone will be after him!'

Suddenly exasperated, the girl gushed:

'Don't give up, I need to get away. I need hope – you're that hope.'

'What do you think this is – Sunday Prayers? You're on a boat with a bunch of desperadoes. What the hell did that Preacher Woman say to you?'

'She told me to stay and run the Mission with a true and open heart or go out into the world and to see what a place of lost souls it is. I can't stand it up on that hill, it feels cursed and cold, a place so dead in heart that my blood runs cold thinking about it; a barren world, full of ghosts from a time long past. So I left and went down to the dock.'

Mawji stared in disbelief.

'After the police station, she told me I had already made my choice and to go straight back out again. I told her what had happened and that you had helped me, but she said you were the worst of the worst and it was my mission to…'

'Save me!' He butted in. 'Christ this is all wrong! You gotta get home. Just think of this as a false start.'

'What arrogance! I'm not trying to save you. That would be a complete waste of my good time. I'm trying to save myself and run away from all I thought I believed in.'

She paused, looking straight at him with blazing open eyes.

Mawji backed away to the door as she quietly added:

'How weak is that? So we both know the ghastly truth about each other now.'

To stop the madness she was spouting, he simply said:

'Get some rest. We've got a long wait for the tide. There's food in the galley and the water's good to drink.'

She knew it was hopeless to talk to a man like him, so she lay back on the bed, letting the world go black and blank.

Mawji closed the door and thought hard about what may happen next. He was tired and hungry but didn't dare rest as he felt plenty of trouble was still yet to come.

Pacing the gangway, he stopped to pull out a photograph from behind the pack of cigarettes in his shirt pocket. The faded colour photo showed happier times: a family in a lush tropical garden, a young Mawji pushing his sister on a swing with their two parents looking on and the airy blue of their old house in the background behind some trees, long before it was destroyed. Studying the photo for a few moments, he put it back behind the cigarettes before going below to the engine room. He flicked on the lights, walked past the loud humming engines and into a small tool room where he pulled out a long, slim box crate sitting on the floor under some shelving. He opened the lid, took out a pistol, two full magazines and a brand new looking passport, which he always kept handy for a time like this, closed the lid, pushed the box back and grabbed an old fishing jacket hanging on the wall. He clicked one magazine into the gun, loaded the breech, flicked the safety on and put it in the jacket side pocket along with the spare magazine and passport. He put on the jacket and went back through the engine room, up the small wooden stair into the gangway where he stopped and looked up the metal stairway into the helm. Seeing he was unobserved, Mawji opened a cupboard door and took out a large holdall that sat amongst some old junk and then went into the galley near the front of the boat. Taking a few small pots, some plastic plates and cutlery, he stuffed them in the holdall alongside dried food packets, tea and powdered milk, and then went to the very front of the boat where his quarters lay. Mawji found some fishing lines, hooks and lures and also stuffed them into the holdall along with some clothes. Catching himself in the chipped mirror hanging next to his bunk, he studied his unshaved face and greasy hair before moving back along the gangway and up the stairs where he slung the holdall to one side near the deck door.

Back in the helm, Joey was turning into Black Shell creek, the boat leaning heavily to one side as he dropped speed and pulled hard into the narrow waterway. The water was muddy brown and sluggish. The thick jungle clad sides of the creek looked impenetrable. A large exotic bird, startled by the noise of the motors, flew up, squawking from its reedy perch.

A few empty beer bottles lay around the deck. Jona and his two men were engaged in a heated conversation but stopped when Mawji reappeared, standing by the doorway.

'Don't let me interrupt the party now Jona. You go right ahead and keep on plotting.'

'Why you need that preacher girl? You found religion or just banging the good Lord's work?'

Trying to keep the conversation from going down to the berths below, Mawji stepped out on deck. Feeling awkward while everybody laughed, he smoothed his hair back.

'What could I do? You nearly got her folks killed by shouting your big mouth off to Scar Face.'

'She's one of them. How can we trust her?'

'No she's not and you know it. Right Joey?'

'Right! She's one like you – way out there.'

Everyone except Mawji laughed again, who stepped back inside and snapped at Joey.

'What is it with you? Watch where you're going, and take that right fork up by the bend will ya.'

'We can't take her with us.'

'Why not?' Mawji answered Jona.

'Coz we gotta get back to port, round up the men and start to fight back.'

'You crazy? If one man can shoot the President and get away from under your nose, what you gonna do against a few thousand like him? They took the country in under twenty four hours!'

'We did it before, never heard you complain then.'

'Last time's not this time. You went bad Jona.'

'And you went worse.'

'I did your dirty work and you know it.'

The engines screamed as the boat hit the shallows, the propellers churning the muddy bottom sending the boat sideways into some bank vegetation.

Below, the girl woke with her face close to the window and saw the wet muddy bank, dense green jungle and the slippery movements of a bright green snake slither into water. She turned over and went back to sleep to the sounds of desperate men.

'Christ! Don't you remember anything from last time? The tide channel runs to the right side of the creek.'

Mawji took the helm. He pulled a cigarette from the packet in his shirt pocket under the old fishing jacket.

'Give us a light.'

Joey pulled out a match, struck it on the doorframe and lit the cigarette.

Both men looked into the other's eyes and Joey whispered:

'We can't live in this swamp forever.'

Mawji indicated to Jona, now sitting down in the tattered armchair.

'What's the alternative? To die fighting for his twisted ideals?'

'It's our country,' Jona quickly answered back, forcing Mawji to show aggression.

'It was their country too and now they're organised and looking for payback. How long before patrol boats arrive? I'll drop you anywhere you want but I don't want any part of this.'

The boat scrapped the bottom and Mawji stopped his rant. Slowing the boat to a crawl, he edged into a small cut between hanging branches, manoeuvring about twenty yards into a deep pool with plenty of tree cover. Cutting the engines, the boat drifted to a halt. The men were silent as the radio chattered from the bridge.

A bulletin told that resistance was patchy but still active and a general amnesty was offered to those who turned themselves in during the next few days.

Mawji looked at Jona, 'Well, there's your chance for a clean break.'

'They might even send me to college!'

'Give you a medal of honour.'

As everyone laughed, Joey asked:

'So where are we going?'

Mawji looked into the tangled mass of dark trees and brilliant green foliage, but before anyone could press him further, said:

'Let's eat and rest up. We could all do with a break.'

MAWJI HAD FALLEN ASLEEP on deck under the mottled shade of the hanging foliage with the gentle rocking of the outgoing tide. Next to him was an empty plate and coffee mug. As he woke from his deep slumber, the boat was still, grounded in the thick mud. Mawji had dreamed of jellyfish, drifting and shining bright as the tide lapped against a muddy creek under a full and ghostly moon, but as the tide ebbed away to expose the mud, the jellyfish were stranded, helpless until the flood returned again.

The girl was sitting next to him. She had cleaned herself up and changed back into her clothing of the previous morning. Mawji looked over at Jona and his two men lounging on the other side of the deck talking in hushed tones, eying the girl. Joey was next to them, standing and looking into the swamp. Mawji noticed more bottles now littering the deck.

'You trust me?' Mawji whispered to the girl.

'No.'

'Wanting to save yourself?'

She looked at him, concerned.

'Then pray hard, real hard.'

Joey was now looking at Mawji.

'What's up Joey?'

'Heard a boat. Tide's still low, so it must be small and already in the creeks.'

The boat rocked a little as the tide started turning.

All the men got up. The girl stayed sitting, head down, murmuring soft prayers.

Jona glared at Mawji, pointing to the girl.

'We gotta get rid of her now.'

'What you suggesting? Get her to walk the plank?'

'Leave her here in the swamps.'

Looking over to the girl, one of the young men said:

'We could have some fun first.'

The girl looked up, ashen.

'Go below. Get ya backpack and grab that holdall on the way back,' Mawji said, carefully putting his hand into his jacket pocket to flick off the gun safety.

He pointed to the bag by the helm doorway and she went below.

'Give her the dinghy and be done with it,' Mawji said to Jona.

'We need that dinghy. Just get her off the boat or I'll shoot her.'

The girl returned and stood in the doorway, pale and frightened.

'Get down that ladder into the dinghy with those bags,' Mawji urgently ordered.

Jona went for his gun but Mawji already had his pistol out, pointing it straight at Jona's head. The two young men pointed their rifles at Mawji but seemed somewhat perplexed and kept looking to Jona for an order.

'Joey?'

Joey put his hand into his pocket and pulled his gun, pointing it at no one in particular, asking:

'What is it with you?'

'I'm leaving with the girl.'

'What you want to do a stupid thing like that for? We can get our country back with a little help,' Jona snapped.

'And how long before you get blown out of the water? Preacher Girl, get to the dinghy and start the motor just like you seen me do it.'

The girl hadn't moved but now went to the side and down the ladder struggling under the weight of the two bags.

Mawji and the men faced each other in a moment of silence as they heard her efforts to start the outboard.

'Give it some choke!'

Joey spoke first to Jona:

If you shoot Mawji, I'll shoot you.'

Then to the two men:

'Put your guns down. You don't know the water and you need me to get you outta here.'

Furious, Jona relented.

'Go with your preacher. You can rot together in this cursed swamp.'

The men lowered their rifles.

'You in love with that freaky preacher?' Joey asked, looking at Mawji who was still pointing his pistol at Jona.

'I just know when to quit, that's all. You coming?'

Joey pointed to the swamp.

'Out there! This is my country, I can't leave it. I gotta try – right?'

Mawji indicated to the three men.

'Drop them off after the old pumping station to sneak back into town. You take the boat down towards the city and anchor up in one of those small harbours before the ridge ends and do a little fishing. No one knows you there…you'll be just fine, and be ready for whatever plays out.'

'But I hate the smell of fish.'

'You get used to a bad smell,' Mawji said, looking at Jona.

Mawji put the pistol back in his jacket pocket at the sound of the outboard catching. Joey kept his gun handy as Mawji went to the side of the boat, pausing only to look Joey in the eyes before downing the ladder and stepping onto the dinghy. Avoiding the girl's eyes, Mawji looked back up the ladder to where all four men were looking down at them. He held the tiller steady, throttling slowly away from the boat along the increasing tide channel, under the overhangs and out of the pool, before looking back at the boat, half hidden by trees. In silence, the girl sat next to him.

Mawji cut the engine and drifted further into the swamp with the tide, which had now started to flood the shallow mud banks. Taking one of the small paddles, he guided the dinghy into smaller and narrower channels until they were undercover of the low leafy canopy, totally lost from view.

The dinghy bumped against a tree, spinning round as it moved with the flooding tide. Mawji moved to the front and guided it along, pushing against the mangrove to avoid getting jammed in between the trees, where they would be stuck and held under by the racing tide. He turned to face the girl whose hollow eyes showed the horror of her decision to leave the Mission. She sat looking at him, her arms around her hunched up legs. He knew they were in big trouble, knew he had taken a gamble and that his hunch that he had kept quiet about may be just a wild goose chase.

Looking at the girl again, sitting opposite and staring him in the eye, he caught a glimpse of the distracting view at the top of her legs. He lost concentration and, as they hit another tree, had trouble keeping the dinghy steady in the strong pull of the current. The dinghy spun around again, making Mawji lose his balance and then his footing. He fell into the muddy water with a splash.

The dinghy floated away as Mawji surfaced, tangled in thick weed. He gasped, desperately struggling to free himself. The girl shouted but he could no longer see her, and, as he broke free of the weed, was at the mercy of the rushing tide.

'Preacher!'

He repeated his shouts and mixed them with curses.

The girl had managed to grab the paddle as Mawji disappeared. She tried to use both paddles as oars, but it was hopeless to row against the fierce rush of tide. The dinghy hit a tree. As it slowed and started spinning round, she threw the mooring rope around the trunk and tied a knot. The rope went taught and the dinghy stopped, tossing with the current. The girl knelt and held on tight.

She had lost her only hope, a man whose reputation was so despicable that she felt she had unwittingly made a pact with the devil. Within this milieu of confusion and contradiction, she was frightened of losing herself, her faith and her sanity; but more than anything, she wanted to find him alive in these muddy, murky waters.

Hearing his shouts and curses, she soon caught view of him being swept down a fast moving channel as he toiled to stay afloat.

While shouting out to him above the noise of rushing water, she attempted to untie the rope, whose knot had locked tight with the pull of the current. Mawji looked over, aimed his body towards a tangle of thick vegetation and struck it hard, jamming himself in as the water tried to push him down. He signalled to the girl who was at least one hundred yards behind, further back towards the sea. It would be minutes before the rising tide washed over and took him down.

The girl desperately pulled at the knot, was almost blind with tears as she struggled to set the dinghy free. She scrabbled around in her backpack, found a penknife and struck the rope. It cut and the dinghy lurched forward with the tide, sending her flying back as it turned and spun with its release. Grabbing a paddle, she steered towards Mawji anxiously clinging on to roots.

Unable to control the dinghy as well as she had hoped, she was soon heading down the channel out of Mawji's reach. On seeing this, he lunged into the water and tried to grab the dinghy as it passed. He missed, but managed to seize the trailing rope and hold on tight, yanking himself half on board as the dinghy spun and turned around again. She pulled him in and he lay exhausted, looking at the sky. The girl battled on, the fierce current bumping them through the narrow channels, deeper into the swamp. By a miracle, she stopped the craft from capsize.

MAWJI AWOKE TO the sounds of birds. Instinctively, he grabbed the gun from his jacket pocket and sat up to see the girl pass him a water bottle. He drank but didn't say a word. Although still wet, he pulled the soggy crumpled packet of cigarettes from his shirt pocket and cursed on realising he would not get a smoke. The tide was full and the brown water still. He remembered his dream of thick black weed chocking and pulling him down, and the warm pink sunlight beckoning him above.

Unloading the magazine, he placed the bullets in a small open compartment in the side of the dinghy. He did the same with the spare magazine. She watched him and when he had finished, asked:

'Are we lost?'

Not answering, he pulled his wet cigarettes out of the packet, also placing them in the open compartment to dry. Remembering the photograph, he pulled that from his pocket, studying it for a brief moment before noticing the girl looking at it; he deliberated before handing it to her. She carefully took it, quickly absorbing its powerful image before handing it back without saying a word. Along with his passport, he added the photo to the compartment.

Mawji looked at his watch to make sure it was still working, nodded and turned to the girl.

'How long was I sleeping.'

'A few hours…are we lost?

He took off his watch and placed it on the sun-bleached seat.

'If the small hand faces the sun.…'

He adjusted the position so the hour hand faced the sun.

'…then north lies between the little hand and twelve o'clock.'

He pointed north. 'It's not that accurate near the equator, but it's good enough.'

'That way's the Pirate Coast, we're not that far from the sea because we have a full tide and…'

He dipped his hand into water and took a taste.

'…the water's salty. Further north is where Tuxedo Man's friends came from – we can't go there and we can't go back.'

He paused. 'Did you hear anything when I was sleeping?'

'Jaffa's engine, I think.'

'Too early, Joey's far too smart to leave before dusk. Which way was the noise?'

She pointed into the swamp.

'OK, we may have a little rendezvous.'

'Where?'

'Black Shells.'

'That's where Freeman said to take him.'

'Who?'

'Tuxedo Man – I remember him from the Mission school. My mother disliked his lot.'

'His lot?'

'Moneyed and arrogant.'

'Troubled and deranged more like. You kept that quiet.'

'You kept our rendezvous quiet.'

'It's just a hunch. We've got a few hours before dusk, so we need to move.'

Mawji checked the watch against the sun again, was lost in thought and calculation, before saying:

'We got an onshore wind, so if we head into the swamp over there, we need to keep the breeze kind of to our backs.'

He indicated a direction.

'Reckon you can paddle and steer? We need to save on fuel and keep our position silent.'

'Why silent?'

'My bet is that Tuxedo Man's out there and I'm not wanting his attention.'

The girl paddled through the dense swamp as Mawji went to work cleaning and oiling his damp pistol with some tools and rags he had to repair the outboard. The air turned cooler as dusk approached and Mawji took over paddling. The swamp became eerie as black shadows crossed the water and the birds stopped singing. Only the odd insect's hum cut the silence.

The current of the turning tide was weak and the girl knew that far away through the swamp in the direction of the setting sun, was the sea.

They came to the edge of a large basin (Mawji called it a lagoon) surrounded by dense wet swamp with no dry land. Dotted about the lagoon were small islands of piled up black sea shells, some with small white inlays that reflected the setting sun like tiny, sparkling mirrors.

'The Black Shell Islands.'

'What are they?'

'Don't rightly know…holy ground built up by my ancestors. My old man used to take me here once a year to fish and add some more shells to the pile. Just said his old man did the same.'

'Why would Freeman come here?'

'Well, he sure ain't piling up shells.'

The girl suddenly grabbed Mawji's hand, making him turn to face her. She pulled her hand away and gestured to the sea of endless green.

'Tell me what we are really doing here?'

Mawji looked away and towards the Black Shells Islands.

'Guess we both made a choice of no return…gotta play it out now…'

'You lost your family, your country, gave up your boat. What can we do out here?'

'Through this swamp, maybe a few months away, there's another country. Know it?'

Mawji pointed northeast.

She glumly nodded at the thought of such a dire journey.

'Ask me then.'

Tying the dingy to a large swamp tree, he focused on a task at hand.

'Come on, we need to eat before the light's all gone.'

IN THE PITCH BACK of night, as the girl lay curled up in the bottom of the dinghy, she woke to the sounds of Mawji snoring softly to the rhythm of the changing tide. He lay on his back with one hand resting on his tummy, clasping the pistol, and the other flopped down by his side. The swamp was strangely silent with only the occasional piercing shrill of an unseen bird echoing across their solitary world. As moonlight glimmered through the moving foliage, she reached out and momentarily touched his hand before letting the ebbing tide rock her back to sleep.

Mawji dreamed he was being shaken in bed: 'Get up, Get up,' his mother said. 'It's time to go, you'll be late for your first day.' Maya grabbed his hand.

He awoke from his deep sleep to the sounds of an engine whirring in the distance and sat up wondering what he was going to be late for. The girl was gone and he flicked the safety off his gun, carefully looking around before seeing her swimming near the boat in the calm of the flooded tide. He flicked the safety back and looked out into the lagoon but couldn't see the boat.

Shocked at her naivety, he stared in disbelief, whispering:

'What the hell are you doing? Things that eat you live in there.'

Pulling herself up into the dinghy, she didn't answer. Having changed before he woke, she now sat dripping wet in shorts and T-shirt. He put a finger to his mouth as they both heard the whirr of an outboard. The girl seemed happy, indifferent almost, and Mawji looked at her, his gun and then to the lagoon. Wisps of mist floated above the water as the first rays of light caught the nearest shells, making their whites dimly flicker orange. At the far end of the lagoon, the ghostly image of a man sitting in a boat was just visible through the fine white film before the mist thickened and all that was left was the ominous whirr.

The girl looked up.

'Freeman?'

He nodded without turning around and kept on looking for another glimpse of their appointment.

Listening and watching, they sat for a while without saying a word. Mawji seemed on edge and the girl asked:

'What is it…with you?'

'Once the mist clears we won't have surprise.'

'Why do you want to surprise him?'

'Because he's dangerous and I wanna know what he's up to. This is my place, not his.'

They heard the engine cut and a moment later the crunch of feet on breaking shells.

Mawji untied the dinghy and paddled silently into the lagoon. As the mist engulfed them, they lost sight of all the shells and steered towards what now sounded like digging.

Through the rising mist, they saw a black shell isle, grey motorboat and the sketchy figure of a man digging with his hands into the top of the mound. The girl hung onto the back of Mawji's jacket, tense and with an increasing sense of knowing – knowing that in this beautiful Eden she had stumbled upon, someone would probably die. She watched the shells come closer as the dinghy drifted in and prayed, hoping the awful inevitable she had just imagined was a bad dream.

Freeman dug deep into the top of the mound, the broken shells cutting into his hands. He remembered the daring plan to shoot the president. Then, making their escape: a helter-skelter dash down an overgrown mountain road before skidding on a bend and crashing through the trees. His reminiscing was interrupted by a noise, the rude awakening of Mawji jumping out of the dinghy and onto the shells with an almighty crunch, before running up the mound with his gun out, loaded and ready to fire.

The mound was steep at the top and Mawji struggled with every stride, sinking and slipping back, losing momentum and any element of surprise. By the time he was close, Freeman was on him, both tumbling down to the water's edge where the gun went flying onto the shells. The two men fought hard and fast with an unnatural fury knowing it must end badly for one of them. However, Freeman being more trained and stronger than Mawji, soon overpowered him and was in the throes of trying to strangle him, when a shot exploded, reverberating across the lagoon. Freeman looked up at the girl pointing the gun at his head; she was shaking and pale and he knew from experience that she was seconds away from pulling the trigger again. Raising his arms, he stood up, followed by Mawji who was soon taking the gun from the girl and levelling it straight at Freeman, who seethed:

'A right Christian soldier Miss…'

'Don't you dare say her name! Turn around.'

Freeman turned around. His suit was ripped and in tatters, covered in a mosaic of white and grey from sticky brine and the fine dust of crushed shells. But the black leather patent of his shoes still had a shine.

'Glad to see your shoes made it. A man's gotta look his best at a time like this.'

He turned to the girl.

'Get up on the mound and see what he's got hidden,'

She crunched up the mound and looked into the gaping hole. Mawji, seeing the golden light of morning reflected on her face, asked again:

'Well?'

A bar of gold landed near his feet, then another and then another.

'Guess you were going to be filthy rich again.'

Freeman said nothing, and then did nothing as Mawji barked:

'Put it all in the dinghy.'

Mawji backed off a little and put his free hand to join the other on the gun, carefully aiming at Freeman's chest.

'Load or die.'

As the girl threw down the bars, Freeman loaded the dinghy. When it was done, there was a sizable stack weighing the dinghy down and Mawji reckoned it was about the weight of a big man.

Sweaty from the work, the girl slid and clambered down the mound to join him.

'We could rebuild your Mission, you could both be part of this new country,' Freeman solemnly said.

Mawji looked at the girl.

'Your choice, but I'm not staying.'

'I've already made my choice.'

Mawji backed away to the boat.

'Reckon you can paddle?'

Picking up a paddle, she embarked. Mawji sat on the edge of the dinghy and pushed off, still carefully aiming at Freeman. Taking one hand off the gun, he grabbed the grey motor boat's towrope and pulled it out into the lagoon.

Freeman dropped his arms.

'You can't leave me here.'

'With a good tide and a lot of luck, it should take you two days to swim back to dry land – that way.'

Mawji pointed south.

'You bastards.'

'Oh and here's a little something – don't spend it all at once!'

Mawji grabbed a gold bar and threw it on the shells. It landed with a crunching thud by Freeman's feet.

They paddled across the lagoon to the east as Freeman cursed at them.

'Thank you for not shooting him.'

'I told you – that stuff's finished now. Ever fired a gun before?'

The girl ignored him, looked at the bullion and then to Mawji.

'What will happen to him?'

'Be tough, but I could get out of here with the right tides and a bit of luck.'

'He's not like you. No one's like you. Don't you want to know my name?'

'Hell no!'

'What is it with you?'

Their laughter drowned out the other noise as the sun broke through the misty cloud. Moments later and lost from view, Mawji let the grey motorboat loose to drift with the last of the rising tide.

2.

BAYONNE DAYS

FREEMAN STOPPED HIS long barrage of abuse as the dense vegetation of the endless swamp swallowed up the dinghy. As the mist cleared and the day showed, he heard the couple's distant laughter and then nothing, only the soft sounds of early morning birds.

It took less than a minute to walk around the edge of the island, and as he did, he viewed the landscape, the black shells crunching and breaking underfoot. It was just as he remembered: small islands of piled up black shells, some no larger than an armchair, others as big as a barn, all made of shells, millions of them piled up by generations of strange sea-gypsies who seemed to come from nowhere. As he looked out across the rippling water of the opaque lagoon glistening in the early morning sun, he tried to remember something important that his father had told him about these islands, something he knew was relevant but couldn't quite catch. Unable to remember, he sat down on the edge of the isle and felt for his gun, but it wasn't there, it was sitting in the boat that was out of view and drifting with the tide.

He felt hopelessly stranded.

It was now late August and Freeman looked back on his long turbulent summer that had started one early morning in May. Before long, he was remembering and picturing everything that had led him to this fateful point.

France, early May 1968

A S THE RISING SUN began to warm the morning air of early summer, a fine and steady breeze blew in across the Bay of Biscay. Freeman stood on the deserted shoreline breathing the fresh and welcome air. He had cycled out from Bayonne through the drabness of Anglet showing grey in the first light of dawn and followed the Adour River to where it meets the sea. He liked to cycle to keep in shape and while away his long and dull days, but it also helped to dissipate the burning anger raging deep inside that slept at night but rekindled with every waking day. He enjoyed this journey on the south side of the Adour where he could see the port that straddled both sides of the river and the sleeping boats all silent and tucked away before the stirring of a new day bought the bustle back. It was in these solitary frozen moments that he felt closest to home, where nothing disturbed his thoughts, when time just seemed to stop and he very nearly forgot.

There were only two fish you could catch here: grey mullet in the river mouth and bass out past the breaking surf. He had long given up on the mullet; they had supernatural powers and never took the bait. He liked the endless casting and reeling in, the pounding of the surf, the wind in his face and hair and, if he was lucky, the strike and play before landing a beautiful silvery bass. He would watch it flapping and floundering on the fine sandy beach before throwing it back from where it came and still belonged.

It was here, during a long cast into the beautiful deep blue sea that the odd accent of a man broke the spell he had so carefully set up. Freeman turned around to see who had done such a thing. As he reeled in, pulling slowly on the rod every few turns to flick the lure through the water, he studied the man standing on the beach behind him. Blocking out the early morning sun, he created a lanky shadow that ended at Freeman's feet.

'What?'

Freeman spoke in French of course but the man replied in English so strange that it seemed pieced together by several different people and accents. Yet only one man stood there.

'In the splendour of the still and early morning light, you cast your line out far and wide like a man waiting for that special thing to rise up and take the bait.'

Freeman understood every word but had no idea what the man was talking about.

'The bass are running and I like to catch them, if that's what you mean?' He replied in English.

'Yes, so I have seen.'

The man moved to the water's edge where the foam of the surf fizzled out, its air bubbles bursting as it was sucked back out again. Tall and slim with very dark mixed features that Freeman could not place at all, he was dressed in pale slacks, smart desert boots and a loud Hawaiian shirt with motifs of boats and waves in crass multi colours, unbuttoned at the neck. The sun caught Freeman's eyes, making him squint.

'You've been watching me?'

'Before the night is cut by day, I motor up the river to enjoy the empty dawn and lapping of the waves.'

'Sound like a man after my own heart,' Freeman coolly said, trying to break the weird feeling he was suddenly experiencing.

'A man with a heart and a passion to fish…and a man with a lot of free time on his hands.'

'You don't sound so busy either,' Freeman defensively parried.

'I suggest morning coffee and a fine Bayonne breakfast.'

Freeman, who had started to feel uneasy by the stranger's odd speech, was suddenly startled as the tension on the rod eased and the red and sliver lure sprung out of the water, dangling at the end of the line.

'We can put your things in my launch and motor up to where the Adour meets the Nive.'

He indicated towards the river mouth where a small boat had been pulled up onto the beach.

'You live in Bayonne?'

'I am living at Itxassou in the Basque country, way up on the Nive, behind some leafy trees and near a rocky gorge.'

Freeman just stared as the strange man continued.

'I moor the launch along the low grassy banks where the shallows and small rapids begin. It's not such a drive to my house from there.'

'You do that every day?'

'In recent days, yes.'

Freeman had lost the urge to fish. The man's strange speech had broken the magic of his early morning and felt he had nothing to lose by taking the launch to town. After all, the man seemed harmless enough albeit slightly odd, and anyway, he could do with some company after all the lonely months spent wondering what to do next after having been routed from his homeland.

Freeman tried to smile.

'Breakfast's on you.'

It was still quiet as the two men motored up the river. The tide was full and the water slow, hardly lapping except for the boat's wake sending out ripples, which broke gently against the river's shored up banks. The port was coming to life, a few clonks and bangs as workers started their day. The journey was short and the men kept an easy silence in a way that only comes with the comfort of a long friendship, which of course they did not have. Freeman watched the approaching town as if something meaningful was about to hatch and perhaps play out in a Bayonne coffee shop.

Old stone steps led up from the large rusty mooring ring secured in the river's stonewall that had been built long ago to protect the town from flood. Here the two rivers joined: the Adour at the end of its long and sluggish trip from the north, and the Nive, smaller and faster flowing with its fresh cargo of early summer Atlantic Pyrenean rainfall, from the south. At the top of the steps, Freeman looked back down at his bicycle and rod lying in the launch.

As the man led the way across a bridge over the Nive, he pointed to a line of cafés that ran a short way along the empty road that followed the Nive upstream.

Outside a café, the two men took a table that looked out over the river to the boat bobbing gently in the turning tide. The man, having noticed Freeman's nervous glances towards the boat, said:

'Nothing will be taken.'

'I've lost a lot of things.'

'You won't lose here. I'm Jaffa, some like to call me Colonel.'

He reached out his hand and Freeman shook it.

'Freeman. Are you an army man?'

'Let me say, I'm a man who understands the use of such things. I'm in mining: exploration and development, mostly the securing of rights.'

Freeman instantly knew that an instrument of war, which tore countries like his own apart, was sitting opposite him. However, instead of feeling disgust and politely leaving the table, he remained seated, for he had fleetingly caught a glimmer of something very similar to hope and it glued him to his seat. He also knew his feelings were now reflected though his face.

'Are you not approving?'

'I'm intrigued.'

'I am thinking that you have a tale to tell.'

'What makes you think that?'

Freeman was on edge and increasingly confused.

'Out there in the breaking dawn, when the world sleeps and the only sounds are those of the sea and wind throwing up and blowing in the spent mysteries of the night, a man fishes not for the sparkle of a silver bass but to find his dreams, shipwrecked and lost on some distant hostile shore.'

'You're one strange sounding jumped-up bunny rabbit whose poetry grates my ears. I think you'd better quit!'

Looking at the dark features across the table, Freeman felt a rising tide of hatred.

'I could do with a man like you. Do you want breakfast?'

Freeman calmed down.

'I'm sorry, you remind me of something I don't want to think about. Don't you speak French?'

'Not much, and anyhow, what use would that be? People say the same rubbish in all languages of which I speak four. Here I can just be.'

Freeman ordered Bayonne ham with eggs and coffee, whilst Jaffa had fresh baguette with black cherry jam and tea. They remained silent during the meal and the easy-going atmosphere that had earlier been disturbed quickly returned long before the waiter took their plates.

Freeman ordered Armagnac with Perrier. He looked at Jaffa with a smile.

'You're driving me to drink.'

'Then it's time to get outside what's churning on the inside, instead of pickling and preserving it with that never ending drink.'

'Do you always speak like that?'

'I find it best and better than saying: spit it out man and be getting it off your chest.'

'What makes you think I have anything to say?'

'A man like you, obviously tough and not so very French, doesn't fish with the abandon and enthusiasm of a boy who's just discovered the wonders of being alone at first light, unless he is searching for a dream, lost and washed out with the endless churning of the tide.'

Freeman laughed loudly, a long and honest laugh that sent the angry echoes back down to settle in the dark pool lurking in his heart.

'I like you Jaffa. So, you want to hear my story, my tale of loss and woe and how it eats me up and drives me to fish that early morning lonely shore. Is that what you want to hear?'

'Very much, but not here – come, let's go up river to while away the day beside a black cherry tree and listen to the river a stone's throw from my home.'

After Jaffa paid the bill, they went across the bridge and down the old stone steps to slowly motor up the full tide river, out of town. The early summer day was warm, the morning light still, soft and clear. Lazy trees dotted the edge of the low banks, their green and sliver leaves shimmering in the subtle breeze.

The two men were again silent; the whirr of the motor drowning out nature's sounds as Freeman relaxed, enjoying his ride, wondering about the stranger at the helm.

It took about twenty minutes to reach the mooring point on the north bank where green fields stretched back to a small rail track and sleepy village looking serene and devoid of people.

Jaffa secured the launch to a washed-out faded grey wooden jetty, the slats all cracked and twisted from the endless ravage of summer sun and chilly winters. Both men carefully walked to the bank as the jetty creaked and moved beneath their feet.

The air was fresh with a slight hint of fragrance, suggesting the vibrant glory of the coming summer, rich in scent and lush with green to intoxicate even the most hardened of men; and today, as the soft cool breeze silently worked its magic, Freeman felt the tacit promise of something good and unusual yet to come.

'My car is sitting behind that barn, under the shade of those two big trees whose name is now escaping my thoughts.'

Jaffa pointed to a stone barn in the field nearby. Two huge trees majestically rose up behind its far side, its branches and foliage covering and protecting the barn from wind and burning sun. Freeman smiled at the odd talk and looked over to where Jaffa had pointed before looking back at his precious bicycle propped up and exposed inside the launch. He deliberated and then slowly followed Jaffa towards the barn through tall grass along a narrow path. The earth underfoot was soft from recent rain and soon insects were flying up and out from the damp grass seemingly annoyed at this sudden and disturbing intrusion into their cosy private world.

The barn was old and completely open on one side. In the dusky shadow under the pitched roof, a light brown cow munched on dry grass and looked nonchalantly at the two men whilst flicking its ears at the occasional, annoying fly. The car sat on the damp mud, in the shade under the huge trees. It was a two-seater red sports car with the roof rolled down, its silver chrome shining brightly where the sun filtered through the canopy.

The subtle magic of morning with its soft sounds of water moving over rock and the gentle rustling of the cow slowly pulling grass from the feeder, momentarily held Freeman. The spell quickly broke as Jaffa spoke:

'The wheel is turning.'

Jaffa now sat in the driver's seat, staring right at him, turning the steering wheel.

Freeman felt an urgency he could not explain and the waves of bitterness echoed back through him. He looked straight back at Jaffa, who fired up the engine and wrecked any semblance of tranquillity Freeman felt. A moment later, as he opened the car door and sat down, Freeman had a feeling of dread. Jaffa drove off slowly down the sleepy track without saying another word.

Freeman spoke, as they turned right into the small village.

'Sweet Chestnut.'

'Ah, yes, they flower very late.'

'How old do you think they are?'

'All that twisting and cracking up...'

Jaffa shot a dead sardonic glance at Freeman.

'...they must have silently witnessed history.'

'And shade your car.'

'Be giving the cow a friendly home.'

'And produce nuts. Maybe even children climb that twisted gnarly bark.'

'Shall we be declaring them a French national monument, Freeman?'

'Long live the mighty chestnut!'

They crossed the Nive and joined the main road. The traffic was light and soon the green hills and dense woods of the low Pyrenees surrounded them as Jaffa turned off right, entering the pretty Basque village of Itxassou. Passing a lone banana tree on their left, just before the road crossed a small bridge over the river, Jaffa turned right into a leafy gravel drive and parked up by a small house. The garden joined the riverbank, which was lined with trees and luscious plants. The soft sparkle of moving water could be seen here and there through patchy undergrowth.

Freeman left the car and viewed the scene. The verdant garden was enveloped by green and hidden from view from the outside. A patchwork of shade and sunlight covered the uncut grassy ground in which small colourful flowers showed prettily and inviting, attracting insects whose humming melded with the sound of nearby flowing water. The air was still and warm and only a soft rustle in the treetops gave indication to any wind that blew.

The house was small, just a cottage really, the walls brilliantly whitewashed and the wood painted oxide-red just like any traditional dwelling in the area. The front door was ajar and the opening covered by a heavy white and blue beaded curtain to keep the flying insects out.

Freeman noticed Jaffa talking to a woman lying down and gently swinging in a framed lounger covered with a white cloth awning that was standing in a sunny part of the garden. She lay obscured by shade with one bare leg hanging down in the bright sunlight, which occasionally pushed at the ground to ensure a never-ending, soothing motion. He could not see her face clearly and scanned her slim figure in a black cotton vest and a wrap-around bright orange coloured skirt that ended at her knees. She suddenly sat upright and stared at him with an empty look that he could not read. She was dark like an Indian with a strong fierce face and twisted braided hair dangling down across her bare left shoulder. He looked hard, as he always did, and clearly saw the raised scars of deep claw marks showing proud within her dark features; her face had been badly ripped and gashes marked her shoulders. A rounded raised dent on her right calf told Freeman it had caught a bullet. Through her afflictions, her dark eyes bore down on him.

His serenity once again mixed with dread as his hairs stood on end and his skin tingled. His stomach felt empty with that disconcerting sense of falling into a black and endless pit.

She rose and walked straight to him without lowering her eyes away for an instant and held out her hand to greet him. Unsmiling and speaking in simple French, she invited him for lunch. Pretending he could see no disfigurement and barely understanding her heavy accent, he feigned a lightness to disguise his shock. Her grip left him cold.

As she disappeared into the house, lost behind the moving beads, he asked:

'Your wife?'

Jaffa didn't answer, only stared, making Freeman feel more uncomfortable.

'Girlfriend?'

'Do you mean…are we having sex?'

'I suppose so.'

Again, there was no reply. Freeman felt so awkward that he gazed up at the clear blue sky.

'I call her Tiger Jane.'

Freeman looked back at Jaffa, who seemed to smile this time.

'Did you find her in the jungle?'

'I did!'

'Does she have a story to tell?'

'She might! Come, let's stroll along the riverbank. This is a good time of year, not too hot with a gentle breeze and the river still full before the summer sun dries the hills above, shrinking the torrent to a gentle flow.'

Not waiting for an answer, Jaffa turned and walked towards the tall trees and vibrant growth that formed the garden boundary. Disappearing through a wall of green, he quickly dropped onto the pebbled bank below. Freeman followed, perplexed at this odd man and the strange day unfolding with every turn he made.

Through the foliage, Freeman slipped and stumbled down the short damp slope onto the riverbank. The bright glare sparkling off the moving water was unbearable and he put on his sunglasses. Jaffa stood close, his relaxed gait and tall slim frame seemed to mirror the gently sway of trees.

Smooth boulders and pebbles formed the riverbank. An occasional grey sand bar broke the higgledy-piggledy milieu of endless piled stones, which until recently would have been covered by the full force of the spring torrents. A warm and steady breeze blew along the river.

A kingfisher swooped low, crossing the sparkling river to disappear into the silvery leaves of tall trees on the opposite bank. Behind the trees stood a small grey rock face at whose top stood more trees and, behind that, the brilliant blue of endless sky.

Wondering why he had never ventured this far into the hills to enjoy the splendours nature gave for free, Freeman noticed a figure move on the grey and sun drenched rock.

'I see you have located our local misfit, taking children up the tricky rock.'

'What makes a misfit?'

'Obvious difference is making such a thing.'

'Does that make you?'

'I am not a misfit but a clever fit, disguised and hidden behind the trees of home sweet home.'

'I'm surprised they haven't run you out town the way you speak,' Freeman smirked.

'They surely would, but as I am not speaking French so very well, no one knows so no one cares. I am polite and never troubling anyone.'

'Only me it seems.'

'When you fish the way you do, out there...'

Jaffa looked up, spanned both hands and opened up his arms to give a sense of space.

'...as light cracks night to day, don't be surprised by the strangeness of your catch.'

Freeman stared coldly at Jaffa with empty eyes, barely holding back the volcano, rumbling deep within.

'And what's that?'

Jaffa removed his mirror shades and stared right back with a look that Freeman could not read but knew contained something monstrous that both repelled and drew him in.

'Have I caught you, Jaffa?'

'Maybe we have both been caught...a brief moment playing itself out in this vast unfathomable world.'

Freeman made a quick decision to see the day out as painlessly as possible and to avoid his early morning fishing trips to the river's mouth. Perhaps he would look for another place to fish to find solace in the breaking surf of dawn.

'So, what sites can you show me in this lovely spot?'

Jaffa changed as quickly as Freeman did.

'Lunch will be soon. However, we have these moments to investigate the opposition.'

He pointed across the river and indicated to the other side.

'There may be fun waiting amongst the leafy trees.'

With a flick of his hand, Jaffa beckoned Freeman. Both men strolled to where the river flowed under the small road bridge. They turned left and up a grassy bank to the quiet road, leaving the pebble shore and noise of rushing water behind them. The breeze vanished, left below to blow with the current and, as the sun pierced Freeman's skin in a way that took him across the ocean and back home, he felt the rising sparks of his burning heart.

Across the bridge, a small road ran to the right behind the tall trees rising up out of the riverbank. Tightly sandwiched between the rock face and the road, a single-track rail emerged from a small tunnel. As they turned into the tiny road, they heard the shouts and easy laughter of children somewhere in the trees and thick lush vegetation.

About a hundred yards down the road, Jaffa turned right down some old and very overgrown steps into the trees along the riverbank. Freeman followed and saw him turn and disappear into an earth bank where a foot tunnel ran under the road and rail track to the trees beneath the rock face. It was dark. Hanging ferns and long leaves shone in the light at the end of the tunnel. It was narrow and Freeman had to stoop, virtually crawl the damp thirty yards along the passageway to the brilliant green luminescence hanging down over the far exit. Jaffa was already gone and out of view. Spiders and remnants of their webs uncomfortably covered Freeman as he pushed through the flora and stood up, sweating in the still and humid air of the dense vegetation. He quickly brushed himself down. All around him were shades of green illuminated by shafts of light.

Freeman hated green. It reminded him of the harsh time he had had in the swamps during his desperate escape from those who had evicted him from his home.

Through shadows of a narrow mossy path, he walked to where Jaffa waited among the trees. A slim, wiry looking young woman stood nearby, her elegant face exaggerated by very short hair. Children ran around, shouting and playing.

The woman slung a coiled up climbing rope to one side. As it landed on the grassy ground with an empty thud, she beamed a wide smile and bellowed out in English cut with a heavy French accent:

'You are wearing a loud and angry shirt – the forest will be upset!'

Jaffa shot the girl an easy smile and gave a light and airy answer:

'I will have to make amends. Will you be forgiving and joining us for lunch?'

'Oh, the forest has forgiven you! I am very hungry and will be joining you for lunch.'

She looked at Freeman who was bemused at her similar Jaffa-like way of putting the language together.

'Who is your handsome friend?'

'I'm Freeman.'

'Oh, it's not often a Freeman comes though my dark tunnel to have adventures in my forest!'

They all laughed together.

'Has he met Tiger Jane?'

Jaffa nodded and she instantly fired a question at Freeman:

'Don't you think her scars look sexy?'

To Freeman the scars were horrific, a reminder of the violence he had left behind in Africa. Looking at Jaffa, whose eyes gave nothing away, he mumbled:

'Disturbing...'

The girl growled, swinging her arm towards Freeman, her hand and fingers open like a claw.

'They both found her in the jungle, but one didn't like her taste.'

Freeman started to feel drained of energy and needed to get out of the shaded forest and back into the fresh air to clear his head of all the madness this day had conjured up. He shot a glance to Jaffa that said 'I quit' and Jaffa responded with a parting comment:

'It's all a question of taste. Lunch must be almost ready…and Freeman, Elsa here does not bite, her growl is just for show.'

'You have spoilt my disguise! Now, I will organise the children and see you at the house.'

With that, the two men left and were soon back on the road, crossing the bridge. They didn't drop back down to the riverbank but continued a few yards more and turned left into Jaffa's leafy drive.

Freeman, feeling overwhelmed by the strangeness of the day, stopped in the drive and turned to Jaffa, firmly saying:

'After lunch, I want you to take me back to Bayonne. Your world is not for me.'

'Understood, but I am asking one favour of you.'

'What?' Freeman felt impatient now.

'Your story.'

Then he felt relief, for such a thing was easy. After that, he would be gone for good. Never again would he make such a foolish mistake and go off with a barking mad stranger. He was sure of that.

'Deal.'

Jaffa indicated towards the secluded garden with his open palm as he veered off towards the blue beading and entered the cottage, leaving the curtain swinging in his wake. Freeman languidly ambled across the grass and nonchalantly plopped himself onto the swing-lounger, quickly finding the solace he so badly seemed to need. He swung as Jane had swung and soon found himself melding with the soft sounds and tranquil shade.

He longed for home.

In the small rustic kitchen, Jane was collecting a few things to lay on the table, which she had placed out in the garden under the black cherry tree. She touched her proud scars and turned from the kitchen window to look at Jaffa, her hand falling from her face before reaching out and finding his dark inscrutable features. They gazed at each other as Jane spoke in a hushed and firm tone.

'Is he the man you've been waiting for?

Jaffa nodded as Jane continued:

'He looks dangerous and twisted up…another desperado, pushing hard toward his own destruction.'

Jaffa laughed.

'Not this one. This one casts far and wide into the ever turning restless tide, hoping to catch a magic wave to take him home to Africa…and needing money, I am sure of that.'

'Then use him. Use him up and play him to the last…and…'

She glanced at Jaffa with a ferocious smirk.

'…if you become his friend, I'll kill him myself.'

Quietly chuckling, they both turned to the window to glance at Freeman, swinging on his own.

As he swung, Freeman shut his eyes, listening to the gentle sounds of nature, which soothed his nerves and settled his longing heart. Although the noise of cutlery and plates being laid and the rustling of bare feet through the long grass somewhat cut into his tranquillity, he chose to remain in the pleasant company of darkness and soon fell asleep.

His cosy cocoon was pierced by the loud and invasive voice of Elsa.

'You cannot sleep. There is no peace for us wickeds! Come, we must be singing for our suppers!'

Freeman's heart sank even lower. As he opened his eyes, the wide grin of this enthusing French girl beamed down on him. He feigned a smile and reluctantly stood up from his slumber, as Jaffa spoke:

'Ah, not all the French are sophisticated and tragic!'

Freeman stared at Jaffa who now sat at the table with Jane. He felt embarrassed at his brief sleep and was perplexed by Jaffa's comment, until Elsa spoke.

'I am Basque, we are happy and strong…how do you say…like clever, hard working farmers?'

'Robust and wily perhaps,' Freeman casually replied.

'A new word for me – robust and…'

'Wily, it means to be smart and cunning, clever and flexible – a survivor's word.'

'I am liking your wily.'

Jane and Jaffa were both laughing quietly, a sight that eased Freeman's sullen mood.

'I'm happy you like my wily, Elsa. It's not a word we use very often.'

'What a shame! It sounds too good to be wasted,' Jane spluttered through laughter.

This was the first time Freeman had heard Jane speak English and recognised a strong eastern inflection. He glanced at Jane, whose mystery he could not fathom, then back to Elsa's open playful features exaggerated by her boyish haircut, and at her strong legs scuffed and scarred from numerous rock adventures. He marvelled at the decadent luxury of a European life, where a scar could mean you had had the best time on earth rather than an unchosen bout with death.

'Are you liking my legs, like I am liking your wily?'

All four erupted in irrepressible laughter, during which Freeman and Elsa moved towards the table, joining Jaffa and Jane.

The table was oblong and Jaffa sat at one end facing the swing-lounger. Jane sat to his left directly in front of the gnarly trunk of the cherry tree whose low branches and airy canopy gave soft and mottled shade.

Elsa pulled out a bleached wooden straight-backed chair opposite Jaffa and offered it Freeman.

He took the chair and tucked himself into the table. Elsa sat down to his left.

They all began to help themselves to lunch. Freeman noticed there was no tablecloth and that the black cherry tree above them was laden with young fruit. He repeated Jaffa's phrase:

'To while away the day beside a black cherry tree.'

Jane looked at Freeman intensely as Jaffa spoke.

'You are knowing trees as you are knowing how to look for lost dreams in the breaking surf of dawn.'

'You surf?'

Elsa poured herself a glass of wine and, whilst waiting for Freeman to reply, moved the bottle towards Freeman.

He shook his head and answered:

'No, the breaking surf of early morning fishing.'

'Surf, trees and lost dreams,' Jane quickly interjected.

'Today is a day for a story of a far away land,' Jaffa added.

'Do tell us Freeman.'

Freeman ignored Jane's request and turned to Jaffa.

'Where did you learn English?'

'On an ocean breeze.'

He turned to Jane:

'And you?'

'Sometimes there is a closed door and you don't know what mysteries, magic and horrors lie behind its battered façade. Are you knocking?'

Freeman had that sense of foreboding again, knew he was getting into something inexplicable and probably perilous, but he was hooked, taken by the wave he had so carefully sought.

'Knock Knock!' Elsa boomed with Jaffa replying:

'Who's there?'

Only the soft breeze rustling the leaves above and the mesmerising rush of the river spoke, as all stayed silent around the table.

'A phantom!' Elsa gasped.

The easy laughter around the table quickly activated Freeman to take his cue:

'A Freeman.'

'A Freeman who?' Jane added.

Flummoxed and not having a witty reply, Freeman struggled between the stable solitude of his empty life and the tacit lure of the unknown and tantalising dangerous.

All eyes were on him.

'You must pay the door keeper.'

Glad of Jaffa's prompt, Freeman wondered why he was putting himself through this torture. Perhaps it was some stifling politeness of his or perhaps he just needed the company no matter how trying it was. He smiled at Jane:

'How much?'

'Your story, of course.'

Freeman told his story without pause or interruption. He told of his country, his struggle, the lost war and the terrible time he had had in the swamps, but he didn't tell about the gold or his fury, hell bent on revenge.

It felt good to offload the burden. He felt easy and light at heart like the breeze playing with the leaves above.

'Freeman, your story is breaking my heart. What happened to your country?' Elsa asked. But before he had a chance to answer her difficult question, she bellowed across the table:

'The door!'

'Which I reeled in from the deep – right?'

'You cast far and wide and with a purpose.'

On hearing Jaffa's comment Freeman knew something bad lay ahead, but bad was good right then and, although perplexed, he made a mighty decision right there and then to go along with whatever was playing out.

'I've paid, so here goes!'

'Open Sesame,' Elsa joked.

They all laughed and unexpectedly, Jaffa asked:

'What use is an American without money?'

Freeman, wondering at the strange change of topic, knew he was now in the play for which he had just so easily bought a ticket.

'None I suppose.'

'You are right of course, but we all have a little American in us Freeman.'

'I am hoping not.'

Freeman suddenly realised he was speaking in that strange way of Jaffa's.

'Are you needing?'

His funds were certainly low and the thought of regular work and a life in France, no matter how easy it could be, wasn't of his choosing, and he forcibly replied to Jaffa:

'Yes, I need money,' wondering what he was setting himself up for.

The garden went into shade as a small brilliant white cloud obscured the sun. The ensuing subtle chill was a reminder that summer had not yet properly arrived. As the insects ceased their humming and the birds stopped singing, only the soft breeze in the trees and the timeless rush of river could be heard.

'A white cloud in a cerulean sky.'

As soon as Jaffa said it, the cloud passed. As warmth returned, insects hummed and chirping birds filled the day again.

'Poetry and magic!' Elsa exclaimed.

She looked right at Freeman who could only marvel at the complexity of what lay around him. Knowing all eyes were on him, he said nothing and studied the table, noticing that he had eaten a healthy lunch but had no memory of doing so. He then spoke without thinking anything through first:

'Spells and witchcraft...why can't you people speak straight and clearly instead of all this...mumbo jumbo...'

He caught himself and added:

'I'm sorry. It's been a long and strange day. I must leave.'

Feeling a prisoner of their inexplicable hospitality, he had an urgency to get out of there as quickly as possible, even if it meant ordering a taxi.

'They are only games, harmless words playing out their tacit mischief,' Jane mused, as Jaffa finished, 'under the shade of a black cherry tree.'

'We are not enemies of life. We are loving every moment, and please excuse me I must be being a good teacher and get back to my children,' Elsa said abruptly. 'Can I be seeing you again?'

'Of course,' he replied – anything for an easy passage.

She leant over and gave him the French greeting: a kiss on each cheek, something he so detested. She left waving, beaming her impish and delightful smile.

'Are you liking the robust and wily?' Jane immediately enquired.

'I am liking but not wanting.' He turned to Jaffa, 'I need to go.'

Jaffa rose and walked towards the car sitting under the leafy shade on the overgrown gravel drive where he waited for Freeman who was trying to say goodbye to Jane.

Before Freeman could say anything, Jane's palm came up and she looked deadpan at him.

Taken aback by her abruptness but also grateful he did not have to go through the motions of kissing her afflictions, he gave a polite bow and strolled over to Jaffa.

The two men faced each other and, after a few seconds of silence, Jaffa placed the car keys in Freeman's left hand.

'But my bicycle and your car?'

'Don't be worrying. Elsa shall drive us to my boat tomorrow and we will be finding you above the fruit shop or in one of the many cafés you seem to frequent.'

Freeman felt uncomfortable at knowing he had been watched; but before he could voice this thought, the familiar feel of cold metal pressed into his right palm. He shuddered and looked down at the gun his fingers wanted to clench.

He looked into the deep and hollow eyes of Jaffa, who, after a moment, said:

'Hesitation makes choice.'

Freeman clasped the gun.

He said nothing as he placed it in his pocket, opened the door of the driver's side and sat behind the wheel, putting the keys into the ignition before slamming the door shut. He glanced over to Jane who was still sitting at the table looking right through him and then to Jaffa who was doing just the same.

The door had opened and he was through. As he fired the ignition, he knew it was slamming shut behind him.

With this certainty, Freeman drove out of the leafy drive and into sunlight.

JANE WAS SWINGING on the lounger, occasionally kicking the ground to keep the motion going. Jaffa joined her and they swung together.

'Jane...'

'Yes Mohamed?'

'Is he to your liking?'

'He is too suave, but perfect for the job.'

'He's also tough, focused and without distraction.'

'You chose well.'

They both stared out and swung in silence, as the black cherry tree trembled in the breeze.

MEANWHILE, Freeman had been driving steadily towards Bayonne, devoid of thought. Focused on the road ahead, he felt a longing that took him far away, across the water, back to his home…to Africa.

As the traffic slowed, his thoughts returned. The sun was low and right at him, the afternoon glare making it hard to see the road. The open top offered no shade and Freeman squinted, pulling the sunglasses from his shirt pocket to place over his eyes. His hand then moved back towards the wheel. Instead of joining the other, it dropped down to the gun.

The narrow streets of the old town with their old tall buildings obscured the sunlight. Freeman pulled off his sunglasses and threw them on the passenger seat. He drove through an arch between two shops, pulling up in a small stone cobbled yard tucked away and out of view from the street.

Switching off the engine, he stared out at a crumbly grey plastered wall covered in faded red-oxide and green Basque graffiti that he could not read. Thinking of his parents who had been brutally murdered as they slept in their bed one stormy, dark and terrible night, he let go of the keys and, in one seething, pleasing moment, grabbed, crushed and bent his sunglasses on the passenger seat next to him before they finally snapped, shattering to pieces.

Leaving the remains of the sunglasses on the seat, Free-man left the car and pulled the soft top up and over to protect it from an early summer shower. With one foot on the ground and one knee on the seat, he lent awkwardly across the driver's seat to wind up the passenger window.

As he was about to shut the driver's door, the silhouette of a person stood in the arch blocking out the dulled light from the road. The silhouette remained motionless but was instantly recognisable to Freeman.

He wanted to stroll in the fading light, collect his thoughts and maybe have a drink or two in one of his favourite night cafés. However, his new hope and refreshed vigour the day and gun had brought, made him focus on the silhouette with different ideas. Feeling bold and sure, he wondered if he could have both things tonight: the easy stroll and the girl whose name he did not know and had never cared to know.

He wanted to change his clothes, disguise the gun from a bulge to the invisible but, as the girl had never been up to his small flat, wondered if he invited her up what it would really mean to her, to him.

The click of the car door shutting was exaggerated in the silence of the yard. As if on cue, Freeman moved towards the girl with verve. Usually he was polite, in some odd way respectful; but in the fading light, he left those lifetime habits in the shadows. She sensed the change, tensed and shuffled back a step. Freeman saw her unease and hesitated, but on remembering Jaffa's words, made a choice.

'Will you come up?'

She nodded, smiling as she followed him to an old battered oak door out in the street to the left of one of the shops – a tatty fruit shop run by an old Basque woman who rented him the flat above.

Freeman peered through the glass front and waved at the woman sitting on a small stool in the middle of the shop surrounded by mounds of fruit and jams, watching a TV above the counter at the back, but she did not see him. He unlocked the heavy door and opened it for the girl. She passed him, her body close, catching his eye for reassurance.

Following her into the dark lobby, Freeman feigned a smile, shutting the heavy door with a thud. The air was still and cool and a dull shaft of light illuminated the area from a dirty window above the first turn on the stairs.

Freeman wanted to follow the girl up, watch her figure move and swing, but he couldn't, as this was all new to her and she was not familiar with the way. He led and she followed, their footsteps on the stone stairs echoing an eerie scrapping sound as they climbed past the turn onto the next level. It was just as dark here and, in the dim unwelcoming light as his key clinked in the lock, he could just see her chest rising and hear and feel her heavy breath from the short climb upstairs.

The main room was well lit by a large window that looked out onto quaint houses in a narrow street, all painted white, green and oxide-red: the colours of the Basque country. On the other side of the room, a window looked out onto the grey wall of the courtyard, and through this window, Freeman saw amber clouds of the nearing sunset.

The girl had sat down on the bed that stood in the middle of the room. Freeman had positioned it such so he could look out at dawn and watch the night crack into day.

He was self conscious of the gun and aware of the setting sun that he wanted to view from the large bridge over the Adour, a few minutes' walk from his flat.

Waiting for a move, the girl looked up, but none came as Freeman collected a bundle of clothes from a closet and disappeared into the bathroom. The girl sat perplexed but somewhat content that she was finally in his place. To her it had meaning.

Freeman quickly changed. He loved his shirts, and although would never go as far as Jaffa's crass coloured choice, had a good selection of colourful ones himself. He put on a short-sleeved shirt with painterly like stripes in sea blue, brown and cream. Leaving two buttons undone at the top, he looked hard in the mirror. He felt stylish and more refined than Jaffa and then wondered if his vanity was a sign of getting too comfortable in Bayonne, or a sign of insecurity in these hopeless times. As he glanced in the mirror again, he saw an unshaven handsome man cleverly disguising a bitter loser. He felt the gun to wash away his insecurities and left the bathroom.

The girl's face lit up as he asked her out.

'Walk with me to the bridge and have a drink.'

They strolled to the Spirit Bridge without speaking and without touching, as was their habit. Freeman stood watching the red glow of sunset change into a multitude of inky fire colours burning through the sky and cloud.

This was as near to home as he could get: a magnificent sunset over a wide expansive sea. Although he could not see the sea from the bridge, he could sense and sometimes smell it with an onshore breeze.

Lost in thought and letting anger rise to fuel his hope of return, he forgot about the girl and went to feel the gun but found her hand instead. He turned, looked, and saw her looking up at him, smiling and enjoying a spectacular sunset with a mysterious handsome man. For one, it was the sunset of home and hope; the other, a sunset of romance.

Freeman let go of the girl's hand and walked to a nearby café where he found an outdoor table overlooking the Nive.

The girl followed and sat down next to Freeman as he watched the remains of the sunset glow above the buildings.

He looked at her features: her glossy, long straight black hair always tied back in some way, her shiny dark and tired eyes, their shadows offset by sallow skin and at lines etched around her pretty mouth.

The waiter came over and Freeman ordered his usual Armagnac and Perrier. The girl seemed delighted in the fact she was able to order whatever she pleased.

She spoke first, softly and with caution.

'Why have you asked me out tonight?'

Freeman felt uncomfortable at the direct question, that a boundary had been crossed. He paused before replying, trying to let his tension fade.

'Why did you look for me tonight?'

'I didn't, I saw you pull up in the red sports car as I was returning home.'

He wondered if she was returning from another client and had grabbed at an opportunity as he passed by in Jaffa's expensive looking car.

'Well, you picked a good night, I'm in a generous mood.'

'Why do you always give me money?'

Freeman felt panic. What did she mean? Surely, that was the arrangement: he paid and she delivered.'

Holding onto his breath, he forced a reply.

'That's what you want.'

'I never asked for money. You offered and we foolishly took it.'

A heavy silence sat between them. Moments later, as the waiter arrived with drinks, Freeman turned towards the river. Studying its dark rippling surface, he remembered his first time with the girl.

HE HAD OFTEN seen her as he wandered around Bayonne. Sometimes she was alone, other times with another girl pushing a baby in a pram. Although he was generally a solitary bird, he badly needed company, as the only human contact he had was with his landlady and the necessary dialogues he had in shops. Then one brave day he spoke to her. She was nervous at first, but the more he bumped into her, the more relaxed and friendly she became. After about a month of these random meetings, he suggested going to her place to be more comfortable. She was reluctant, but he pushed and charmed her until she relented, leading him to a rundown part of town and up to an apartment.

Her sister was sitting on a threadbare couch holding the baby. The place was clean but scant; devoid of the all things he imagined people to have. He simply took her poverty as a reason for need.

She had gone into a bedroom and Freeman followed. She had tried to close the door before he entered but he came through anyway, and when she tried to talk, he kissed her, pushing her down onto the bed. As he lifted her skirt to pull at her underwear, she went rigid and tightly shut her eyes. He felt her breasts, whose warm and wet told him it was her baby, so he rolled her over to take what he was about to pay for.

Afterwards, he went straight to the bathroom and on returning to the main room found the girl dressed and sitting ashen faced on the couch next to her glaring sister. The girl gave him an empty stare and Freeman, who thought he was adept in these particular situations, pulled his wallet from his trousers and offered money.

'Something for the baby.'

The sister reached out and pulled the money from Freeman's hand. In that awkward moment after the transaction, he took his leave, saying he hoped they could meet again.

He didn't see the girl in the street for a week or so and when he did, she avoided his eyes. Freeman thought nothing of it as he had no care, but soon she started smiling back again and the whole thing started over, except for one thing: she would insist they went for coffee and chat about mundane matters first. Freeman didn't understand this, but with time on his hands and the relief that some undemanding company gave, he was happy to go along. The sex became easier and the visits became as frequent as Freeman dared afford. Aware that this was a decadent luxury, no matter how cheap it was, he needed to hang onto his francs.

FREEMAN SAT AT the table with the girl staring at him. Knowing he had grown fond of her, he also wondered how he had become so blinkered, unable to read the simplest of situations, but he knew how.

HE MUST HAVE BEEN thirteen or fourteen when his father left the family estate for a year to study oil and gas in Brazil. It had been decided that he and his mother would join him and Freeman would attend the International School in Sao Paulo. To safeguard their future, petroleum prospecting in the vast swathes of unused land on their estate had been commissioned.

Freeman was excited at first. As an only child, he was lonely. Although he had thousands of hectares to explore, there was no one to play with. The locals were off limits and the Mission School he attended, when his mother could be bothered to drive him, only knew the bible and eternal damnation. Generally, he preferred to stay at home. He could drive, shoot, round up cattle, fix a broken door and mend a flat tyre. He could even do his sums. His parents were liberal and besides, it was assumed he would one day take over the family estate.

Sao Paulo was far from what he had expected. As a farm boy from a little known and distant country, he did not fit or mix very well. To him, the other boys and girls were worldly wise, travelled, educated and easy with themselves. They were also the meanest people he had ever known.

After school each day, the boys had a ritual of kicking a football along the empty leafy streets of the diplomatic quarter. For Freeman, it was a double edge sword. The fun, play and company were marvellous, but the taunts, jeers and ridicules were a nightmare.

'Farm Boy.'

'Monkey Fucker!'

This he could take, but what he found hard to swallow was:

'Freeman the Virgin.'

He would protest at the sheer audacity that he was some-how not a man, take umbrage but mostly he was just plain furious. At home, the local boys would not dare say such things. Their families were dependent on the employment and good will of Freeman's father.

His parents understood, told him it would all be over soon and anyhow, none of those boys knew how to grow the coffee their parents drank or raise the cattle for their steaks. He ought to remember that. It helped somewhat, but his pride was hurt and he foolishly took the bait.

'I've got girlfriends back at home.'

'Monkeys you mean!'

One devastating day, the usual football kicking started, except the taunts were silent, you could even say the gang was subdued. Thinking nothing of it, he was simply glad that he would have an easy playtime. The football was kicked down a side street, not one that they usually went down, and the gang went charging after it, passing the ball to each other across the empty street. Knowing they were at about the edge of where they were allowed to play, he expected them to turn around and kick the ball back the way they came. However, one of the boys suddenly kicked the ball hard into the air. Landing a long way from where they were, it rolled into the front porch of an old house that once must have been grand but now had that quaint look of age and pleasant decay.

The boys stopped and turned to him, one of them saying:

'Go get it chicken.'

Not understanding the cutting remark, he just simply strolled up the street and into the porch. A woman sat in an old wicker armchair by the open door; she was brown with long black hair and wore bright red lipstick. Her skirt was too short and he could clearly see the curly legs of the black widow spider all bunched up, tight and springy just like his mum's when he saw her in the bathtub.

'Looking for your balls?'

Turning around, he saw the other boys close in on him, huddled together in a group with open and expectant faces. One of them ran past him, picked up the ball and then ran back to the group. Another shouted:

'We collected out pocket money and now you prove to us you're not a liar.'

He felt empty and perplexed and turned back to the woman as the ugly chant began:

'Freeman's a virgin, Freeman's a virgin.'

The woman got up and said:

'You're not going to let your friends down – are you?'

His mouth was dry as she grabbed his hand. Dutifully, he followed her into a large hallway where a few other women sat smiling, one even giggled as he glumly walked by and up the stairs.

The room was cheap looking with a cheap looking bed and had net curtains to hide them from the street. He heard laughter from the boys and the sound of the football bouncing off a wall. She sat on the bed and he stood before her. Catching the smell of stale cigarettes on her breath, he felt the blood rushing in his head as she undid his trousers and started playing with him.

She was speaking. He didn't really hear what, and then she laid back, her skirt hitched high, the black widow all open and ghastly looking like nothing he could have ever imagined. She pulled him down on top of her, saying things as he felt her skin and moisture, moving him back and forth like a slow bucking bronco. It seemed an eternity before he heard:

'Time's up, big boy.'

He remembered the other women with their wide smiles as he left the building and all the boys standing together open mouthed as he walked back to them, knowing he was the only one of them to be a fully paid up member of that mysterious thing the boys had called The Pink Alley Club.

The boys had left him alone after that, seemed almost in awe of him, but he was still lonely and yearned for home.

That was how and that was why.

FREEMAN TOOK HIS EYES away from the river and his memories, looked at the girl studying him and then to the inky sky above the dark river shimmering the reflection of town lights.

He wanted to tell the girl his story, explain himself, excuse his behaviour, but he could not. All he had ever known since that fateful day in Sao Paulo was sex for cash. He had never known it any other way.

'You treat me like a whore.'

Freeman refrained from saying that he had thought she was a whore. Instead, he tried to appease her, somehow make things neutral, as he knew he couldn't make them right. He couldn't make himself right, not now, not yet and anyway he had no clue how.

'Why did you take me home that day?'

'Because you were pushy and you had smiled at me so many times. No one smiles at me and certainly not a man…'

She paused, and then continued with a certainty that Freeman admired but was also intimidated by.

'…like you.'

Freeman took a sip of his Armagnac. It was spoiled by the conversation and he signalled the waiter with a raised hand, asking for the bill.

The evening air was cool, almost chilly and, as they strolled back across the bridge, he noticed the girl shiver slightly, clenching her arms to her body. Feeling he was decent deep down, he was about to offer the girl his jacket when he remembered the gun; he awkwardly placed his arm around her shoulders instead. Her hand instantly rose to find and join with his, and she moved her body close.

Freeman felt strange, it didn't feel right at all and one part of him wanted to run into the darkness while another part told him that if he did, he was doomed.

'What's your name?'

'Jacques Freeman.'

'Not French, not English…where's it from?'

He told her his country, that some people spoke French, others English and that the locals spoke many different languages of which he knew one.

The girl had vaguely heard of Freeman's country.

'I'm Rebecca.'

He couldn't ask questions. It was not his habit and they remained silent until arriving at the heavy oak door.

Sex without money was like a menu without a meal and the situation put Freeman at a loss.

'I need to give you something.'

'Have you never been in love? Have you always paid?'

He said nothing because he didn't understand such a thing as love with a woman.

'Yes, you can give me something,' she sighed.

In the apartment, Freeman felt tense. Rebecca sat on the bed smiling at him; she looked tired and washed out but also sexy and Freeman went on automatic, pulling out his wallet and handing her the usual wad.

'You can pay for two months in advance.'

'I don't have those funds.'

Rebecca pulled the wallet from his hand and put the money back, keeping a well-worn ten-franc note for herself. She then handed him the wallet back.

'Ten francs. That's ten unlimited weeks where I have to pay you back in love…and you mustn't be having other girls.'

Smirking, Freeman couldn't think for the life of him why he would want the hassle and expense of having other girls when he had one right here in front of him. He liked Rebecca, she had something and she had taken the money; even though it was a minuscule amount, it did the job. He now wanted to collect for what he had just paid.

Freeman flung his jacket on the bed and went quickly to the bathroom.

In the room, Rebecca decided to tidy up the jacket by hanging it on the fixed peg she had noticed on the door. She dragged the jacket off the bed.

In the bathroom, Freeman heard the thud of the gun as it fell out of the pocket and hard onto the wooden floor. He froze as Rebecca froze, transfixed on the terrible object. He then heard the door shut and her running down the stairs. After the reverberating sound of the heavy oak door being slammed, he listened to her fading footsteps echo down the empty street.

Freeman picked up the gun, placing it on a small table. He lay on the bed knowing love was a dangerous thing, but that also being Freeman was a lonely stroll across a twilight bridge to drink alone at an empty, dark and troubled table.

He closed his eyes and dreamt of home.

THE STREET WAS GREY as Freeman peered out of the window. Still lying on the bed after a restless night, his clothes were crumpled. He was deciding exactly what to do.

MEANWHILE, as the grey light of dawn was lifting over the river, the small boat cruised downstream. When the first sparkles of light bounced off the ripples, Elsa spoke loudly over the engine:

'Are you sure he will be up?'

Jaffa looked at her across the bicycle to where she sat at the front looking back at him. She was dressed in a crass green and white tropical shirt half covered by a ripped and scruffy light grey jacket, brown slacks cut high above the ankle and leather sandals. Jaffa wore a yellow and grey shirt with racing cars zooming across his back and chest.

'The man has routines. I am guaranteeing he is up, heading to a coffee shop to have his eggs fried on one side only and to sample the freshness on Bayonne bread and…'

'Shut up and tell me about Freeman.'

'Are you wanting him to spend time inside that petite and rather flat belly of yours?'

'So crude, but oh so true!'

They both laughed loudly.

'I am thinking he is a man who prefers to pay for such a pleasure.'

She screwed her face up in disgust.

'When did you meet this troubled soul?'

'Only yesterday, as he cast his line into the silver surf of dawn where the river joins the sea.'

'Yesterday! But you played and whiled away the afternoon like long lost friends. I had never seen you so…normal.'

Jaffa gazed past Elsa towards the approaching outline of Bayonne looking dim in the early morning light. He then looked her in the eye and she looked back, waiting for a response.

'Yesterday his lunchtime story was breaking your heart.'

'I have a heart!'

'And what does it feel?'

'A lonely man wanting to go home?'

'So what's he needing?'

'A miracle.'

'And before God's intervention?'

'Money and friends.'

'Exactly Elsa.'

'What care is it to you?'

'I am needing such a man.'

'But is he needing you?'

'That is the question.'

'You want to catch him?'

'I do!'

'And why would a man like him want to live in Jaffa's cage?'

'Because he may sense a miracle glinting with every breaking day.'

'And you want my help to trick and trap this elusive beast?'

'You are not stupid.'

'Why should I play such a dirty game?'

'He may find his miracle and your heart would be mended!'

They both laughed again.

'And?'

'He may want to spend time in your petite and rather flat belly.'

'Oh!'

'A rare bird comes by so rarely.'

'I shall be his friend but leave me out of your riddles. And one more thing...'

'Yes?'

'Your story.'

'Be thinking of my story as payment for your co-operation.'

'A lousy deal but I accept so long as Jane still cooks me lunch.'

'Lunch is free.'

'It's never free.'

They were still laughing as Jaffa docked the launch by the old stone steps.

FREEMAN WAS IN a quandary. Having dismantled the gun and put it back together, it was once again lying on the small table. As it looked and smelt brand new, he figured it had never been fired. With a full magazine, it was ready; but for what, he had no idea. The feelings of the day before had gone, and now, as he sat on the bed in the clear light of morning, staring at the gun, knew he had been expertly played. Blind hunger for home had left him open, stupid even. However, he had felt something real and strong and couldn't let that slip away.

And the girl! What was he doing? He had bought ten weeks of unlimited love from her for the price of a few good drinks. He liked the deal, but he didn't like what was happening to him. Was he getting soft?

She had seen the gun. That could only mean trouble and he had to fix it somehow. But she had taken the money, not left it on the bed.

He left the gun where it lay and headed for the door.

The streets were almost empty, only the odd shopkeeper unlocking a door and a few solitary shapes unenthusiastically heading to work greeted Freeman as he hurried through the chill of early morning to Rebecca's dreary block.

It had been easy in his head to rehearse a speech and make it right. Nevertheless, as he stood outside her building looking up at grey windows and her closed front door, he was no longer sure. Doubt was a new feeling he didn't like and, as he couldn't shift it, felt it was a burden.

He banged once and waited self-consciously for some reply. Toying with the idea of heading to one of his favourite cafés, the laboured scrape of a sash window opening above, startled him. He knew what he had to do: explain the gun and make things right.

The sister peered down, studying Freeman for a while before disappearing back into the apartment. It was a few minutes before she appeared again to drop a bunch of keys on the pavement. She hadn't said a word. Without hesitation, Freeman immediately started trying them in the lock. Pushing the door open and ascending the stairs, he found the sister waiting by the threadbare couch, glaring at him. Rebecca's door was shut.

'She's in there. Why don't you barge on in and take her like the brute you are?'

Freeman had never been spoken to like that by a woman and was stunned and lost for words.

'She doesn't need a man like you making her feel special before turning her to prostitution.'

Rebecca came out, closely holding the sleeping baby.

'Your boyfriend's arrived – The Bayonne Beast. I can't stand him here.'

With that comment, the sister left the apartment, violently pulling the keys from Freeman's hand and slamming the door shut.

Clearly seeing through Rebecca's negligee, he felt uneasy, near ashamed and sat down heavily on the threadbare couch. Without saying a word, she swung back and forth, kissed the baby's head and stared right at him. He stared back, studying her, disturbed by a thousand things he couldn't voice.

'Your shirt is the same as yesterday and crumpled.'

'Did you tell your sister about the gun?'

She shook her head and placed the baby gently in a cot at the end of the couch.

'I can explain.'

'Whores and guns – what's there to explain?'

'The gun's never been fired and....'

'What's it for then?'

Rebecca had pulled out and set up an ironing board. She plugged in an iron.

'I don't know...maybe to give me hope that someday I'll get my home back.'

'Your shirt.'

Puzzled, Freeman started unbuttoning his shirt as Rebecca added:

'Keep your guns and whores away from me.'

He passed the shirt, which she took and placed upon the board.

'It's one gun and there are no whores.'

'And me? What am I if not your whore?'

Freeman couldn't answer and Rebecca deftly ironed Freeman's shirt, placing it neatly at the end of the ironing board.

'So am I your whore or your girlfriend?'

He said nothing.

'Trousers.'

Staring at her thinly veiled nakedness, he proceeded to take off his casual shoes and summer socks before unbuckling his belt and standing up. Although he knew this wasn't about sex right now and that they had more to talk about, he felt aroused and bashfully removed his trousers. Handing them to Rebecca, he sat back down. She set to work and then looked up.

'Am I your girlfriend?'

Unable to respond, he just looked back.

'Would you like me to speak?'

Alarmed and barely managing a near inaudible 'yes', Freeman listened as Rebecca proceeded as if it had been her who had rehearsed a speech.

'I am your girlfriend and in ten weeks' time you can pay me another ten francs. That way you feel normal and I know where I stand...and Jacques, you can't be having other girls.'

Freeman still had no idea why she thought he would want other girls.

'As my sister can't stand the sight of you and as I have a baby to look after, you can't come here anymore unless it's to pick me up or to leave a message.'

Freeman nodded. So far, nothing was awry.

'It's your place and I want a key.'

'A key?'

'To come whenever I want unless you have someone else there of course.'

Again, he couldn't fathom why he would have the complication of another girl.

'There's no one.'

Feeling hopelessly out of his depth, Freeman struggled with ideas he had never considered. Lost in his own confusion and badly needing clarity, he blurted out something he could understand:

'That's the deal?'

'Yes, that's the deal. You seem to like deals.'

The baby gave a low cry and Rebecca left the trousers to crouch down by the cot. Close to Freeman, he caught her scent. He looked straight down at her crouching body and she looked up, emphatically saying:

'Cut a key and the deal's done.'

Quickly dressing, Freeman brushed past Rebecca to hurry out into the easy air of the morning street.

ELSA LENT ON a rail overlooking the Adour near the Hotel de Ville. Jaffa joined her and they both gazed out across the slow water of the turning high tide. On the opposite side of the river, behind the tightly packed riverfront buildings glowing in the morning sun, they heard the whistle of a train.

'We have been to his house, seen the car and have looked in every café twice. I am recommending breakfast and a miracle.'

'Yes, the miracle.'

'Does he really need Jaffa for his miracle? Maybe he has other plans.'

'He surely does, but right now he must be with his special friend.'

As a train left Bayonne station heading for the hills, the whistle echoed once again.

'The call for breakfast – it's on you today!' Elsa exclaimed.

'It's not free you know.'

They laughed, left the rail and moved on up the street towards the centre of town.

THE BUNCH OF KEYS lay on the middle of the stained wooden table where Freeman had placed them some ten minutes before. He gazed at them with an empty mind; things were going fast, and his slow routines lost since Jaffa broke them with the breaking surf of dawn, yesterday. Breakfast came and the waiter moved the keys to the far end of the small table to make space. Refocusing his eyes on the keys' new position, he slowly ate without interest, ignoring the bustle in the street where his table sat. The coffee tasted bitter and Freeman wondered if it had always tasted bitter; his senses were waking up, and he somehow felt more alive.

He pondered Rebecca, whose continued affections lay in a key he had not cut, and thought of Jaffa, the strange man who had cleverly placed the gun in his hand, giving him hope that he could somehow find his way back home.

These deep and silent thoughts were suddenly washed away by the almost familiar French accent of Elsa's strange and funny English.

'A very late breakfast! May we be joining you to feast ourselves?'

Glad they had found him, Freeman needed answers fast.

They sat down on either side of him and Jaffa spoke.

'A fine day to break a habit…'

'How long have you been watching me?'

'A few months now.'

'What makes me so popular?'

'I was telling you yesterday. I need a man like you.'

'I'm all ears.'

'In time, it takes time you know...of which we have enough. As a fisherman you must be knowing that.'

'Riddles, always riddles,' Elsa sighed.

The waiter came to take their order. As Freeman had already finished his breakfast, he took the opportunity to excuse himself and head to the locksmith across the street. He grabbed the bunch of keys and left. Elsa and Jaffa watched him intently as he disappeared into the shop.

'He is lost in his own thoughts today,' Elsa tutted.

'A key, it's all about a key,' Jaffa smiled.

'Oh, his special friend...shall we ask him?'

'You ask, make him feel at ease.'

Jaffa peered deep into Elsa. She replied to his stare:

'Your deep and empty eyes hide many secrets which I know I must not know, but imagine Freeman, all confused and pretending to be cool.'

'My wily little Basque...'

FREEMAN RETURNED, placing the keys on the table; two were new and glistened in the bunch.

'New keys...a special friend?' Elsa coyly enquired.

'A business colleague.'

Jaffa laughed and feigned a choke.

Freeman knew that Jaffa must have known something about Rebecca, but knew he couldn't know that much. Maybe he had seen them together, noticed the short time he spent inside her flat.

'A girlfriend.'

Now he had said it and that was that.

'A business girlfriend?'

'Yes, I'm in business with my girlfriend.' After all, they had made a deal.

Jaffa pushed the joke a little more:

'What kind of business?'

Freeman was now stumped and Elsa quickly came to his rescue.

'Oh, I'm sure you have some private business with Tiger Jane!'

Elsa and Jaffa laughed but Freeman, feeling the madness of the day before creeping up on him again, barely smiled. After a moment of silence, Jaffa looked deadpan at Elsa.

'Be driving my car back home. I will take the launch upstream.'

Freeman led the way to the old fruit shop where the old woman sat on her stool in the middle of the shop. She waved a toothless grin as they went into the courtyard behind the shop.

Freeman handed over the car keys to Elsa who unlocked the driver's door and adjusted the seat before getting in. This gave Freeman just enough time to roll back the folding roof and quickly grab the broken sunglasses, which he discarded on the courtyard floor as Jaffa stood and stared.

The two men watched Elsa reverse and turn before driving through the arch and down the narrow street. Freeman turned to Jaffa.

'We need to talk.'

'Then talk we shall. Do you want a job?'

'You know I do.'

'It might be dangerous.'

'I need the gun?'

'For the job, no. To be giving hope, yes.'

'To get my country back?'

Jaffa completely ignored the question.

'We are not needing to be whiling away the fine and pleasant day, but come back to the house and all will be revealed, discussed and hopefully concluded.'

Freeman thought of Rebecca and the shiny new keys, but knew this may be his only chance and she would have to wait. He was sure she would.

Strolling in silence through the late morning, they stopped at the top of the old stone steps and looked down at the boat bobbing in the receding tide.

'Ah, your bicycle…shall we be taking it for another cruise to the old and leafy chestnut trees?'

'I need to be back by tonight.'

'The keys?'

Freeman felt his old-self return. The rising tide of hate, which had been calm and low, now showed in his face. Before he could voice irritation at this intrusion into his private world, Jaffa intervened.

'Good Freeman! That's what I need, your spitting volcano which never blows, but sends all and sundry to take cover from its boiling rage.'

'You sure have a way with words.' Freeman couldn't help but smile now.

They embarked and, as Jaffa pulled the cord to start the engine, Freeman released the mooring. They headed upstream.

Feeling apprehension, Freeman sat in the front of the boat looking back over the forgotten corpse of his bicycle to the mirror-shaded Jaffa and the disappearing town.

They moored to the rickety wooden jetty. The ground underfoot had dried a little, the soft damp earth now having a fine crust that broke and crumbled as the two men made their way through the tall grass towards the barn and chestnut trees.

Under the shadows of the mighty trees and looking much like a long abandoned farmyard wreck, sat a beat up old blue Renault car.

'She needs a new car,' Freeman remarked.

'Oh no, this is perfect and exactly to her taste.'

Jaffa opened the unlocked passenger door.

'This is the only door that works.'

His lanky frame crawled across the passenger seat, neatly righting on the driver's seat. As Jaffa started the engine, he looked over at Freeman sitting next to him.

'Chestnuts never lie – their branches point the way to heaven and their roots to earth.'

Looking back, Freeman knew there was more to come.

'How is your sense of direction? Are you remembering the way back home?'

Freeman nodded. He had started to like some of the absurd poetry that Jaffa constantly spewed.

'Who taught you to speak like that?'

'My mother.'

'You had a mother!'

'I have a mother.'

'Where?'

'Over the chestnut trees and far away.'

'You're not telling?'

'Exactly Freeman, exactly.'

Jaffa drove slowly along the dirt track to the small road that ran through the empty, sleepy village. Following the small rail track, he turned right towards the river, as Freeman gave directions.

'First, you must not be speaking with anyone of what I am about to tell you. Secondly, Elsa: she is smart and knowing far too much already. So please be stringing her along in anyway but truth.'

Freeman nodded: so far, so good.

'I fix and secure contracts for mining exploration. Sometimes other factors are involved.'

Not so good, as Freeman knew this business. His country was surrounded by strife of this making; endless wars and skirmishes, stirred up by interested parties only out for themselves.

'Other factors?'

'Dacoits and undesirables.'

'You hire men to clear them out, hence the secrecy?'

'It's a legitimate business. I pay tax you know.'

'Tax! Where?'

'If I don't say, then you can't tell.'

'Then don't say. What's the job?'

'Negotiate a contract with whatever tools I give you.'

'Will there be killing?'

'That's not your job.'

'You said: it might be dangerous…'

'If it goes all wrong.'

'And the money?'

'Enough to buy a sailing boat and cruise an ocean breeze, maybe for a year or more, maybe even more.'

Freeman was flabbergasted. The sum seemed outrageous and he knew there had to be a catch, but he badly needed money and this route just might lead him home.

Jaffa followed Freeman's dry instructions, crossing the bridge over the Nive and turning left towards Itxassou.

'What's the catch?'

'If it's going wrong, you are well and truly on your own.'

'That sounds bad.'

Jaffa stayed silent for a while and then said, nonchalantly:

'A day's work for a few years sailing…not bad I say.'

'A day!'

'Of course it might not be such a breeze you know.'

Freeman felt that fate had dealt him a dud and dangerous hand, which he now had no choice but play.

'I can handle a strong breeze.'

'Best prepare for a hurricane.'

'That would blow me right off course.'

'So, you're in?'

'I'm in.'

The pale blue sky was becoming increasingly dotted with small white puffy clouds as the Renault drove past the lone banana tree towards the overgrown gravel drive.

'Which country?' Freeman innocently asked.

'It will be written on your ticket.'

'Of course it will…'

The car crunched on the gravel and came to a halt behind the open top red sports car.

Jaffa switched off the engine and both men gazed through the still and warm midday air at the two women swinging on the lounger.

'Elsa.'

'Yes Freeman, Elsa.'

'Play her, right?'

'As she plays you.'

Elsa waved and smiled as Freeman left the car and headed towards the women.

'Do you like my sweet little car?'

'It needs attention.'

'I call her Julie after my little sister.'

'Don't you like her?'

'Yes, she's cute.'

Jaffa went straight inside, the beaded curtain swaying as he disappeared from view. Jane deftly jumped from the swinging lounger and followed him, leaving Freeman and Elsa alone, facing one another.

'Swing with me a while.'

Freeman, glad of the invitation, sat himself next to Elsa, who immediately spoke.

'You play a dangerous game.'

'And you?'

'I worry that you will be swept away...'

She tried to find the right words and Freeman helped her:

'...by the ruthless tide of deception.'

'Yes, how succinct.'

'Let's not talk Elsa.'

'But I feel it Freeman, your story, your pain and those two devils making plans and tricks to lure you to your death.'

'How can you know that?' And what do you know about me?'

Freeman turned and looked at Elsa with open eyes and a weary heart. She looked right back at him.

'Because I feel it...can't you feel it?'

'What?'

'Life and what's all around.'

Freeman said nothing for he only felt the burning desire to take back what was his.

Elsa, now staring out at the black cherry tree, continued:

'Don't let your anger blind you from the truth.'

'Which is?'

'You're being used.'

'And you?'

He looked away and he too stared at the tree.

'I'm the fool, the idiot who amuses the devil in his court.'

'Stop it, Elsa.'

'Freeman...'

He looked back at her looking back and straight at him. She was close and her breath on him.

'Kiss me.'

'I can't.'

'Why not?'

Grabbing him, she forced him down onto the cushions, smothering his face with hers.

JANE WAS LOOKING through the net curtains.

'We should kill them both.'

Jaffa joined her and gazed at the swing-lounger.

'Freeman, what an easy lay.'

'Do we let them fuck the afternoon away or stop this mating game?'

They both smiled and Jane added:

'Are you sure of Freeman?'

'Anything to get his homeland back.'

'And the French girl, Mohamed?'

'Elsa only guesses and besides, she is most robust and wily.'

As they laughed, outside on the swing-lounger Freeman tasted coffee on her tongue. He thought about the devils that had played him so very well.

Jaffa's shout broke the spell and Elsa let Freeman go, sitting upright to swing once more. Freeman joined her.

'Drinks?'

'Do you think they saw?' Freeman asked Elsa.

'They don't care so long as you do whatever they will ask.'

Freeman shouted back:

'Thanks.'

'Do you want me Freeman?'

Freeman didn't know the answer. He was in the thick of something and couldn't see anything clearly.

'I don't know.'

'Yes you do, I felt you hard against me.'

Freeman said nothing.

'Your special friend?'

'We have a deal.'

'Then break your deal.'

'A deal's a deal.'

'Until it's broken.'

'But it's not broken.'

'Then break it soon.'

Freeman wondered about this free sex business. It took up lots of time and nothing was straight or clear. He also wondered if Elsa was playing some unknown game. Best stick to deals where things were clear and straight and where he had promised not to be having other girls.

Jane and Jaffa came out of the house, Jane carrying a tray with long, cool refreshing drinks. Putting the tray down on the wooden table under the black cherry tree, she looked up at the increasing cloud cover and listened to the leaves rustling in the subtle breeze.

'You have made the sky broody.'

She looked at Elsa and Jaffa chuckled:

'The poetry of truth.'

Elsa blushed but it quickly passed.

'The poetry of life,' she parried back.

A sudden clap of thunder echoed across the hills, prompting Elsa to add:

'It agrees!'

They all sat around the old wooden table sipping their drinks. It had grown oddly humid with the heavy sky suggesting a downpour. The wind suddenly ceased and Jaffa spoke:

'A sultry sky.'

'Sultry?' Elsa enquired.

'Moody and expectant, a passion that sits heavily, waiting to explode like this heavy sky and oppressive warm close air, or that sultry look in your dark and moody eyes.'

'I'll fuck Freeman if I want!' Elsa snapped, defending herself.

Freeman felt the façade of decency crumble around him and his body tensed.

All eyes were on him and, in the sudden and unexpected humidity, a bead of sweat rolled down his brow and landed on the table for all to see.

For Freeman an awful moment of silence was broken by Jaffa:

'Has the neighbour's cat been getting at your tongue?'

'What's the matter?' Elsa joked.

Freeman managed to utter his shock and disgust at the wayward conversation.

'It's not decent.'

'But it's life and truth.'

'Not like this,' Freeman stiffly answered Elsa back.

'Such decadence is not to your liking?'

'There's a time and place,' Freeman curtly snapped at Jaffa.

'How civilised and courteous of you to be putting your raw and dangerous nature in a box.'

'Yes Jane, we can be labelling it: do not open, dangerous and disgusting!'

'You know what I mean Jaffa: if we let things slip, things fall apart and….'

In his moment of deliberation, Jane finished:

'Go back to the jungle.'

Freeman eyed the scar on Jane's leg as she sat crossed legged on a small bench at the end of the table at an angle to him, and Jane looked right back at him.

Raising both palms, Freeman managed a phoney smile.

'I surrender. You win.'

He turned to Elsa.

'Yes I'm wanting but I stick to my deals.'

He then looked at Jaffa and said:

'As I hope others do.'

'Let me be telling you all a tale,' Jaffa said, taking off his mirror sunglasses.

'Each day, the jungle crept closer towards the decaying but once magnificent colonial mansion. On this particular day, the hot and sweaty sultry sky, dark with the expectant storm, bore down oppressively on the lunchtime guests. I sat at one end of a huge table, which was covered in a heavy linen tablecloth full of fine china and polished silver cutlery. The men were dressed up for this midday meltdown in starched collared shirts, crème jackets and, of course, the obligatory black polished shoes. Dressed in haute couture laden with sparkling jewels set in shiny metal, the women were heavily made up, like dolls, so they could be played with later on.

We all melted along with the stinking cheese rotting and swimming on the plates from the sweat rolling off our brows and, as endless courses came, we had polite talk about a Paris no one longer knew and how the lazy good for nothing staff knew absolutely nothing of the decent things in life.

As we ate this huge lunch and over-filled our poor stomachs in the sweltering heat, which the overhead fan did little to ease, outside, not so very far away, guns rumbled and shells exploded, sometimes shaking the house, as the country fell and tore itself apart.'

Jaffa paused and added to the expectant faces:

'That was decadence.'

'And their undoing,' Jane added.

Freeman frowned, knowing the comment was aimed straight at him.

'I don't like cheese.'

With another thunderclap, the first cool drops of rain splashed onto the wooden table, easing the tense and close air the day had conjured up.

'Oh, magic rain to wash away all that smelly and rather embarrassing cheese,' Elsa quickly jibed.

Laughing, they soon took cover under the black cherry tree. Large heavy raindrops splashed the leaves above, showering them in tiny droplets. On glancing over to his open top car, Jaffa jogged over to roll the roof up to protect it from the wet.

Elsa gazed at Freeman through clear dark eyes and smiled through neat white teeth. As he looked hard back wondering what to do or say next, Jane spoke:

'Elsa, what is it about Freeman?'

'So very old fashioned and totally removed.'

'Like an antique.'

'A treasure rarely found.'

'What did you call him?' Elsa asked, shouting over to Jaffa.

'A rare bird.'

'Yes, a rare bird indeed!'

'To keep locked tight in a cage,' Jane goaded.

'Can I keep you in a cage?' Elsa teased.

Freeman longed to escape this absurd theatre and be back home or at the very least inside the simplicity of Rebecca's embrace, but he played along.

'Perhaps I'm already in a cage.'

'Whose?' Jane pursued.

But Elsa wasn't having that.

'Oh Freeman don't be a fool. You have no keeper.'

'I can't win with you people. You have me every time.'

Jaffa strolled back smiling through the light rain, saying:

'That is what we are liking about you – your raw and honest simplicity.'

'I'm not sure how to take that.'

'Did that pussy also get your sense of humour?' Jane turned the screw a little harder, with Elsa adding:

'Along with your heart?'

Freeman's eyes seethed at the endless dry and rude humour, but he quickly contained himself, and, before he could invent some meaningless sentence to parry the remarks, Jaffa spoke:

'Perfect Freeman.'

'Perfect for what? Endless jokes and riddles?' He replied, exasperated by the conversation.

'We have lured you and played you, and now that my mission is complete, I must be going home…and Mr. Jaffa…you are owing me your tale,' Elsa concluded.

'Of course! And thank you for your expertise. Feel free to collect it anytime.'

Astonished, Freeman looked at Elsa.

'They had you in on this too?'

'Oh not really, I only played you for myself. I am living behind the lonely banana tree – you will see my car. The door is always open for you to break your precious deal.'

Elsa moved close to Freeman and, whilst standing on tip toes and pulling at his shirt to ensure his head met hers, kissed him ritually on each cheek. Freeman felt her wet cheeks and damp hair on him as he gazed at her small figure turning away, walking towards her car. Without thinking, he followed the car to the end of the drive and watched it for a hundred yards before it turned, disappearing into a tangle of garden behind the lone banana tree.

Freeman looked at Jane and Jaffa dripping rain drops under the cherry tree, staring right at him. He too was wet, but as the rain was cool and the air warm, found it comforting and refreshing.

Jaffa shouted over to Freeman:

'You have a passport?'

'Yes.'

'Are you ready anytime?'

'Yes.'

'Then it is done.'

'What, that's it?'

'That's it.'

Perplexed, Freeman gave a resigned nod as Jaffa strolled towards him.

'Let's journey back to where the solitary cow munches on the hay and gently cruise to the old stone steps that lead you back to home.'

'The cow is still there?' Jane enquired.

'Would you like to say hello?'

Jane hurried over to the car and entered the open front passenger side, crawling over the seat to position herself in the rear. Jaffa was soon in the driver's seat and, before Freeman had had a chance to sit down properly and shut the door, they were slowly driving off. He pulled the door shut and looked to his right as they passed the banana tree and caught a glimpse of Elsa's car parked down a long grassy drive.

'Are you needing to be knowing where she lives?' Jaffa comically asked.

'I just may.'

As they both laughed, Freeman caught Jane's stare in the badly positioned rear view mirror that she had knocked whilst getting in. She wasn't laughing: just staring cold at him.

They drove in silence, the windscreen wipers scrapping and squeaking in the slight but steady rain. Patches of blue sky showed between the grey clouds, hinting that the rain would pass. Freeman did not fancy the boat ride in the wet.

Pulling up under the huge chestnut trees whose thick leafy canopies had kept the ground under fairly dry, Jane immediately went into the old barn and up to the light brown cow. She started singing softly in a language Freeman did not recognise. The cow stopped chewing and seemed to listen to the soothing words.

Freeman and Jaffa stood under the trees. Jaffa spoke first.

'The rain will soon abate, so let us wait before we journey on.'

'Do I just wait…not for the rain to stop…I mean, for the job?'

Jaffa's wry and bemused smile infuriated Freeman but he kept it in, knowing any outburst would be further ridiculed.

'In a week, perhaps much sooner, I'll be bringing you some freshly pressed hard cash money in any currency your burning heart desires.'

'French francs will do just fine. All the money?'

'A third up front, the rest paid into a Swiss account once I have the contract you shall so effectively get signed.'

'You seem so sure of me.'

'A rare bird comes so rarely.'

Looking over at Jane and listening to Jaffa, Freeman mumbled: 'Strange.'

'Not strange but lucky. That cow is a very lucky cow indeed!'

Freeman nervously laughed and Jane shot him a nasty look.

The rain eased and only splashes that had accumulated on the leaves still fell. The sky was blue once again, the dark gloomy grey disappearing over the hills across the river.

They left Jane with the light brown cow and walked through the long grass, sinking in the wet squelching mud to the old wooden jetty. Even though it had been a brief downpour, the river had risen enough to pull the boat out into the current. The mooring rope was so tight that hauling the boat back to the jetty by hand was impossible. Without ado, Jaffa immersed himself into the cool water, wading out waist deep to push the boat back alongside the old jetty. Freeman stepped onboard.

Watching Jaffa looking passed him over the bicycle to the river ahead, Freeman asked:

'Aren't you cold?'

'A wet and chilly body, drying in the comfort of a warm delightful day…'

Jaffa lifted his sunglasses and looked straight at Freeman.

'…is pure rewarding luxury, and nothing less than…sorcery.'

He flipped the glasses down.

Freeman chuckled at the absurd speak, looked over and saw himself and the bicycle reflected in the mirrors of Jaffa's sunglasses, an image that was soon joined by the rough outline of Bayonne buildings.

'Were you in the army?'

'A few years of military service. Nothing much, just patrolling around the estates. But then the uprising put everybody in the army.'

'You saw action?'

'Everyone did.'

'Good Freeman.'

'Good?'

'Yes, and you were knowing how to get out, right?'

Freeman didn't like that remark one bit and replied gruffly: 'I'm here now.'

'Yes, here to while away the days with a special friend and friends anew. What is it about home you are so missing?'

'The empty open spaces and an uncomplicated life where rules are only talked about but never really known.'

'That's because they are written in your head where they cannot be seen, only acted on.'

'You know what I mean – living without forms and regulations and God knows what!'

'But God doesn't know what. God left confusion to the world of men.'

'And God is now just whiling away pleasant days somewhere under a black cherry tree, right?'

'Exactly Freeman, exactly.'

The stone steps welcomed Freeman and, as he clumsily disembarked with his chattel to negotiate the steps, Jaffa waved once before heading back upstream to the car, chestnut trees and Jane talking to a light brown cow.

BAYONNE WAS QUIET, the traffic low and people scant with only a few slow moving shapes on the bridge. Freeman looked at his watch. Seeing it was now three-thirty, he decided to wait until evening to eat in one of the quiet side street cafés.

He tied the two pieces of his fishing rod to his bicycle, put the small pack on his back and pushed the bike home through the narrow streets. He felt tired, drained of energy, as recent events had been confusing and exhausting.

He decided to carry on as normal. If he never saw Jaffa again, then so be it.

Pushing the heavy oak door open, he carried his bicycle over the stone step into the lobby and left it in the shadows under the stairs. He headed upstairs to his apartment.

The gun still lay on the table. As Freeman placed the pack down, he eyed it with disdain. Yesterday he had felt its power, but today, its magic spell had run its course and all he saw was the terrible object Rebecca had heard falling on the floor. Picking it up, he placed it in a drawer, out of sight.

SOMETIME LATER, after Freeman had showered and changed, he organised his fishing pack for the following morning. Between Rebecca and her key, Jaffa and the gun and Jane talking to a light brown cow, let alone the lure of a mysterious and dangerous job, he badly felt the need for some semblance of normality again.

The light in the room dulled as the grey wall at the back of the courtyard obscured the sinking sun. He switched on the artificial light he so detested.

He had laid the lures and traces in a neat row on the floor. The silver and bright colours shone under the electric light. Freeman had this ritual of laying out the gear every evening before a fishing trip. It made no sense to him, as picking a lure was more a matter of luck than measured skill, but the need for order was paramount and kept him focused. He studied every piece, knowing that the big fish had been caught. However, he couldn't stop thinking it was he that had been caught and expertly played, soon to be dumped upon an unknown foreign shore. Jaffa's job filled him with such apprehension that he half hoped it wouldn't happen.

He packed the gear away as he always did and shut the pack ready for the morning. Listless and at a loss, he picked up the keys and headed out into the evening, hoping to catch the last rays of sunset from the bridge. His small narrow street was full of shadow and the air unusually chilly. Changing his mind, he hurried through the dimming light to Rebecca's front door. Knocking hard twice, he looked up at the dirty kitchen window, waiting for the scrapping sound of sash. He heard the sound and Rebecca peered down. Moments later, her quick light footsteps rushed downstairs to meet him. She smiled through large white teeth, the lines clearly showing around her mouth and eyes. Freeman eyed her nervously. She wore a black dress buttoned down the front, ending between her ankles and her knees; her hair was tied back tight and Freeman thought she had some makeup on but he wasn't sure, as he didn't really know about those things.

She eyed his denim.

'You've changed your shirt.'

'Exactly…'

Trying to shake off Jaffa's speech, he added:

'…I had to.'

They stood staring at each other for a moment with Freeman wondering what was next. On remembering, he said:

'I have the keys.'

Rebecca beamed a smile, threw her arms around him and kissed him on the lips and neck, making Freeman realise a key was so much cheaper than the hard cash from his wallet. He wondered what else came free.

'Want to eat?'

'I have to bring the baby as Chloe, my sister, is out with her own Bayonne brute.'

Freeman looked uncomfortably away.

She shot upstairs and moments later came down carrying the baby in one arm and a fold-up pushchair and small bag in the other. A shawl hung over her shoulders. Erecting the pushchair, she placed the wide-eyed baby inside, wrapping it up against the early summer chill.

The marvellous sunset of the evening before was nowhere to be seen and he felt good about not having headed to the bridge for a disappointing view.

They ate modestly at an outside table near the Cathedral, away from the traffic and early evening bustle that Bayonne attracts when the weather is fine and settled. Freeman admired the old, strong stone buildings of the area, so unlike those at home where the constant wet, baking sun and gnawing insects ensured that every building had to be constantly renewed. They had engaged in small talk about his farm and life back home and his early morning fishing trips to the breaking surf of dawn, before he changed the topic to the job he had been promised, which would take him far away for a short time.

'Where is this job?'

Having no idea, Freeman froze.

'Is it to do with the gun?'

'No, no, it's just that I don't know where. I get told at the airport.'

'Why the secrecy?'

'A tricky contract, I suppose.'

'Don't you find it odd? It's not normal.'

'Nothing's normal about those people.'

'Then why do it?'

'Money…and these people just might get me home.'

'But hasn't home been burnt and plundered.'

'Not in my heart.'

Rebecca stretched out and touched Freeman on the chest.

Both mother and baby gazed intently.

'Be careful what you wish for Jacques.'

Freeman knew that somewhere in the not so distant future, the devil beckoned with an easy grin. He said nothing.

'I don't know what you are involved in but it worries me.'

'Me too,' he chuckled to dismiss his own concern.

'I suppose that is who you are.'

'It's not! I only want to get back home,' he retorted.

'But it's not there anymore'

'Then I'll make it there.'

Changing the subject, Rebecca asked:

'Why don't you ask me questions?'

'Because the future's uncertain and I may not be around.'

'But life is now, not in some faraway sketchy plan.'

'I can't be involved.'

'You are.'

'What's the baby's name?'

'He doesn't have one yet.'

Freeman said nothing.

'Is that it?'

'That's it for now, Rebecca.'

'Jacques, that's the first time you have used my name.'

Freeman took out his key ring, carefully pulling off the two new shiny ones and pushed them across the table to Rebecca who smiled before reaching out to touch his hand.

'Take me home. I want to try my new keys.'

THE FIRST KEY turned the lock rather stiffly but the ensuring click sent a shiver through Rebecca as she looked up smiling at Freeman who was feeling very unsure of himself. Along with her bag, she carried the dozing baby over the threshold into the dark lobby followed by Freeman carrying the folded pushchair. He flicked a switch and the gloomy staircase lit with an unearthly glow that created stark ugly shadows. Soon they were moving upwards where the second key undid its lock.

Freeman, getting used to being at a loss with Rebecca, knew in these awkward moments where he felt like a broken spare part, she would work everything and show him what to do.

Carefully placing the baby on the bed, Rebecca smiled and looked over to Freeman who was standing at the end of the bed.

'The deal's done,' she said, adding the two new keys to her own key ring, which she had just plucked from her bag.

'Look after the baby Jacques while I use the bathroom.'

Giving Freeman a reassuring smile, she picked up the bag and headed to the bathroom,

Freeman stayed glued to the spot, looking at the baby peacefully sleeping on the centre of the bed and waited the ten minutes or so until Rebecca re-entered the room. She was half-undressed.

'The bathroom window's too small and the electric light makes everything so ugly.'

'Does it?' He had never noticed.

'Yes, it's horrible...do you have a spare blanket and a sheet so I can make up a small bed on the floor?'

Freeman opened a drawer and pulled out a woollen blanket and spare sheet, handing them to Rebecca who quickly made a small cot on the wooden floor next to the big bed. She placed the sleeping baby carefully on it.

She laid her dress over the one and only wooden chair in the room and then went over to the bed, pulling back the sheet. She sat cross-legged, looking up at Freeman who was still standing fully clothed in the middle of the room.

'Turn the light off and collect your part of the deal.'

He flicked the switch and did as he was told.

FREEMAN WOKE BEFORE DAWN. The room smelt of sex and he untangled himself from her clinging body, got up and started to pull out some old clothes to wear. Rebecca stirred.

'Where are you going?' She mumbled.

'To fish the river mouth at dawn.'

As she drifted back to sleep, Freeman left the sleeping couple, quietly closing the door. With his pack fastened to his back, he went downstairs to collect his bicycle and fishing rod.

THE GREY OF DAWN, before light shows the world once more, was a joy to Freeman. He always aimed to arrive at the beach before any sparkle hit the waves so he could cast out into the magic that was neither night nor day. He pushed hard at the pedals of the old bike and felt his legs burn and his heart pump. The shadows of Anglet passed him by as he raced towards the sea.

The surf was subdued and the fish not biting. As light broke, showering the ripples with a glinting sheen, Freeman decided to pack up and head back to the new company he had so yearned but never understood.

The journey back was always the same, cycling through the waking town with its sleepy inhabitants going off to work. They were lost in their own thoughts and unaware of this stranger fishing while they slept, as he cast to catch the sunrise before it vanished to another day.

Just before home, Freeman always pushed his bicycle through the narrow potholed streets to save his wheels and tyres from being wrecked.

Suddenly, a white Mercedes pulled up next to him and two men rushed out. Freeman, having the terrible times of the uprising still with him, quickly placed the bicycle between him and the men. They abruptly stopped. These men weren't French or Basques but North Africans and the one now ranting, looking quite deranged, had a nasty scar across his forehead and left temple.

'Stay away from Rebecca.'

Freeman said nothing and took one hand off the bicycle.

The man spoke again in an ugly harsh tone:

'If I see you with her again, I'll slit your throat!'

Freeman still said nothing.

Incensed by the silence, the man pulled a knife from his pocket as the other launched himself at Freeman who was quick to respond, pushing the bicycle into his path. The collision sent both bike and man sprawling onto the empty road. The knife slashed dangerously close to Freeman's face and he kicked out at the knifeman's knee. The man tensed and wobbled, allowing Freeman the chance to jab him hard in the throat, sending him back against the car where he collapsed down by the front wheel. The other man was up but Freeman was already on him, cracking his ribs with a well-placed punch.

Seeing his chance to escape, Freeman picked up the bicycle and quickly disappeared around the corner. Soon, he was slamming the heavy oak door shut behind him.

He checked his rod, relieved to see no damage.

Rebecca was sitting naked on the bed playing with the baby. She smiled inquiringly at Freeman, who was visibly shaken up and tense.

'What's the matter?'

'Who's the Arab with the scar across his forehead?'

Rebecca blushed, picked up the baby and held him close.

Freeman wasn't angry but needed answers.

'Now I'm asking questions.'

'A bad and dangerous man. What happened?'

'Two of them just attacked me. I nearly got knifed. They said to stay away from you…well Rebecca?'

'He forced himself on me – I was terrified, and now…'

She stopped.

'Is he your boyfriend?'

'Of course not! Who do you think I am? He's a local gangster that everyone's afraid of. Even when the Separatists threaten him he doesn't seem to care.'

'What's that to do with me?'

'It's his baby, and now he thinks he owns me and threatens to cut me and the baby.'

She looked frightened and Freeman puzzled.

'Ahmed is crazy and I won't give him sex, so now no one else can be with me. Can you imagine what it is like for me? I can't go home because the shame it would bring my family and I can't live here.'

'Home?'

'Algiers.'

'I think I hurt them pretty bad.'

'Now they will kill us both.'

She started crying.

'Why didn't you tell me all this?'

'Would you have wanted me if I had?'

Freeman was very unsure and said nothing.

He couldn't go to her and she knew it. Holding the baby, she crawled across the bed, reached out and grabbed him, pulling him down so he could hold her as she sobbed.

A LITTLE TIME BEFORE, Jaffa stood in the narrow streets of Bayonne watching the white Mercedes speed off up the road. He had planned to drop off Freeman's money at his apartment but now thought better of it and headed back to the stone steps where his boat took him back to the chestnut trees and the drive back to Itxassou. Jaffa was lost in thought and plans.

The sun had burnt off the early morning chill and any remaining dew sat in the heavily shaded parts of the garden. Jane stood barefoot in the long wet grass softly singing to the light brown cow, which was wandering around its new surroundings. Occasionally, it gave a loud mooing and somewhere in the meadows between the patches of forest among the steep green rolling hills across the river, the sounds of cow companionship echoed back.

Jane wore a small black vest and a pair of creased and wrinkled loose white shorts in stark contrast to her dark skin. Her hair was tied with a band and hung down across her shoulder where she absent-mindedly played with its ends.

The red sports car crunched the gravel and came to a halt near the house. Holding a large brown paper bag stuffed full of French francs, Jaffa got out the car and looked across the garden. Jane stopped her lullaby and stared.

SOMETIME LATER, Jane sat cross-legged on the swing-lounger looking out across the garden to the light brown cow happily munching grass and clover. As Jane watched the cow, she spoke to Jaffa, sitting on one of the old wooden chairs under the black cherry tree.

'Love is dangerous thing. Are you sure of everything?'

'Yes, Freeman is a man of habit. He'll be there.'

'And the others?'

'Their blind rage will take them to wherever he is.'

'We need to talk with Freeman.' She changed topic, focusing on things at hand. 'The cow needs a friend. I'm going to the hills to find another one.'

BACK IN THE APARTMENT, Rebecca had dressed. Her ashen face reminded Freeman of the first time they had had sex. He knew that he too had forced her. They both remained sitting on the bed as he tried to ease the tension.

'What brought you to Bayonne?'

'My sister works here for the Municipality. I was visiting her.'

'And your family?'

'They think I work for the Municipality too now.'

'You can stay here with me, at least until it's safe.'

'I'm sorry I wasn't honest.'

Freeman felt sorry too but about the whores and the money and was about to explain his time in Brazil when Rebecca asked:

'What brought you to Bayonne?'

'We used to holiday here once a year and when I was old enough my father occasionally took me to the casino by the Virgin's rock. The bathroom had shocking green and black paisley wallpaper, which he absolutely loved. He managed to get a few rolls with which he decorated the farm office. God it looked like a brothel!'

Freeman abruptly stopped, and Rebecca asked:

'Why whores?'

He told her about Sao Paulo, the schoolboy chants and jokes, the black widow spider and how one seemingly ordinary day had shaped his entire relationship with women.

'But that's changed now. Like you, I too want to get home, and for me that means being married to a good man.'

Freeman was speechless, knowing there was more to come.

'I can't love you...'

The baby sat between Rebecca's crossed legs and they were both looking at him.

'...your desire to go home and mine are so different and incompatible.'

Freeman suddenly saw a way and said:

'Let's make a deal.'

'Another?'

'I'll fix this problem with the baby's father and try and get you home.'

'Is that possible?'

Freeman nodded but he wasn't sure at all.

'And what do I do for you in this deal?'

'Be around.'

'Deal,' Rebecca smiled.

THE FOLLOWING DAY Freeman woke long before dawn and gazed at Rebecca with the sleeping baby in her arms. He knew he could easily get used to this, but also knew that that would be a foolish thing; he had to keep his focus and enjoy this only while it lasted.

They had stayed in the apartment all the previous day. Freeman found it slightly amusing to be holed up with scant supplies in a civilised and luxurious part of Europe with a woman and her baby, keeping low and hidden from the twisted actions of a deranged psycho.

Having a need to exercise and think things through in the solitude of darkness, Freeman left earlier than usual. The cycle ride was covered in the shadow of the night as he pedalled hard towards the crashing waves. The beach was grey under the fading starlight and the ocean dark and endless. The rhythmic sounds of the rolling surf soothed him as Jane's strange language had soothed the lucky light brown cow.

Freeman sat on the hard damp sand with his pack, bicycle and rigged rod next to him. It was too early to fish and too otherworldly to think and he just stared at the inky sky listening to the sea.

Just before dawn, as twilight showed a cold horizon, dividing sky from sea, Freeman cast out hard and far. In the eerie light that was neither night nor day, he felt a soft cool breeze and the hairs rising on the back of his neck. He abruptly turned and saw the two men near him, their footsteps inaudible on the sand and against the pounding waves. He dropped the rod and saw a gun and the vague outline of a knife. Trapped against the water, they were too close for him to splash through the rolling waves and get out into the shadows of the sea. He went for his gun but his pocket was flat and empty. He had left it lying in the drawer.

Knowing they would play with him before killing him, he immediately decided to rush the man with the knife that he could now see clearly in the increasing light.

Two muffled shots cracked out. Freeman watched the bodies fall and thud on the hard compact sand to briefly writhe and moan before another two cracks, as Jaffa dispatched any life left in the dying men.

'Love was a dangerous thing.'

Jaffa unscrewed the silencer and put it in his pocket along with the gun.

'Don't be moving or touching anything.'

He disappeared towards the river mouth. Freeman, who was both bewildered and relieved, heard the outboard motor start and saw the silhouette of Jaffa heading out to sea. The boat turned and Jaffa opened the throttle full, coming in fast and hard, aggressively cutting through the rolling surf to beach with a tremendous thud upon the shore, a few feet away from Freeman. Once out of the water, the motor briefly screamed before Jaffa turned the engine off. He then jumped out of the boat.

'Help me with the bodies. We don't have much time before the sun rises.'

Freeman went on to automatic, roughly loading the two bodies, gun and knife into the boat. As Jaffa held onto the boat, now being pushed around in the shallow surf, he spoke slowly and clearly to Freeman.

'In half an hour the tide will rise and wash away this bloody sand and you will drive their car to Saint Jean de Luz and be leaving it unlocked with the keys in the ignition in a rundown part of town. Wait for me at an outside table near the square of Place Louis XIV – and don't be going home first.'

He handed Freeman some old gloves from the boat, which he took without saying a word.

Jaffa felt the pockets of the man nearest to him and found the car keys, handing them to Freeman.

'A few miles out, the Atlantic has a current that will swallow this fish bait far and deep. Be passing me your bike, pack and rod – time for a fishing trip!'

'Rebecca's expecting me back.'

'Be leaving it all to me. Where's your gun?'

'In the drawer in my room...don't shoot her please.'

'I am looking after my assets. What good would that do me?'

Freeman reeled in the line and awkwardly loaded the stuff into the small boat before pushing it out into the surf. Jaffa jumped in, pulled the starter cord and throttled hard, crashing and bouncing his way through the waves, out to sea. Freeman heard the engine silence and could just make out the shape of Jaffa throwing the bicycle overboard before continuing on his way. Freeman stood there until the noise of the engine became lost amongst the sound of the breaking waves; he then looked down at the bloody sand being lapped at by the surf.

It had all taken a few minutes: the long cast far into the breaking waves of dawn, turning to see two shadowy figures and the sketchy outlines of their weapons and for Jaffa to shoot coldly before collecting the boat to beach upon the shore. Then another few to load the men, bicycle and gear onboard before Jaffa motored into the shadows of the early morning sea.

Feeling a chill, Freeman looked down at the water swirling around his wet boots. He saw and felt his soaking legs from pushing the boat and knew Jaffa had been right, for the tide was rising and the twilight disappearing fast, as the light of a new day threatened from the east.

Freeman walked towards the white Mercedes. He could just see the car roof behind the top of the sandy dunes about two hundred yards to his right. Instinctively, he knew they had driven in without lights, cutting the engine early to roll silently to a stop. The easy life of France had made him soft, perhaps even romantic, and it had very nearly cost him his life. He put on the gloves and tried the door. It was open and he put the keys in the ignition. A moment later, the engine whirred before spluttering into life. It was an old car for a cheap gangster. Freeman read the fuel gauge. It was low, and he hoped the car would make it as he had no cash; even if he had, he knew to stop at a gas station would be a foolish thing to do.

Things were very different being in a car than on an old bicycle; he heard the whirr of the motor and felt the bumpy road cushioned by suspension. Although he had the window open, the rush of air was not the same as when he pedalled through the morning chill. The joy of his bike trips in wind, rain and shine was lost inside this steel cage. Suddenly, he had the clear vision of his bicycle rusting on the ever-turning seabed near the river's mouth. Was it to ease the load on the boat and create more room, or was it another tacit message on how not to live his life? One thing was for sure, Jaffa had saved his life and he was thankful for that; however, he also knew that an enormous debt would be collected in the job, which now seemed terrifyingly real and extremely close.

THE RIPPLING SEA shimmered in the sunrise as Jaffa cruised into the strong current that made the water look dark and heavy. He scanned the sea before looking back towards the decadent shoreline luxury of Biarritz and southwest France. He moved further out into the current to be out of sight but more importantly to ensure these dangerous waters took his quarry all the way to Spain. As the boat turned, drifting with the tide, he rolled the men overboard to splash, sink and disappear into the deep blue sea. Scooping up the ocean with the bailing bucket, he poured it over the patches of blood dotted about the boat to wash away any trace of damming evidence. He then headed back towards the Ardour, the fishing rod sticking overboard, the lure swinging from its end.

Two hundred yards offshore, about in the same place he had dumped the bicycle, Jaffa cut the engine and picked up the rod. He knew the early morning light made perfect fishing unlike Freeman's strange obsession to fish the gloomy grey of dawn that only kept his dream alive. As Jaffa cast the lure, he knew Freeman would be driving apprehensively, understanding he'd been helplessly caught.

It didn't take long for Jaffa to hook a good size bass, playing it coolly and landing it in the boat. Before long, he had another and was soon heading back up the Ardour to the rusty ring and old stone steps.

Jane was waiting for him at the top of the stone steps and, on hearing the familiar sound of the outboard, came down to meet him as he came around the bend where the Ardour met the Nive. She wore a long dark linen skirt and a green and white, short sleeve batik shirt with a light brown shawl the colour of the cow around her shoulders. Her hair was tied back, clearly displaying and exaggerating her startling scars, which she held with pride.

They didn't speak as Jane took the rod and pack. Jaffa had bagged the fish in an old leather holdall and followed her up to the narrow stone quay where he opened the bag to show his catch.

'Two very nice fish, Mohamed.'

'But in return, I was having to throw two back into the deep and moody water that never tells its tale.'

'A fine morning's work.'

'A rather smooth and neat affair.'

'And Freeman?'

'Oh, I am afraid someone stole his bicycle and he is looking for it far and wide. Alas, I'm fearing it has gone for good.'

They both laughed with Jaffa adding:

'At Freeman's request, I am needing to be seeing and probably assuring his one and only friend.'

'Then you must deliver her a bass.'

The red sports car was parked a few yards away from the top of the stone steps. Jaffa placed the larger of the two bass in an icebox, which sat on top of the spare tyre in the trunk.

Jane placed her hands on Jaffa's, which were still holding the bagged bass, and lent forward putting her mouth close to his ear. She softly sang the strange words of the light brown cow lullaby. Jaffa nodded, turned and walked into the narrow streets of the old town, carrying the bag and rod, the pack fastened to his back.

Gazing after him, Jane watched the outline of a man about to deliver his morning catch.

JAFFA SOON STOOD outside the old fruit shop, looking in through the window at the old woman as she organised her store. On seeing Jaffa, she smiled and waved, came out to greet him like a well-acquainted friend. Jaffa had spent many hours keeping her company and occasionally tended the shop when she went out to run an errand. Of course, he had been enquiring about Freeman who had caught his eye being new in town, looking sun burnt, gaunt and wild-eyed; obviously not from Bayonne but perhaps from a country that not so long ago had splashed the headlines with its turmoil and demise.

Jaffa explained in awkward French that Freeman's bicycle had been stolen and that he was now scouring the town in hope of finding it. He had asked Jaffa to return the rod and deliver the freshly caught bass to his fiancé up above the shop. Of course the old woman, whose name was Eve, knew all about the girl and baby; after all, gossip was rife in Bayonne's old town. Happy that Rebecca had found a good man and that Freeman had finally found someone to do his washing, as he always used the expensive dry cleaner around the corner, Eve was soon opening the heavy oak door to ascend the gloomy stairs to knock on Freeman's door. As Jaffa waited on the pavement by the open door, he heard whispering voices echo down the hall and stairs. Quickly back, Eve said Rebecca would be down shortly and that he could wait inside the old fruit shop.

Jaffa eased the pack off his back, placed it alongside the rod inside the lobby under the stairs before joining Eve in the sweet and musty smelling shop where he put the bagged fish down. He then helped Eve by moving some boxes of fruit, which were sitting on the pavement, inside the shop.

Holding the baby, Rebecca entered. Still dressed in the same black dress, for she had not felt it possible to return to her apartment, she stood silently swaying, staring right at Jaffa's dark features.

Jaffa spoke slowly in French, introducing himself as Freeman's fishing friend. With some difficulty, he then explained that they had been out fishing and on return, the bicycle was gone, probably taken by kids. Freeman was now searching the town and had instructed Jaffa to return the gear, deliver the fish and take Rebecca out for breakfast. He picked up the bag and opened it, showing Rebecca the bass.

'What a good sized fish…let me take it upstairs to the fridge.'

She took the holdall and disappeared with Jaffa shouting for her to keep the bag.

Rebecca was some time upstairs and when she returned, she had her handbag, shawl and fold up pushchair with the baby ready for an outing to a nearby café.

As soon as they moved away from the shop, Jaffa changed from French to Arabic.

'Jacques is wanting me to tell you that your problem's gone for good.'

Rebecca, trying to hide her relief, changed the subject.

'You speak a strange Arabic…'

They strolled in silence to the Nive. Rebecca felt relief that it was safe to walk the streets; she was famished and happy she would eat.

WHILE FREEMAN HAD been driving away from the beach along the gravel track, the first rays of sunlight appeared over the urban scene in front, making him squint. He felt the warmth it brought and realised he was shivering from the cold wet and exhausting reality that had just played out on the deserted Bayonne shore. He knew he was in thick and deep, involved with things he could not explain and that Jaffa would have planned this all impeccably. He had no choice but to follow through as instructed.

He drove through Bayonne, past Biarritz onto the open road, heading for Saint Jean de Luz. The fuel gauge was on empty and Freeman toyed with the idea of pulling off the main road and abandoning the car on one of the numerous dirt tracks that criss-crossed the countryside. But he would then be stranded miles from his destination and probably miss his rendezvous with Jaffa.

As Freeman approached the town, the car started spluttering. He turned across the carriageway into a tiny road, grinding to a halt as the engine stalled in a dirt lay-by at the bottom of a hill next to a small deserted farm. He sat for a moment looking at the empty road before opening the glove compartment to look for cash. On finding none, he searched the floor before getting out of the car to search around the back seat and then the trunk containing a leather bag, which he riffled through. Discarding a handgun and some spare magazines, he found twenty francs. He slammed the trunk shut and headed up the road to where he thought the town must lie.

Glancing down the hill at the white Mercedes looking small and lost, he now felt safe, as no car had passed. Climbing over a gate and crossing a damp field on his right, he squeezed through a small opening in a hedge and was soon in town. Briskly walking west, he threw the gloves on the first rubbish heap he passed.

HAVING ENJOYED A hearty breakfast, Rebecca now sat looking out towards the Nive. She felt it safe to ask a question.

'How do you know Jacques?'

'Oh, we met one fine and early summer's morning on the sandy shoreline where the river meets the sea – right where Jacques likes to fish the gloomy light until dawn is broken into day, and, as the world awakes, he quickly cycles back to while away his endless Bayonne days.'

On hearing the strange speak, Rebecca almost laughed. However, her baby's sudden need dampened her amusement and she excused herself to go inside the café.

Jaffa gazed out across the river to the closely packed buildings on the other side, brightly lit by the morning sun. He felt it time to visit Freeman, who was now probably pacing the streets of Saint Jean de Luz.

Rebecca returned. As Jaffa paid the bill, he nonchalantly asked:

'What's the baby's name?'

She didn't answer, briefly blushing as they strolled in silence back to the heavy oak door.

'When will Jacques be home?'

'Oh...cook the bass for six, I'll have him back by then.'

She smiled and Jaffa was pleased she didn't have the habit of the French kiss greeting as he didn't want to smell Freeman in her hair.

A FEW MINUTES LATER, Jaffa approached the red sports car where Jane sat at the driver's wheel. He rolled back and secured the soft roof before joining Jane, who headed south, pressing her foot hard to the floor. The rush of wind roared in their ears.

She slowed the car down as they drove into town, passing the small road on the left where Freeman had dumped the white Mercedes, and turned into the narrow streets of Saint Jean de Luz. Soon they were in the small port, parking on the quayside.

Jane opened the car trunk and Jaffa took off his jacket with the gun still in the pocket and placed it next to the cooler with the bass. Jane then slammed the trunk shut again, handing over the keys to Jaffa. The day was balmy and they walked slowly to the old square with its fine church. They soon found Freeman sitting by an outside table at a corner café with an empty coffee cup, a newspaper on his lap. He looked shifty, his eyes darting back and forth until they caught the gait of his rendezvous strolling through the shoppers.

BEFORE ARRIVING AT the table where Freeman waited apprehensively, looking right at them, Jane remarked:

'He looks a fine mess.'

Jaffa quickly scanned Freeman, saw his muddy shoes from crossing the damp grassy field and the patches of dried blood, which Freeman was obviously trying to hide, showing on his light and scruffy slacks under the edges of the folded newspaper.

Freeman said nothing, only looked up and stared as Jaffa turned to Jane.

'What size trousers do you think he wears?'

'Small fish size…any particular style or colour?'

The sarcasm went straight over Freeman's head and he seriously replied:

'To match my shirt will be just fine.'

Amused, Jane took notice of the brown and crème check shirt and walked away, disappearing into a narrow street leading off the square.

Jaffa pulled out a chair next to Freeman and sat down, looking over at the sunny square and church.

'Once upon a time, Saint Jean de Luz was full of pirates dropping off their loot and swag, hiding out until their next debauched venture out at sea.'

Freeman looked hard at Jaffa.

'Where are you from?'

'From where the poet's whisper mingles with the endless singing breeze.'

'Where the hell is that?' Freeman seethed.

'To where you drift when the anchor breaks.'

Realising it was useless to push the matter further, Freeman pondered for a moment, tried to calm down, knowing his anger wasn't helping anything.

'Thanks. How did you know those guys would come and find me?'

'Only luck – it comes with endless patience and intent.'

'And Rebecca?'

'She had a fine Bayonne breakfast, not dissimilar to your own favourite taste.'

'Did you tell her what happened on the shore?'

'Now that would be being, being stupid. Does she know about the gun?'

'She found it, but don't worry she won't talk.'

'No, she's not the type. But now, to be safe, we are needing a second fix.'

Freeman felt anxious and blurted out:

'What are you going to do?'

'Nothing with Rebecca. What about the car?'

'It ran out of gas so I left it on the edge of town unlocked with the keys in the ignition and dumped the gloves on the first rubbish heap I found. No one saw me.'

Jaffa didn't speak for a while, just stared at the changing light as a cloud passed overhead, dulling the colours of the square. The silence put Freeman on edge, forcing him to say the first thing in his mind.

'There was a gun in the trunk.'

'Do you like bass Freeman?'

'You know I do. I fish for them enough!'

'But you are not eating them but throwing them back to have another chance, as it is not fish you seek but the answer to your dream.'

'Not now Jaffa, I don't want to hear your riddles right now.'

Speaking clearly, not to be misunderstood, Jaffa looked hard at Freeman.

'We met at the river mouth and fished the early light of dawn in the boat not too far out to sea, catching two bass. On returning, your bicycle was gone and we went to town where you looked hard for your precious early morning transport. Failing to find it, we drove down here with Jane to have an early lunch. That's it, nothing more.'

Freeman took it in and nodded.

'You must want me pretty badly.'

'You are crucial.'

'Why don't you do this job yourself?'

'They're not wanting to see a face like mine, but one like yours: suave and civil, pretending moral virtue and, of course – completely white.'

'That's just nonsense.'

'Exactly Freeman, exactly!'

Jane returned and handed Freeman a paper bag containing some new trousers. He hurriedly went to the restroom to change.

Having washed and flattened his thick mop of dark hair, Freeman returned wearing his new and stylish khaki slacks that matched his shirt. He carried the bag, which contained the blood stained evidence.

'How did you know what size I am?'

'Because you're so obvious,' Jane remarked dryly.

Jaffa led the short distance to the small port where the parked car was outside a scruffy quayside café and bar. It was well lit with two large folding French doors hinged open to the outside. Freeman smelt a waft of strong tobacco. To protect the premises from sun or a sudden shower, there was a grimy green awning over the entrance, under which a few wooden tables and chairs sat in the shade. Inside, a long bar ran horizontal to the quayside and a few more tables and chairs lay ramshackle about the place. The only customer was a drunk smoking at the bar, singing quietly along to a scratchy record playing Basque songs.

On seeing and recognising Jaffa, the café owner left the drunk and followed him to the car. The trunk was opened and the bass from the cooler carried to the kitchen out the back.

Jane and Freeman had waited near the open doors without speaking before joining Jaffa at an outside table overlooking the harbour and the small fishing boats lined up against the quay. In front of them on the quayside lay an assortment of pots, nets, chains and coloured buoys. The view gave Freeman memories of the harbour back home: its old square opening out to the dock with its deep-water jetty and old wooden pontoons littered with a messy jumble of fishing things, and, when the soft breeze blew, that unforgettable smell of engine oil and rotting fish.

Freeman was wondering what they were doing sitting in the small run-down harbour of Saint Jean de Luz. He knew they had a story, an alibi, and someone was probably cooking the bass right now, but he also knew there was more coming than just fish, and urgently asked:

'What's the second fix?'

'It takes two fixes to fix your stupidity,' Jane curtly answered.

Freeman looked confused so Jaffa spat it out:

'The gun – Rebecca needs not think your gun played any part.'

'It didn't.'

'But she knows you have a gun.'

'Rebecca's gangster hasn't taken to the high seas out of some sense of decency or because you said pretty please,' Jane added.

Freeman looked out to the Bay of Biscay whose tranquil surface hid many things. He felt stupid and then angry and tried to vindicate himself.

'How the hell was I to know any of this would happen?'

'Love is a dangerous thing,' Jane replied, forcing Freeman to snap:

'Where the hell did you get those savage scars and that bullet in your calf?'

'From a tiger that didn't like my taste and a bullet from those who don't like tigers.'

'Pah – riddles, always riddles.'

'Alas, the truth walks right by you Freeman,' Jane softly remarked.

'Look, you are needing us as we are needing you.'

Freeman calmed down and replied to Jaffa:

'You're right. It's been a bad day and I'm feeling it's not over yet.'

Jaffa shook his head and smirked:

'Two deaths before dawn and no breakfast.'

'Jaffa caught the bass. We need to eat your alibi,' Jane mocked.

'My alibi!'

'Ours Freeman,' Jaffa said reassuringly.

Once again, Freeman's anger made him feel in control, but he knew he was more than one-step behind whatever lay ahead.

The café owner brought the bass out. It had been cut into strips and pan-fried. They ate in silence, listening to the squawking gulls and fishing boats clonk and splash against the quay. Freeman had felt famished and soon polished off his plate. As he was finishing his salad and drinking the sharp tasting chilled white wine, Jaffa asked:

'How's your alibi?'

'Freshly caught, well cooked and gone for good.'

'Perfect Freeman,' Jane smiled.

'Phone call,' the café owner shouted out in broken English.

Jaffa went inside and picked up the heavy black receiver that was lying on the bar.

Freeman looked at Jane.

'The second fix?'

'Don't ask because you won't get told.'

Freeman felt a spell working inside him like a poison without a cure.

'What are you doing to me?'

'Only what you want, but couldn't do yourself.'

Before Freeman could ponder this, Jaffa returned and pointed to the car.

'Time to be going to the hills and not so far away.'

Freeman noticed they had no bill to pay and that the rugged café owner was standing under the awning watching them closely as they got into the car. Jaffa stepped over the side into the back and Jane took the wheel. Freeman sat next to Jane and, as she turned to take the keys from Jaffa, he studied her proud and furrowed scars.

'You have the bag?'

Freeman nodded without looking back.

'Where's the car?'

Freeman told them and they drove down the hill near the abandoned farmhouse, seeing the white Mercedes on the left in the dirt lay-by. They drove on by.

'Do you think it will be stolen?' Freeman asked.

'Saint Jean de Luz still has pirates looking for swag and old tin cars!' Jaffa swiftly replied.

In silence, they drove along deserted roads, skirting the foothills and coming out near Itxassou where Jane turned, driving up under craggy rocks where the Nive cut a small gorge. Freeman looked down at the narrow swirling river, its current forcing a way though rocky boulders, and then up to the steep, tightly packed wooded hills of the Atlantic Pyrenees. They veered off uphill, the road twisting steeply through shadows of overgrown leafy foliage, to meet an isolated farmhouse or lone barn before dropping back to the river, now edged with watery meadows and leafy, tree lined banks.

They entered the pretty village of Biddary, crossing a fast flowing tributary of the Nive via an old short and narrow bridge. Jane turned right, following this stream into a labyrinth of forested hills. The sports car slipped and spun on the tiny track, loose gravel noisily hitting the underside of the car. Coursing down a steep hill, braking hard and crunching through the gears, she stopped where the track forked. One track followed the stream over a stone bridge by an abandoned building, which Freeman thought might have once been a customs house; the other, to their left, followed a small torrent gushing out of a narrow wooded gorge. Jaffa pointed left. Spinning through the dirt, the car climbed as the valley narrowed, leaving the torrent to rush among the dense green trees below.

In front of a ramshackle stone farmhouse with old barns and long discarded farmyard junk, the car came to a sudden halt. The track had run out; the way blocked by a wall of trees.

Jaffa broke the silence from the back:

'We're here!'

'Where?'

'Spain.'

Freeman got out of the car and looked around. The farm buildings and immediate area sat on a terrace overlooking the steep wooded slopes of the wild river valley. A fresh breeze blew downstream.

It was obvious that no one was about for the peeling oxide-red shutters of the house were closed and locked. The only sign of life was a tiny track full of muddy footprints following the valley upstream and vanishing among the trees.

Jaffa turned to Jane, who was still sitting behind the wheel looking up at him, and said:

'You have a friend to pick up.'

On hearing that, Jane picked up Freeman's bag and tossed it hard towards his feet. She then turned the car, slowly crunching down the gravel and loose stone back towards Biddary.

Freeman picked up the bag and followed Jaffa along the path into the shadows of the dense forest. The air turned damp and chilly. Occasionally, in small clearings where a tree had fallen, shafts of light broke through, illuminating the forest floor. They pressed on, higher up the valley and deeper into trees.

As the valley narrowed, the steep slopes forced the path back towards the stream where they found themselves close to the noise of rushing water. Through the trees, Freeman saw a large well-kept barn in a green field full of cows. He checked his watch – it had taken nearly an hour of good steady pace to reach this spot.

At a gate into the field, a Basque farmer stood waiting. He was short and stocky with rugged features and the typical unkempt black curly hair and heavy stubble of these rural people. He wore a well-used dirty white pullover, ripped pants and muddy gumboots. Freeman looked at his own muddy wet feet for the second time that day and then to Jaffa and saw the same.

Freeman thought that robust and wily was a perfect description of the man now looking at him with a fierce expression and furrowed brow.

They stopped at the gate and Jaffa immediately requested that Freeman 'Look hard at Luk and not forget his rugged Basque-like features.'

Luk smiled, instantly losing the rough exterior Freeman had first seen. Knowing all Jaffa's riddles had some hidden meaning, Freeman looked as he was asked.

Speaking in English with a very heavy accent, Luk stepped back, opening the gate:

'Open Sesame.'

No sooner had Freeman and Jaffa gone through the gate, Luk pushed it shut. After the reverberating clonk of the closing gate, he spoke directly to Freeman.

'In the barn there is a fire for your things.'

He pointed and Freeman took this as his cue, trundling across the wet field made muddy by the heavy hooves of cows.

At the entrance, Freeman turned and saw Luk and Jaffa still standing by the gate face-to-face, intent and involved in conversation. Turning back, he stepped into the cool interior of the barn. At the rear, two men sat on long crates, their rifles next to them leaning up against the wall; in front, stood an old oil drum with small flames showing over the rim. Freeman heard the crack of a combusting twig. One of the men quickly stood, walked over and took the bag from Freeman, pulling out the trousers and turning the empty pockets inside out before flinging them with accuracy into the oil drum followed by the screwed up bag. He then smiled at Freeman, indicating with a sweeping gesture of his palms that the job was done.

Freeman looked out across wet grass glistening in the sun and saw a man up in the corner of the field, a rifle slung across his shoulder, smoking a cigarette and staring down at him. He headed back towards Luk and Jaffa who had both stopped talking, and by the time he arrived, Luk had opened the gate.

As Freeman followed Jaffa through, the gate shut hard behind them. Jaffa didn't stop and headed fast towards the forest. Freeman briefly saw another armed man leaning against a tree but he was soon gone, lost amongst the trees as they moved at pace around the twists and turns, heading back to the old farmhouse on the terraced hill.

Out of the damp shadowed forest, the sun was warming and the air fresh. Freeman noticed he was breathing hard and slightly damp from exertion. Looking at his watch, he realised he was behaving as he had during the uprising: checking time and working out the next manoeuvre – not that it had done any good, as they had lost the war and were now dispersed across the globe. It was three o'clock.

After unlocking the old wooden doors of a large shed opposite the farmhouse at the end of the dirt road, Jaffa turned to Freeman.

'You can be telling Rebecca that you heard a whisper on the street that may have sent her gangster boyfriend into ground or out to sea.'

'He's not her boyfriend.'

'Don't be touchy.'

'I heard a rumour that things were going bad for him – right?'

'But nothing more.'

Jaffa pulled the doors wide open and Freeman saw a pristine metallic turquoise car sitting in the gloomy light. Jaffa took some keys from his pocket and threw them to him.

'Be driving me to home.'

Freeman entered the shed and walked towards the open top sports car that looked expensive and new. Opening the driver's door, he picked up the car documents lying on the seat. After he had adjusted the seat and placed the key in the ignition, he handed the documents over to Jaffa who was now sitting next to him. Freeman stopped, held onto the documents, as Jaffa clasped them, and clearly read his own name as the car owner with his address above the fruit shop. Jaffa pulled the papers from Freeman's hand and placed them in the glove compartment. Freeman stared, totally lost for words.

'Are you liking your new car?'

Freeman said nothing.

'A present from Luk.'

'But I don't even know him. What's this all about?'

'Ah, you know, those Basque farmers are needing just like you.'

'Needing...what?'

'Money and their homeland back.'

'They work for you?'

Jaffa only smiled.

'What have you got me into?'

'Not knowing means not telling. You must remember that.'

Once again, Freeman knew it was useless to continue with the conversation so he started the car and carefully drove out the barn onto the dirt track where he stopped. Turning to Jaffa, he demanded:

'What's the second fix?'

'The gangster has a most troublesome gang who may now come looking for an explanation which only you know and keep.'

'You know it too.'

'But they are not knowing me.'

'They'll come again?' Freeman asked irritably.

'The fates are smiling, for what was a headache for you, becomes a reason and a blessing for the rest.'

'How can killing those two guys be a blessing for anyone except Rebecca?'

'Just enjoy the car, it's legally yours…and forget the rest. Your job here is done.'

They drove in silence back to Biddary, but instead of turning left across the old narrow bridge, they drove straight on into another part of the village where Jaffa had Freeman pull up outside the shell of a burnt out building.

'The owner of that restaurant was kindly giving Luk his car before hastily retreating back to Paris with his not-so Basque cuisine.'

'Did they run him out of town before or after he burnt the toast?'

Both men laughed. Driving across the Nive, taking the main road back to Itxassou, Freeman felt pleased that something was finally happening in his life, but he also felt the familiar dread that he was now associating with Jaffa.

HAVING CROSSED THE small rail track and river bridge, they pulled up behind a farm truck with a small animal trailer in tow that was blocking the road and their access to the overgrown gravel drive. There was a bit of a commotion going on. With shouts and whistles, Elsa and Jane were trying to herd another brown cow in to the garden, as the farmer stood in the road to stop it stampeding into the village. Refusing to move, the cow stood in the small road swishing its tail. Freeman automatically got out of the car to help, clapping his hands and shooing the cow behind the trailer where it had no choice but to charge into the garden. Amused, Freeman turned to Jaffa, who was now standing next to him, and asked:

'From the chestnut trees?'

'Oh no, Chestnut is already here. This is a friend whose calls echoed down the hill.'

Jane handed over a small wad of cash to the farmer who seemed pleased at the generous payment. Instead of driving off, he immediately unloaded large pieces of planed wood from the trailer and proceeded to assemble a gate for the drive. Peering down the road between the trailer and the hedge, the farmer eyed the turquoise car. He shook his head, flashing Freeman a knowing grin.

In the garden, the two cows mooed at each other with Chestnut disappearing through the trees to the riverbank. The new cow followed.

Elsa was concerned.

'They will get lost!'

'They are not people you know,' Jane reassured.

'I think that cow is pregnant,' Freeman dryly commented.

'Are you really knowing cows?'

'From the farm back home. You need to watch her,' Freeman replied to Jane.

Jane smiled, and Elsa turned to Jaffa.

'Now be telling me your tale. You owe me that.'

On hearing Elsa's words, Freeman inexplicably felt dazed and started drifting off. He came to, hearing the loud bangs of a gatepost being hammered into ground. Elsa was shaking him vigorously by the arm.

'Jaffa wants you to tell me where he's from.'

Somewhat bewitched, Freeman spoke, lucidly and without ado:

If the anchor breaks
And throws you out to sea
Hold fast the rail
No compass, no sail
And pray you'll make it'

Freeman paused and looked at the faces, all smiling and expectant and he finished, as he knew he should:

*'To where the poet's whisper mingles with the endless singing
breeze.'*

'What beautiful nonsense!'

Elsa pulled him down by both arms and kissed him on the
lips.

As Elsa let him go, she said:

'You can lie like that to me anytime.'

But Freeman knew he had somehow spoken truth, but for
the life of him couldn't remember where he had heard the
poem.

Elsa, looking at Jaffa, said laughingly:

'Well, I suppose that's as close as it will ever be!'

'Like a sail to the wind,' he replied.

She slowly walked to the half-finished gate followed by the
others and, as she stepped into the road, noticed the turquoise
car.

'Oh Freeman, those devils have really caught you now.'

Staring hard at the car, she proclaimed:

'It's a snake!'

'A horse,' Jaffa corrected her.

'Then why has it got a cobra on its side?'

'Because some horses are really snakes,' Jane answered.

Elsa started walking up the road. Briefly stopping, she
turned, beaming a huge smile, shouting back to Freeman:

'Now you can really break your deal!'

Freeman dismissed the comment as he watched the farmer
deftly drill holes for the large hinges of what was now almost a
five bar gate.

He looked at Jane, her dark eyes shining in the late afternoon sun, and asked:

'Why cows?'

No answer came and Freeman looked up the street to where Elsa had disappeared behind the lone banana tree and then back to the Ford Mustang Cobra parked behind the truck and trailer. He then looked to Jaffa and Jane standing close, staring blankly at him with the two cows mooing somewhere along the riverbank below, and then to a Basque farmer fixing hinges to a gate.

'A snake, a horse and two brown cows?'

There was no answer to his rhetoric and Jane simply asked:

'The cow may need a veterinary. Can you be getting Elsa's sister Julie from their house?'

AT THE HOUSE, Elsa was speaking to her sister. Lounging on the couch, they sat looking out the open doors to their garden, full of scent and early summer colour.

'It's hopeless. Now I am aching and soaking wet. This Freeman drives me crazy.'

'I'm so jealous, I saw him drive past with your strange friends. He's very handsome.'

'He's useless. Now I need to find someone else to press their love home hard tonight.'

'Oh Elsa, don't be easy! Anyway, I don't want to hear you wailing like a cat on heat. It's unbearable!'

'Well, you spend time with him and you see what he does to you!'

The gravel crunched on the girls' drive and moments later Freeman appeared, looking in through the open doors.

'Freeman! You have come!'

'Jane wants Julie to look at the cow.'

'Oh,' sighed Elsa.

Freeman peered at Julie who fiercely blushed, quickly sitting upright and pulling her skirt down flat across her knees.

'See!' Elsa joked.

Julie tensed, got up, walked right passed Freeman without catching his eye and crunched her way down the gravel drive and out of view.

'Now my sister wants you,' Elsa complained.

'What?' Freeman replied, confused.

'Fuck me Freeman.'

He did, right there and then as she sat on the couch, passionate and desperate. It was noisy and soon over, Elsa out of breath, shaking and crying out victoriously:

'Oh, to break a deal – break it again,' she demanded.

He no longer wanted to see her contorted impish face, so he turned her around, was harsh and mean, but she only cried out for more, lapping up everything he had to give.

Afterwards he felt vacant just like he had been with the whores.

Elsa interrupted his thoughts:

'That's all I wanted.'

'And now?' Freeman asked, re adjusting his clothes.

'Nothing, it's done and gone.'

Pleased and relieved at her answer, for he was still unsure about this free sex business, he left without saying goodbye. As he took the first crunching footstep on the gravel, Elsa blurted out:

'What did it feel like…'

Freeman looked back at Elsa sitting on the couch, her legs up, all open and exposed, glistening and trickling, full like a satisfied wild beast that had just devoured another living meal.

'…to break your deal?'

'I think it was already broken.'

'Oh,' she mumbled, sounding disappointed.

Knowing the curse of some Sao Paulo brothel was finally gone, Freeman turned away and felt the crunching underfoot go right through his empty body.

THE FARMER HAD gone and Jaffa was waiting, leaning on the finished gate, watching Freeman amble down the lane towards him.

'The green hills moved!'

'You heard?'

Freeman stood facing Jaffa on the opposite side of the gate and heard the cows mooing as Julie and Jane shooed and whistled, herding them back into the garden.

'But I'm sure the rushing torrent drowned the echoes from the hills,' he added.

Freeman was relieved. He felt it was no one's business but his own.

Over the gate, Jaffa handed Freeman the paper bag.

'One third up front.'

Freeman peered in. On seeing the amount, was speechless.

'Rebecca is expecting you in thirty minutes.'

Freeman looked over to Julie and Jane examining the cow. Julie flashed a glance back, once again blushing, making Jane stare hard and dismiss him with an annoyed wave.

JUST OUTSIDE BAYONNE, he pulled up at a gas station and asked the pump attendant to fill the tank. Clutching the paper bag under one arm, he got out the car and opened the trunk, dropping the bag down next to the spare wheel. He discreetly removed a note from one of the bound bank wads. Freeman noticed an envelope sticking out from under the spare tyre and could clearly see his name written on the front; he snatched it, stuffing it in his pocket before slamming the trunk closed and returning to the front of the car to pay for his gas.

'Don't you have anything smaller?'

Freeman then noticed the huge denomination of the note just handed over and awkwardly said:

'No.'

The attendant shook her head and went inside the shop. He immediately pulled the envelope from his pocket and hurriedly tore it open. There were a few scrawled lines in French saying that on a certain date he had bought the car from a Parisian in Biarritz and had paid cash. Under this brief message was a hand drawn map with many small-interconnected streets but only two buildings were marked – a bar and a hotel – and underneath the map was written: 'memorise and destroy.'

Freeman studied the map but was unsure whether to memorise the route from the bar to hotel or the hotel to bar; however, he decided one way was enough and carefully took in the route from the hotel to the bar. He repeated the route several times over in his head. As the attendant returned with his change, he thought he just about had it. Before driving off, he had one last look before tearing the paper into many small pieces, letting them fly with the wind as he thundered into Bayonne.

In the courtyard behind the old fruit shop, Freeman sat staring through the windscreen at the crumbly grey wall. Although he felt a chill in the shadows of the yard, he didn't move; the effects of the long exhausting day, full of love, death and mystery, held him transfixed. But the smell of fish frying, wafting down from his open window above, reminded him the day was far from over and he still had more to do.

Struggling for clarity and clutching the paper bag, he walked up the dark stairway; and then, he was looking at Rebecca's beaming smile as she stood cooking at the stove.

'You're just in time! What happened to your shoes?'

Freeman looked down at his shoes and trousers caked in mud from the forest walk, which now seemed an age ago.

'Jaffa's wife bought a new cow and we had to herd it in with the other one.'

'They have cows! He's an unusual man.'

'You can say that again.'

Freeman plonked the bag down in the room. Not caring if she saw the money, he grabbed some clothes and went to the bathroom to erase the mud and any last trace of Elsa.

Feeling slightly clearer as he re-entered the room, he noticed that Rebecca had been home to change. Gazing at her bare shoulders and evocative red dress, he knew this was all so different from the empty void he had found with Elsa. She smiled.

'Did you find your bicycle?'

'No...so I bought a car.'

'A car! Where?'

'Err...Biarritz.'

'Biarritz! It must have been expensive!'

'Well, I got paid some of the money for that job.'

He then remembered he had left the soft-top open.

'I'll show you later.'

She had laid the small table and Freeman found himself sitting opposite her, eating bass again and drinking a good wine, which he knew she couldn't afford.

'Did you catch it?'

Freeman shook his head.

'Jaffa did.'

'He spoke Arabic to me.'

On hearing this, Freeman perked up slightly.

'He can't really speak French, where's it from?'

'Oh, I don't think it's his mother tongue…Red Sea, east coast, very old fashioned, like…'

She struggled to find the words and Freeman said:

'…an odd poet.'

Rebecca looked bemused, but before she could comment or continue, Freeman changed the subject.

'The talk down at the docks is that Ahmed's been run out of town.'

'Good, then one half of the deal is done.' Rebecca eyed him cautiously.

'Deal?'

'To fix the problem and get me home.'

Freeman looked nervously across the table to Rebecca who instantly reassured him.

'It's ok. I know you meant well, but it is up to me to find a way home – as it is for you. Do you think we'll make it?'

Dog-tired, Freeman thought of the open car below, wanted to sleep but also knew he had somehow to finish this long and strange day. He didn't want to let her go but knew he had to; had to help her as she was helping him. Abruptly leaving the table, he grabbed the paper bag, emptying its contents on the bed. Freeman gazed at the pile sprawled about before him as Rebecca gasped and sat spellbound, fork in hand.

'Take whatever you need.'

Freeman sat on the chair in the middle of the room watching Rebecca count the money. He had no idea how much was there and when she told him, he laughed nervously.

'It must be some job!'

Rebecca looked up and straight at him.

'Show me the car.'

The courtyard was dark and chilly, the damp air hurrying Freeman to close the soft-top of the car.

'Ahmed drove an old Mercedes which had once been a taxi. You have an expensive foreign car, a gun and a big bag of money for a mysterious job from an odd sounding poet. What's going on Jacques?'

Rebecca pulled her shawl tight around her shoulders and stared at Freeman. Suddenly feeling nervous and full of newfound doubts, he pulled her close and held her tight. After they had kissed, she said:

'Drive me to where you fish the silver surf of dawn.'

'Now you sound just like him!'

Freeman didn't want to take Rebecca to the river mouth and made the excuse that the gravel track may be too rough for the car and best they went elsewhere. Instead, he drove south, past Biarritz to where the desolate surf beaches lined the shore all the way to Saint Jean de Luz.

Rebecca had insisted he take the fishing rod, which he had placed in the trunk along with the gear. They now sat parked in a secluded spot, the sandy beach and sea stretching out before them. The moon was half-full and ripples sparkled in the darkness as the surf endlessly pounded the shore a stone's throw from the car.

Rebecca had Freeman in her arms as he lay across her, and before he fell into a deep black sleep, he murmured:

'Where's the baby?'

Rebecca kissed his forehead.

'Safe with Chloe.'

He awoke face down on her lap and felt the warm soft skin of her thighs on his face and smelt her lingering fragrance that stuck to him like glue. The next thing he noticed was a banging sound. Stretching his neck, he looked up and saw a policeman staring in through the window. As Freeman sat up and away from Rebecca, she pulled her dress back down. They both got out the car.

There were two policemen. The one who had knocked spoke in Basque and was surprised when Freeman said he only spoke French. They wanted to see the car's papers, which Freeman obligingly pulled from the glove box. After studying them, they enquired how he had come to own the car. He told them that he had bought it in Biarritz from a Parisian who was in a hurry and heading back to Paris. They looked bemused and asked where he was from. On hearing of his country, they seemed to sympathise and handed him the papers back. They then drove off. Freeman knew he was in the clear and that yesterday was gone, washed out with the endless turning tide.

Rebecca looked at Freeman with sleepy eyes.

'So it really is your car.'

Freeman nodded and cricked his stiff neck. He looked at his watch – six thirty – dawn had passed and the fishing would be good right then. He went to the trunk and started assembling the rod. A few minutes later, he and Rebecca stood in front of the white breakers looking out at the deep blue sea and pale sky of a brand new day. Laying the rod on the hard wet sand, he pulled Rebecca down. They had sex. As the tide rose, the water was at their feet, but they didn't quit until a breaking wave showered them in swirling surf. Soaking wet and standing up, they laughed as another wave chased them up the beach.

With the fishing put on hold, the wet couple drove south towards Saint Jean de Luz. Freeman wondered if he should dare visit the quayside café without Jaffa and with the Parisian restaurateur's Mustang. Before he had finished mulling this over, he was pulling up outside the green awning and heading for the wooden tables outside the open French doors. The sun was warming and the shivery feeling of the soaking sea soon passed.

A few fishermen lolled around the boats, quietly chatting among themselves. They soon stopped to stare, eyeing the couple and the car.

'They like the car Jacques.'

As Freeman eyed them back, wondering if his daring had been such a good idea, the café owner appeared, also looking at the car. Turning to Freeman, he smiled, teasingly stating:

'Very stylish.'

He slapped Freeman on the back and offered them breakfast on the house. As the café owner went back inside, Rebecca whispered:

'I feel wet and rather sticky.'

Freeman pulled out the change from the gas station.

'This is a good town to buy clothes. Behind us near the square.'

Before she disappeared into a side street, Freeman watched her swing along the quayside, her soaking red dress clinging, revealing the contours of her body.

Slowly drying himself out in the morning sunshine, he viewed the port, smelt the sea and thought of home, which he knew was somehow within his reach.

'The boss wants you.'

The café owner pointed inside and Freeman turned and saw the big black telephone with the hand piece off the hook, sitting on the bar. Heading inside, he wondered if someone was angry that he had returned to the café. He lifted the receiver and spoke in French. The reply came in English.

'Freeman.'

'Yes Jane.'

'You are needing to be going to the big printers across the Spirit Bridge and down the second street on the right.'

'How did you find me?'

'Everybody knows you.'

The phone went dead. Freeman turned around and saw the few customers in the place stare at him. He took his seat outside the open French doors trying to ignore the curious looks. The café owner appeared again and offered him the local morning paper.

HE WAS STILL staring at the front page of the newspaper as it lay on the table in front of him when Rebecca returned from the shops.

'What do you think Jacques?'

With the quayside behind her, she stood smiling, facing the table with her arms outstretched. Looking up, he saw a shopping bag between her feet with the red dress poking out. She now wore dark blue slacks and a white cotton button up top.

Nodding, he feigned a smile, as she sat down.

'Don't you like the clothes?'

Freeman handed her the paper.

Rebecca stared at the grainy photograph of the white Mercedes riddled with bullet holes and covered in Basque slogans standing next to a burnt out warehouse with Anglet showing behind the Ardour in the background.

Rebecca quietly read out the headlines:

'Separatists kill three and run drug smugglers out of town. Gang leader missing, presumed dead.'

She looked up.

'So it wasn't you?'

He shook his head.

'What do I tell the baby Jacques?'

Freeman didn't answer. Once again, the café owner was at the table, looking over Rebecca's shoulder pretending to read the report, nodding and shaking his head before finally saying:

'Someone did us all a great favour running that scum out of town. Can't imagine there'll be much of an investigation.'

As he left again, Freeman knew he was only doing as he had been asked. Rebecca, looking pale, stared right at Freeman, who said:

'Tell the baby the truth Rebecca.'

'What's the truth?'

'He went missing, presumed dead during a skirmish at Anglet port. Keep the paper to show him one day.'

'Yes, I will.'

'Are you upset?'

'Not about Ahmed. It's just all so horrible.'

But to Freeman it was the perfect end to what had been a very bad day yesterday and he smiled at Rebecca, saying:

'You look fabulous.'

She too smiled, knowing he was trying to be nice.

AFTER DROPPING REBECCA back at her apartment, he drove steadily across Bayonne, focused, with all the wobbly emotions of the past days seemingly still and settled.

He felt like Freeman again, well almost, there was something new in him, something he liked but kept suppressed; whatever it was, he knew he couldn't afford its luxury right now.

At the printers, a brusque Basque woman curtly ushered Freeman into a near empty and well-lit room, sat him down on the only chair and quickly shot a few frames from a large camera sitting on a tripod before showing him the door. They had not exchanged a word.

Minutes later, as he stood listless outside the printers, the car parked next to him reflecting the late morning sunshine, he knew the waiting would soon to be over.

3.

110 DEGREES

THE NEXT FEW WEEKS found Freeman spending all his time with Rebecca, swimming in the pale blue sea and being carefree in a way he had long forgotten. She had refused his offer of free money, saying she would take some if her needs were so.

Freeman wasn't sure, but he did wonder if this feeling of newfound domestic bliss was a thing to cherish, hold onto. After all, he was sensing something like happiness, something that seemed to make him nearly forget. But, one early silent morning, whilst the town slept at about the time he used to fish the empty morning shore, the unwelcome sight of Jaffa stood looking in at Freeman who had just answered the door, sleepy and half-awake.

'Where is your heart on such a still and expectant morning?'

Freeman felt anger. At first, anger at being disturbed by this freak at such an early hour and then at Jaffa's features that now reminded him of those who had taken his home and stolen his life.

Freeman then looked out at hope, and in that empty moment, Jaffa spoke:

'You leave today.'

After a brief exchange of words, Jaffa was gone and Freeman felt the chill of dawn as he stood looking out and down the empty shadowed street. A lone bird chirped as if encouraging the break of day and Freeman stepped back into the cool dark interior of the hall, shutting the heavy oak door behind him. He stood silent and still, pondering the moment. This was not a day he particularly wanted to encourage. However, it was time: the waiting over and his mysterious job, on.

He crept back up the stairs to the apartment where the sight of Rebecca sleeping and the smell of sex greeted him. Wanting her urgently, he forced himself to get dressed before doubt and heartache got the better of him. Jaffa had said to leave the gun locked up and to bring only his passport – no clothes, except the ones he chose to wear that day. He moved with speed and care, wrote Rebecca a scribbled note – told her to keep the money and to wait for his return, but by the time he was in the yard, starting the car and heading east into the breaking sun, he was already forgetting the note, Rebecca and his Bayonne days.

BACK IN THE APARTMENT, Rebecca opened her eyes. She had heard the inevitable and overdue knock at the door – Jacques's calling – and looked over at the sleeping baby with a tear in her eye, knowing that Freeman's heart was somehow driving him home.

THROUGH THE OPEN WINDOW, the cool rush of breeze numbed his face, held back his thoughts and roaming mind as he focused on the empty road. He drove slowly, savouring the calm before pulling into the gravel drive whose crunching broke him from his trance.

He stepped out of the car and strolled into the garden, stopping under the shadow of the black cherry tree to look pensively at Jane. She sat in the lounger pointing a handgun at him with what Freeman thought was a terrifying ease; with her other hand, she held and spoke into the big black hand-piece of a telephone that sat conspicuously on the grass between them. She spoke quietly, confirming Freeman's flight details, as Jaffa's gait swayed gently between the gravel drive and house, his features blotted out to Freeman by the strong morning sun, very much like the first time they had met on the deserted early morning shore. Jaffa looked on in silence.

The hand piece clonked heavily down and Freeman took his eyes away from Jane and stared at the black object sitting in the green grass. He looked up at Jaffa's silhouette and then spoke to both of them in a low gruff voice trying to suppress his increasing anger, his eyes darting from one face to the other.

'What's this?'

As Jane lowered the gun, she dismissively remarked:

'A reminder, that the breeze may yet become a storm.'

Freeman's pained scowl was eased by Jaffa's light and easy movements as he moved into the garden. Standing by the wooden table, he asked for Freeman's passport. As Freeman pushed it over the table, Jaffa handed him another, which he took and looked through with great curiosity. Flicking through the pages, he stopped at the photograph taken by the brusque Basque woman and read the name aloud:

'Marcel Malo?'

'He was available.'

'Is he real?'

'Of course you are real!'

'And who am I?'

'Monsieur Malo, only you can be knowing that!'

Laughter eased the tension but it never went away; and, on the long drive to Lyon-Bron airport with Jaffa at the wheel of the Mustang, Freeman breathed in deeply, trying to relax his pent up body. He looked sideways at Jaffa's deadpan features.

'Tell me what I need to know.'

'You will be being met by someone at the airport and taken to a hotel where there will be a change of clothes and an invitation to dinner. A car will pick you up and you will then get a signature for a contract I will hand you later. You will then be calling me on this number.'

Without taking his eyes off the road, Jaffa produced a small white card from his pocket and handed it to Freeman. After Freeman had read the hand written Parisian number, Jaffa told him to memorize it, which was simple because the number was short. He handed back the card.

'That's it?'

'Unless it all goes wrong.'

'What then?

'Only a Freeman will be knowing that!'

'You mean Marcel Malo?'

'Oh no, he'll be dead by then.'

Freeman said nothing, almost felt like sulking, knowing this was all of his own choosing.

After the long boring drive, they parked the car in the open lot near the entrance to the terminal and Jaffa proceeded to lead Freeman into the busy building and through the milling crowd. They stopped at a rather deserted check-in desk.

'Your ticket.'

He handed Freeman his oblong pass to danger. He reluctantly took it and read the destination. His heart sunk. At least the return date was for two days after his arrival and he found that part reassuring.

After the brief formalities of check-in, during which he had to keep reminding himself he wasn't Freeman but Malo, whose character he needed to invent creatively long before touch down, they ambled towards immigration where Freeman half-whispered and half-hissed:

'There's a bloody civil war going on there.'

'And you are an expert in just that.'

'What the hell do you expect me to do?'

'You'll be doing whatever it takes to get you home again.'

Freeman knew he was being played, squeezed to compliance, risking his life for his burning desire to get his home back, and he knew he was going right along with it, come hell or high water.

'You have it all worked out.'

'And so have you.'

Jaffa handed him a large envelope. Nonchalantly examining the drab brown, Freeman knew that somewhere inside was a blank space demanding a signature that he must secure. What if he couldn't get it and it was left blank – what then?

Smirking, he looked up but Jaffa was gone, lost somewhere among the crowds. He had timed that perfectly Freeman thought, no further talk or reassurance and certainly no goodbyes. It was up to him now – walk through immigration or walk away.

He handed his passport to the surly looking official who stamped it without utterance or change of expression and Freeman was through, into that no-man's land between leaving and arriving where one just sits it out and impatiently waits.

It was going to be a long flight where Freeman hoped he could sleep and be ready for whatever was waiting in that despicable country to which he was now heading. Sitting down in departures, he became aware it was his face conspicuously sticking out from all the other passengers.

The envelope wasn't sealed and he pulled out the contract. In fact, there were two identical contracts – one for him to take back and one for the despots he had yet to meet. Flicking through it, noting the blanks where the interior minister had to put his scribble, he digested the main points: the rights to drill and export oil for an obscene amount of money deposited upfront into a Swiss account on agreement and signature and the assurance that rebels holding the drilling area were quickly removed.

Freeman thrust the document back in the envelope. Besides various company names he needed to know no more – money and soldiers to make more money and probably a lot of dead soldiers. This was how this stuff always worked. He was disgusted with himself, with Jaffa and with just about anyone he could think of. This is what he had become – a stooge for big business and corrupt dictators. He quickly blanked this useless moral turmoil from his mind and felt his own rage, his own quarrel and self-righteous need to use anything at his disposal to take back what was his.

West Africa, June 1968

I T WAS THE KIND OF FLIGHT where everyone talked loudly to hide their fear and concerns, as turbulence shook the plane all the way to a bumpy landing in a vast and empty landscape. He had seen the delta, swamps and endless green, before parched soil told him they would be landing soon. He hoped dry land would offer a smoother ride.

The engines ceased whining, the propellers stopped spinning and Freeman was soon walking the hot tarmac towards the terminal in unbearable heat and searing light. He squinted and loosened his shirt collar. By the time he remembered his sunglasses, he was inside and alone in the alien entry channel, facing another hostile looking official, as all the other passengers had formed a separate queue.

The immigration official studied the passport. He eyed Freeman with suspicion and disdain before asking in English:

'Mr. Malo, what is your purpose?'

Freeman had forgotten to invent Malo during the long bumpy flight and now quietly panicked whilst making a huge effort to stay composed.

'Business...'

But it didn't matter, as a slim and tall, well-dressed man approached and intervened. His modern European demeanour immediately told Freeman this was a well-travelled sophisticated man unlike the brute sitting at the desk before him.

'We have been expecting you. Follow me please.'

He barked an order at the immigration official in a language Freeman did not recognise and the official stamped and handed Freeman his passport back.

Freeman learned that the man was Abiade and was taking him to his hotel. During the slow drive in an official car with an official driver through city streets devoid of traffic but thronging with people, Abiade made polite conversation. He spoke about Paris and particular French women he had intimately known but Freeman was sleepy and only half listening and hadn't even noticed that they were now speaking French until he heard – 'Marcel' – and then he knew he had better answer, watch out and not get caught out. The only French girl Freeman knew was Elsa and he didn't think she fitted into the complex sophisticated type he was now being told about, but he nodded and said the right things or rather what he thought were the expected things.

They didn't have proper hotels in this country and the decaying colonial mansion whose steps they were walking up now served as some kind of club for foreign interests. The large foyer was impressive, its high ceiling with large lazy fans and its sweeping curved staircase looked down on worn sofas, cushioned chairs and a long wooden polished bar with a smartly dressed barman that was typical of this kind of place. After this facade, Freeman knew it couldn't function as a proper hotel and everything would be shabby, dark and very unwelcoming.

After signing in, Abiade insisted on drinks. The bar area was full of tough men, mostly European, an indication to the war and the constant hired help it required. They were drunk and silent, grateful that they were somehow still alive, blanking off the horrors of tomorrow. Their guns were leaning against the foyer wall, away from the bar but close enough to reach. Freeman scanned the scruffy war weary bunch, eyeing him with empty stares. He decided not to talk to Abiade about his country's mess and Abiade made no reference to it.

Not in the mood for pleasantries and only caring about a signature and speedy exit back to France, Freeman put one hand on the envelope he had placed on the table between them, and came straight to the point.

'I have the contract, we can proceed anytime.'

There, that was clear.

Abiade nodded, appearing lost in thought.

Freeman looked towards the hired men and then back at Abiade who had still not spoken and seemed to be in a dilemma, and when he did finally speak, he was agitated. Freeman sensed that whatever Abiade's plan had been, it was changing fast – perhaps Freeman or rather Malo was not what had been expected and a different tact was needed. Abiade stood up, high and proud, saying, 'I'll pick you up at six,' and left the hotel with a curt goodbye.

Alone and worried, Freeman sat looking about him. One of the hired men made a nasty comment about Abiade's colour to which the others laughed but Freeman didn't share their sentiments – he knew their type well, had sometimes felt the same but had long mellowed, unless it was to do with home.

He felt caught between the lure and promise of what the mission represented for him personally and for his absolute revulsion towards the dirty business that drove it all. Freeman knew this quandary was weakening his resolve and that he had better quit any moral sensibilities still lurking in his angry heart.

Deciding to retire, he followed the sweeping staircase into the gloomy shadows of a dark corridor. Quickly shutting himself off in his stuffy, cheerless room, only the noise of a spinning fan and the disagreeable smell of disinfectant kept him company.

HE DIDN'T REMEMBER MUCH, certainly not flopping on the bed and falling into a dead sleep. When he came to, he had a moment of slight panic; the whirr of the fan, the unfamiliar surroundings and the knocking at the door frightened him and he jumped up off the bed, crashing into the side table, knocking the old telephone to the floor where it made a thud and clanking noise.

A maid was at the door, looking up and speaking something Freeman couldn't quite catch.

Speaking to her in French, he realised she was speaking English, telling him that the officer was waiting for him downstairs. She had a white shirt, black tuxedo and bow tie over one arm and a pair of shiny black shoes and socks in the other. She just stared and he realised she was waiting for some response, acknowledgement, so he nodded and she entered, placing the clothes carefully on the bed and the shoes on the floor below. She then just stood there, looking at him.

Dismissing her with the type of wave he had not used for a long time, he went to the bathroom with his evening's attire. After he had taken a cold shower, as the hot was non-existent, had had a shave and dressed, he looked into the mirror and almost felt like Freeman once again, but knew he was somehow different, changed in a way he dare not fathom.

Picking up the contract, he left the room, taking himself down the sweeping staircase to the lobby. The other men had gone, leaving only the barman, receptionist and Abiade who was finishing a telephone conversation and staring up at Freeman. He was immaculately dressed in an army uniform. Freeman caught his eye and received what he thought was a tacit look of approval, which meant that he, Freeman, was looking just right, as Jaffa had prescribed, to be negotiating a deal and getting it signed. Well, that was Freeman's fantasy, as he finished his dashing descent into the lobby, and was encouraging enough to get him going and proceed into the labyrinths of the waiting night.

The car drove slowly through the dusty streets in the dimming light and the two men remained silent until the old palace appeared down a long tree lined avenue. Having a slight headache, Freeman felt relief that this time there was no conversation. Soldiers guarding the entrance waved the car through large open metal gates and they stopped outside the impressive colonial residence. As the car doors were opened by more soldiers, Abiade spoke:

'It's a party. You'll be called soon enough. In the mean-
time, enjoy yourself.'

The evening had turned to night and interior lights shone
brightly through the windows of the impressive curved facade.
Inside, through the glass, Freeman could see the typical
ostentatious fixtures and fittings that these places always
seemed to have; he also saw the shady guests with whom he
would shortly be expected to mingle. Abiade gestured towards
the entrance and Freeman found himself inside, alone,
wandering from room to room, smiling at uncomfortable
faces. Clutching his precious envelope, he ended up at the rear
of the house where stone steps dropped down to a lawn and
formal garden. Here more people milled, some sitting on
chairs and benches fanning themselves in the increasing
humidity, which reminded him of home. A fountain and stone
pool caught his attention and he found himself heading
towards its delicate sounds and cool ambience. From a waiter
he managed to secure a glass and jug of water that he downed
in minutes. As the sweat started to drip from his pores, his
headache lifted and he observed his surroundings.

Hired men were on the perimeter and he could see and
sense many security agents among the guests who were mostly
men, as was usual at these events, with an occasional wife in
tow. Good time girls mingled, providing lewd entertainment
on demand for those with such a taste. He knew that every
single one of those guests were like him in some way, drawn
there only for profit and without care for the country
crumbling around them.

He remained by the fountain, which lay slightly too far out
into the lawn to be attracting other guests, for he did not want
to be questioned on his business. He still imagined the
welcome breeze would not become a storm.

Watching shadows dance on the lawn from various candles burning on the stone steps, he enjoyed the flutter of night moths attracted to these phoney moons. Lost in the moment, Freeman did not notice Abiade approach from the dark recess of the garden.

'You are a very strange man Marcel.'

Freeman turned and saw Abiade as a man with silent power, his face softly gleaming in the light that just managed to reach them from the house.

'After such a long stuffy journey, I needed the fresh air and open space.'

He gestured around and looked up at the vast African night sky, empty of moon and full of sparkling stars. Abiade too looked up but seemed unconcerned at things that he had no influence over.

'The minister will see you now.'

Indicating to the house, Abiade eyed the envelope that Freeman held. They both walked across the small lawn, up the stones steps into the house that was now heaving with people, full of laughter and drunken chatter. Waiters were speedily moving around refilling glasses and offering an abundance of tasty looking snacks whose sight and smells exaggerated Freeman's own hunger.

As Abiade led the way to the front lobby and up the main staircase, a band started up from one of the main function rooms and swing music filled the house with its easy style. Freeman liked this, felt himself being sucked into something pleasant, numbing, and with the envelope firmly in his hands – dangerous.

He found himself in a large wood panelled room and heard the door click shut behind him. The music and din of guests was still very audible but soft enough so not to shout. A large man sitting on a sofa with two scantily dressed girls on either arm said, in a jolly booming voice:

'Marcel, please join us.'

He indicated to a comfortable armchair opposite. Although they had not been introduced, Freeman knew this was the minister. Before he took his seat, he gave a small bow, knowing a handshake would not be wanted.

A serious looking man with black rimmed glasses, dressed in an immaculate ivory coloured suit, sat at a desk peering up at Freeman. A guard stood by the door and another girl was slumped in an armchair next to Freeman, her eyes shut; either drunk or drugged, her dress straps had fallen down over her shoulders making her dress so loose it showed her black nipples. One of the girls freed herself from the minister to sit on the arm of Freeman's chair. She smelt of perfume and sex: the smell of brothels he had once enjoyed, but now revolted him. It reminded him of a public toilet where the smell of scent tries to disguise the stinking smell of piss.

'Meet Titilayo.'

Titilayo put an arm around Freeman and started playing with his hair. Tensing, he faked pleasure, attentive that he had to see this through. Abiade looked on bemused, malevolently adding:

'How's your maid, Marcel?'

Freeman pained a smile, knowing that he may fool everyone else but that Abiade wasn't fooled by very much at all.

'Fine…I guess.'

'So you like the smell of the country?'

The minister laughed at his own joke, and everyone else followed suit.

Abiade drove the malice home.

'You can do anything with her. Once she's finished ironing your shirts, she's surplus to requirements.'

The minister turned the screw a little tighter:

'As with Titilayo.'

Through the mean laughter, she squeezed his shoulder tight, causing him to feel her fear but also his own fear, aware that these evil jokes cloaked a warning aimed at him.

There was a soft knock at the door. Whilst the laughter was subsiding, a waiter came in with a trolley loaded with food and drinks and, much to Freeman's relief, served him a large plate of assorted snacks, which he immediately started eating.

The man behind the desk, who introduced himself as Toby, asked Freeman for the contracts. On receiving the envelope, he pulled both contracts out and started to examine them in detail.

The minister took his hand out from under the remaining girl's skirt, making Freeman ever so glad he had not shaken it, and pointed a finger at the contracts being scrutinised on the desk.

He almost barked out an order:

'Tell us what you know about oil?'

He felt he could handle this question easily and told them about his father's farm, how they had built a small platform to pump oil out the swamps into coastal tankers.

They seemed surprised at learning his country and Free-man astutely dismissed its importance by adding that he had left for France long before the troubles and how it now lay wasted and abandoned. He had no idea if anyone knew Jaffa, thought it best left alone and merely mentioned the oil company he was pretending to work for; this seemed to satisfy everyone, for now. Freeman got the waiter to pour another drink.

A side door opened and a man came into the room, quick-ly exiting through the main door. He was followed by another girl who plonked her exhausted body on the sofa close to the minister and looked blankly out of joyless eyes towards Freeman. He looked her over, saw bruising on her thighs and a badly swollen cheek.

The long drawn out uncomfortable process of being in the room and waiting for the contract to be approved and signed was starting to put Freeman on edge; he would soon be showing it and badly needed a way out of the room. Wanting the lavatory but knowing that would be too short a trip, he did what he thought was probably expected: he pointed to the side door and stood up, grabbing Titilayo by the wrist.

'May I?'

'Of course.'

The minister chuckled. A moment later, they were through the door and into a bedroom where Freeman immediately went into the bathroom to relieve himself. On his return, Titilayo had stripped naked and was sitting on the messy bed, looking up at him with frightened expectation. He opened the window to be rid of the stink the room had accumulated. Looking out onto the grounds below, he saw a patrol of hired men. He pulled the curtains shut.

During a lull in the music, Freeman took the opportunity to slap one hand hard against the other. As the harsh sound filled the empty space, he whispered:

'Scream.'

He repeated the fake slap and she yelped loudly, making a convincing sob and, as laughter echoed from the room next door, Freeman loudly snapped:

'Get around!'

As the music started up again, drowning out the laughter, Titilayo had done as she was told and was on all fours putting her head down and her skinny haunches up. Freeman sat down in the only chair. As Titilayo turned her head around to look at him, he shook his head but she did not move. Freeman just looked on into the entrance of The Pink Alley Club, knowing he was no longer a member of such a mean and sleazy business; but how easy it was, he thought, to be blank and mean and then pretend it was the manly thing to do.

'Get dressed,' he whispered.

She needed no more than that and was up, slipping her dress back on and staring at Freeman who wanted none of what she had no choice but offer.

When the band had finished their number and the house went quieter, he pushed his foot against the bed and made it bang hard against the wall that joined next door. He mouthed the word:

'Moan.'

She did with an amazing expertise that would have fooled almost anybody, and when the music started up again, she knew to stop for now she knew his game. She almost found it amusing, but something more urgent was on her mind.

'Take me back to your hotel.'

He shook his head.

She implored again to find his silence.

She sat on the bed in solitude as he waited and, when he thought the contract had been examined enough, went to the bathroom, pulled his handkerchief from his top pocket and rinsed it under the tap. He squeezed out the excess water and returned to the room, handing it to Titilayo. She stubbornly refused to take it, only saying 'please' again.

'Maybe,' he retorted.

She shook her head.

Not wanting to blow the stupid game he had started, he reluctantly agreed.

She took the handkerchief, knowing exactly what to do – she placed it against her cheek and started to sob, which Freeman knew was fake, but boy was it convincing. They re-entered the main room. He took his place in the comfortable armchair as she sat on the sofa opposite, feigning a painful sitting position and snuggling up to the girl next to her who remained quite indifferent.

The minister laughed.

'Oh Marcel! Now she is useless! We'll have to throw her out and get a fresh one in!'

He gruffly spoke to the security guard in a local language who then made towards Titilayo, who looked up at Freeman, terrified.

'I haven't finished with that one yet.'

Although he didn't feel sorry for her, he certainly didn't want to be involved in her misfortune. Freeman understood that he was being paid to play a role and had to keep this farce going, until back on a plane and heading home.

The men in the room laughed and the minister dismissed the guard. Titilayo quickly went and sat on the arm of Freeman's chair. This time her arm around him held on tight.

Toby had decided that the contracts were in order and soon the signing was completed to the satisfaction of everyone, especially Freeman who now felt he was half way home. However, Abiade reminded him things were far from over.

'There's a telephone in the other room.'

He opened the room's main door and Freeman followed. Titilayo slunk down in the chair.

Music was in full swing and the party as lively as before. As they walked along a gallery over-looking the busy hall below, he saw Luk amongst some hired men looking up at him with that wry smile he remembered from their meeting in a Pyrenean cow field. Freeman knew he must not acknowledge him.

Shown into a small empty office containing only a table on which the telephone sat, he lifted the receiver, imagining it was there just for this occasion. Immediately, an operator asked for the number. He knew he was probably being listened to, and by the time the number had rung a few times, he had heard a few suspect clicks.

'Freeman?'

'Yes. It's been signed.'

'Their call will come in soon...' Jane paused. 'A storm's been forecast, it will be a bumpy ride back home. Hold on tight to your precious cargo.'

The phone went dead and Freeman looked at the door, which he now knew would open into something that made all that money he was earning make perfect sense.

Why had he said yes?

Abiade opened the door and Freeman left, their eyes coldly meeting for the briefest moment. He did not look down to see if Luk was still there, he doubted it anyway and knew events were somehow about to take a turn.

Abiade did not follow him back to the waiting and expectant room.

The minister was happy to see him and snapped at Titilayo to move out of the seat but Freeman indicated for her to stay, helping himself to another drink from the trolley.

On edge and desperate for the phone to ring so he could get out fast and collect himself, he felt like pacing. Whatever was about to happen, he knew he would have no say.

Everyone in the room was tense. No one spoke. After what seemed an age but was less than a minute, the telephone shrilled. Toby picked it up. A moment of silence passed as he listened with intent.

'Yes,' he said, placing the receiver down and looking up at the strained faces. 'The money's been deposited.'

The minister smiled, clicked his fingers, ordered champagne and immediately the mood changed to a party atmosphere, which Freeman found terrifying.

After a wax seal pressed down hard on the last signature of the contract, it was handed to Freeman. It was done and he inspected every page, carefully noting the official seal.

'I'll join the party for a while.'

The Minister approved and Freeman quickly took leave followed by Titilayo who grabbed his arm so hard he practically dragged her down the stairs. He never returned to the party but exited straight out of the main entrance to look around for his car and driver.

On finding them, he ordered the man to take them to the hotel. He barely noticed Titilayo shaking next to him.

He had the contract, now he only needed to get on a plane in the morning. What could be simpler?

He relaxed slightly as they drove away and entered the deserted city streets. About half a mile from the hotel, he told the driver to stop and he leant over Titilayo, opening the door, indicating that she should leave. Their deal was done. She didn't wait a second, disappearing into darkness.

He left the car a block away from his hotel, walking to the back of the building in darkness. Although he had done his job, they had the money and all he needed to do was leave, he still felt the need for caution. Jane's weather report bugged him and he understood that something might be coming for him soon – but what, and what could he do about it anyway?

The hotel's back door was locked and he realised he would have to enter from the front, but as he had his passport, ticket and some cash, wondered why he needed to go back – he would not be able to sleep anyway. As he stood in the dusty street looking up at the entrance, pondering what to do, he saw car headlights way down the avenue coming straight towards him. He decided to go inside. A few hired men hung silently around the bar, eyeing him coldly as he stepped into the lobby, their weapons close to hand. Collecting his key from an unsmiling receptionist, Freeman quickly ascended the sweeping staircase. He didn't take the risk of looking back.

In the shadows of the corridor, darkness stalled him and he stopped. Placing himself out of sight in an alcove, he tried to think. Was he just being paranoid or was there reason for his fear.

The hotel was silent, not a sound and he dared not move. He could feel his heart pounding and the rush in his ears. Then the car squeaked to a halt and doors banged. Moving up the corridor, he found the maid blocking his way. She looked terrified, shaking her head, pointing a finger to his room. He knew someone must be there and that he had walked into a trap. As the stairs below creaked, he grabbed her arm in desperation, tacitly communicating his need to get out of there fast. Her own survival took over and she pulled him to a service door, pushed it open and, in total darkness, led him down a tiny staircase to a laundry room. They stopped, heard shouting, doors opening and slamming shut.

'Get me out of here,' he seethed.

A small window gave enough light for him to see her take a key from her apron pocket and unlock an outside door. He looked out, saw no one and dashed across a yard into an area of old sheds and junk. In the shadows, listening to the noises coming from the hotel, he noticed her by his side.

Desperate, he implored in a raw whisper, 'Which way?'

Her response was a worried stare.

Stuck and with no hope of help, it would be moments before the hired men found the open door. Freeman tried to remember something useful, anything that might help to save his life. A man appeared at the door shouting for his colleagues. They had found his getaway. It then came to him: that map he had memorised from the boot of the Mustang – hotel to bar. Needing to get across the avenue, they left the shadows, hurrying across a track to a small patch of scrub. Squatting down, trying to buy some time, a lone dog started barking. As armed men stepped out of the laundry door, Freeman frantically moved to the edge of the long avenue. Having only a scrawny tree and the shadow of the night to stop them being seen, he gruffly hissed:

'Run.'

They both dashed across the road. Near to the other side, shots rang out but they were in the shadows once again, running down an alley. Freeman had the contract still firmly in his hand.

It was difficult to find the way with all the manoeuvring they needed to do to stay ahead and out of sight, and once, when the men were close, they had to get off route and hide. Having backtracked to get back on track, he saw a bar, a shack really, half-brick half-mud and dashed inside. He had no clue if it was the right one or not.

It was empty except for a barman, who seemed indifferent to their entrance. On seeing them, he turned the TV on, which sat at the end of the bar. A grainy picture slowly emerged with accompanying sound. The barman totally ignored them.

They were both perspiring and breathing hard. Not wanting to lose Freeman to find herself alone and at the mercy of those in pursuit, she held hard onto his arm. Freeman felt the urge to run again.

As if sensing that, the barman spoke:

'The show will be on in a minute. Want a drink?'

Freeman didn't want a drink – his head was still swimming from all the drink at the palace meeting.

His wound up anxiety nearly turned to explosive anger when a news bulletin came through. It was Abiade giving news that the President had been assassinated and that a curfew was in force. The Minister, whose signature Freeman firmly held, was now in charge. His anxiety soon turned to horror: the picture of him, taken by the brusque Basque woman in Bayonne, was being displayed on the screen, telling the entire country that Marcel Malo was responsible for the murder and must be shot on sight. He had some valuable government documents in his possession whose safe return was subject to a large reward. Abiade held up the other copy of the contract that Freeman now furiously clenched.

'Want that drink now?' The barman brought two beers over.

The news bulletin kept going with Freeman's face constantly appearing as a wanted man, preferably a dead one. He was speechless. The maid and barman said nothing as they kept looking from the screen to him.

Ignoring the beer, feeling wired and desperate, he followed his racing heart and stepped towards the door. Not wanting to lose him, she hung on tight, holding him back. Before Freeman had time to shake her off, the barman pointed to a back room.

'Wait in there.'

In a dilemma between his instinct to run and Jaffa's little map telling him there must be some sort of a plan, he deliberated. She pulled and he followed, the pair soon finding themselves in a small storeroom without a door. A kerosene lamp gave off a dim and flickering light. In the shadows of the corner was the silhouette of a man, half-sitting, half-slumped – a European riddled full of bullet holes.

The maid gasped, holding a hand over her mouth. Freeman looked hard in the faint light and saw that the face was badly mutilated. Not wanting to know anymore, he sank down on some hessian sacks full of something hard like corn. This could only get worse.

They were followed in by the barman who had now locked the bar room door and turned the lights and TV off. He sat down on a small chair by the lamp and, whilst looking into the dim burning orange flame, softly said.

'Wait.'

Freeman said nothing, was angry, exhausted and bathed in cold sticky perspiration. It was now very clear to him that Jaffa had set him up, but Jane had also warned him on the phone of some impending danger. He couldn't fathom a thing and the more he thought the more confused he got. When he finally came out of his useless thoughts, he saw the barman smoking a cigarette, looking right at him with large indifferent eyes. He learned the woman's name was Jeneta as the barman started softly talking with her in yet another language Freeman couldn't understand. Sitting right next to him, huddled close, he noticed that she wasn't wearing shoes. He turned and looked at the tiny, fierce looking woman who had probably saved his life. She now looked older, her bushy hair and gold-hooped earrings not fitting with her long khaki coloured dress and dirty apron still tied around her waist.

They fell silent as shouts and running footsteps passed the bar. The barman lifted the lamp glass and blew hard, leaving them in complete darkness. Freeman felt his heart thud and Jeneta's breath upon his neck. Smoke from the extinguished wick stung his throat. The glow of the barman's cigarette soon vanished and the stubbing scraping noise of his foot gave way to the rattle of diesel engines. Headlights of patrolling vehicles occasionally illuminated the bar room in front of where they sat.

This went on for about fifteen minutes before all went quiet. Only the odd dog bark cut through the silence of the night. The air was offensive, a mix of stale alcohol and strong tobacco and, lacking a window, the room hot and confining. Freeman became aware of Jeneta's sweet and sickly smell, which he knew was fear. The unbearable tension was broken by a soft knock at the door. The barman left the storeroom and they heard a door latch click. Freeman pensively stood up and Jeneta did the same. As they apprehensively clung to the darkness, the brief sound of footsteps came back to where they stood. A match was struck and in the flare, before the kerosene lamp was lit again, they saw the shapes of men around the open doorway and then the orange glow revealed the visitors.

Freeman stared in disbelief as Luk and a few heavily armed men, who looked like Basques, peered around the room. Jeneta gave out a frightened gasping sob that everyone ignored.

Freeman spoke quietly in French to Luk.

'What the hell's going on?'

'You have the contract?'

Freeman pointed to the floor where it lay in front of the hessian sacks.

'Did you kill the president?'

'Marcel Malo did,' Luk shrugged.

However, there was no time for explanations as the hired men had already dragged the body into the bar room and had stripped him of his clothes. Luk then requested Freeman do the same and, as he stood almost naked looking at the unidentifiable corpse being dressed in his own evening's attire with Marcel Malo's passport and air ticket stuffed inside a pocket, he realised he was helpless and at the mercy of some big double crossing plan.

The body was dragged outside and along the dark street. At the door, Luk turned and quickly wished Freeman all the luck there was and said he was going now to fight a war but wasn't sure for whom or who against. Then he was gone and the door latch shut again.

It all went dark as the barman blew the lamp again. Freeman fumbled to the sacks with Jeneta, shaking badly, following his every move. Everybody was tense, even Luk and his men who had worked with measured urgency had been tense, and Freeman suspected the barman who was now puffing away at another cigarette was more than tense.

They heard shooting, which Freeman instinctively knew to be Luk pumping the tuxedo full of holes, followed by shouts and whistles. As a truck pulled up, more men spoke and a walky-talky sprang to life. For a long time they sat in silence listening to the noises, until the night turned still once more. Far off in the distance, another lone dog barked.

The lamp was lit and the barman beckoned Freeman to the bar. On the counter was a backpack that Luk or one of the other Basques must have dumped. The barman gestured to the pack. Freeman immediately emptied out the contents onto one of the wooden bar room tables. He heard the familiar thud of a pistol as it fell onto the floor. There were some clothes and boots that he quickly fitted. Once dressed and feeling less vulnerable, he checked the remaining chattel: a blanket, water bottle, compass, sun hat, spare magazine, knife, a few boxes of matches and a wad of local currency. He bundled them all back in again, picked up the pistol from the floor, quickly checking its condition before putting it in his pocket. Then he remembered the contract, which was now sitting on the bar, and added that, pulling the backpack straps tight shut.

The barman handed him a note. It was written in French – maybe it was from Luk, he didn't know. It merely gave the name of a town followed by a compass bearing of 110 degrees, a river to cross and then a certain spot for him to wait.

Freeman re-read it and no sooner had he finished, the barman snatched it back, setting it alight, tossing it to the floor where it curled and blackened before his foot smeared it to oblivion.

Freeman looked up and almost barked:

'Where's that bloody town?'

The barman pointed east before pointing to the door with an unforgiving glance.

'On the highway, two days walk.'

From his experiences back home, he knew that he couldn't afford to hang around, wait for morning or any hope of help.

He picked up the pack, slung it on his back and walked to the bar room door. Pulling the bolt, he eased the door towards him and peeked outside. Jeneta was speaking rapidly to the barman who only uttered indifference back, but said to Freeman:

'She's going with you.'

Freeman chose not to hear this remark and was soon outside, adjusting to the darkness and nervously looking up the empty street.

She was right next to him but he didn't meet her eye as he stepped out across the street to hide among the shadows of a small deserted house. Turning back towards the bar, he saw her staring at him with the door shut tight behind her.

Damn, he thought.

As he deliberated his next move, she crossed the street. He looked into her eyes and saw himself standing helpless in the hotel corridor before she led him out to safety.

Although he knew no one would be looking for them now, they walked cautiously through the darkness. On the edge of town, she led the way towards the highway. A cold clear band of light cut the horizon to the east. They could make out the dark shapes of bush and scrub that would soon show as empty rolling wilderness as morning broke.

They had been walking for a while on the hard compact mud until the increasing light told Freeman it best to stop, lay up and take stock of their surroundings. He found a small rocky escarpment full of rounded boulders. By the time they reached the top, the sun was up and they hid among the rocks. About a mile or so behind them was the edge of town; down the hill in front, was the dusty highway cutting through the endless bush and disappearing into haze.

As Freeman scoured the landscape, Jeneta sat down and leant against a rock. Feeling it was safe, he too dropped his exhausted body to the ground. He turned to her.

'Jacques.'

She repeated his name several times aloud.

Asking her to buy what they might need for the two day hike, Freeman emptied out his pack, handing it over with a small amount of cash,

She left with him wondering if she would return.

When she did, Jeneta found Freeman fast asleep, curled up against a rock. Only after the smell of her cooking made his stomach pang, did he wake. Without moving, he watched her crouching over a small fire, stirring a pot, occasionally looking down at him.

She had bought a second backpack, jammed full of things for their journey, and he pensively asked:

'Were you noticed?'

She shook her head and he felt relief.

Around midday, when most people would be hiding in the shade, they walked in silence, down towards the highway. Again, Jeneta led the way, carefully placing her feet to avoid the sharp debris that lay strewn between the thick scrub and bush. Freeman followed a few feet behind.

The occasional vehicle passed along the highway. They couldn't see them through the dense bush but could clearly hear the engine splutters and tyres crunching on the broken road before the smell of diesel wafted over, lingering in the still and silent air.

Arriving at the edge of the empty road, Freeman looked hard left and right. Incessant heat and endless downpours had cracked the road; now, it was nothing more than broken stones. Nothing was visible, only the road disappearing into the heat of a wavy mirage. If a truck or car appeared then they had ample time to step back and disappear into its thick bush perimeter.

Hiking along the deserted highway, listening for any sounds that might indicate a vehicle, Freeman fiddled with the compass inside his trouser pocket. Turning events over in his mind, he ignored Jeneta trailing in his shadow.

As the long day bore down on them, the only change in their rhythmic steps was to meld occasionally with the bush, as a truck full of soldiers passed back towards the city, or to stop and sparingly drink. The monotony was finally broken by Jeneta.

'I need rest.'

Freeman felt it too and without any need for eye contact or further prompt, they headed across the road into the bush until a suitable boulder offered shade. They both sat against the rock, their legs pulled up to make sure they were fully protected from the sun.

Whilst looking at the thorny bush, Jeneta asked:

'Where are you taking me?'

Freeman turned and looked at her profile. Before turning away, he answered:

'I'm not taking you anywhere. You followed me.'

'Where are you going?'

'110 degrees from the next town.'

'The barman told me only ghosts and vultures live out there…'

Freeman turned and stared.

'…but as your dead body was already in the bar when he arrived, he said you must be a ghost.'

Freeman smirked. Not wanting to be bothered by such idiotic talk, he turned away again, lost in his own thoughts, waiting for the road to pull them back.

THEY MARCHED ON towards the haze until their shadows grew long, stretching way out in front. Freeman stopped and turned to see Jeneta's looking up at him, the low orange glow behind her minutes from giving up the day. Her face was in shadow but her eyes shone in a way that unnerved him.

'Let's camp.'

He chose to get way off the road so a fire couldn't be seen from a passing truck or car. Just before darkness blanketed the bush, they managed to find a good spot and settle for the night. The silence of the day gave way to shrills, shrieks and a disconcerting cracking twig.

Freeman felt the chill of night and a shiver of the un-known, as she spoke:

'Did you hear that?'

'What?'

'Ghosts.'

He couldn't stand this superstition, had had enough of it on the farm back home, and blurted out:

'Anymore mumbo jumbo and you'll be on your own!'

Pulling the blanket from the backpack, he lay on the ground and placed it over him, raising one side.

'Come on, forget about the ghosts…'

She got under and rigidly lay facing the stars above.

'…go to sleep, we need to rest.'

'Do they have these stars at home?'

Glad at the change in conversation, he looked up.

'Not in France where I live now.'

'Why not?'

'It's too cold for them. You know France?'

'From the atlas and they live across the border where you want to go.'

He fell asleep as she watched the stars, listening to ghosts around the camp.

HE WOKE BEFORE DAWN. Feeling chilly, he pushed up against Jeneta's back; he was hard and felt confused. He smelt her now familiar scent.

He got up and she spoke without moving.

'The ghosts came last night.'

He went to the bush to pee but also collect himself and shouted back to humour her:

'What did they say?'

She didn't reply and when he returned, she was gone. He picked up their things ready for the day's walk. Cold and needing to get going, he indicated towards the road as soon as she came back. She stood staring at him.

'They told me to keep following you.'

'But you're not a ghost.'

'I'm Osu, so I am a ghost like you.'

She saw him staring, not knowing what she meant.

'Go home. The fighting must stop sometime soon.'

'The fighting never stops while men like you are in the world.'

'I'm just a man trying to get home.'

He told her of his country and she looked into the bush, pointing.

'When the wind blows maybe you can smell your country, follow it home.'

'It's more complicated than that.'

Looking at her looking right at him, he knew that if he looked more like her then getting home might be easy, but he didn't, and, as a vast silence consumed the moment, she picked up her pack and went towards the road.

WAITING FOR THE SUN to appear over the murky horizon to warm their bodies, took about an hour. Freeman was glad to be moving, not only for warmth but also to get away from his physical predicament with Jeneta. He had never actually slept next to a local, not even in The Pink Alley Club days. Then, it had just been brief blank visits, and her talk about ghosts had unnerved him. He knew how much they believed in all that stuff.

The day was much the same: a long hike down a hot and empty broken road with the occasional passing truck that had them hiding in the thick cover of the bush. They didn't speak except for necessities and, at about midday, when their shadows were at their feet and the water nearly gone, they rested under the shade of one of the few tall trees they had come across. Jeneta climbed the smooth bark, clutching at small branches until she was high up, looking out at the vast vista, which Freeman couldn't see. Back down, she told him that nearby, in a dip in the road, lay the town and that some small dwellings were even closer and that meant water.

Driven by thirst, they moved at speed until the bush petered out and they were standing in a small clearing. Tethered goats sat munching cut leaves under a makeshift lean-to between two small trees. Nearby were huts and a small stone well. A man sat on the stone sides with a rifle leaning next to him. Facing away, he hadn't seen them. Instinctively, they both stepped back into the cover of the bush.

Desperate for water, Freeman knew exactly what they had to do. Turning to Jeneta, who was feeling just the same, he whispered:

'Follow me and collect as much water as you can.'

He handed her the canteen and they moved silently through the bush. Freeman pulled the gun, flicked the safety off and pointed it towards the man who turned on hearing footsteps. He froze with a look of dumbfound shock.

Freeman was right on him, pressing the gun hard against his forehead. Pulling the bucket from the well, Jeneta filled the canteen before filling some glass bottles she had seen, lying on the ground nearby.

When she was done and had the bottles packed away and the pack back on her back, Freeman roughly grabbed the man and pushed him over the stone surround into the well. They heard a cry and the resounding splash.

Freeman grabbed the rifle and peered into the well. Attempting to haul himself up the broken well walls, the man dropped back down as he glanced up at Freeman's silhouette. They left, quickly reaching the road, crossing over and walking deep into the bush. They headed towards the town.

Stopping, they drank a bottle each, panting and gasping as the cool fluid poured life back into them. A bead of sweat rolled down Freeman's temple as Jeneta put the empty bottles back. He examined the rifle. It was old and heavy, a burden to carry so he left it where they stood. Moving on, he knew they would be followed. Without delay or complication, they had to reach the town and set the compass bearing. Only then could they find the river and hopefully some safety.

As the bush became thinner from the constant cutting of firewood that the town demanded, the view to the town below became clear. At the top of a group of jumbled boulders, Freeman found the perfect vista where he could peer out, hidden amongst the smooth red-grey stone. Slinging his backpack down, he rummaged for the compass and took a bearing, knowing they would have to get right inside the town to make it accurate.

Roughly pointing in the direction of the bearing, Freeman asked her to go down and find out what she could before buying anything they might need for their journey from the information she obtained. Emptying his bag, he handed it to her with all the money he had left. After she had looked down on the sprawling jam-packed town, she looked at him oddly, compelling him blurt out that he would wait and that they needed to leave while it was still light enough to find their way.

He knew she would return. The ghosts had spoken. This irritated him, but he needed her now, more than he could admit.

As there was no shade in the rocky hideaway, he lay on his back, his hat covering his face from the burning heat. Reckoning the well-owners would be now be on his trail, he dared not move or make a sound.

Before long, he heard their chatter, increasing until they arrived at the maze of boulders where he hid. The air went still and silent; then, he heard the scuffle of their feet, as the men looked around for footprints or any other sign. Freeman already clutched the gun, the safety off, waiting for that moment where he would have to squeeze the trigger.

A cry pierced the tension and he heard the sound of running feet, knowing they must have found Jeneta's tracks. Peering over the rocks, he saw dust kick up as angry men followed her bare prints to town.

Even in a busy town like this, an outsider, especially a woman, would probably be easy to locate. It took him a few moments of vivid imagining to realise what would happen if they caught up with her. Quickly tying knots with the opposing corners of the blanket to make some kind of sling, he threw in the spare magazine, precious compass, contract, knife and canteen and was soon following the well-men's tracks.

Moving fast, he saw them about three hundred yards ahead talking to some herders by a wooden cattle stockade. They were all armed.

Studying the town, Freeman wondered if hired men were down below. If so, he could easily feign being one of them; after all, Marcel Malo was no longer a wanted man. If not, then his appearance would mean arrest at the very least.

Deciding to take the risk, he detoured around the thin bush and entered the edge of town where the highway cut it into two. In the centre of every town like this would be a hotel where hired men might be. Near to that, a barracks and a market. He moved fast towards the centre, collecting stares and sensing danger, for hired men never went alone or without a heavy arm. Seeing the hotel and the unmistaken look of nervous hired men, their guns close by as they drunk themselves towards the night and ghastly waiting day, he entered the tatty place without issue. He was one of them after all. They sensed his desperation and total solitude as he took a seat at an empty table by the open, battered doors.

The well-men came by but didn't stop, just stared and murmured. They knew they were too late with Freeman and any confrontation with him may end in their demise. As they disappeared up the road, Freeman knew Jeneta wasn't safe. This was a lawless place where guns and tribal clans meant everything.

With increasing anxiety, he gazed up the road at the bright colours of the market. He saw her walking towards the hotel and made a dash, grabbing her by the arm and dragging her up the wooden steps to the hotel terrace. However, the well-men had already spotted her and came rushing over, pointing, shouting, brandishing their arms.

Hired men were up, confused and cursing, clutching their weapons and, moments later, just as the tension reached its peak, Freeman pulled his gun and fired into the air. As people scattered, ducked or hit the floor, Freeman pulled Jeneta inside the shadows of the seedy hotel bar. He saw a shaft of light through a half-open back door and seconds later, in the empty alley behind the hotel, he set the compass bearing. Following it to the edge of town, shots and screams rang out behind.

They didn't stop or talk, each now carrying a loaded pack with Freeman clutching the gun, the blanket slung across his shoulder.

At the brow of a hill they stopped, perspiring and out of breath. They looked below. All shadows now stretched east. It was nearly dusk and Freeman realised it had happened all so fast. He could hardly remember the town or tiny streets as they had rushed away to safety.

Trucks were coming down the highway, probably from the war zone, and although he knew the calamity they had caused at the hotel wouldn't follow them here, felt it best to move and not tempt fate.

Freeman gave her one more chance to leave but she refused, defiantly staring, stating, '110 degrees.' They carried on, only stopping with the setting sun.

Not daring not to risk a fire in the dark, he went through Jeneta's shopping pack in the last of the dimming light. There seemed a lot and he asked if she had learned something about their route.

There was a moment of silence.

'Ghosts and vultures.'

She added that they might find water under reeds in dry riverbeds.

He noticed her canvas shoes, which she must have bought, and, as he stared, she simply said:

'My feet are the same as yours.'

Slightly embarrassed, he turned away.

The night was chilly, the air crisp and the stars clear and bright. They didn't talk under the blanket, each lost in their own thoughts and dreams, occasionally interrupted by the sound of distant guns.

WHEN FREEMAN AWOKE, it was already light. His body ached from the hard ground and, as he sat up and stretched, saw Jeneta blowing the flames of a newly made fire.

'Is that a good idea?'

'There's no one here. No war, no soldiers, no well, no people, no animals…'

Not so sure, he added sarcastically:

'Did the ghosts come and tell you that last night?'

'We are the ghosts,' she replied coldly, ignoring his insecurities. She knew where they were heading, and knew that if he knew he really wouldn't like it.

The terrain became arid, devoid of trees and the ground hard underfoot, helping them stick directly to the bearing.

They found water by digging under reeds growing in a depression. Jeneta had dug, knowing exactly where the water ran closest to the surface.

They spent two days hiking this terrain without seeing a living soul or any wildlife, except for the odd sliver of a snake and the high circling of huge winged vultures. They spoke less and less; the need to talk extinguished as they hiked slowly in the heat, hoping that all this would lead to some respite.

ON THE THIRD DAY, as far as they could see, the now red earth was all cracked like a dried out mud pond. As they trekked hard, toiling under dazzling sunlight and a stark and empty blue sky, the dust kicked up, caking their shoes and legs in a fine film of soft powder. They hung their heads low to avoid the harsh midday sun and to be constantly following the bearing on the compass, which every now and then Freeman had to blow clean of the annoying dust. He was thankful that the wind was still and only hot air filled his nostrils and not the choking dust of a desert blow that would have had them lying down and wrapping up.

It was here, during this long and lonely tramp across an unfriendly and inhospitable landscape, with plenty of time for thinking and reflection, Freeman tried to hatch a daring plan to seize his homeland back.

He turned the plan over and over in his mind. Changing it, amending it and even re-inventing it, nothing seemed to work. It was all fantasy. He needed Jaffa, if their paths ever crossed again.

They had just about enough water to keep them going but Freeman felt parched, wrung out and frazzled from the incessant heat pouring down on them. He knew he couldn't go on much longer and that Jeneta must be feeling much the same.

Listening to the silence, they sat in shade against a large rock under a small lone scraggy tree.

'Let's walk at night.'

He knew it made good sense for the waxing moon would give enough light to read the compass.

Jeneta sat looking at him. She was dusty; her frizzy black hair sprinkled with fine red and grey particles. Her face was coated too and her dress badly ripped on one side. She saw him stare and looked right on back at his dusty features with its heavy black stubble showing proud on his wrinkly sunburnt face. She looked passed him into the haze and asked him to show her how to use the compass. Freeman did and she was soon standing, turning the dial so the needle pointed north and the marker to one hundred and ten degrees.

'Only ghosts walk together in a place like this at night.'

'Stop that nonsense!'

'Can't you see it?'

'What?'

He was too tired to be angry.

'You could have joined the men at the hotel, found a way out through them, but you didn't. You took me here.'

She pointed to where the bearing disappeared into the hazy desert horizon.

'It was on the note. It's the plan.'

'What plan?'

Flummoxed, he spoke candidly to her for the first time.

'I don't know. Some crazy guy from France set the whole thing up. I don't know the plan.'

'The devil leads you.'

'What?'

'To where you want to go.'

Freeman smirked. She couldn't know a thing about Jaffa.

'If the devil's here, why come too?'

She said nothing, only stared, and Freeman asked again. 'Well?'

Jeneta walked away, disappearing behind a group of near-by rocks.

Freeman slunk down again. He really needed to get out of there. He feared he would lose his mind if things carried on like this.

He dozed and later awoke to the familiar smell of smoke as Jeneta blew to start a fire. As the fire caught, she stood, her silhouette blocking out the afternoon sun. At first, he couldn't see what was different but knew that something had changed. Her outline looked the same, but then, as she took a sideways step, exposing the sun's glare, he clearly saw what she had done: she had ripped the sleeves off her shirt, exposing slender arms, heavily pocked with protruding scars of small round tribal marks and, having tied the bottom of her shirt up, her small round belly showed; her dress had been torn apart to manufacture some loose fitting, flimsy shorts.

She stood proud before him.

Freeman stood up and looked down on her now squatting by the fire. Her attire was completely revealing and, as he stared, wondering what she was up to, she stared right on back.

He busied himself collecting dry wood for the fire, not because they needed any, but because he wanted to feel useful, as he suddenly had the sense of having lost control with absolutely no clue of how to get it back again.

JENETA HELD THE compass and followed the bearing as Freeman walked beside her. She had the blanket over her shoulders, as the night was cool and would get chilly later on. The moon gave an eerie light: the subtle shadows and monochrome landscape open and two-dimensional. Freeman eyed Jeneta. Turning to meet his gaze, her eyes shining, he thought she might be smiling. That would have been a first since they had fled the hotel to find Luk in a small rundown city bar.

He asked her if the stars had names, her names, but she whispered that they mustn't talk and to respect the silence of the night.

It was still dark when they stumbled upon a dry riverbed. Jeneta's hands dug deep into sandy soil until water shimmered in the moonlight. Freeman thought it best to hold up; they badly needed rest. Without waiting, Jeneta collected scrub wood and soon a fire burned, warming their aching muscles, stiff from the long and endless hike.

At dawn, under the blanket and very cold, they lay close but didn't touch. As Freeman dozed, he could smell Jeneta. At first, it had been the smell of the women from his farm back home; then, as she became familiar, it was just her; but now, it seeped into him, strong and potent, playing with him, breaking down some life-long taboo he didn't want to think about.

He didn't want to like it, got up and squatted by the embers of the fire. As she looked on, the smell of smoke filled his nose and he started missing what he had just tried to get away from.

They just stared at one another and he wished he could say something. Then she spoke.

'Is it a long way home?'

He pointed south.

'If by a miracle, you made it through the swamps alive, a few months, give or take.'

'Yours is back the way we came.' He vaguely pointed west.

'The sun has set on that.'

Again, Freeman felt uncomfortable and blanked it from his mind.

THAT EVENING, as they hiked through the ghostly landscape, the ground underfoot changed, becoming soft and grassy.

Morning twilight showed the bush, but this time it was green not parched. They didn't stop, kept on going, pulled by some invisible force towards a pre-set destination. As birds began to sing, Freeman turned to Jeneta, who was clearly smiling this time, and grinned, hoping their ordeal would soon be over; but she was smiling, knowing that ghosts had told her true.

Although exhausted, they marched hard into morning. Just before they were truly spent, they saw the river, vast and slow, meandering towards the delta many days away.

The river was below them, flowing south before a sweeping bend took it east. On their side of the river, the landscape was a fertile looking plain that ran along the riverbank. On the other side, a dense barrier of tangled green tropical forest lined the riverbank. Behind them, the strange desert they had just managed to get across. Freeman, careful not to let his enthusiasm stray from the bearing, followed it right down to the river's edge.

The river was chocolate brown, the strong current taking wood and foliage around the bend and out of sight. Across the water on the line of the bearing, a jumble of vines and creepers clung to a dense wall of trees. A slight and welcome breeze blew along the river. As Freeman wondered how they could get across, Jeneta stripped naked and started washing in a shallow pool. He gazed as her intently, before shouting out:

'Can you swim?'

She didn't answer, pointing to dark shapes lurking in midstream.

He looked out into the current and then studied the river upstream. He heard the rustle of the flimsy khaki fabric and when he turned back towards her, she was adjusting her makeshift shorts. He didn't understand the woman dripping before him. In fact, he didn't even try. Right then, all he felt was urgency to cross the croc-infested water.

'There must be a village upstream. Look at all the floating wood.'

Freeman shook his head.

'We're still in the wrong country.'

Making a raft seemed the only option and they started examining the wood and broken trunks spewed along the banks. It took a while and a lot of work to lash together a ramshackle raft; after which, they laboured hard, pushing it upriver a hundred yards or so before jumping on to join the current. Having roughly fashioned some paddles, they furiously tried to get to the other bank before they passed and missed the bearing point. The craft smashed into the opposite bank close to their intended landing spot, coming apart in a jumble of twisted creepers and wet vegetation. As they fell, splashing into the shallows of the muddy river, Freeman desperately held his pack up high so not to sully the precious paper contract. They stood relieved, knee deep in reeds, but moved on into the dark forest, as a crocodile surfaced nearby.

The close and humid air was overwhelming and they were soon perspiring, drawing hard on each breath. Before exhaustion got the better of them, they stopped in a tiny clearing where a tree was down, to make their camp. Too tired to speak and barely able to eat, they sat around a smoky fire listening to the sounds of croaking frogs. A sudden onslaught of biting insects forced them under the blanket. Soon, they were sound asleep.

Freeman found himself half-awake and half-aware, thinking of Rebecca, was on her but it wasn't her. It was Jeneta. She shuddered, clung on tight, crying out in a language he couldn't understand. Freeman didn't stop when he realised what was happening but carried on until exhausted. He looked up at the last rays of sunlight penetrating the gloomy dark green canopy as Jeneta gripped him hard, shaking in the fading light.

Freeman uttered the only thing that made sense right there and then:

'110 degrees across a chocolate river to a town called...' but he couldn't remember.

She squeezed him tight before falling into sleep. Freeman felt slimy and sticky, full of her scent he couldn't and didn't want to shake.

IN THE SILENCE of the forest dawn, she lay across him, cold sweat sticking them together. He looked down his body to her staring back at him. He felt content, somehow home again and tried to stop a lifelong habit that meant casting her away.

Having been completely naked, she now dressed in her makeshift flimsy gear. Not uttering a word, she didn't take her eyes off him. By contrast, Freeman had only loosened his clothes and even had the boots still on his feet when he rose and stretched, before blowing at the embers to start the morning fire.

The day was long and humid and the bearing difficult to follow in the mud and twisted creepers littering the jungle floor. They didn't speak a single word all day as they slipped and struggled, fought the insects and were wary of any sound that may be some kind of dangerous animal.

They caught a mild waft of smoke. Roughly on the bearing, they followed its trail out of the forest into thick bush until the sketchy outline of a village showed.

Freeman stopped walking, sat on a broken trunk and pulled the wet gun from his pocket. Taking it apart as much as he could, he checked it, emptied the magazine and then put it all back together, hoping it would still fire after all the mud and dirt it had collected. Jeneta took the blanket from his pack, wrapping it around her middle to hide her flimsy shorts. Inside his pocket, Freeman nervously held the gun.

The locals merely stared, didn't run or show aggression and Freeman asked Jeneta to find out what she could. They spoke her language, said they were displaced from all the fighting and that many foreign soldiers were up ahead in the next town. Jeneta pointed along a deep rutted track showing imprints of fresh tyre marks. Freeman checked the bearing: five degrees out, but that would have to do.

Although exhausted, he was glad to leave the village – it was poor, dirty and no doubt full of desperation. They pushed on, following the track.

The town was so packed, swarming with people coming and going from the war, that looking for someone seemed impossible.

'Stick to me like glue.'

Having seen the girls hanging around the bars, she knew the trouble she might have and held tight onto his shirt as he moved among the crowd.

Unsure of what to do next, he asked for any information on the whereabouts of Luk or Jaffa from hired men hanging around the dusty streets, but they were distracted by all the commotion and couldn't help.

They found the only hotel. It seemed to have been built recently, two floors of roughly cut timber and no glass in the upstairs windows. The terrace outside the hotel entrance was crammed with hired men and again Freeman asked for Luk or Jaffa. Their replies were negative as they eyed him suspicious-ly. He knew he must look a mess.

He then had a thought.

'Where's the Colonel?'

After he spoke, someone briefly went inside and came back out again, indicating for Freeman to go inside.

To avoid staring soldiers, Jeneta hung her head down low. Still holding tight, she followed Freeman's boots inside.

Jaffa was sitting alone at a table. A map and some papers lay before him. He had a pistol in his hand that he placed on the table when he saw Freeman.

'You have a brought a Bush Baby back with you!'

Laughter erupted from a group of men propping up the small bar by the door.

Freeman felt uncomfortable as he saw them sneering at Jeneta.

Behind the bar was a mirror running along its length. At first, Freeman didn't quite get what he was looking at; the reflection showed a sunburnt, wild-eyed, bearded skinny man with torn clothes, clutched by a tiny woman wrapped inside a blanket. He was shocked at what the journey had done to him.

'You're looking like you've seen a ghost.'

Freeman looked at Jaffa.

'The devil,' Jeneta murmured so only Freeman could hear.

Freeman felt a sudden rage, dropped the pack off his back and rummaged for the contract. On finding it, he pulled it from the envelope and barbed:

'Is this what you want?'

Jaffa said nothing and Freeman walked over to where a wood fire sat smouldering under a pot outside the open back door. He knocked the pot off in an angry sweep and held the paper over the flames.

'Why the theatrics? That's your ticket home,' Jaffa mused. 'It was a job which you completed admirably.'

'My face was on the television and I very nearly got killed.'

'But you did get killed. Luk saw to that.'

He thrust the contract inches from the flames.

'Once they had the Swiss francs they were always going to send you up to join God's light, rip the contract up and sell the drilling rights to yet another dirty bunch. That contract's a legal paper and you really spoiled their day.'

'Who shot the President?'

'Marcel Malo, it was you, of course!'

Freeman knew it was hopeless to unravel these events. He had done his job and had earned a small fortune. He just wanted to be out of there and forget the whole event.

He stood up, walked over to the table and dropped the contract in front of Jaffa who examined every page. Freeman sat down and Jeneta joined him.

'Perfect Freeman. You have earned every penny.'

'Why didn't you tell me I'd have to run like that?'

'If I had, you would have never gone.'

'Did Abiade kill the President?'

'If you don't know…'

'Then I can't tell…damn you!'

'There's a room upstairs. You could be doing with a wash – that's quite some smell you've been collecting.'

Jaffa smirked, which made Freeman slightly relax, before asking:

'I need some cash money.'

Jaffa pulled out a large wad and handed Freeman a chunk of it.

'When do we leave?'

'Tomorrow morning.'

Freeman took Jeneta upstairs to an empty room where he threw their bags onto the floor before going out into the busy street. They bought clothes and toiletries.

With the low sun shining through the glassless window, Freeman watched Jeneta walk down the corridor to where a cold tap served as a shower. Having already washed, he left

Jeneta to her chores, shouting out that they would meet downstairs. He joined Jaffa at the table, who said:

'Nourishment is coming.'

Freeman smelt the cooking, wanted it so much that his stomach ached and gurgled, making Jaffa laugh.

'You're a bit thin but looking most ready for your Bayonne days again.'

He handed Freeman a letter. It was from Rebecca:

Jaques,

I've returned to Algiers…

Freeman read the note, dropped it on the table and left to find solace on the overcrowded terrace. Lost in thought among drunk and desperate men, he watched the last rays of sunset. As kerosene lamps were lit, the hotel became a strange mix of dancing shadows and eerie lights.

Jeneta was sitting near Jaffa. She had picked up the letter insisting Jaffa translate Rebecca's French as best he could before Freeman returned to stand and ponder at the door. He looked on as Jaffa showed her something with the compass on the map.

Freeman, all mixed up from the note, yet distracted enough by food being brought out from the kitchen behind the bar, sat down and ate in silence. Jaffa entertained them with another ludicrous story about some absurd and lavish French cuisine.

IN THE EARLY DAWN, Freeman joined Jaffa in an open jeep to drive inland along a dry and rutted road. He barely remembered flopping on the bed as Jeneta's potion wove its magic spell. Her scent was still with him, but he thought it must be in his mind, as wind blew coolly through his hair and over his mixed up head.

As the day warmed and rolling hills dotted with forest brought peace to Freeman's angst, he asked:

'What's an Osu?'

'An untouchable whose ancestors were assigned to God. They're considered possessed.'

'Like a ghost?'

'Is your Bush Baby an Osu?'

'So she said.'

'Now she will be haunting you no matter what!'

Freeman had to smile.

'What were you showing her on the map?'

'Even ghosts have to be having somewhere to go!'

Freeman changed the subject.

'I've got a plan.'

'And I have ears.'

'I own a pumping station and all the drilling rights around it near my home town.'

'That sounds like something I can sell.'

'There's a lot of oil.'

'But can you prove it's yours?'

'I've got the deeds hidden deep in a diabolical swamp, under in a pile of...'

Freeman paused.

'...black shells.'

Much to Freeman's bafflement, Jaffa said nothing. Before long, they hit a roadblock. Two soldiers pointing guns waved them down.

'What do they want?'

'Money for the road to salvation.'

Both men chuckled, Jaffa adding:

'Do you have some left?'

'But you are fighting a war here. They can't be serious.'

'Not here, over the river and far away.'

'I gave all my money to Jeneta – you must have some.'

'I gave her some too.'

'For what?'

'To get her home of course.'

The police were aggressively asking for money in French.

'What do we do, Jaffa?'

'Use your great diplomacy.'

He said they were short of cash and could they please carry on, but the soldiers, seeing only two hired men, ordered them out of the jeep. They were angry and of course drunk.

Freeman had no patience, pulled his gun and was on them just like Jaffa on that deserted Anglet shore, but Freeman didn't pull the trigger. The men froze and Jaffa immediately pulled away as Freeman kept them covered.

'Diplomatic enough for you?'

Jaffa drove as if nothing had happened and didn't speak until pulling up outside the airport terminal.

'Welcome back,' handing Freeman his own passport back.

Freeman left the gun on the seat and strolled towards the terminal entrance where he turned to see flying dust of the disappearing jeep.

His ticket was waiting at the check-in desk. Sitting in the empty departure lounge, he smelt Jeneta as if she was there under the blanket with him. Confused, he opened up his pack to find her flimsy makeshift shorts. She must have put them there to haunt him, as Jaffa said she would, and knew he wouldn't do a thing about it, packing away his cargo once again.

WITHOUT A HITCH, Freeman arrived back and walked straight out of the airport terminal into the cool air of a summer morning. Lacking cash, he looked vacantly out at the airport road, pondering his predicament. The red open top sports car pulled up and Jane beckoned him with an open palm. Unlike Jaffa's laid-back style, Jane raced out of Lyon–Bron, heading back to the Atlantic Pyrenees. Freeman closed his eyes and listened to the wind.

He slept for a few hours. On waking, he studied her scarred face. They hadn't yet spoken, not even the obligatory hello uttered when they met. As they sped down some empty tranquil country road, Freeman realised he only knew a fraction about this strange and formidable woman who had had a hand in all that had recently transpired. Not wanting to say anything that may provoke her, and run the risk of having to hitchhike back to Bayonne, he kept things neutral, by asking:

'When's Jaffa back in town?'

'Just wait. You have money. What else is there for you to do? Just keep out of trouble this time.'

She was defensive, almost aggressive and he had learned it best to back off and let things be; after all, she was right – waiting, no matter how tedious, was the only thing to do.

Staying silent, he fell asleep again, waking only to the sound of crunching gravel as the car jolted to a halt. Freeman stretched, got out and saw Jane disappear into the house. Soon returning, she handed him his keys and a piece of folded paper before reversing out the drive so he could get the Mustang out. He knew this was his cue to leave.

The two brown cows stared indifferently, munching on the sweet lawn grass, as Freeman turned into the road, driving past Elsa's house behind the lone banana tree.

Under a still cerulean sky, the slow and easy drive towards Bayonne told Freeman that this was the perfect place to wait; no-one to bother him or ask questions, the food and climate pleasant and with Rebecca now gone, no distractions whatsoever. He turned into his courtyard and stared at the fading Basque graffiti wall.

Knowing he was avoiding going upstairs to his flat, he opted for distraction and opened the folded paper of paper. It was a Swiss bank account number. Reluctantly picking up his pack, he headed to the front of the shop. Eve was there but didn't see him as he unlocked the heavy old oak door and entered the gloomy hall and empty stairs. Inside the apartment, he sat on the bed trying to forget Rebecca, but it wasn't easy; he would just have to let her go.

Freeman opened the windows on both sides to let the breeze blow through and take Rebecca far away. He washed and shaved, changing into clothes that made him feel all right again.

He shut the windows, opened up the pack and emptied its meagre contents on the bed. In fact, there was very little besides Jeneta's haunting gift. He didn't know why he had had to bring her home, but he had; as her scent replaced Rebecca's, it pulled him back to Africa.

Not given to or liking sentiment, Freeman tried to shake it off by opening the drawer, taking out the gun and placing it in his pocket. He then noticed the bag sitting on the chair. Emptying it, he once again marvelled at the amount.

Had Rebecca taken what she needed? He would never know and wouldn't have cared if she had had the lot. She needed it much more than him.

As there was enough of the day left, he needed to do two things. Grabbing the bag, he headed out. First, he knew he had to talk with Eve, pay some rent and tell her he had been working overseas and that Rebecca had gone home. He hoped she wouldn't want to chat about it.

Happy to see him, Eve told that his strange but charming Indian-looking friend had already been to see her, had paid the rent and had explained that he was away. She enquired if he had the note his girlfriend left. That was that, Jaffa pulling all the strings behind his back.

The bank was still open and after numerous phone calls, he was handed a piece of paper with a figure on it that shocked him. He didn't even need to transfer any over; his bag was loaded full. About to deposit the cash into his Bayonne bank, he thought better of it, not wanting local gossip to blow any discretion he might still have.

With nothing much to do or needing to be done for some time to come, Freeman strolled across the main open square in the hot and lazy afternoon sunshine. He drifted through the small streets full of tourists and, before long, found himself in an empty part of town staring straight at Rebecca's old front door. It had been less than two weeks since he had left Bayonne, but right there and then it seemed an age ago.

Without thought, he knocked hard but no one came down or opened the sticky sash-window above his head.

Freeman felt a pang of remorse, some kind of regret at being alone and with himself again. Turning to head back towards the square, he saw Chloe staring at him from across the street. He went nervously over to her.

'How's Rebecca?'

'Fine.'

'Back home?'

'You know she is.'

'Does she need money?'

'She took what she needed from your big fat piggy bank.'

Freeman didn't know how to continue or even if he should, but Chloe finished it all off with one final sweeping cut.

'She only wanted you because you took an interest and look so damn bloody suave – but you were mean and not so nice but then protected her from Ahmed whom I'm sure you killed, so thanks for that – but she's gone and happy now. She's where she needs to be.'

Freeman said nothing, felt her wrath and pleasure at telling him the truth and, as he was about to leave, she added:

'She named the baby Jacques, so you must have something good that I can't see, but don't kid yourself she's missing you and wants you back.'

He knew she was deliberately being mean but also knew she was right and it was history.

Mumbling something about if she needed anything just to ask, it fell onto deaf ears and only served to appease his battered sensibilities.

As he walked away, she continued her barrage:

'Go back to your jungle! Freaks like you don't belong here.'

Freeman felt small and hurt as he hurried back to the main part of town. Rebecca must have spoken to Chloe about his desire to get back home and he suddenly realised that they must have seen him in a way he had never imagined.

Who was he now? He wondered. No good could ever come of asking things like that. That was decadence.

He walked the streets until exhaustion manifested, his body refusing to go on. He found a café where he ate and drank his favourite Armagnac until he found himself again.

Later, he entered the apartment and was overwhelmed by Jeneta who had totally infused the space. Feeling slightly drunk, he flopped down on the bed. The gun fell out of his pocket, hard onto the floor. The familiar thud made him laugh and he was soon giggling, releasing all the pent up tension in a way he never could. In between gasps, as his laughter slowly petered out, he was astounded by his light and easy newfound qualities. He hoped it wasn't weakness that would stop him getting home.

IN THE MORNING, Freeman woke with a start. He had been deep in dreams, lost in a fusion of green foliage and sticky heat with someone calling out his name; but on waking, found only silence. He was drenched in sweat and breathing hard.

He had to get a grip.

After washing and changing into a favourite shirt, he put the gun in his pocket, knowing it would become his constant companion and left the apartment. He wandered down the dark stairs to the small hallway where he spied his now obsolete fishing gear, for he had had his catch. Then continued, slamming the heavy oak door behind him as he squinted in the early morning light.

What would he do whilst waiting? How to keep resolve, not go soft or out of his mind as the long summer days dragged on? Jaffa may be a while yet and he needed something to occupy but not distract him from his task. Seeing Elsa only meant some messy business and he dared not visit Jane to face a tiger's wrath.

Hoping an inkling of an idea would come over coffee and cherry jam baguette, he went out to find breakfast.

The morning sun showed white in the soft reflections shimmering in the high tide of the Nive. Freeman felt calm return after the turmoil of meeting Chloe in a deserted Bayonne street. A few gulls had flown up from the port, noisily disturbing the precious peace before the midday rush of people filled the streets.

Freeman wondered why he couldn't be content. After all, he had enough money now to buy a small house and perhaps set himself up in some easy business. But he couldn't, and

Chloe had been right: freaks like him just didn't belong and only one place, no matter how fraught with difficulties, was for him.

When the idea came, he rushed home to collect the car and drive to Saint Jean de Luz where he pulled up along the quay next to the pontoons and fishing boats. The quay was quiet except for the odd boat owner and occasional tourist.

The café owner sat outside the open doors at a table with several weather beaten rugged men whom Freeman thought might be fishermen or farmers. They were softly speaking Basque and drinking coffee. On seeing Freeman, they stopped their chatter, greeted him in French and silently stared, knowing he had something important to say. Hesitant and awkward, he swept a hand across his brow and hair.

The café owner offered him a seat and Freeman took his place, looking at the expectant faces, wondering if they wanted news of Luk. He used that as a starting point.

'Luk wants you to know that he and the guys are all ok.'

The men relaxed, chattered for a bit in Basque until the café owner finally remarked that Luk's wife would be pleased. They all laughed, sharing a private joke that Freeman knew he would never understand.

They didn't ask questions and Freeman knew better than to get involved with their private world of wives and war so he just put forward his idea of keeping occupied for the coming weeks or months.

'Luk says I can help out on the farm while he's away. I used to have a farm.'

He left it there.

The men smiled some more, chatted away in Basque, seemed to take it seriously and Freeman wondered if he had stepped over the mark in some hidden way.

'But why?'

'I need something to do.'

They all burst out laughing.

'But you can swim and fish.'

'Eat good food and go to bars,' another said.

'Pick up girls in your fancy car.'

'Go to the casino and spend your money.'

'Read a book.'

'Go to Paris.'

'Buy a boat.'

'Learn to speak Basque.'

They found that hilarious and Freeman laughed too, knowing his idea was daft. After the laughter and jokes had subsided, still at a loss of what to do, he thought he would give it one more try.

'I'm waiting for Jaffa to return.'

He thought that that may do it but it produced a response that he was not ready for.

'From where?'

The jokes and snappy talk continued as before.

'I heard he was born in the Mombasa slums.'

'All hot and angry.'

'No, it was out in the bush with his redneck missionary mother that twisted him up like that.'

'But he's Muslim!'

'No, he's not! He was raised by sharks in the Indian Ocean.'

'Became a pirate, got lost and drifted up the Nive.'

'Good job for us he did!'

With this laughter, Freeman knew the secret world of Jaffa, Jane and the elusive Basques would remain a mystery. He was an outsider, but so was Jaffa and he just couldn't get his head around that.

He left the Basques to their beaming smiles and headed off to be alone again.

4.

The Mission

France, late July 1968

H E HAD BEEN BACK more than a month, spending his days mainly in Biarritz. It had been the place of his childhood holidays and somewhere he could easily get lost amongst the summer crowds. It was also somewhere he wouldn't bump into Chloe or Elsa. He had gone to see Jane a few times but the house was always locked and the car just sitting in the drive. Once, he saw Julie and Elsa feeding the two brown cows in the garden but he drove on by, not needing that type of company as he waited Jaffa's return. The café owner down at Saint Jean de Luz, whom Freeman had dropped in on twice since the Basques had laughed at his idea of working on a farm, had said that Luk and others had not yet returned but that was not unusual.

He had swum a lot, progressively getting better until he could go out into the surf and swim from one end of the beach to the other in almost any conditions the summer sea produced. But he avoided going around the Virgin's rock where the current battered things against its deadly jagged reefs.

The more he waited, instead of calming down and relaxing into an easy pace of life, the more agitated he became. The sole focus and purpose of his life was to get back home.

On this particular day, instead of going up to the apartment in the afternoon, where the scent of Jeneta still held on enough to remind him of his continent, Freeman got back into the car and drove straight back to Biarritz. He didn't want to be alone and let lamenting get the best of him.

His car and rugged good looks fitted neatly into Biarritz and he was seldom bothered or even given a second glance. With this anonymity, he headed to the old harbour in the warm and breezy air.

Sitting under the shade of a large umbrella, eating sardines and drinking the local wine, an occasional wisp of pure white cloud blotted out the sun's warm rays; but it was the cold shadow of a man stretching out across his table that made him shiver, seek reassurance from his gun. He looked up at his unexpected lunchtime guest.

'Whiling away the last ebbs of peace...'

Freeman said nothing as Jaffa took a seat, admiring the view of small harbour boats and, further out, wild white surf in the wide blue sea.

'...as the fuse you so easily lit, smoulders to its end.'

The two men sat in silence, Freeman slowly finishing his lunch before pouring himself another glass of the agreeable wine.

'Drink?'

'Most amusing.'

'Might lighten up that dark heart of yours.'

Jaffa took off his black mirror shades and exposed nut-brown eyes. Freeman thought they would have been smiling if they had not been set in a permanent sardonic sneer. He wondered at the funny stories the Basques had told of Jaffa's origins. He bet they really had no clue either. All Freeman knew was that the man sitting next to him was somehow his ticket home.

'If my heart was light like those delicate wisps of cloud floating high up in the lifting breeze, what use would I be to you?'

The wind had risen slightly, enough for them to notice but not harsh enough to turn them away from the quaint harbour and swelling sea.

Freeman wanted to ask a thousand questions but only the simplest came out:

'How's Luk?'

'Farming the green hills of the Pyrenees.'

'I foolishly tried to work with those guys to occupy my time.'

'Yes, they were telling me your request to be a Bayonne cowboy.'

Feeling embarrassed, Freeman changed the subject:

'Did Jeneta get off safely?'

'I was giving your Bush Baby the gun and map. She had your compass around her neck like an amulet from outer space.'

'What the hell did you give her the gun for?'

'To get her home, of course.'

'But she didn't want to go home!'

Jaffa changed the subject as Jane approached along the narrow cobbled road to where they sat above the old stone harbour in a small narrow alcove, below the cliffs.

She sat opposite Freeman, away from the sea with the sun behind her shadowing her face. She stared at him with that defiant proud look that he had only really noticed in the car back from Lyon-Bron.

Freeman pondered, before asking Jaffa:

'How long have you been back?'

Jaffa ignored this and stared far out to sea.

'Oil and minerals puts your country on the most wanted list.'

'And without the riddle?'

'Marcel Malo has a job to do and some important deeds to collect and sign to finalise the deal.'

'But Marcel Malo's dead.'

'He's been resurrected! Besides, you're still available!'

It transpired that Freeman was to attend an exposition under some disguise and then shoot the President, escaping and hiding out while others came and took his country back. With the old government reinstated, he could sell his assets and do as he pleased.

'Is that all! Jesus Christ, what else do I need to know…to perform this miracle?'

'As little as possible.'

As Freeman heard Jane's words, he turned and looked out towards the darkening horizon, knowing a storm lay somewhere out to sea.

THE FOLLOWING WEEKS saw Freeman in a state of perpetual flux and excitement. He found it hard to sleep but when he did, had vivid dreams and woke up bathed in sweat. In fact, his whole waking life seemed to be an endless dream from which he would only wake when his feet touched the ground of home.

He had called his friend Ralph in Paris, another exile from his homeland, as Jaffa said that he would be needing help this time. A few days later, Freeman sat at the wheel of the open Mustang with Ralph sitting next to him. The car had just pulled up on the gravel drive in Itxassou. Both men stared out across the garden to where both Jane and Jaffa sat swinging in the lounger, staring right back at them.

'You never told me he was black.'

'He's not…'

'Sure looks like it to me. Where's he from?'

Freeman wanted to say something about a poet and a whispering breeze, but dared not.

'I don't know,' he nonchalantly replied.

'And her?'

'I don't know.'

Ralph angrily turned to Freeman.

'And what do you know?'

'What I told you.'

'And you trust him after the fiasco of getting that contract signed?'

'Yeah, I trust him.'

'Well, that's good enough for me right now.'

'Use English – he doesn't really speak French.'

Both men got out of the car.

Jane had the handgun next to her, her finger playing with the trigger.

'He's brought one of those men.'

'Be trying not to shoot him, Tiger. It would unnecessarily upset Freeman.'

Ralph watched the odd couple kick the ground to swing a while before kicking once again to keep the motion going. Next to them, in the shadows of riverbank trees, the two brown cows and a small calf also stared, quite indifferently.

Ralph spoke quietly:

'A couple of freaks if you ask me…you sure about this?'

'Quite sure.'

Freeman led the way, but shortly before they arrived in front of the lounger, Jane had the gun on them.

For Freeman this seemed almost normal, but Ralph froze. Perplexed, he shot Freeman an urgent glance.

'It's okay Ralph. It's what she does.'

Jaffa deftly jumped off the lounger, leaving Jane to swing and point the gun. He handed Freeman a rather tatty Marcel Malo, two air tickets and two formal invitations to an exposition and a presidential party. Jaffa kept his hand held out in front of him, making Freeman realise he was to hand over his own passport again. Jaffa placed it in his pocket, saying:

'Just like before, a presidential party, or let us be saying a shooting party where this time the contract must be signed in blood.'

Ralph was the one who responded to Jaffa's comment.

'Where do we get the guns?'

'A rather helpful waiter will be slipping you some tickets for the shooting show.'

'What the hell does that mean?'

'He speaks in riddles.'

Freeman then turned to Jaffa.

'How do we get out of there?'

'The same helpful waiter will be showing you dessert.'

'And then?'

'It's your country,' Jane dryly remarked.

'I suggest lying low for a week, after that we can negotiate a price for your deeds,' Jaffa concluded.

'What deeds?'

Freeman answered Ralph:

'The pumping station – I'm selling it. It's part of the deal.'

'And the farm?'

'That's mine and I want it back, just like you want yours.'

Ralph looked at Jaffa:

'I'm going to kill every black face I find there.'

A shot rang out, the noise echoing across the Nive and bouncing back from the green hills of the Pyrenees. Jane had not put the silencer on and, following an eerie silence where the birds stopped singing and everyone was momentarily deaf to the gurgling river below, Ralph clutched his left shoulder with his right hand. While looking into Ralph's shocked eyes, Jaffa quickly spoke:

'Let us not be spoiling such a fine and tranquil morning with another loud and perhaps devastating bang.'

Freeman pulled Ralph back to the car and placed him on the passenger seat, his big muscular frame tense, fury burning in his eyes.

'You alright?' Freeman asked as he backed out of the drive and drove off towards Bayonne.

Ralph had taken off his sports jacket and was examining his ripped and bloody shoulder. He aggressively tore the sleeve off his shirt and used it to mop the blood.

'Flesh wound. If she did that deliberately, she sure can shoot straight. Fucking bitch, what the hell did she have to do that for?'

'Why did you have to say such a dumb thing?'

'Because it's true – I'll kill anyone I find on my farm. And if I see that bitch again, I'll rape her before cutting her up for shark bait.'

Ralph spat out of the car in a fit of seething fury.

'What the hell have you turned into?'

'Don't you want to get home?'

Both men were shouting as the roar of the wind washed over the speeding car.

'Not like that! Christ, what's happened to you?'

'You've got soft. You need to be more like that ripped up face bitch back there.'

Freeman said nothing and Ralph added:

'I'm not surprised someone tried to rip her face off.'

'It was a tiger that didn't like her taste.'

'They don't have tigers in Ceylon,' Ralph mocked.

'Ceylon?'

'Yeah, I'm sure she's from Ceylon. I did a job there a while back. You should have been with me instead of lounging round Bayonne and going fishing.'

Both men didn't speak again and Freeman eased off the pedal of the racing car, trying to calm himself down before they entered town. He drove Ralph straight to the hospital.

While Ralph was getting his wound looked at, Freeman went to the public telephone in reception and called Jaffa.

Jane answered.

'Yes Freeman.'

'How did you know it was me?'

'Because…'

She didn't finish and Freeman heard Jaffa's voice.

'How is the loose cannon?'

'I could ask you the same question. He's fine…getting a stitch. Why did she shoot him?'

Ignoring the question, Jaffa asked:

'Have you checked the tickets?'

Freeman pulled the tickets from his jacket and read the date.

'Tomorrow!'

'As Jane said, it's your country. No surprises this time.'

'When do we meet again?'

'Are you missing and lamenting me already?'

'I feel uneasy.'

'Then be careful what you wished for.'

The phone went dead.

Freeman stood in the reception looking out through the glass doors into the car park and sunny blue sky, blank and empty when Ralph took the receiver from his hand and placed it back.

'You've gone soft.'

'What did they say?'

'It's nothing. I told them it was a fishing accident.'

'Yeah, you never know what you might catch. We leave tomorrow.'

RALPH HAD PICKED UP some new clothes from Freeman's apartment to replace his ripped jacket and shirt and both men had bought tuxedos for the coming presidential party in two days' time. They now sat under the awning of a café near the Ardour, Ralph breaking the usual and familiar silence between them.

'I can see how it was easy for you to get soft here. I could almost get used to this myself.'

He laughed at his idea and Freeman nodded thoughtfully.

'It's an easy place, but like you said – I got soft.'

'Good that you did, otherwise you wouldn't have met those freaks back there.'

'Where do you think he's from?'

'Freaksville. That was some story you told me about escaping from the hotel and finding some shack of a bar in the dead of night you remembered from a drawing, then those Basque guys turning up. That was really something.'

'Yeah, his timing and planning is impeccable.'

'So what else do we need?'

'Nothing, he will have worked it all out. All we need to do is shoot that bastard and get out of there.'

'And if we make it, where will we hide? Half the country will be on our tails.'

'You remember that abrasive, scruffy fisherman down at the port?

Ralph briefly reflected.

'Owned the cruddy bar in the open square and ran fishing charters in a ridiculously large boat?'

'That's the one. Do you think he's still there? We could charter his boat and get into the Black Shells from one of the creeks.'

'If he's still alive, he's there, stuck in a rut and probably desperate.' Ralph paused, smirking meanly. 'We stole that gold, remember. We'll have to get rid of him afterwards.'

Freeman said nothing, knowing if they made it that far, they would be untouchable.

Ralph pulled out his wallet, rummaged through some cards and dropped one on the table.

'Here, ring him.'

Freeman picked up the card. Leaving Ralph at the table, he headed down the street towards the post office where he could make the call.

It took some time to connect, and after many rings, was answered.

'Mawji's Bar.'

'I'd like to charter a fishing boat for Thursday morning.'

'Hang on.'

Joey placed the heavy black receiver down on the bar and went outside. He saw Mawji smoking, sitting on a lobster pot near the floating pontoons, looking up at the hills behind the port.

Joey shouted out across the square:

'You got a charter – on the phone now.'

Mawji flicked the cigarette and hurried across the square towards the bar.

'Who the hell would want to charter a boat in this god forsaken place?'

Mawji went in and picked up the receiver.

'Two hundred dollars a day plus expenses.'

He hadn't even bothered to say hello.

'That's fine, Thursday morning for about five days.'

'I need the money before we leave.'

'Sure. There'll be two of us.'

'How did you get my number?'

Freeman hesitated.

'You were recommended by a friend.'

'Thursday.'

Mawji put the receiver down.

'I keep seeing troop movement on the main road and now someone wants to go fishing – two hundred a day no questions asked.'

'Trouble and fish.'

'Trouble and fish don't mix Joey. I'm going to anchor Jaffa off shore and use the dinghy.'

Both men looked out at Jaffa moored to the quayside of the deep-water port left of the old pontoons.

'You know, he had a local accent.'

'Maybe someone's coming home.'

'That'll be one hell of a coming home party! You got the gear packed up?'

Joey nodded knowingly.

ON RETURNING TO the café, Freeman was greeted by Ralph's expectant stare.

'It's done – Thursday morning at the port.'

'What do you do about girls around here? Where's the action?'

Freeman had not told Ralph anything of Rebecca.

'I don't bother with that stuff here.'

'You used to be partial to a whore or two back home.'

'It's not the same here. I don't feel the same after the revolution.'

'Don't call it that!'

'OK, but I don't know where the action is…maybe the casinos down in Biarritz.'

'You always were fussy. That hotel spook didn't know how safe she was with you.'

Ralph laughed but Freeman didn't, barking back:

'Her name's Jeneta and she saved my life!'

'Got a soft spot for her have you?'

'Cut it out Ralph.'

'We weren't hard enough. We got soft, that's how these things happen.'

'We need to get on with them. They're people too, you know.'

'So, you want to shake that President's hand, do you? He'd shoot us on the spot if he knew who we were.'

'Point taken. Come on, I'll take you to Biarritz.'

They stopped off at the apartment and dropped off their shopping.

'That strange smell in here Jacques…reminds me of…'

'Home…'

He was feeling all mixed up. Ralph was his childhood friend and they had often played together when their parents visited each other's farms for a party or a shoot. These regular visits, lasting three days or more, had bonded them. During the troubles, they had fought and escaped together. Freeman, now wondering what was real and what was past, dared not show confusion. He badly needed Ralph to help get back what he'd lost.

Before driving to Biarritz, he showed Ralph the gun. Any doubt Ralph may have had over Freeman's commitment to get them home, quickly disappeared.

Listening to Ralph's debauched adventures overseas, Freeman wished he could enjoy them and have the good time girls again; but as those things were gone, he only felt a muddle of emotion. Lamenting his past, Freeman suspected home might be hanging on in a pair of khaki shorts and no place else.

HE DRANK IN the casino, saw that the ghastly paisley wallpaper in the toilet was still the same, gambled some money and had small talk with Ralph who was drinking and enthusing, a pretty girl by his side.

Unable to join Ralph's high spirits, Freeman left the casino. Drifting to the old harbour, he found a secluded table outside one of the small restaurants. Listening to fishing boats clonk with the lapping tide, he looked far out to sea at passing ships twinkling in the dark.

Waiting for his head to clear from all the casino drink, he sat and pondered. He knew he had to do it, had to see what was left of home. It was what he wanted – his farm and African life.

Refreshed and feeling more confident, he headed back to the casino. Ralph was playing roulette with the pretty girl still by his side. Her sallow skin and tired eyes reminded him of Rebecca, but it was her fragility that he knew Ralph would never see or care to know.

Ralph, drunk and enjoying himself, fitted in with the crass decadence. He even looked part of the place: big and strong, fashionably dressed, confident with that uncaring swagger that made Biarritz what it was.

'I'm leaving.'

'I'm not.'

'It's a late afternoon flight. I'll pick you up.'

Freeman looked at the girl who looked back with her unchanging smile and said nothing until he asked:

'Where do you live?'

She told him and then he left, entering the welcome solitude of night.

Back in the apartment, Freeman packed the things he thought they needed. Taking the bags down to the trunk of the car, he knew that if it all went wrong, they would be dead, but if it all went right, he would be home. Still erring on the side of caution, he posted some rent through Eve's letterbox.

Satisfied all was in order, he placed the gun in the drawer, took out Malo's passport and lay back on the bed. Feeling nervous and alone, he shut his eyes but couldn't sleep. It was all too real. He had wanted it all so badly that now it had actually come, he had no choice but to stare through the door he so willingly opened. Tomorrow he would be stepping through.

Freeman shivered, pulled the blanket over his head and wrapped himself up in a cocoon. He smelt home and it terrified him.

HE AWOKE AT DAWN, the grey light showing through the window to the street. Still in his clothes, he went to the bathroom. Trying to look the part he and Ralph were about to play, he changed, only daring a cursory glance towards the mirror. Leaving the apartment, he suddenly stopped, turned around and grabbed Jeneta hanging on the wall where he had placed her. Pulling the khaki shorts off the hook, he stuffed them into his jacket pocket and ran down the stairs into the dark lobby, exiting the building with a bang of the front door. Moments later, in the yard and close to panic, he fumbled with the car keys, desperate to get away before an increasing doubt held him fast and stopped him in his tracks.

Relieved to be on the move but having time to spare, he drove through the morning light on the empty road towards Itxassou. He passed the lone banana tree and stopped by the gravel drive where the two cows and calf pulled hay from a feeder connected to the closed gate. The red sports car was nowhere to be seen and Freeman drove off, across bridge and rail track onto the main road. His stomach churned and he belched. Hungry and nervous, he drove back to Bayonne to drink coffee and eat a croissant; he knew if he had been a smoker, he would have had half a pack by now.

He easily found the house, set back from the main town in a small street, and honked the horn twice. The front door opened and Ralph dawdled sleepily to the car. He looked slightly worse for wear. Standing in her underwear, the girl stared out from the open door. She didn't smile as they drove slowly off.

'Did you give her money?'

'Of course I gave her money!'

'Did she ask for it?'

'No.'

'How did you know she wanted any then?'

'What?'

'She wasn't smiling.'

'What the hell are you talking about?'

'Forget it – just a bit of nerves.'

Ralph slept the whole way to Lyon-Bron and Freeman parked the car near the main terminal building.

Having checked in, they sat in the departure lounge. Still jittery, Freeman asked:

'Aren't you nervous?'

'What use would that be? I just don't think about it, and if I do, I remember all my murdered family. Night of the black knives, I call it – then I feel fury, hatred and nothing matters…only this…'

'…miracle,' Freeman forlornly finished; but Ralph wasn't going to let Freeman's woe and doubt spoil his day and offensively thrust out his hand, staring cold into Freeman's eyes. Freeman stared back at his friend's unwavering and ruthless focus. He knew this mission was of his own making and that Ralph had been his first and obvious choice; a good choice, as he wasn't now going to let Freeman's sentiment weaken and sink their plan before its job was done. Success was against all odds and, as Freeman pondered this, more doubt crept in and he recognised he badly needed Ralph. Lost and having no option, he shook Ralph's hand.

Bottling up his angst, Freeman opted for distraction. Knowing Ralph's interest lay in facts and action only, he told him about the cover he had used on the last job and they both concocted a story and names of companies if they should be asked.

West Africa, 26th August 1968

BY THE TIME THEY LANDED, they had a corroborative story and Freeman had his purpose back. However, at immigration after landing, it was their invitations that sped them on without questions; and before long, they were through, bags in hand, staring at each other.

'How easy was that? Welcome home,' Ralph whispered.

'It's become a very dark place.'

Ralph laughed at Freeman's joke and they headed out into the warm morning sunshine to find a cab.

The two men silently viewed the landscape as the taxi lazily approached the city through a dusty landscape. Having opened his window to feel the warm rush of air, Freeman breathed in deeply, lounged back and closed his eyes, picturing the farm and a happier time.

Ralph tugged at Freeman's jacket and he awoke with a start, felt for his gun, which wasn't there of course, and found himself looking at the entrance of the Grand Hotel that he knew would be full of double-dealing money grabbing opportunists.

Later, in the late afternoon, they sat in the garden of the hotel bar, the sun low yet still strong enough for them to seek the shade of a table umbrella.

'I had almost forgotten how warm it is here.'

'Not me! Paris is bloody freezing for most of the year – not that I was there that much.'

They looked around at the other guests, some at tables and others propping up the bar in the lounge, which opened onto the garden.

'You wouldn't know anything had changed,' Ralph sneered.

Freeman looked around.

Bar girls arrived and Ralph became interested in one playing with an empty glass, throwing the two men vague looks now and then.

'Don't even think about it!' Freeman chided Ralph.

Both men laughed.

The waiter came over with some more drinks and, after he had returned to the bar, Freeman said:

'Did you see that surly look? Bet he was just dying to throw the drinks in our face.'

'Probably was, but doesn't dare.'

'Yet.'

'I came here a few times before the troubles. It was a lively place. People showed respect.'

'How organised do you think they are? I mean do you think they'll fight back?'

'Sure they will…wouldn't you? Aren't you?'

To stop Freeman from musing further, Ralph changed the subject:

'What was it like spending time with that freak?'

'He's like a magnet that I got stuck to, strange things started to happen. I even started speaking poetry.'

'Bah, you'll be wearing dresses next.'

As the two friends sat drinking and making jokes, carefully avoiding the topic of tomorrow's mission, Freeman privately knew his business with Jaffa was far from over, knew there was much more, over which he would have little or no control.

THE FOLLOWING MORNING as they ate breakfast outside on the hotel lawn, the two men hardly spoke. They took a cab to the exposition on mining, oil and development, which both men knew was nothing more than an auction of the country's assets – their assets.

The war still clearly showed in bullet holes that peppered decaying walls of abandoned burnt out houses. It was obvious that very little reconstruction had been done and they remained silent, sharing sadness and a fury that drove them on.

The exposition was a series of stalls, some showing what could be bought and exploited in the country and others, mostly foreign, offering services to undertake the task. There were lectures on development and both Ralph and Freeman knew that deals would be thrashed out behind closed doors and vast sums of money exchanged in the coming months. They even saw a drawing of their farmland cut up into parcels for sale alongside the old pumping station – just about everything that could be sold, leased or exploited in every corner of the country was on display.

At lunchtime, just as the buffet was served, the two men left the building.

'I can't stand it, it sickens me. Did you see those familiar faces? Some of our own guys involved in the whole thing.' Ralph was beside himself. 'In a few weeks, a few months, it will all be over, everything sold and lost for good. Your freak sure has his timing.'

Any doubt that Freeman had was immediately washed away and by the time they got back to the hotel he had focus and a blankness that he silently acknowledged as an asset for the coming event that evening.

Ralph was fuming, pacing around the hotel room like a caged wild animal, cursing and accusing Freeman of not caring about what was happening to their country.

'You were soft as butter in Bayonne, now you're cool as if nothing matters.'

'Nothing will matter if we don't do the job right. Calm down. We need to focus.'

'Calm down? Did you see what they are doing with our farms?'

'We need to change and get to the county palace for eight. How long do you think it will take?'

Ralph paused his ranting and stopped in the middle of the room between the two single beds.

'Assuming the roads are good, three, maybe four hours.'

'So we leave at four. We can have lunch here. See you downstairs.'

He left the room and went to the garden bar. He sat inside away from the harsh light, ordered coffee and looked at the menu.

Still upset, Ralph followed.

'I didn't need that cruel reminder.'

'He's winding us up, turning the screw to make sure we don't get cold feet before its time to pull the trigger.'

'Cold feet, what does he take us for?'

'If we do the job right, we get our homes back and he gets his assets.'

'That oil's your birthright. I'd pull the trigger on your freak and bitch, anytime.'

Freeman didn't comment and both men went silent, lost in their own thoughts.

After lunch, as afternoon wore on, the bar and garden emptied. Only birds disturbed the peace.

'The calm before the storm.'

As Freeman said it, he noticed Ralph looking at him, studying his paisley shirt.

'You always were a bit of a dandy.'

'What are you saying?'

'Bayonne's turned you the other way.'

Freeman's calmness of before quickly eroded and he became incensed.

'Cut it out Ralph! I'd knock you for six if I didn't think you were joking.'

'Girl talk, Jackie.'

'What did you call me?'

'Jackie – it's a girl's name.'

Freeman threw the cold remains of his coffee cup straight into Ralph's face who spluttered before furiously lunging across the small table. Grabbing Freeman's shirt collar with both hands, he ripped the buttons clean off, toppling Freeman and his chair. Ralph was quick, his hands around Freeman's throat, squeezing hard. As he struggled for air with no time to spare, Freeman smashed the bottom of his china cup against Ralph's face, making him cry out and lose his grip.

'Dandy your bloody self!'

Freeman was up, looking at Ralph sitting on the floor nursing his bruised cheek.

The waiter and barman stood looking at the pair and Freeman barked over to them:

'What the hell are you looking at? High jinks never hurt anyone.'

They sheepishly turned away.

Ralph was up, looking at Freeman with his open ripped shirt showing his tanned torso.

'That shirt didn't suit you anyway.'

'Yes it did – and it was expensive.'

Having drawn too much attention to themselves, they avoided any more members of staff by going back up to the room using the sweeping stairs instead of the lift.

On the staircase, Ralph was still rubbing his cheek.

'You sure can pack a punch.'

'What was that nonsense all about?'

'That exposition really wound me up.'

'Me too, but we need that anger for later.'

'Sorry.'

'Face ok?'

'Does it show?'

Freeman stopped and looked.

'No, as handsome as ever.'

'You sure you're not a dandy?'

Both men laughed until they got into the room.

As RALPH SHOWERED, Freeman changed, pulling Jeneta out of his jacket. He caught her fading scent before stuffing her into his tuxedo pocket. Suddenly feeling dizzy, he sat down on the bed in slight sweat. He saw green and the glistening of water.

Ralph came out of the shower.

'You look like you've just seen a ghost.'

Freeman came to.

'It's nothing.'

AFTER MAKING SURE they had everything they needed, for no matter what happened that night they would not be coming back to the hotel, they ordered a car from reception.

'We can't talk about this once we get in the car. We need to just get on with it.'

They were standing in the lobby, speaking in hushed tones, looking out through the glass doors on to the bright dusty busy street, thronging with people going about their daily business.

Ralph didn't look at Freeman, just stared out into the street, and after a long pause, said:

'Who takes the shot?'

'Does it matter?'

'I'll do it.'

Freeman shrugged.

The two men fell silent, the moments slowly passing. Every sound, flicker of light and sensation were exaggerated, stretched out to the point of unbearable. It was some relief when the car pulled up and they could drive away.

They sat in silence, each man looking out of his rear passenger window as the taxi slowly drove towards the main road through crowded pot holed streets. They would then drive across a long undulating plain into the hills and presidential country palace.

Traffic was light and they soon reached the main road. Suburbs, small settlements and villages quickly petered out and only scrub and an occasional tree showed in the vast landscape. Far ahead in the distance and half-hidden by haze, the hills of their destination looked small, dwarfed by the huge, brilliant blue sky.

They stopped at a heavily guarded roadblock next to a fortified enclosure housing a small garrison. Freeman and Ralph looked at each other, didn't speak and produced their invitations. They were asked to get out of the car and both men sat down on a bench by the empty road. Inside a hut, a soldier made a call whilst another stared at them through an open window.

'They're expecting something,' Freeman whispered.

'They're always expecting something.'

Before long, the barrier raised and the two relieved men took their seats. Leaving the plain behind, the taxi continued, climbing up through overhanging dense damp forest. Foliage soon enclosed the hard clay road. On a steep sharp turn, the vegetation briefly cleared to give a passing view west, towards the small port hidden behind an imposing jagged ridge Rain clouds lingered out at sea. Their farms lay behind this ridge, sandwiched between tall crags, the port itself and the vast swamps on the far side that followed the coast north, edging the rocky escarpment before the rock petered out and only a tangle of impenetrable jungle, stretching to eternity, remained.

'Looks like rain,' Ralph nonchalantly commented.

'It is always raining over there,' the driver answered back.

'Where?'

'The small port,' the driver answered Freeman, pointing in the general direction of their farms.

'What's it like…over there?' Freeman feigned ignorance.

'They say the farming used to be very good.'

'Used to be?' As he said it, Ralph sat bolt upright, his tension clearly visible.

'Since independence no one farms anymore.'

Sensing an outburst from Ralph, Freeman exclaimed loudly:

'Independence – now there's a word!'

'Oh yes, democracy is good.'

The driver paused, his false enthusiasm waning as he looked back at Freeman in the mirror, seething a whisper:

'Except we have no freedom.'

He went silent, turned the radio on and highlife music softly filled the car. The two men tacitly looked at one another before looking out of their respective windows once again.

As the sun dropped into the low cloud and disappeared behind the hills, dark shadows engulfed them on the gloomy forest road. Before long, the two men were looking out at endless stars twinkling in the tropical night. Freeman remembered Jeneta asking about the stars back in France and he chuckled, prompting Ralph to ask:

'What's so funny?'

Freeman told him but Ralph didn't find it funny, looked away and at the stars he had missed so very much.

In the darkness, waving red lights ahead told of yet another checkpoint. As their car slowed to a crawl, torches glaring harshly in their faces, the barrier raised. A minute later, lights of the country palace shone before them.

Rain drizzled down the windscreen, diffusing the view, and the two men watched the smeared vision of their fateful dinner location come closer until the car jerked to a halt right outside the stone steps that led up to the open front door.

Freeman had déjà vu as he stepped out the car to be greeted by a man holding an umbrella, eager to escort him to the entrance. Ralph followed under the protection of another and they were soon standing in the covered porch producing their invitations. They were curtly frisked before being allowed to proceed.

It was a lavish affair, almost identical to the one before; rooms filled with men, some with wives, smartly dressed bar girls hung around pretending to be sophisticated and crooks of every description were there, waiting to seal a deal and strip the country bare. A band played somewhere, the lively music unobtrusively giving things an easy air. As Ralph and Freeman circulated around the numerous rooms, seeing faces they recognised, smiling and making the right conversation, they tried to spot a waiter who would show them what to do. However, nothing materialised and the two men stood by a window, feigning interest in nearby conversations.

Nervous and perplexed, not daring to discuss it, Freeman broke away and went to the bathroom to find some calm and get a grip.

He stood peeing, looking ahead at the white tiled wall when Ralph suddenly appeared next to him. For a moment, they did not talk, just stared ahead as there were others around and an attendant sitting on a stool.

Ralph spoke first.

'I hope dinner's good.'

'With a just dessert,' Freeman replied dryly.

They spoke no more and returned to mingle with the crowd again.

A waiter moved through the room banging a bronze gong he held in one hand, announcing that dinner was about to be served in the main hall. Freeman and Ralph eyed him expectantly but he just moved on through the crowd, disappearing into the next room. As the stateroom emptied out, the two men stood alone. Ralph, flummoxed, looked to Freeman who only shrugged, turned and followed the crowd into the banquet hall. Hundreds of people milled around looking for their places at the scores of neatly laid tables placed around the enormous room; at one end, a stage hosted the band that had now ceased to play.

It took some time for everyone to be seated, the noisy chatter echoing through the room and off the high, decorated ceiling where fancy chandeliers hung.

Freeman found his name on a long table near the stage and took his place. Ralph sat opposite, several places down the table.

The President and some bodyguards appeared, sitting down at a separate table not too far from Freeman, his ugly face hidden from view by guests and guards sitting next to him.

Both men knew that any speeches would be held immediately after dinner and after that, music, dance and drink would shake the house, cleverly obscuring the shadow world of scheming hanky-panky where the deals of the exposition would be finalised; and by then, any chance of performing their miracle would be lost.

The room murmured with polite conversation as the hors-d'oeuvre arrived and both men felt utter disappointment, but also great relief that the plan had not materialised. They too made conversation with those around them, forgetting that they had had a mission to complete, as now the time was nearly passed and the moment almost gone.

The main course arrived. Plates were placed in front of the guests by numerous waiting staff. As Freeman's plate was presented to him he realised it had a silver lid covering the food and that the waiter was whispering in his ear that the door behind him was an excellent place to view dessert. As Freeman stared at the dull silver coloured lid, lost in the moment, he heard the noise of a chair falling back and saw Ralph standing up with a handgun pointing at the President. He then witnessed the terrible moment when Ralph squeezed the trigger and the gun refused to fire. Time seemed to slow down and an instant hush fell over the table as Ralph's other hand frantically went to fiddle with the gun. However, Freeman had already flicked the lid off his own plate, had grabbed his own gun and was standing up, pushing his chair back to take the shot. By the time Ralph started firing, the President had already slumped down dead.

Chaos followed, people screamed, some ducked down, some stood up and some just ran towards the front door. The room was a mass of moving panic and Freeman ducked down too, moving towards the door the waiter had mentioned. He seemed lost in the milieu and looked back towards Ralph who was nowhere to be seen. Aware that guards would soon be on him, he reached the door; it opened, a pair of hands grabbing and dragging him through. As he quickly turned, he saw Ralph desperately scrabbling out from under the table. Freeman let a few rounds fly to buy Ralph time as he dived through the open door. Shots rang out as the waiter banged the heavy door shut, turning the lock as splinters showed where bullets hit the other side.

They ran behind the waiter, along a narrow corridor and turned into a small room where another open door led down some stone steps into a dark basement. The two men followed the sound of footsteps along a damp smelling, pitch-black tunnel, their hands against the walls to keep them steady before they saw the night sky behind an iron gate. It was unlocked and the waiter led them up stone steps into the palace grounds, hurrying them across a small dark lawn to a large black car, its engine running. Behind them, they heard the door being battered down and the screams and shouts of chaos they had created and left behind.

Ralph went straight to the driver's side. The waiter ran in front, opening a gate that led onto a small track.

Wasting no time, Ralph drove fast downhill, knowing that pursuit was inevitable. Shots rang out as the waiter held the guards at bay.

'Jesus, that was close!'

As Ralph said it, Freeman turned around and looked back up the pitch-black road, wondering if the waiter had nine lives. Turning back, he saw a shape moving on his right.

'Watch out!' Freeman screamed, as a small antelope jumped and ran across the road in front.

Ralph braked hard, stopping just in time, sending Freeman flying into the dashboard.

'Where the hell does this track lead anyway?' Freeman grunted.

Ralph eyed Freeman's surreal silhouette in the seat next to him.

'Probably works its way back to the main road...somehow.'

Both men looked out through the drizzle on the windscreen at the headlight beams illuminating soft rain and the dark road edged by thick black forest.

'We won't last five minutes there.'

'You remember the old mountain road before the main road was built? It must run off to the right somewhere.'

'Be in pretty bad nick by now, besides, it would take forever.'

'Got a better idea?' Ralph mumbled as he headed down the hill, wheels spinning on the wet shale track.

Above them to their left, they saw lights of vehicles speeding up the main road towards the palace. Cutting the headlights, they crawled along at a snail's pace, the road hardly visible in the low moonlight.

'There! That must be it.'

They had just passed a small overgrown turn, which Freeman barely noticed. Ralph immediately backed up, turning into the abandoned narrow mountain road.

After the car made some sharp turns, Ralph switched the lights back on, increasing speed as they tore around the bends, heading towards the port, still many hours away.

They drove in silence and hours later, when they were feeling calm and safe, Freeman asked:

'What was it with the gun?'

'Safety on – boy was that close!'

'Sorry you missed your chance.'

Ralph laughed.

'You remember those songs we used to sing during the troubles?'

As the car raced downhill in the wet, Ralph and Freeman started singing, both raucous, loud and completely out of tune. Sometime later, as the two men were laughing, reminiscing the good times, Ralph lost control on a hairpin bend. The car left the road, hurtling down between the trees. Smashing into small boulders, the two men were thrown and dashed around the interior until the car took off over a small drop and crashed hard to the ground before rolling to a stop.

As Freeman sat there dazed, he noticed the encroaching twilight, his panting breath and Ralph slumped forward against the wheel.

He got out, stumbled in the shadows to the other side and opened the driver's door. Ralph fell out, thudding to the ground, his lifeless body telling Freeman the terrible thing that had just occurred.

He fled towards the darkness.

5.

THE BLACK SHELLS

West Africa, 30th August 1968

FREEMAN BROKE FROM his memories of Bayonne, Jaffa and the events that had led up to Ralph's demise a few days before. He had wasted too much time indulging and felt a sudden urgency to act, to do something, anything to get him out of rotting in this cursed swamp.

If he tried to swim, the racing tide would be sure to catch him, take him down or maybe dump him somewhere out to sea. Everyone who lived in the port knew about this place and no one ever came here – it was far too dangerous and full of ancient superstition. It had been the perfect place to hide the gold and deeds, or so he had thought – he had forgotten freaks like that strange sea-gypsy had made and sustained this ghostly place. He looked up the mound and realised that his deeds were probably still there, the girl having been blinded by the gold. He scuttled up, looked inside the hole and clearly saw the plastic wrapper where his and Ralph's deeds were safely packed away. He pulled the package out and examined it carefully. It was still sealed and in perfect condition.

He crunched his way back down the mound and looked out into the still waters of the silvery lagoon. Skimming a shell across the flat water, the ripples spreading like a fading echo, he realised the tide was full. Without hesitation, he removed his shoes and dived into the water, swimming across the lagoon towards dense vegetation, the plastic wrapper held tight between his teeth. Entering the narrow tangled passage-ways of the swamp, he followed the movement of the turning tide. Before he was lost to an increasing rush of water, he grabbed a root, hauling himself up to perch in a woody maze of mangrove. The torrent below turned into a gurgling demon that no man could endure.

Sticky and exhausted in the rising humidity, he lay uncom-fortably among the rough branches and wet salty vegetation. His only respite was from the small breeze the fast moving water generated in its furious pull towards the open sea. Freeman knew he didn't want to end up to the west and out to sea, where strong currents and dangerous fish lurked, but south towards the port.

As the breeze softly swayed the leaves above, bright sun-light filtered through the canopy, forcing Freeman to remove what was left of his jacket to cover his face and head. Staying still and silent, he waited for the tide to slow so he could have another try to get as far as possible before it turned again.

TO THE EAST and deep in the swamp, Mawji and the girl struggled through the shallow waters of the dropping tide.

'It's no good, we can't paddle when the tide's low with all this gold weighing us down. We need the high tide to takes us on.'

'Why not dump the gold?'

'Are you crazy, what use are we without money? We need to buy our way out of this mess, if we ever make it through this hellhole.'

'What use is the gold if it holds us in this swamp? How long can we last?'

'Longer than you think, Preacher Girl.'

'I'm not preaching.'

'And I'm not quitting!'

The dinghy grounded in the muddy shallows. Mawji sat facing the girl. They looked straight at one another.

'We need Jaffa, then we could go wherever we pleased.'

'Why did you give her up? You didn't have to.'

'What choice was there? It was a desperate moment.'

'You could have left me to walk the plank.'

'Walking the plank would have been the least of your worries.'

'So?'

'Don't ask dumb questions! It's done and Jaffa's gone.'

'But why give it all up just to save me.'

'I don't know – because you remind me of my sister, no you don't – you just needed the help I couldn't give her. What does it matter? Just quit this pointless talk.'

The girl looked away, out in to the endless green and then looked back at Mawji who was obviously uncomfortable and still staring back.

'And where would you take Jaffa now?'

He laughed, easing his tension and answered without deliberation:

'Indian Ocean, South China Seas – it's where we're from. My old man wanted to take us back, find my sister a husband. We just got stuck here for a while.'

'Fishing?'

'And living.'

'Did he want to find you a wife?'

'What is it with you? Always in my business like a badger after honey.'

'I like that,' the girl laughed.

'OK, Honey Girl! How does that suit you?'

'Just fine!'

'So here's the choice: struggle on, which will be a living hell, or we can go and find Jaffa if we can, which will be dangerous. Either way I'm not dumping the gold.'

'Will you take me with you?'

'Where?'

'Indian Ocean, South China Seas.'

'Around the Cape and thousands of miles of hostile sea just to visit some shacks built on stilts on some godforsaken sandbar in the middle of the ocean! Why the hell would you want to do a dumb thing like that?'

'Well?'

'What's in it for me?'

'What are you asking for?'

'No more stupid questions.'

'I promise.'

'You are crazy.'

Mawji started to laugh and Honey Girl laughed too until they were in stitches, letting out tensions they never knew they had.

When the laughter had subdued and their sides ached, Mawji said:

'We can move when the tides returns, but the gold's heavy and we need to take care when we reach the fast moving tide of the outer mangrove. Besides, I nearly drowned on the way in.'

'YOU SHOULD HAVE been looking where you were going.'

'Instead of looking up your skirt you mean.'

'That's exactly what I mean.'

'Is that why you changed into shorts?'

'Do you want me to change back again?'

'Hell no! I might not make it back!'

They laughed again, both pretending they hadn't just said those things, and settled down to wait for the flooding tide.

TOWARDS THE PORT and deep in the dense twisted mangrove, Freeman lay perspiring in darkness under his tattered jacket, listening to the softening sounds of the weakening tide. He lifted the sticky material and peered below at the water still swirling around exposed roots. Judging it safe to try another bout before the tide turned and rushed back in again, he was about to discard the useless jacket when he felt and remembered Jeneta sitting in a pocket. He pulled out the wet and muddy material. Although her scent was gone, just mud and salt now filled his nose, he held onto her tantalising and infuriating smell that was somehow home and had helped to keep his dream alive. He stuffed her into a trouser pocket. Remembering the passports, he pulled those out too; they were wet and soggy but good enough to keep. However, the air tickets were a useless mess and he threw them with the jacket into the swirls below.

He dropped down and splashed into the warm water. It was shallow and he waded through the easing tide to where he thought south must lay. He soon found himself in deep water and had to swim again. To stop being driven mad by thirst, he found distraction in mulling over recent events, but it always ended with Ralph's demise. Unable to find a happy thought, he turned over everything and anything in his mind to drive the thirst away. Occasionally, he laughed aloud, sometimes speaking to an imaginary companion and once, when he really thought he was lost and would perish in the swamp, he pulled Jeneta from her rest and asked her to take him home. A soft breeze blew, like a lullaby whistling through the canopy. Freeman laughed as he remembered Jane singing to a light brown cow. He thought of Jaffa and then remembered hearing that freak and his friends talking in the bar about a boat called Jaffa.

The breeze stopped and Freeman stopped. He was walking once again in the shallows and stood in disbelief at his stupidity. Jane had said that the truth walks right past him and maybe it did, for he couldn't quite get the connection between Jaffa the man, the boat and the freak paddling to a better life with that deranged bible basher across a hellish swamp in a dinghy loaded full of gold.

Laughing at the madness of it all, he then hollered at the top of his voice for help before collapsing down in the water on his knees. He lay back and floated for a while, occasionally catching the brilliant light blue sky through the dense leafy canopy as the last of the ebbing tide slowly moved him on. The tide went slack and his drifting stopped. Freeman shot up out of the water knowing he had better get a grip and move on further before the rush of the coming flood. Somehow, he had managed to keep hold of the precious plastic wrapper during his derangement and he held it tight as he soldiered on, despairing at his thirst.

'YOU HEAR THAT?'

Honey nodded. 'Do you think it was him?'

'It's a long way off, maybe one of those screecher birds.'

She watched Mawji lighting one of the crumpled cigarettes that he had managed to dry, and he watched her back as he dragged on his smoke. After he had blown back out, he said:

'You like to look.'

'And so do you.'

'Give me a hand. Tide's turning.'

He stepped out of the dinghy into the knee-deep water and she followed, helping him move the craft into the middle of the small slack channel. They turned the dinghy around.

Once the returning tide had raised the dingy clear from obstructions, they boarded, heading back the way they came.

Sitting side by side at the front to counter balance the weight of gold piled up at the back, they paddled silently through mottled shade and flickering light, listening to birds, insects and the plops of jumping fish. An occasional snake slithered through the shallows.

Honey looked at Mawji.

'It's beautiful.'

He merely grinned, looking straight ahead.

Clouds appeared and broke the sunlight streaming through the gaps in the dense leaves and vines. Before long, raindrops splashed the water and soon a tropical downpour forced the couple to moor up under a dense tangle of green to shelter as best they could. Mawji caught water in a pot for cooking and with another he constantly bailed out the dinghy to stop it sinking under all the weight.

'How much is there?'

Mawji stopped his chore and looked over at the gold.

'Fifteen stone – hundred kilos, something like that.'

'Is that a lot?'

'Sure is a lot to me,' Mawji laughed.

Honey looked at him questioningly.

'So you're interested now, eh? That's about a hundred thousand dollars sitting there, give or take,'

'You're rich,'

'Not me – us! If we ever get it out of here.'

Mawji looked over at her sitting on the side of the boat, her soaking t-shirt tight and wringing wet, catching all the drips running down her face from the leaking canopy above.

'You're soaked.'

'I know,' but she couldn't tell him it wasn't just the rain.

Her heart beat fast and her body tingled and the aching fire gasping below made it unbearable for her to sit still and watch him work, so she jumped down into the shallows to feign going to the bushes, so to speak, so she could momentarily disappear and cool herself by dipping in the water.

When she returned the rain had abated and she saw Mawji sitting where she had sat, looking towards her as she came back into view. His wet shirt was stuck fast to him and he puffed at another cigarette. Waving to her, he shouted over, 'Ahoy there,' making her feel those things again.

BACK IN THE MANGROVE, Freeman felt euphoric when the first drops of rain began to fall and he quickly found a gap in the canopy to get the full force of the downpour. Turning his head skywards, he caught the cool liquid inside his open mouth. He stuffed the plastic wrapper inside the top of his trousers and cupped his hands to catch and drink some more. Although the rain burst was brief and he felt relief, he wasn't satisfied. His thirst kept him to the shallows, where he waded through the flooding tide, drinking any water that had collected in the dips and troughs of the densely tangled woody vegetation. He was soon in deep water and the flood started to push him back inside the swamp, forcing him to find and climb another high and uncomfortable perch until it slackened once again.

The sun was harsh and high. As any raindrops still left in the small depressions of the mangrove started to evaporate, the humidity rose steadily. Freeman was soon bathed in sweat again. Turning to face the rushing water to keep any sunlight out of his eyes, he watched the multicoloured crabs that littered these swamps scuttle up the bark to join him in his wait. Now missing the shade of his jacket, he felt the sun spike his head and neck as it found its way through the gaps between the leaves. Remembering Jeneta, he soon had her out and wrapped around him, the wet material cooling and protecting him from sunburn. She was still a useful companion and he fell asleep wondering where she might have gone. He dreamed of green and a swamp more hellish than the one he was in and woke with a jolt, remembering his escape with Ralph; not to the east where that freak and bible basher had just gone, that was pure insanity – hundreds of miles of dense jungle and mosquito hell with crocs so big they could swallow a cow – but to the north where he and Ralph had struggled to reach a friendly country that he now hoped was sending boats and troops to help his fellows out.

Drowsy and fighting sleep, something overpowered him and held him down. Unable to breathe, he ripped Jeneta off his face. Gasping for breath and stuffing her in his pocket, he almost fell down into the gurgling froth below. He didn't dare fall back to sleep. Not only was he scared of falling into the water, there was also something waiting in his sleep. It so terrified him that he pinched himself hard on the arm and took a couple of big gulps of air to clear his muzzy head and stop from going mad.

SOMETIME LATER, the dinghy sat under the dense swamp canopy at an opening into the lagoon.

'Do you think he's still here?' Honey whispered.

Mawji answered as he scanned the lagoon for movement while listening out for any unusual sounds.

'I wouldn't be.'

The dinghy bobbed in the flooding tide. Under the vegetation, Honey held the craft steady by pushing forward on the paddle. She sat at the front apex of the boat.

Mawji stood behind her, holding the gun in his right hand.

'Take it out to the left, follow the vegetation and circle round to the other side. We don't want any surprises.'

He pointed with the gun and she pulled hard on her paddle, struggling against the tide as Mawji watched out for Freeman who he thought could be hiding out and preparing for an ambush.

Honey found it difficult to make progress but Mawji was in no hurry as she laboured to circle around the edge of the lagoon. Her increasing gasps of breath mixed with the sounds of the paddle pulling through the current until she stopped, exhausted, and the boat drifted back with the tide towards the centre of the lagoon. They clearly saw the gold bar glinting on the shells.

She steered the boat in. As they bumped and scrapped along the shells, Mawji jumped out, crunching down by the shiny black patent leather shoes sitting neatly near the bar of gold. He grabbed the rope and held fast as the dinghy swung around with the tide, making the craft come to a halt as it hit the shore.

He handed Honey the rope as she stepped out over the side to join him.

Wasting no time, Mawji quickly circled the shells before heading to the top where he scoured the lagoon for any sign of Freeman.

'He's gone. Must've been feeling desperate to leave those shoes behind.'

Mawji put the gun down and started filling the gaping hole at the top of the mound by pushing shells with his hands and

feet until it was full and he was satisfied. He then picked up
the gun and joined Honey below.

'Where are all these shells from?'

'Out at sea there's a reef.'

Mawji pointed west.

'At certain times of year, depending on the phases of the
moon, sand bars are exposed with millions of black shells –
that's where we get them from – only in the past they had
feasts with them before throwing the shells away to make
these mounds. Hell knows why we keep the tradition alive.'

'Your ancestors?'

'Sea-gypsies. I don't know any more.'

Honey looked intently at Mawji.

'What if we had found him here, still on these shells?'

'I knew he'd be gone.'

'And if he makes it back?'

Mawji smiled.

'Then pray hard, Preacher Girl.'

'Pray hard yourself! I left that girl way back in the swamp
there!'

Both of them laughed as Mawji threw the shoes out into
the water and tossed the bar of gold in with the others before
they both got back into the boat. He pulled the cord a few
times before the motor spluttered into life.

Heading slowly across the lagoon in brilliant sunshine, the
boat made big ripples as it met the returning tide. Inside the
narrow watery passageways of the dense mangrove, Mawji
throttled back the motor to a crawl. The increasing tide
pushed floating debris through the swamp, bumping it against
the boat. Not wanting to crack the propeller on a piece of
wood, Mawji cut the engine.

In silence, they paddled slowly under dense and twisted
vegetation, their skins wet and sticky from humidity. An

occasional shaft of bright sunlight cut through and sparkled on the ripples.

Listening to the birds, insects and the scuttling sounds of multicoloured crabs, there was an easy air between them. When their arms lightly touched, Honey felt goose bumps and a new shiver sensation that she liked. Mawji looked over as if he knew it too, but he didn't say a thing until they were labouring hard against the tide.

'It's too strong. Best moor up while we still got light.'

He caught a branch and they moored the dinghy fast from bow and stern; but soon the rushing tide spilled over, filling the over-laden boat. As Honey frantically bailed, Mawji pulled hard on the ropes to get the boat as high up in the water as possible. Once the flooding tide had eased and the spill had ceased, they both stacked the gold neatly at the back to give them room to cook and rest.

The light was fading as they ate. By the time darkness fell, the sounds of the mangrove dropped away. Honey sat changing at the back, sitting on the gold, which briefly gleamed as Mawji lit a match to light a cigarette.

Lying in the bottom of the boat looking up at blackness, he knew the moon would soon appear to give this place the ghostly hue it so deserved. Honey watched the red ember glow as she crawled across the gold to join him.

There's always a first time and this was hers, not his, but he could hardly remember his own escapades as they were long ago, washed away with tide and time.

As she lay beside him in that skirt which nearly had him drowned, not talking and lying so close he could feel her breath against his cheek, he knew that she was sure and ready to seal the bond they had both so unwittingly made.

Mawji dragged on his cigarette and flicked the butt out into darkness where they both heard it fizz in the flat water of the high tide.

The boat swayed gently.

Sometime later, they both lay looking up at moonlight penetrating the foliage. The gold, some of which had tumbled down from its neatly piled stack, flickered and flashed in an unworldly way. The pair lay drenched in sweat, sticky from the sex and high humidity.

'Will it always hurt?'

Mawji wanted a cigarette, but not wanting to break the intimacy of the moment, was on her again.

'You tell me.'

FREEMAN HAD HEARD THE NOISES, was unsure of what they were. They sounded spooky, especially as the swamp had begun to show strange moving shadows, some dancing in the water where the tide rippled and others locked deep inside the vegetation where leaves trembled, making the moonlight flicker dark and sombre shapes.

Feeling tired, he didn't dare sleep. His hunger and thirst were so bad that he wanted to drink the salty brackish water and chew the leaves he could smell and feel beside him.

He heard the noise again but this time there was something else behind it, something coming for him out of the vast and endless swamp. Not a noise but an entity. He then had a vision of The Black Shells and something waking up, or rather something he had woken by digging into that mound; something he disturbed sleeping deep below.

Freeman felt a pang of fear, lost all concentration and slipped off his perch, splashing hard into the dark water below. The tide was full and he easily pulled himself back up and into the mangrove, the plastic wrapper of his deeds still safely stuffed inside his trousers.

'WHAT WAS THAT?'

They were once again lying side-by-side staring up at the dark canopy cut here and there by moonbeams. The temperature had fallen and the blanket over them with Honey snuggled up to Mawji.

He left it a moment and then replied:

'Not sure, the crocs don't like to come this far out into the racing tides.'

'Was it him?'

Mawji shrugged.

'Could be anything. Strange things happen out here.'

'In The Black Shells?'

'This place is one big riddle. My grandfather spoke in riddles, said he would show me its secret one day.'

'Do you miss him?'

'Miss him? Sure I miss him. He's out there somewhere floating on an ocean breeze.'

'That's a nice way to remember him.'

Mawji sat up and looked at her, the moonlight dancing in her pale face. He pulled a cigarette from the crumpled pack in his shirt pocket lying in the bottom of the boat and, after lighting it, dryly said:

'He's alive just like me and you, out there and waiting.' He dragged on the cigarette. 'That's where we're going, if we ever find Jaffa again.'

'Where do think Joey's gone?'

'Wherever it is, he sure ain't fishing.'

Mawji pulled the blanket away, exposing her silvery nakedness, all mottled and patchy in the flickering moonlight.

'Honey and gold...'

Before he could finish she had pulled him down hard on to her.

AS THE SOFT BREEZE of the turning tide swayed the leaves above, Freeman heard whispers, mumbles, and thought he heard the word Jaffa. He knew he was going mad and had very little time to get back to the port before he gave up the ghost; on thinking that, he remembered Jeneta saying they were ghosts already. Freeman laughed aloud, a deep reverberating laugh that echoed through the swamp.

'That's him alright.'

'What shall we do?'

'Wait till morning. He's not going anywhere, only into madness perhaps.'

WHEN THE PENNY FINALLY DROPPED, Freeman felt a cold shiver of realisation as the memory came back: his father had told him it was The Jaffas who had built The Black Shells. He was soon covered in perspiration and shaking as a mixture of fever and terror overtook him. He used all his waning strength to hang on, hold on and not lose his mind or fall into the sea.

AROUND FOUR IN THE MORNING, the tide had rushed back out again and the water flat and low. Freeman jumped down into the shallows and, with some effort, got his aching legs and stiff body to follow the gentle flow towards the sea.

Mawji had spent the night adjusting the ropes to the level of the tide, making sure the boat was neither stuck half way up a tree nor being flooded out. As he adjusted the ropes for one last time before trying to get some sleep before dawn, he heard Freeman's splashing footsteps slowly coming by. He picked up the gun, nudged Honey who was sleeping on the floor, and looked out into the moonlit swamp. Honey heard the noises and quickly dressed without saying a word. They silently waited until an illuminated ghostly silhouette appeared and crossed in front of them.

A moment later Freeman stopped, turned slowly and stared. A few yards away, under the shadows of the swamp canopy, he saw two dark shapes sitting in a gleam of gold. In the stillness no one spoke, all of them frozen until a strange breeze softly blew, disappearing no sooner had it come.

'What are we going to do?' Honey whispered.

'It's that way,' Mawji shouted out, waving the gun towards the south.

Freeman just stayed put, looking at the freak that may just have an answer to his burning question.

'What ya waiting for? You'll miss the tide and have to spend another night out here.'

'What's a Jaffa?'

'My boat,' Mawji sneered.

'My father told me The Jaffas made The Black Shell Isles.'

'So now you know. Go while you still have strength. You want to risk another night out here?'

Freeman sat down exhausted in the shallow water.

'Where do you think these antics will get you?' Mawji snapped.

'To where the poet's whisper mingles with the endless singing breeze...'

He said it softly, but both Mawji and Honey heard it clearly. Mawji didn't waste a second and was out over the side of the boat splashing through the water towards Freeman who was too tired to do a thing about it.

'Who told you that? I'll shoot you right here and now. Who told you that?'

Mawji was right up to Freeman, the gun inches away from his face, shouting and beside himself.

Freeman chuckled and lay back in the shallow water, his head and back lightly touching the muddy bottom of the channel.

'Jaffa told me that.'

Mawji said nothing and Freeman looked up at him in the twilight of the fading night, before sitting up and asking:

'But I don't know where it is. Do you?'

Mawji took a step back and heard Honey splashing through the water to join him. When she was by his side, he said:

'He's going mad.'

'Are we going to leave him here like this?'

'Do you?' Freeman asked again.

'Sure I do.'

Mawji whispered to Honey:

'He's been touched by one, I bet it was him digging up the shells that did it.'

'What are they?'

'I'll tell you later, but this guy must have met the devil himself.'

On hearing that, Freeman collected himself somewhat.

'Jeneta said the devil leads me.'

'What did you have to mess with those shells for?'

'They're just shells.'

'Do you think it's an accident that you met a Jaffa?'

'I met him fishing on a lonely shore at dawn.'

'Trouble and fish don't mix. I don't know what you caught on that lonely shore, but I bet things have been pretty strange ever since.'

Freeman looked at the freak in front of him and chuckled:

'Stranger than the strangest fiction...'

'We can't leave him like this. He won't make it.' Honey was concerned.

'We should shoot him like a dirty dog.'

'You said that stuff was over for you.'

'This is new stuff. He's got nine lives and a whole heap of trouble following him.'

'Maybe it's just swamp fever and the rest all mumbo jumbo.'

'Bah, maybe, but I doubt it. He can't come with us though. Once the tide runs, the boat'll be too heavy to manoeuvre with him on board. We'll get swamped; besides, he'll have us overboard before we know it.'

'You can keep the gold. I've got what I came for.'

He pulled the plastic wrapper from his trousers and held it up.

'The deeds to my farm.'

'What about the gold?'

Mawji waved the gun menacingly.

'I don't need it anymore. You keep it.'

'I sure will. It's that way.'

Mawji pointed south once more.

'Take me with you. I won't last another night.'

'Sure you will. Your Jaffa's not finished with you yet.'

'We can't leave him,' Honey said firmly.

'Get some rope and tie his hands.'

Honey went back to the dinghy, returning with a short piece of rope and proceeded to tie Freeman's hands. As she squatted down to tie the rope around Freeman's wrists, he looked straight in her eyes, laughing in a deranged way.

'You've been touched too I heard.'

'Not by the devil!'

'God damn! Make sure it's tight. He's cursed remember.'

The flood returned as dawn broke, the light chasing away the eerie shadows of the night to show the swirling mud brown water and endless green vegetation of the swamp.

They had tied Freeman to the back of the boat, his hands fastened to the mooring ring, his head and shoulders up and out of the water resting on the rubber side next to the motor with his legs and body floating in the tide – like a prisoner ready to be dragged through water.

Both Honey and Mawji waded through the increasing tide, pulling the heavy dinghy into deeper water before boarding and paddling south towards the large creeks. Freeman dragged behind.

Freeman drifted in and out of consciousness, his thirst was bad but he didn't ask for water; somehow, he just didn't seem to care.

They paddled in silence, pushing hard against the rising tide. To Honey, the night before was still burning deep inside and she glanced at Mawji who was lost in thought and only eyed the water out in front, except for when he turned around to check if Freeman was still secure.

The tide increased, moving faster and lapping over the edges of the dinghy. Freeman coughed and spluttered as the water splashed his face, making him cry out.

Honey looked behind at Freeman struggling to get his body higher onto the boat. By doing so, he pulled the back down, slowly filling the boat with water.

'We're sinking!' She screamed.

Mawji grabbed Honey and lurched forward to the apex of the boat to counter balance the weight, but the water still splashed over and they were close to losing all the gold as the back angled down.

'Cut him loose!'

Mawji handed her the knife and Honey crawled over the glowing mass being pulled down into the tide and put the blade hard against the tight rope through the ring.

There was a slight crack as the rope cut, releasing Freeman who fell back into the water, moving away with the flooding tide. Honey caught his helpless eyes looking straight at her as Mawji desperately shouted:

'Quick, get back over here!'

As Honey slid back over to join him at the front, the boat lifted at the back and she went to work bailing out all the water in the bottom of the boat. Mawji secured the craft to a sturdy trunk.

'Shit, that was close. We nearly lost the boat.'

'We lost Freeman.'

They both stopped what they were doing and looked back at the swirling water that would soon become a torrent for they were now near the sea where the tide ran hard and fast, and saw nothing. He was gone, lost in the maze of endless green.

'I killed him.'

'No you didn't. If the boat had gone down, he would have gone down with it. At least he's got a chance now and we've still got the boat.'

'The gold you mean.'

She looked at him defiantly and he immediately became defensive.

'Don't be like that. Things like this just happen and before you know it it's all out of control and…'

But he didn't finish, just stared at her and she stared back, saying:

'He's still a human being.'

Mawji looked at the racing tide behind the boat.

'Maybe he's still got some of those nine lives left.'

Honey fell against him with a sob and he held her tight as the dinghy bumped about.

NOT HAVING SPOKEN much since Freeman's disappearance, they lay together looking up at the morning light filtering through the lush green leaves. In the rising humidity, waiting for the tide to ease, Honey spoke.

'What's a Jaffa?'

'Kind of witchdoctor.'

'Like the ones my mum just loves to hate?'

'No, not that kind,' Mawji chuckled. 'More like strange beings who drift in on an ocean breeze only to mysteriously disappear again.'

'And the poetry? It was beautiful but made you so angry.'

'It's like a spell. I heard it once before, a long, long time ago.'

Honey turned and looked at Mawji, making him turn to focus on her enquiring eyes, half hidden by matted hair tousled over her sweaty sun tanned face.

'My grandfather said it.'

He grabbed the last cigarette from the pack in his shirt pocket and lit it, throwing the empty pack down towards the gold. Momentarily studying the gold piled up by their feet, he looked back at her, softly muttering: 'You're pretty.'

She went to hold him, but he was already up, undoing the mooring rope.

'Tide's slacking. We need to get to the creek before it races back again.'

'Let's look for him. I want to feel we at least tried.'

He hesitated with the rope and she knew he would do it just to please her. She smiled when he said:

'What is it with you?'

Turning the dinghy, they paddled to where they had last seen him, scouring the twisted roots and tangled vegetation for a sign.

They didn't have to wait long.

Freeman saw them approaching through misty eyes. He could hear them talking but couldn't catch the words as the dinghy bumped against the mangrove next to him and rough hands pulled him up and pushed him into the boat. Shivering, he lay facing the gold reflecting the morning light.

They stared down at Freeman, wasted looking with lank hair and dark stubble, his empty eyes staring out at nothing.

'That's what ya get for messing with the devil.'

'You sound like my mum!' Honey laughed.

'Pah, give him some water if he can drink it, and see what he's hiding in his pockets – we don't want any surprises.'

Mawji handed her the water bottle and she went to Freeman sprawled across the gold. Holding his head up, she put the bottle to his lips, letting a small amount in to his mouth. He spluttered as the swallowing reflex of his dry throat started to revive and the water went down, first slowly and then in great gulps as he became aware of the girl and his aching throbbing head. Finishing the canteen, he lay panting as Honey turned out his pockets.

'A few soggy passports.'

She looked at the photographs.

'He's calling himself Marcel Malo these days. There's a wad of money.'

'For the charter I guess – anything else?'

'An old green rag. He's burning up with fever.'

She wet the rag and, as she went to place it over his forehead, Freeman giggled as he saw the green coming straight towards him. He closed his eyes and laughed some more.

'He's possessed.'

'Now you really do sound like my mum.'

'Sooner we dump him the better. Come on, we need to get paddling.'

FREEMAN WOKE AND CAUGHT the sunlight reflecting off the gold. It made him squint and turn his head. He found himself looking at the freak and bible-basher sitting in the front of the boat staring right at him.

'How are you feeling?'

Honey handed over the water bottle, which he took and downed in one long continuous gulp.

'I've felt better,' he said, panting for breath.

They were moored in a small basin adjoining a large creek and were protected from the strong tide now running hard out to sea. Clutching his throbbing head, Freeman felt Jeneta, warm and moist, and reassuringly pulled her off his head. He lent over the gold to wet her once again in the muddy water of the basin.

'I'm not gonna fish you out again,' Mawji shouted out.

Freeman lifted Jeneta out of the brackish water and wrapped her around his head like a small turban, thinking the others staring at him had no clue about her whatsoever; but he was wrong.

'Who's Jeneta?' Honey asked.

Freeman was shocked and touched his dripping turban.

'You've been saying her name.'

'She's Osu.'

'What's that?' Mawji asked.

Freeman felt like laughing but he didn't. His head hurt too much and the freak wasn't smiling, just staring in that hostile way of his. Having no clue how to answer, he blurted out:

'A Bush Jaffa.'

'Very funny, any more of that and you'll be swimming back to port.'

'I've got no quarrel with you. You've got the gold. All I need is help getting back.'

Mawji tapped the gun in his pocket.

'No funny business now.'

'Just one thing…'

Mawji said nothing and just waited for the one thing.

'Where is it?'

'What?'

'Where the whisper meets the breeze.'

'What is it with you? You're another one who just can't quit. It's here in the shells, out there on an ocean breeze, it's anywhere they come and go from.'

Freeman looked at the freak angrily spouting his words. Mawji stopped, pausing before driving his point home:

'And you messed with it and it took you right to one of them, but seems you hit the jackpot! You must have met a Kali Jaffa – A Black Jaffa.'

'Messed with what?'

'Those shells of course. That's sacred ground. It was like digging a hole in his mother's head.'

'His mother!'

Mawji spat into the water and finished his rant:

'You've lived here all your life but couldn't see what stared you in the face when you went to bury that gold!'

Honey touched Mawji's arm, saying:

'Stop it! I feel the devil at work here.'

'You're not wrong there. We'll take him back to port and be done with it.'

Handing the gun to Honey, Mawji dropped into the water and swam a few yards to untie the mooring rope. Still feeling very weak, Freeman looked over at the freak, now pulling himself out of the water and up the muddy bank by the taught rope, and shouted out:

'He got me my country back. What do I care what he is or isn't?'

'Your country...'

Mawji untied the rope and pulled the dinghy alongside the vegetation.

'Pass the gun and push hard from the back.'

She jumped out and handed Mawji the gun, pushing as he guided it through a small gap into some very dense watery undergrowth.

'We'll push it through this lot to the pump house. Don't wanna be stopped by a patrol boat with all this gold, even if we are carrying the national hero of the day with us.'

The couple pushed and pulled the dinghy through the shallow water of the dense swamp full of mosquitoes and biting insects. Mawji and Honey were protected by splashing through waist deep water but Freeman, with his ripped up shirt and bare feet, cursed and swatted, as he became a bloody feast. He was soon in the water, walking aside Honey.

Mawji looked back at Freeman stumbling in the water, gaunt and wasted looking, knowing he would remain harmless for a while, but wanted shot of him as quickly as he could.

The tide ran gently in this part of swamp. It was protected from the sea by the dark ochre sand banks and shored up enough by the thick vegetation to miss the full force of the tidal creeks. They made slow but steady progress, sometimes doubling back when the foliage was too thick or when the boat grounded in a shallow spot, until they stopped under a high and wet vegetated bank that blocked their way.

'You know where this is?'

Mawji had secured the boat and stood in the still and brackish water looking at Freeman who had flopped over the edge of the dinghy, his torso resting on the gold and his feet in the water.

He shook his head.

'Over this bank is your dilapidated pumping station where we can hide the gold and motor back to port.'

They sat in heavy shade. An occasional sunbeam flickered through the thick canopy and sparkled off the stagnant water. Honey and Mawji used the last of the supplies to make a meal, as Freeman lay wasted on the boat, dripping sweat he could not afford to lose. The humidity made breathing a laboured chore.

Honey passed him the last of the water, which he drank down in one making him pant and sweat even more. He could barely eat, each mouthful ending in nausea, but he somehow managed before laying back and falling into a deep and empty sleep.

Honey and Mawji had climbed the wet bank and now sat at the brow looking down on Freeman curled up amongst the shiny gold. Honey spoke first:

'He's lucky we found him.'

'Lucky for us too, with him around no one much will bother us.'

'So long as he stays on side. You had better start being nice to him.'

'I've forgotten how.'

'No you haven't.'

'I'm sure not kissing him!'

They laughed together and then she asked:

'What's a Kali Jaffa?'

'They use the dark. One thing's for sure, he's not helping Freeman for nothing.'

Mawji turned around and looked down on the old pumping station. It was nothing more than a large wooden platform holding a pump house and secured to the creek bed with thick posts. Leading away from it and out to sea, ran a large rusty pipe supported by blocks that ended a few hundred yards out from the creek mouth.

The wooden platform was slightly lower than the top of the earth bank and about six feet out; the water was twenty-five feet below in the slacking low tide.

'We'll have to throw the gold over and lower the boat into the creek somehow.'

'That doesn't look so easy.'

'Nothing's easy out here.'

They woke Freeman who reluctantly dropped in the swamp. It took a lot of hard sweaty work to get the gold out of the boat and up the bank, struggling and slipping on the wet earth to get the bars up to the brow. They all sat, sweaty and exhausted, looking down at the platform.

'So this is yours?'

Freeman nodded to Mawji.

'We never got it working, all the trouble put a halt to sinking wells further up the creek and in the swamps.'

'You own that too?'

'Some of it. Here, take a look.'

Freeman handed Mawji the plastic wrapper. He figured friendliness was the best way forward; after all, the freak had saved his life, albeit reluctantly. There was no point in lighting his short and volatile fuse again. He was too weak to fight back or go it alone right now.

Mawji opened the wrapper, pulling out the deeds and boundary maps. He and Honey studied them in detail.

'You'll make an absolute fortune from the oil, no wonder you don't care about the gold.'

'I don't care about the oil or the gold, I've got money now. I only want my farm back.'

Mawji looked up from the maps.

'So you're just leaving it all under this swamp then?'

'I made a deal with Jaffa. He set this all up so long as I would sell the drilling rights to this cursed swamp.'

Mawji pointed to a place on the map. Both he and Honey studied it with curiosity. Suddenly Mawji looked over to Freeman and started laughing, loudly and uncontrollably. Honey followed suit. Freeman felt agitation, confused by this unexpected spectacle. It wasn't until the laughter had subsided that he cautiously asked:

'What's so funny?'

With tears running down his face, Mawji almost choked as his words spluttered out:

'You're about to sell The Black Shells to a Kali Jaffa. They'll never drill for oil here now – never!'

Mawji started to laugh again making Freeman mad.

'What's so bloody funny?'

Honey knew as Mawji knew and said, smiling:

'The Black Shells – he wanted the shells.'

'And to get them legally and keep them for good, he needed the government changed. You did a grand job at that. He must have great faith in you,' Mawji added.

'He didn't know I owned the shells. In fact, until you just told me neither did I. Pass me that map.'

Honey passed it over and Freeman saw that he did indeed own The Black Shell Isles and all the swamp around. As he studied it, Mawji said:

'He knew all right. He caught you good and proper.'

'Well, what does it matter? He kept his part of the bargain. Now I'll keep mine. He can have his shells.'

Freeman looked at the swarthy freak, staring and smiling at him, saying:

'Glad to hear it. Come on! Let's get that gold into the pump house.'

Mawji leaped out across the gap between the earth bank and platform and landed with a thud on the wooden planks, shaking the entire structure that had been weakened by storms and relentless tides.

He gestured to Honey and she threw a bar across. It banged down and slid along the damp planks, stopping just before the other side and a fall into the creek. Freeman threw the next one with care but it still slid on the damp planks forcing Mawji to stop it with his foot.

When it was done and the gold lay strewn around, Mawji hid the bars in the disused pump house. He slammed the door shut and looked down into the swirling creek below, then to its exit out to the sea where the creek ran over a shallow reef creating turbulence and waves. Pointing to the reef, he shouted up to Honey and Freeman looking down at him from the crest of the earthy bank.

'We've still got an hour before low tide. After that, the tide will run back hard and churn up the water over the reef. We'd sink in seconds, so best we catch the flat water or we'll be stuck out here for another night.'

It was late afternoon and they had no time to waste. Mawji leapt back onto the steep earthy bank and struggled to the top before they all slid down the other side to haul the dinghy up. Weakly, Freeman helped Honey push from the back whilst Mawji pulled hard on the mooring rope from above; all working hard, sweating and grunting until the craft and engine lay on the brow with everyone flopping by its sides. Honey went back down to collect the bags and saw the gun lying on a log. She hesitated, then slung the packs over her shoulders and picked it up, heading back up the bank, slipping all the way to the top.

Freeman watched her arrive.

'You were always quite a shot.'

'What the hell do you mean?'

Honey saw the concern reflected in Mawji's face and quickly placated him.

'I used to shoot at the Mission. We all did actually. It was what we did, shoot at targets.'

'Better than Sunday prayers I guess.'

Then, looking at Freeman, Mawji asked:

'You went to the Mission school?'

'As little as possible. I didn't need to learn about the devil or take a shot at him.' Freeman scoffed.

'We only saw him now and then,' Honey conferred.

'Guess you're shooting for the devil now. At least you know what side you're on.'

'He's not the devil, just a guy who sorts out others' dirty work. So stop complaining. He just helped you get rich,' Freeman snapped back, pointing to the pump house.

'You've got no idea what you've landed yourself into here. Sure you've got your country back and sure I've got the gold, but don't kid yourself that's the end of it. He owns you now.'

'You sound like that Osu woman – full of mumbo jumbo.'

'Stop it!' Honey intervened, letting a shot fly causing both men to jump and then stare blankly at her.

'We need to get out of here before it drives you both mad.'

Nobody spoke as Mawji tied two mooring ropes together to get a long length so they could lower the dinghy down into the water. All three of them held the rope tight, letting it move slowly through their fingers until the dingy was hanging nose down just above the water. Mawji hitched the rope around a tree and then jumped across the gap onto the platform to descend the rusty access ladder to the sea. He stopped at the bottom rung and shouted up for Freeman to release the hitch. As the craft flopped into the water in the narrow gap between the earth bank and the platform legs, Mawji leaped out, crashing on board as the current pulled the craft out towards the creek mouth. He fiddled with the engine and pulled the starter, and by the time it caught, he was in the swirling turbulence where the river met the sea, tossing around until he turned and headed back to the platform to pick the others up.

It was a leap of faith for Honey. She took a short run and threw her body towards the platform where she was propelled into Mawji's waiting arms. They lay sprawled out on their backs, winded, coughing and laughing. The thud of Freeman's feet nearby broke the moment and Mawji was up, heading down the access ladder to where he had secured the dinghy.

They didn't head out to sea but slowly motored up the creek.

'In a few minutes the tide will be static. We'll drift then back and then head out to sea.'

Freeman pulled the tied ropes out of the water and slung them down on deck. He looked back and out to sea. The harsh low sun made him squint. Between the silhouettes of the couple at the back staring at him, he saw the dark shape of a boat.

'Patrol boat,' Freeman said solemnly. 'Better turn around or they'll get the wrong idea.'

The dinghy turned and motored slowly to the creek mouth, catching the last rough water of the tide.

Freeman stood up and waved. All three of them could clearly see the big gun trained on them and the captain looking through binoculars.

'It's ok. It's from up the coast.'

'Guess that makes things just fine.'

Freeman laughed at Mawji's sarcasm and felt a semblance of normality return as they closed in on the boat. He soon remembered Jeneta and quickly pulled her off his head, stuffing her in a pocket, and, as he looked down at his cut bare feet and ripped and ragged clothing, something like shame showed on his face, making Honey laugh and blurt out bluntly:

'Sorry we didn't save your shoes.'

As Mawji smirked, Freeman gave a painful scowl that was soon replaced by a look of fresh determination as they pulled aside the boat where he introduced himself as a returning farmer. Soon on board having his hand shaken, Freeman peered back down at the couple waiting in the dinghy.

'Want a tow back?'

'You go ahead, we'll be fine.'

Freeman shrugged, but before he turned away, Mawji asked:

'Can you stop off at the bar? If Joey's dumb enough to be there, tell him I'm on my way.'

Freeman nodded and the patrol boat turned towards the port.

'Good riddance.'

Honey hugged him, putting her arms around him from behind, whispering:

'It's just us now.'

6.

GHOSTS

West Africa, 31ˢᵗ August 1968

REEMAN LOOKED LIKE a long upright shadow waiting to join the night as he stood still in the twilight outside the bar.

The captain had given him some black overalls and scruffy boots, and now, as he leaned against a wall still warm from the afternoon sun, felt invisible and safe, watching and listening to the busy port in the last moments of the dimming light.

As darkness quickly enveloped him, the smell of food wafting from the bar pulled him inside. He was soon squeezing himself into a space along the bar between a girl hanging onto a drunken soldier and a group of locals whose eyes shone with drink and the excitement of it all.

The place was packed with soldiers celebrating victory and probably hard won cash, and others, mainly returning exiles, celebrating justice.

Thankful he had not been recognised, either as Malo the hero or as Freeman the returning farmer, he sighed with relief that his mission was over and he could somehow return to what he knew and liked best. The bar mirror reflected his scratched up bristled face; he looked gaunt and sweaty but was happy that this appearance kept him hidden from endless questions and remarks.

'Guess I got you to thank for this?'

Joey indicated to the busy barroom.

Freeman didn't smile.

'You've got your country back again.'

'Never lost it.'

Freeman rested his elbows on the counter and momentarily put his head in his hands, knowing Joey had spoken the truth.

'He's on his way back; should be here within the hour, so long as the fuel holds out.'

'You've seen Mawji?'

Freeman nodded.

'Why would he be dumb ass enough to come back here?'

'He said the same about you.'

Joey looked perplexed and, before the moment became uncomfortable, shrugged and indicated to the beer taps.

'What ya drinking?'

'Water, and bring some food – lots of it.'

'And there was me thinking you'd had your last supper.'

Freeman's smile brushed aside the sarcasm, making Joey turn away to deal with the order at the other end of the bar.

A LITTLE TO THE NORTH, just outside the breaking surf rolling and crashing onto the dark shoreline, Mawji pulled hard on a paddle and Honey on the other.

'We should have said yes to that tow.'

'You're not wrong there. At least it's calm.'

'My arms ache, how much further is it?'

'Round the corner and we're straight into the harbour. Can't you sing a song or something?'

'You usually ask me to pray!'

Mawji laughed and started singing, making Honey cover her ears and scream out.

A little later, as the harbour lights flashed green and red ahead, they both let out a whoop of joy.

The port had completely shut up by the time they tied the dinghy to the old pontoon. Only a few soldiers guarding the quay showed in the shadows but seemed indifferent to the disembarking couple. A party was in full swing across the square by the bar.

'He sure is a dumb ass alright.'

Honey glanced at the dark shape of Jaffa moored against the quay of the deepwater dock.

'Glad he is.'

They looked across the festive square, milling with people in the midst of raucous celebration, towards the noisy bar, jam-packed, heaving and full of drunks.

'Quite some party.'

'They have something to celebrate.'

'For now.'

They jostled towards the bar through the drunken crowd and peered in through the large open windows. They spied Freeman hemmed in at the counter, gazing at an empty plate. Although lost in thought, he sensed something beyond the racket of the crowd and turned to see the couple staring in. He raised his glass in salutation.

'Looking like a real winner that one.'

Mawji gave a slight nod of recognition before turning to Honey by his side.

'This is all too cosy for me. Let's go to the boat, clean up and...' He didn't finish as they went towards the welcome sight of her new floating home.

In the bar, Freeman had been recognised, not as Malo but as himself. Soon embroiled in conversation with some farming neighbours, he asked about life here at home and them about his exile. He learned that what the taxi driver had said was true; farming had almost ceased and that trouble stayed around long after the revolution. He worried what he may find on his own farm, sandwiched between the port and ridge behind the bar.

Soon the topic of conversation changed to Malo, the mysterious hero and his dead companion who had been found incinerated in a burned out car behind the port on the other side of the imposing ridge.

Who was he? Was he still alive? Did Freeman know anything?

Freeman just feigned ignorance, knowing that public recognition just might attract his own swift assassination. He shot Joey a stern look that told him to keep his mouth shut, but Joey had no intention of telling anyone. He knew that ignorance was a man's best friend in a place like this and that Mawji had been right; he would be a dumb ass to think it would all blow over and things turn back to normal.

The woman cooking stared at Joey and then at Freeman. Having noticed their tacit exchange, she softly whispered in Joey's ear:

'Is that him?'

'Just a ghost, Mbela, just a ghost.'

'Then don't disturb the dead.'

Freeman felt the passports tucked away inside his overall and felt the urge to run; but instead, he ordered beer to join the celebrations and help hide his mixed up feelings and any doubt he had.

Joey popped the bottle cap. Before handing over the bottle to Freeman, he muttered to Mbela:

'And let's not join them either.'

As a slight and refreshing breeze blew in carrying the smells of the port, Freeman caught the muddy brackish scent of the swamps and saw green. Feeling the rag in his pocket, he quickly distracted himself by laughing to a joke he had not heard, along with others at the bar. Faking joy and jubilation, he took a swig from the bottle that was warm and tasted foul.

BACK ON JAFFA, Mawji sat in the old armchair supping a beer. He offered Honey the bottle.

She shook her head. 'Makes me light headed.'

'That's the idea – numb out that self-deluded din.' He looked out over the square to the bright lights of the bar, listening to the shouts and songs of triumph.

Honey stood and looked out across the square.

'When do we leave? I don't want to hang around too long.'

'Might change your mind, huh?'

'What is it with you? No chance of that now.'

'Glad to hear it. A few days…we need supplies, check the engines, get spares, and you need to get your stuff from home.'

'I'm dreading that.'

SOON AFTER DAWN, Mawji headed to the bar. As far as he could see nothing much had changed; the colour of some of the soldiers' faces was different and the obvious pot marks on the buildings from recent gunfire had merely joined the old ones from other times when things went bad. No one stopped him or even gave a second glance.

The place was a mess. Soldiers lay around; some on the floor, others slumped across tables and a few still drinking at the bar. Mbela was cooking at the stove, her bright eyes now red and tired as she struggled to keep awake. Joey was slowly cleaning up the spilt food and broken glass, carefully avoiding the guns littered about the place, some still held in sleeping soldiers' hands.

He stopped as Mawji entered and Mawji stopped too, taking in the scene with one big sweeping glance.

'They all pay?'

'Everyone…except him.'

Joey pointed to Freeman sleeping in a chair, his legs stretched out and his head hung forward, leaning to one side.

'He don't count. Any trouble last night?'

'Nope. What is it with him?'

'We found him in the Shells.'

'Felt sorry for him, uh?'

'Preacher did.'

'Bullshit! You may have fallen for her, but you're not that dumb.'

'I need the boat, we're getting out of here. You coming?'

'We're broke…just the money from last night.'

Mawji hesitated.

'Two days at the most Joey, then I'm out of here for good. Once the honeymoon is over there'll be endless trouble and killing. You feeling lucky or something?'

'Only a dumb ass feels lucky in a place like this. Hey Mbela, get Mawji some breakfast. Where's your preacher?'

'She'll be over soon.'

'Alleluia!'

Mawji looked around.

'Where's the commanding officer?'

'They turned the school into a barracks.'

Mawji swore as he left the bar.

The walk behind the bar up to the old mission school took about twenty minutes. A few cars were still smouldering and rubble lay strewn across the narrow street. Mawji gripped his pistol, listening to the sound of distant gunfire echoing across the hills.

The last piece of road was steep. Below him was the harbour and the north, the swamp; and hidden in this endless sea of green, the black shells and abandoned pumping station. Above him stood the ridge, its jagged peaks and sheer rock walls sweeping south before disappearing into another haze of green. The early morning breeze gave him a chill and he wasted no time in looking for the officer.

The school had been turned into a makeshift field hospital and the soldiers slept in tents behind the burnt out church that was overgrown and full of singing birds. Mawji wasn't challenged by the guards whom he could clearly see weren't locals but hired hands. He knew that once they left the real fighting would begin.

He found an officer and soon a couple of men were heading down towards the port. Before he could follow them, he came face to face with Honey's mother.

They both just stared at one another. As Mawji was about to walk past, she spoke.

'What are your intentions with my daughter?'

'Heterosexual – and yours?'

'Don't be so disgusting.'

'Everyone comes from sex, even you, Preacher Woman.'

'The devil made you.'

'Maybe he did, but what made you? An act of self-righteous fornication over the alter? Maybe that's why your church burnt down.'

A wry smile came over the formidable face of Honey's mother, her blue eyes piecing into Mawji. He turned to stare at the shell of the burnt out church.

'If you can forgive those who did those wicked thing to Maya, maybe I can forgive you too.'

'For what? Taking your daughter or for all those things I did looking for my sister's killers?'

'You are welcome to my daughter. To see the world through your eyes must be quiet a thing and she just might turn you right. No, for all those wicked acts.'

Mawji laughed.

'You like extremes, uh?'

'It gives me purpose.'

'I call her Honey.'

'I suppose you like the taste.'

'You're not the naïve bible bashing freak people say you are.'

'And you're not the twisted monster you think you are.'

'You trying to save me?'

'Save yourself and take your Honey with you? There's only trouble coming here.'

'You're not wrong there.'

As Mawji turned and left, she uttered, so he would hear:

'Sometimes it takes a monster.'

FREEMAN WATCHED THE SOLDIERS LEAVING. He had woken with a jolt as the two men from the barracks had started shouting and kicking men to clear them from the bar. His neck was stiff and his head slightly throbbed. By the time he had stood up and stretched, the bar was empty except for Joey, Mbele and the bible basher who sat near him eating breakfast.

Mawji came back and spoke to Joey.

'Can ya get the key to the engine shed? We need to sort the gear out.'

Joey went upstairs to fetch the key. Mawji stood next to Honey, looking at Freeman trying to shake the fog from his sleepy head.

'I need a rifle,' Freeman stated.

'You know where they are.'

He pointed to the back room and Freeman headed straight to it. Turning to Honey, Mawji whispered:

'You didn't mention the gold to Joey did ya?'

She shook her head. 'Did you?'

'That's our ticket out of her. The less anyone knows the better.'

'Is he coming with us?'

'If he's got any sense left he will.'

Freeman returned with a rifle and a couple of magazines and went outside without a glance or comment.

'I met your Mum. She blessed me.'

'My God, the sooner we leave the better!'

AWARE THAT SPORADIC shots were being fired in the direction of the farm, Freeman stopped at the edge of the square to place a magazine in the rifle.

Passing the burnt out church, he walked towards the hills along a brown red track still soft from the rain.

The landscape was unchanged, every large tree familiar. Even the breeze catching him on a bend was exactly as remembered. Only the silence was different. The sounds of the working farm gone and the endless shouts of children now just an echo in his head. Between these moments of quiet solitude, gunshots reverberated across the hills. The skirmish was taking place among the rocks behind his farm. He hoped it would stay there so he would have enough time to get a measure of the place.

The farm gates were gone, not a trace of metal left, and the ditches on either side of the track, silted up and full of weeds. He looked far down the road to where the buildings, still standing, were shaded by tall trees.

His pace was slow and his eye keen, watching out for anything suspicious. All seemed quiet and soon he was in the farm compound. He stopped, taking in what was left.

Every building had been ransacked, all machinery looted and anything worth having, gone. Even some of the large timbers had been removed from the farm buildings and every window in the house was missing along with the front door.

Freeman flicked the safety off and edged around the yard. Not a living thing seemed to inhabit the place. Everything was gone, even the intense feelings he had, seemed to evaporate with every step.

Standing blank among the ghosts of his memories, a light wind kicked up the dust around his feet, swirling it into his eyes and open mouth. Coughing and stumbling, he moved involuntarily into the house and saw her lying on the floor. Near naked, gaunt and skinny, her ribs clearly showing, she clutched the compass around her neck and held the gun in her other hand.

He knew she wasn't dead but before he could assemble any sense, the world went blank. Later, he only remembered crashing to the floor.

On his back, staring up at the decaying ceiling, which had once held the brilliant whitewash of their kitchen room, he squinted and turned his head to avoid the morning rays streaming in through a piece of broken roof. He faced Jeneta leaning against the wall opposite him. In her hand, she held the rag she had taken from his pocket.

Freeman knew what she had done: she had arrived, defying death at every juncture, by following a bearing given to her by some barking mad freak who no doubt had risen from the swamps himself.

'What happened?'

She spoke, her shiny black eyes looking right into him.

'The ghosts left you.'

Freeman let out a small cough as he laughed.

'And why would they do that?'

'You brought them home.'

Before he had time to ask another question, he felt something shift inside and briefly caught her smiling eyes before blacking out again.

Again, he awoke with the sun in his eyes, but this time he immediately stood up, wobbling a little on his feet. Feeling light and empty, he knew some terrible burden he had carried was finally gone.

Looking out through the doorway into the yard, he saw her sitting in the shade of one the big trees, holding the rag and gun, staring right at him.

Freeman turned and wandered through the house, room to room. He looked for anything that might connect him back to this place. Hurrying up the splintered, broken stairs to the upstairs landing, he looked into the wrecked room where his parents had once slept. Vividly remembering the horror of finding their ritually butchered corpses, he rushed back down the stairs and out into the farmyard. He stood before Jeneta, who was putting the ragged shorts back on and tying them into place.

Instead of panic and despair, he only felt emptiness.

'They're gone.'

As he stood in the middle of the yard in the bright searing sunlight, he knew she was right, and was at a total loss at what to do.

BACK IN THE PORT, Joey and Mawji were shifting through some gear in their metal lockup container behind the deep-water dock.

'It's my home.'

'It's gonna turn ugly. You're not exactly Mr. Popular, are ya?'

'Out there, across thousands of miles of water to find some shacks on stilts stuck on a sandbar god knows where…anyway, how do you know he's still out there?'

'He's there alright. He even made sure we got money enough.'

'Don't start all that Jaffa talk. They upped and left at the first sniff of trouble.'

'They just knew when to quit, that's all.'

'And he quit a long time ago.'

'He's my grandfather and I'm telling you, he's still out there waiting.'

'For you maybe.'

'If you feel a little lonely bring Mbela along.'

'She thinks you're nuts too!'

'And you're not?'

'You'd better take the lot, including the welding and aqua gear.'

'Expecting a leak are you?'

Both men stared at Jaffa partially visible between the sheds. Mawji shrugged and resignedly said, 'You're right, it's a long way and if we make it, the boat ain't coming back.'

UP AT THE FARM, Freeman had picked up his rifle from the house and slung it across his shoulder. He stood with Jeneta, examining her gun before passing it back to her. She tucked it into the tie of her ragged green shorts.

'You've let a few fly,' he said, looking at her questioningly, but she just stared back. He knew she would have died fighting rather than give anything up. Was it luck, magic or sheer tenacity that got her through the swamps? She didn't say and he didn't want to ask; she had come for him, against the odds.

'Why Jeneta?'

She pulled up her torn and ragged dress, showing him the green threadbare faded shorts.

'Why did you carry me with you?'

'I guess you got inside me.'

'And you brought me here.'

He thought he might just be beginning to understand something now.

'The ghosts told me everything before we found the big bend on the Cross river.'

He hadn't known the name of the river, just the bearing to get across. As the image of the chocolate water came to mind, he dismissed remembering. Something more pressing was at hand. Grabbing her wrist, he hurried around the house to the overgrown garden, abruptly stopping at the spot where he had buried his parents. The headstones were gone and the only evidence that two graves lay under the red mud soil were the white stones that had once edged the plot, kicked out of place and strewn around the bush.

Without a word, Freeman moved towards the track. As hired men fell back towards the farm, reinforcements arrived from the direction of the burnt out church. He knew the farmyard would become a battleground before the day was out.

Jeneta hung on tight the whole way back. By the time they made it, the heavy guns had started.

There was a big commotion around the barracks as soldiers hurriedly organised themselves for the offensive around the farm. Freeman scoured the crowd until he caught the unmistakable outline of Honey's mother.

By the time he had pulled Jeneta through the camp, Honey was at her mother's side, both looking at him in that familiar and unfriendly way. For a moment, Freeman wondered if they expected him to join the men, defend his farm and land, but he knew their looks were the same as when he was a child: the look of blame, telling him who he was and how somehow it was his entire fault. However, he had other things to think about than ponder on the past.

'Can you fix her up? You know, clothes, food and…'

They just stared at him and he knew they would do the right thing. He turned to Jeneta who seemed at ease, relaxed between the chaos and strangeness going on.

They hadn't spoken since the farmyard.

'They'll point you to the port. I'll see you there.'

With that, he was gone, into the crowd and heading down the hill towards the sea.

Honey's mother left and the two young women briefly stared at one another. Honey introduced herself and led Jeneta to the house where she shut the door to muffle the distant sounds of shots.

'Who are you?'

'Jeneta.'

Honey examined the small, worn out, ferocious looking woman barely covered in ripped up rags, with a mixture of confusion and curiosity.

'But where are you from, come from? I mean, you're not local.'

Jeneta named her people and her country.

Honey heard and stared in disbelief, knowing that her next question already had an answer.

'You came through the swamps?'

Jeneta touched the compass around her neck.

'That's not possible…how…?'

Jeneta didn't answer.

Honey lost interest. She had had her own swamps to contend with, and went and fetched some of her old clothes, quickly showing Jeneta the bathroom before leaving the house to find her mother.

'She came through swamps all the way from Biafra to be with him!'

'And you? How far would you go to be with Mawji?'

'We're going to sea to find his grandfather.'

'I'm glad you're getting out of here. His grandfather was an extraordinary man.'

'You knew him!'

'Occasionally he helped out here at the Mission. He even showed you how to catch a butterfly.'

'I don't remember. What happened to him? What was he like?'

'A very strange man. It was if he were just biding time, waiting for something. Then one day he had a visitor. After that, we never saw him again.'

'Who?'

'Another just like him, but very young…had the darkest of hearts and I asked him to leave. I clearly remember his charming smile, odd sounding speech and awfully loud shirt…he…'

Honey's mother deliberated and then changed tact.

'You seem to have experienced a lot with Mawji these past few days.'

Honey blushed and then blurted out her story of the swamps, avoiding any talk of romance.

'The Black Shells, maybe they can look after them better than we did this church.'

'Why didn't you tell me all this stuff before?'

'Did you believe in mumbo jumbo?'

'I do now!'

'So it's now you know.'

'And you?'

'Shells or a church, what really is the difference?'

The conversation ended there as Jeneta strolled towards them. She wore Honey's clothes, which were far too big for her, had rolled up the bottoms of some dark slacks with the green rag clearly showing over the waist hem. The gun bulged in a pocket. A white shirt hung loose about her skinny frame and canvas shoes were stretched by her wide feet.

The sun was high and Jeneta's shadow bobbed between her feet. She stopped in front of the two women staring and waiting, their faces screwed up from the harsh midday light.

'Do you love him?'

Giving a surprised shrill giggle, Jeneta touched the compass still around her neck.

'He's Osu like me.'

Honey turned to her mother, who smiled, saying:

'Touched by the spirit.'

FREEMAN HAD ENTERED the empty bar. Despite the light breeze blowing in the aroma of the sea through the open doors and windows, the disagreeable smells of the night before still lingered in the tropical midday heat. This, along with the sounds of the distant gunfire and whirr of the overhead fans grating on his newfound sensibilities, made the place oppressive. He felt an urgency to do quickly what he had come to do and leave.

He demanded the telephone from Mbela who stood watching him from behind the bar.

Clearly seeing the tension in his sweaty face and knowing he was the presidential killer, she didn't ask a thing, pushing the big black phone across the bar to where he stood glaring at her.

He lifted the receiver. When the operator answered, he gave the Parisian number, after which he placed the receiver down and waited for the connection ring.

The tedious wait under the annoying whirr was broken by the sounds of scuffing feet making Freeman turn quickly and point the rifle towards the open door.

'Not up there fighting for your country then?'

The two men were standing in the doorway staring right at him. Before any abuse came back to answer Mawji's sarcasm, the telephone rang loudly and Freeman turned fast to answer it.

There was a pause where only distant gunfire and whirring fans dared speak.

'Jaffa?'

The others stayed still and silent, carefully listening to only Freeman's side of the conversation.

'Congratulations! Marcel Malo has now quite an international reputation.'

'What do I want with him? I need my own identity back.'

'But you're the brand new hero and still available.'

'I don't care…anyway, there's nothing here, it's gone and…'

Freeman stopped his lament.

'I have the deeds.'

'Go to the bank in the capital right next to the hotel you stayed in with Ralph.'

'He's dead.'

'They build monuments for dead heroes. Watch out they don't build two.'

'I need some cash.'

'For what?'

'To come home, no, back… I don't bloody know. I have Jeneta with me. Why the hell did you have to send her here?'

'She made it? Even Jane will marvel at that!'

'It's not possible for anyone to cross those swamps.'

'With a little push from me and a mighty tug from you.'

Freeman saw green and before he was overwhelmed, Jaffa had changed the subject.

'And the gold? Have you given it to the angry fisherman?'

Freeman turned and looked at Mawji still standing in the doorway.

'Yeah, I gave it to him. How the hell did you know that?'

'Go to the bank…and Freeman, wear a rain jacket.'

The phone went dead.

'He's got you good and proper hasn't he?'

'He called you the angry fisherman.'

As Mawji laughed, Freeman asked:

'Do you know him?'

Mawji shrugged.

'You expecting a storm?'

'Not the season.'

Freeman turned back to the bar with resignation to ask Mbela for a beer.

UP AT THE MISSION, Honey gave her mother a hug and picked up her bags to go down to the port with Jeneta.

'I should say good luck, but you won't need it with your...'

Honey put down the bags and turned. Her mother's unassailable composure gave slightly, a mischievous glint appearing in her eyes.

'...Jaffa.'

THROUGH THE OPEN WINDOWS, Freeman stared at the sky and sea. It was a hot and humid afternoon and he was soaked just sitting at the bar, drinking a cold beer that had now gone to his head.

'You sure you're not expecting a storm?'

'Like I said, it's not the season.'

'I need to get to the city. Guess the roads are far too risky.'

Mawji, who had just finished sorting out a small arsenal to load on to Jaffa, was about to head out the door.

'Suicide. If you wanna ride just ask. I'm leaving as soon as she gets back.'

'I'm asking.'

'Then help me load.'

The gunfire had subsided, but the few shots that still rang out were close and right on the edge of town. The two men arrived at the heavily guarded deep-water dock where Joey waited for them, smiling and looking up at the town.

'Jona's got them running in circles up there,' he mused.

'They'll be a thousand self-deluded Jona's picking up guns right across this sick country.'

Both men looked at Freeman who snapped back.

'Like you said, no one's mourning that old dictator. I did everyone a big favour up at the mountain palace.'

'Well you better call in your favours fast because the town will be burning this time tomorrow.'

Freeman looked horrified and stared coldly at Mawji, as he asked:

'How can you know that? And how can that freak Jaffa know I gave you the gold?'

'Because they know everything before it happens and that Jona's out there. He knows every inch of this land and won't quit at anything. He'll give your boys hell alright.'

Freeman felt furious. 'There're not my boys.'

'You're not wrong there, you've only got him now.'

But Freeman knew he had someone else as well and that time was running out. As he rushed across the dock, through the square up towards the Mission, the nearing sound of gunfire told him that the fight was on the edge of town. Feeling panic on seeing Honey and Jeneta coming towards him in the street, he shouted out:

'Hurry…he's waiting at the boat! Keep him there until we return.'

Honey moved as fast as she could under the weight of her bags towards the harbour and Freeman pulled Jeneta through some alleys to the police station. He held on to her as he pushed his way through the guards to enter the ramshackle building.

There was a familiar face at the counter, smiling and greeting him, glad he was back and once they had routed these louts things could go back to normal.

In no mood for war or victories, Freeman produced Ralph's passport demanding some identification papers for Jeneta as Ralph's full blood sister.

The man laughed, Ralph was white and she was black and not even local as far as he could see and anyway it wasn't true so no papers could be made. After all, things were decent here once again.

Freeman threw Marcel Malo on the counter and seethed:

'You owe me.'

With one look at the name and photograph, the man went pale and softy asked for a name and date of birth. Freeman looked at Jeneta, who simply said:

'Osu.'

He figured she was under thirty and gave a date to suit.

Before long, Jeneta was putting her inky thumbprint on the card that was then stamped and signed. Freeman handed it over to her as they left the building without any further exchange.

As they hurried back to the harbour, Jeneta read her name aloud:

'Osu Lafont.'

Freeman smirked as he pulled her along, knowing time had run out and that his lift might just be heading out to sea.

A small navel boat had landed and a dozen or so armed men ran passed them across the square towards the church. Mawji had the engines running and, on seeing the couple dash along the quay to jump on board, shouted down to Honey. She released the mooring rope. They both jumped, landing with a thud as Mawji reversed hard out of the dock, throwing them both face down on the deck. At the harbour entrance, the boat turned, heading north towards the creeks.

As Freeman and Jeneta entered the bridge, Mawji spun around. He stared hard at Jeneta clutching Freeman's arm, and she stared back. Turning back around to watch the sea, he declared:

'He's got you too, eh!'

Jeneta stayed silent and Freeman, confused, asked:

'Who's got who?'

'That Jaffa, he's got you both good and proper.'

Jeneta looked at Freeman and whispered:

'He's a Jaffa.'

'My boat's Jaffa, not me, damn it!'

'My mum said you were a Jaffa.'

Mawji quickly turned and focused on Honey sitting in the big chair behind him and then at the others. Everyone was staring.

'Jesus! My grandfather's one, not me. Now pack it in.'

He turned to face the sea again as Honey spoke.

'How do you know he's got Jeneta too?'

Mawji stayed silent, pulled a cigarette from the pack in his shirt pocket and fumbled around the console area for a light.

'He doesn't know what he is.'

Honey answered Jeneta's rhetoric:

'That's what we're going to find out...sooner rather than later, I hope.'

Freeman saw the matches lying on the floor, left the bench he was sitting on and struck a match against the metal frame of the open deck door. The moment the flare lit the end of the cigarette, Mawji spoke to Freeman.

'There's no going back now. You gotta do everything he says if you wanna get out of this in one piece.'

'What does he want with her?'

Freeman looked over at Jeneta and then back at Mawji, who felt exposed with no place to hide.

'She's a present to you...and she's gonna make you just like him.'

'A Kali Jaffa?' Honey exclaimed, looking concerned.

'Hey, not me! I'm no Kali Jaffa.'

He turned to Freeman.

'But he is.'

Freeman sat back down and looked out at the open sea with its small white caps and brilliant horizon.

Mawji let rip.

'How the hell do you think you pulled all this off, it's not just the help he gave you. He's changed you, every single part of you. You just wait and see, you'll be as terrifying as him soon!'

He looked at Jeneta.

'And so will she.'

'And you, what will you be?'

Mawji looked at Honey's face, close to his, and into her asking eyes.

'An angry fisherman.'

Jeneta let out a shrill squeal and for a brief moment, everyone stared at her. Mawji looked across at Freeman, lost in the madness of it all, and laughed.

'You better get used to it. She's touched alright.'

Freeman felt the hard grip on his arm and looked at her looking up at him with her crazy smile. About to ask her what was up, he thought better of it and just watched the rolling sea as they headed to the swamps.

There remained an empty silence on the bridge and no one spoke as the boat moved smoothly through the water a few hundred yards out parallel to the shore. The distant sound of shots became more frequent and the sudden whirr of a passing bullet made Mawji briefly look out to his right at the densely vegetated low green hills before taking the boat further out. By the time the dark sand of the desolate beaches gave way to the mangrove swamps, they were more than a mile out and Mawji turned the boat hard towards the mouth of pump house creek.

The tide was ebbing, creating swirls around the legs of the pumping platform, so he overran the platform and let the strong tide pull the boat back to bump against the rubber mooring tyres.

The gold was still stacked as he had left it and it was with speed and urgency that three of them loaded. Jeneta stared in disbelief at the glinting metal piled up on deck, occasionally prodding it with her foot to check that it was real and not some kind of magic trick.

With Mawji at the helm, they left the platform. The others took the bullion down to the engine room where they stacked it neatly from port to starboard to spread the load. When it was done, Honey swiftly left to join Mawji. Freeman sat down on the gold. He could see the soft golden hue reflected in Jeneta's shiny dark face, wet from work and the heat being thrown out by the motors.

'Is it true?'

She was looking deep into his eyes; and when he focused on her eyes, he could see the gold reflected there too, moving up and down as she rhythmically nodded with the throb of engines and bumpy tide.

'I don't want to be like him,' Freeman glumly mumbled.

'Does the leopard care when it takes the farmer's cow.'

Freeman heard the odd riddle taking him straight back to Jaffa. Before he could assemble any thoughts, she was on him and he was lost, taken by that thing he had felt and feared when alone and lost in the swamps.

UPSTAIRS ON THE HELM, Honey was uneasy.

'What's keeping them?'

'Making out I guess.'

He seemed happy and pulled her close.

'What, down there in that hot smelly place?'

'They got a lot of catching up to do, anyway she don't smell too good herself.'

'You're right there! And they're so weird. What's happened to them?'

'Christ knows what he's done to them, but they're not of this world anymore – that's for sure.'

'We won't become like that will we?'

'No chance of that!'

He put his arm around her waist.

Mawji turned the radio on and they focused on the frequent bulletins between the light and easy music. Within the fifty minutes that it took to be level with the port, they learned that things were far from stable and resistance was fighting back in the north, soon confirmed by the billows of smoke lifting from the port. He had taken the boat far out of range and now slowed the engines to a crawl, taking in the port vista through binoculars.

'They'll fight this out for months.'

'And then what?'

'Nothing, just the usual mess once they all run out of steam.'

'And Joey?'

'It's his country, not ours. He and Jona got more right to it than any of us.'

'But he's not safe.'

'Nope, but he's staying put.'

'We can't leave him there.'

'What you suggesting? Press gang him into service?'

He stopped looking out to the shore, placed the binoculars down and turned to Honey.

'Can you get him? He oughta see this.'

DRENCHED AND DRIPPING IN SWEAT, Freeman lay on the engine room floor staring up at the dirty light bulb swaying with the rocking rhythms of the boat. Jeneta was on him, whispering something in a language he didn't understand. He let out a sigh, expelling the oppressive hot and heavy air whilst trying to fight off the feeling of going blank and back under that relentless spell he had so helped conjure up. But it was useless, and it took him to oblivion.

Waking with a start, the pounding engines vibrating every fibre in his body, he sat bolt-upright pulling Jeneta with him. He felt wet and sticky and the room was full of the smell of them. She clung on, looking right at him, still whispering her mysterious words.

He didn't panic, just stood up and she followed. As he adjusted his clothing, he noticed her naked, still staring and still whispering. Having become used to her strange ways, he was about to leave the room when he noticed that the whispering was familiar, like a song or a prayer he had heard before.

'Say it louder,' he demanded. And she did, her eyes smiling, full of life, as she changed tone from a whisper to a softly spoken lullaby.

'Who taught you that?'

But she just continued weaving her spell, forcing him to snap:

'God damn it Jeneta! Where the hell did you learn that?'

'The ghosts of course,' she laughed.

He didn't have time to react for Honey was at the open door, her hand clasped over her nose and mouth as she speedily exclaimed he was wanted on the bridge, before hurrying back to the clean sea air above.

'God, it smells disgusting down there.'

'Yeah, must be hell alright.'

They were both laughing as Freeman appeared, looking confused and sweaty, only too pleased to be catching the breeze blowing in through the open door.

'Take a look.'

Mawji handed Freeman the binoculars as he stepped out on deck to view the smoking town. The boat was too far out to take a hit but close enough for the fierce firefight to be heard.

Mawji shouted out from behind the wheel.

'Welcome home.'

'There's no place…' Freeman mumbled softly, but no one was listening as Jeneta appeared, still whispering her spell.

'Hope you left the door open. I have to work down there!' Mawji quipped.

'What's she saying?' Honey asked.

'God knows, but one thing's for sure – she's finishing him off good and proper now.'

Unable to concentrate on the skirmish at the port, Freeman slumped down on the bench. Knowing resistance was futile, he closed his eyes, let go and gave in to whatever she was doing to him.

When he woke, the two women were gone. Mawji turned to him.

'They're down below making food, if that's what ya thinking.'

Freeman studied the coastline for a minute. He knew this journey to the city, passing small harbours and long deserted beaches hemmed by the dense jungle that formed a formidable barrier until the outskirts of the city, whose lights would show later that night.

The boat headed south, the evening sun glaring in through the starboard windows.

'Do you know what she was saying?'

Mawji turned away from the shimmering sea, as he cautiously replied:

'Nope, but I heard that language before.'

'Me too, Jane sung a lullaby to a light brown cow,' he muttered to himself.

Mawji hesitated before turning back to the last rays of sunlight reflecting off the swell. He tried to sound casual and indifferent, pulling a cigarette from a pack lying on the console.

'Did she collect the cows she sang to?'

'You know her!'

Mawji didn't look back. Freeman was now on his feet, agitated, wanting any information Mawji had to offer.

'Well?'

Mawji abruptly turned.

'You don't need my help. It's far too late for that.'

'Your help! You only succeeded in nearly killing me.'

'It's your stupidity that nearly killed you.'

'So who the hell is she?'

DOWN BELOW IN THE GALLEY, the two women had finished preparing the meal. They had not spoken but the raised voices above made Honey break the silence.

'Will they fight?'

'They're like brothers who have yet to recognise each other,' Jeneta sniggered.

Honey quickly ascended the stairs with two loaded plates, as Freeman once again demanded:

'Well?'

With the unlit cigarette still in his hand, Mawji faced Freeman in a standoff, but the welcome plates of food seemed to placate both men. Freeman sat back down and Mawji returned to the twilight of the sea where, momentarily distracted, he turned the navigation lights on. Thinking better of it, he flicked the switch back off again.

Ten minutes later, Honey broke the silence.

'Who is she?'

After the flare of a striking match and a long smoky exhalation, the dry reply came back,

'My uncle's wife.'

No one spoke after that.

Twilight gave way to darkness and no lights showed on shore or out to sea. The only illumination came from the instrument panel where Honey watched the small radar for any sign of other boats.

THE DISTANT DIM GLIMMER of city lights slowly appeared on the portside shoreline. Small boats showed on the radar, all anchored safely out at sea. No boat would dare dock under darkness and risk surprising frightened, trigger-happy soldiers. Like Mawji, they would wait for the first rays of light to sail into port.

Freeman woke to the splash of the anchor and the clonking of the running chain before Mawji's dark shape stood before him, handing him a rifle. Until first light, it was Freeman's watch; after which, Mawji would run them both ashore.

Honey followed him down to their cabin. Mawji bolted the door and pulled a loaded rifle from the rack to prop up against the bed before flopping down and falling into a deep and heavy sleep. Honey viewed the sparkle of the starlit sky through the large open portholes as she joined him on the bed, hoping daylight would finally take them far away from the troubles of this place.

On the bridge, Freeman had turned the radio on. Between the chatter and the hi-life, the news told of stability, safety and of a resistance that was doomed. He switched it off and cursed, realising that most things he believed in were a total pack of lies.

Jeneta giggled. He turned and caught her ghostly eyes staring at him. After a long pause, she exclaimed in that crazy strange way of hers:

'Now you know.'

Somehow Freeman did understand that that thing, which was now in him, had changed and transformed him, with almost nothing of his former self, remaining. All that useless doubt and self-delusion which had held him prisoner for so long was gone, left behind in some hellish swamp further back the coast.

Finally, he was free. He started laughing, waking the sleeping couple below.

'We'll be hearing poetry next,' Mawji whispered softly before falling back to sleep.

MUCH LATER, as the inky sky softened and the stars began to fade, the black sea turned sombre grey. Dark shapes of other boats slowly showed until the first rays of sunlight made them whole again. Freeman then examined every last one through binoculars.

Jeneta was down below in the galley and it was the smell of coffee that woke Mawji and Honey. Honey touched Mawji who turned to look at her with dark clear gleaming eyes, his unshaven face partially covered with hair made unruly from his sleep.

'Your uncle…' she started.

She hesitated as she saw him self-consciously looking back at her, instinctively running his fingers through his hair to slick it back into place again, before reluctantly saying:

'My mother's brother, saw him once when I was little, and then…'

He paused and looked up at the thick white shiny paint on the cabin ceiling before quickly continuing.

'…when my folks and sister got killed, he just appeared one morning, out of nowhere. That was strange.'

He turned to face her.

'…but you want to know what the really freaky thing was?'

Honey opened her eyes wide creating frown lines on her forehead as she nodded.

'…that he had hardly changed. He even wore the same ghastly tasteless shirts…'

Once again, he stared upwards. Honey knew better than to stop his flow and remained silent, as he remembered and reflected.

'…wanted me to go with him, but I said no way. What…become like him?'

'Is he Freeman's Kali Jaffa?'

'Reckon so, and once that demented couple step off this boat they'll be stepping into darkness alright. Probably suit them both just fine.'

'She said you were like brothers who didn't know each other yet.'

Mawji seemed shocked at this and laughed loudly.

'Jesus Christ! Welcome to the family!'

With that, he leaped out of bed and headed straight to the engine room.

On the bridge, having eaten breakfast in silence, Mawji radioed the harbourmaster. Not wanting to be the first boat in, he had left it awhile before requesting permission to drop off an important passenger.

Permission was granted and Jaffa followed the line of green flashing buoys alongside the old harbour arm, which was broken and beaten up from years of neglect and relentless battering from the sea, towards the pontoons recessed in the port.

Small naval boats patrolled the harbour entrance and soldiers guarded the coasters and larger ships moored to the main
cargo dock. Mawji slowed the engines to a crawl to come
alongside some floating pontoons where a small party of
armed men had waved him down.

From a holdall he had brought up from below, Mawji
thrust Freeman a bar of gold and a brand new handgun.

'Here, I owe you these.'

Quickly dropping the gun and the gold inside his overalls
to join his precious deeds, he grabbed Jeneta's hand to lead
her off the boat. Freeman then saw her gun bulging in her
trouser pocket. Unable to voice his concern, as the curious
soldiers were now within easy earshot, Freeman hesitated, but
Honey was already tying the oilskin jacket around Jeneta's
waist as Mawji bumped the boat against the pontoon.
Moments later, the couple dropped down to the shaky
pontoon with a wobble and a thud.

Mawji didn't look or wait for instructions, just reversed
and turned, heading for the open sea, whispering to Honey
not to look back and give any cause for concern. These were
dangerous times and a boat a very valuable commodity.

Freeman had recognised the need for Mawji to make haste
and no sooner had his feet touched down was he producing
Malo, creating great excitement, confusion and of course
distraction. He turned and glanced at Jaffa heading back
towards the harbour entrance, as the officer in front of him
nervously examined his passport. He was speechless and
proudly saluted Malo who now spoke rapidly in French, saying
all the stupid things he was meant to say to the officer before
excusing himself to find a hotel and some decent clothes
before reporting to the city police.

With that, he walked away.

No one seemed to consider Jeneta as she closely followed him along the rickety pontoon, up the steps of the harbour wall into the port and on towards the city centre.

She had tried to hang onto him but he shook her off saying Malo could have a companion but she couldn't touch him here in public.

It was early and the streets deserted except for a few soldiers who totally ignored them due to the colour of his skin. He was pleased about that, as he didn't want to draw any more attention to himself, which would inevitably identify him as Malo the hero to those in charge, or Malo the assassin to those waiting in the shadows.

Tall palms stood proud in the avenues, their dusty fronds catching the morning light, reminding Freeman that this had once been an elegant place; but a split and shot up trunk ahead soon revealed the truth.

Not wanting to lament, he wasted no time and headed straight for the bank, knowing that although it would still be shut to the public it would be open for its staff. Passing the Grand Hotel where he had stayed just a week earlier, he quickly eyed its decaying facade before hurrying on, not wanting to be reminded of his last days with Ralph.

The bank had been well maintained, showing neat and clean against the decay and neglect of all the other nearby buildings. Looking completely out of place and time, it stood a few doors down from the Grand Hotel on a corner overlooking a small crater pocked square. A guard stood outside the closed heavy polished wooden doors. He wasn't visibly armed and seemed reluctant to engage with Freeman who was facing the door and looking straight at him. The guard mumbled that the bank was closed to the public until sometime later on. Freeman knew this man would run at the first hint of trouble so he placed his hand inside his pocket and blatantly toyed with the gun.

'I have an appointment.'

Immediately pulling the doors wide open, the guard let the couple in. No sooner had they entered the expansive hall, he shut the door behind them with a bang.

The noise startled the staff behind a long counter protected by a row of heavy black metal bars. In the strange silence that follows a loud and unexpected noise, they froze and stared before continuing their preparations for the working day.

Another guard sat on a wooden chair, his rifle leaning against a nearby wall, conveniently out of reach and mind and he simply pretended Freeman and Jeneta weren't there, even when Freeman boomed:

'Where's the manager.'

A man appeared from an office at the back of the large hall and introduced himself. When Freeman told his name and produced the deeds from inside his overalls, a reply parried back:

'I've been expecting you.'

He gestured to the office and handed Freeman an envelope. Freeman stopped, turned his back and ripped it open. It was his passport. Relieved, he quickly stuffed it in a pocket before turning around and entering a large room, handing over his deeds.

The papers to sell his swamp and drilling rights were ready and waiting. It was a long drawn out and boring affair of reading, checking, signing in triplicate, witnessing and sealing until the transfer was done. The land had been split in two: his farm, which it appeared he was keeping, and the swamp below the escarpment, which included platform creek, the black shells and much more. In the tedium of reading through the documents, the manager asked for Freeman's passport and he almost handed over Malo by mistake. He knew he would have to shake that burden before the day was out.

Before the seal was stamped into place, the manager made a call. He then asked Freeman if all was in order. Freeman nodded without looking up. He was selling to some trust based in Zurich for a sum he couldn't quite believe. He kept staring at the numbers until the thud of the seal brought him back to face the manager who was passing him his copy, saying the money was already in his Swiss account. He pushed the phone towards Freeman, but Freeman shook his head. He didn't need confirmation about the money. He knew it would be there. He needed Jaffa and asked the operator to call the Parisian number. The call remained unanswered and he despondently placed the hand piece down.

It was done. Even if the money never materialised in his account it didn't seem to matter, as all he felt now was a pressing need to leave the country. That seemed simple enough, but to take Jeneta with him was tricky and something he had been mulling over ever since he had found her at the farm, wasted and worn out from her journey south to seek him out. The risk was enormous and she seemed to sense his difficulty as they stood at the door of the manager's office, Freeman shaking his hand, saying nonsense like what a pleasure it had been.

Although he had asked her not to, she held on tightly to his arm. As her grip released his tension, he relaxed and let the gold bar slip. Sliding out of his overall trouser leg, it thudded on the floor.

All three of them looked down and the manager smiled for the first time, exclaiming:

'You have laid a golden egg!'

'And what's the going rate for such a rare and exquisite, fresh laid beauty?'

It was mid morning by the time they left the bank with the land sale contract and a large amount of French francs stuffed tight into a carry bag. The day was hot, the bright sunlight making them seek shade as they headed to a modern hotel where Freeman hoped hired men would be and somewhere they would be temporarily safe.

He was right. Behind the reception was a cocktail lounge with sleepy half-drunk men propping up the bar, their guns close to hand. Out in the garden, he could see more men, some asleep on the neat short grass.

There was no fuss with checking in and soon they were upstairs in a room overlooking the garden where a perplexed gardener stood still, holding the end of a watering hose, not daring to turn it on and risk sprinkling the sleeping demons on the lawn. Freeman laughed out of the open window making the gardener turn, look up, drop the hose and walk away and out of sight.

The funny moment was short lived as Jeneta, standing next to him and also looking down into the garden, half shut the window, saying:

'It's nearly closed.'

Knowing she was right and that her window of opportunity was closing fast, he dropped the two guns, Malo and his own passport into the carry bag of cash and hid it under the bed.

With no time to tidy up, he knew they looked a mess, but this was war and how could they look any different. He hurried out of the hotel and down the street as Jeneta held on tight. He didn't stop her this time, as they passed soldiers on patrol and locals feeling brave enough to venture out. They didn't speak until they stopped outside the embassy.

'You have the identity card?'

She nodded and he took her to the main door where some armed French guards frisked him, glaring disapprovingly at Jeneta, before allowing them into the building.

At the bottom of a grand sweeping staircase where a huge chandelier hung above the reception room, he and Jeneta sat waiting in silence. There was nothing to say. Everything now rested on a hunch he had, a wild card he had no choice but play.

Summoned to an office, they ascended the majestic staircase.

A guard was at the door and another inside along with the ambassador and an official. Everyone was French and no one was smiling.

Freeman had already handed over Jeneta's identity card to the official downstairs and they knew exactly what he wanted.

The ambassador spoke.

'We don't issue passports to locals, even if one parent is French.'

He looked at Jeneta and then continued.

'Anyway she's not local and I am guessing the ID's fraudulent. Anything else I can help you with?'

Freeman handed Ralph's passport to the ambassador. He studied it, lost deep in thought, before looking up.

'He's not the problem. We have his body. It's the other man everyone is after.'

'Even you?'

The ambassador knew the game Freeman was flirting with and answered back:

'A real embarrassment for France, this is the second time he's shot a president.'

'Maybe he works for the government.'

'I doubt it. His passport's a Legion issue, been missing for years until he surfaced...'

He didn't finish and, while holding up Ralph's passport, asked:

'Where did you get this?'

'Found it on a dead man.'

'And you are?'

'Henri de la Mer.'

'How amusing, I could have you arrested.'

'No you can't. I'm local not French. I don't even have a passport.'

The ambassador nodded to the guard who was soon going through Freeman's pockets and on finding nothing, shook his head.

'Then why does she want one?'

'She's Ralph's sister.'

'One last time, what do you want before I throw you out?'

'A passport in exchange for Malo.'

There was silence and Freeman quickly added:

'What have you got to lose?'

'Nothing, if you are telling the truth.'

'I'll meet you at the Metropolitan in two hours. You have the passport and I'll have Malo. No Malo, no passport – deal?'

The ambassador looked at the official and impassively ordered Jeneta's passport, dismissing Freeman with a curt wave.

It took only a few minutes for Jeneta to have her photo taken downstairs and then they left as quickly as they could. Freeman knew this wasn't over and expected some kind of double cross was yet to come.

BACK IN THE HOTEL ROOM, he put Mawji's gun in his pocket and handed Jeneta's back to her. With the carry bag, they headed down to the hotel restaurant where Freeman looked around. On spotting an officer, they went and sat nearby.

After ordering food, Freeman got talking. The officer was sober and so were his two companions. They were a mix of races, and none of them French. He told them he had been fighting up north but as he didn't have the time or patience to concoct a story, he just put a large amount of money on the table and asked for their protection. He knew there had been no time for any law and order and, at that moment, these men with their most effective guns and total disregard for others' lives, ruled supreme.

The money quickly disappeared.

Quickly explaining that some men would be arriving soon, Freeman asked the hired men to make very clear who it was in charge. The men shrugged. They didn't care.

Through the net curtain of the hotel restaurant where they sat, Freeman noticed a white car with two men inside parked on the opposite side of the street. He wondered if they were French secret service and requested the hired men to see them off straight after the exchange of passports had been made. It was to Freeman's surprise that the embassy staff had come early, not the ambassador, he would never get hands this dirty, but the official and three guards, armed and looking trouble-some.

Freeman saw them hurrying up the street, but before they were even inside the hotel lobby, the three hired men were up, aggressive, their weapons ready, revealing the mean despera-dos they really were.

There was a brief standoff where nothing happened. Eve-ryone was still and silent and before Freeman could speak, he heard the click of an automatic weapon. He didn't know who had done it, but there it was – that noise which woke every drunken hired hand. In moments, the restaurant and reception lobby filled up with nervous, panicked-looking men not needing much reason to squeeze their triggers. The embassy guards dropped their weapons and raised their hands.

Wasting no time, Freeman took the passport from the frightened official, flicking through it to make sure it was genuine. Satisfied, he handed it to Jeneta. Keeping his part of the bargain, he pulled Malo from the bottom of the bag and handed him over. The official tried to hide his shock as he glanced at the passport photo before looking for the entry stamp of Malo's first assassination. On finding it, he nodded sheepishly. Sneering, Freeman told the hired men to disarm and collect the two men from the car outside.

Producing some more cash, he encouraged the hired men to have a drink on him and to make sure that their embassy guests didn't leave the hotel until sometime after midnight, preferably intoxicated. A cheer went up and the French contingent was rudely pushed into the lounge. As the high jinks started, a shot rang out, the chaos of the men unleashed.

Without further ado, Freeman grabbed Jeneta and headed out the door to the white car. The keys were still in the ignition.

The day had been relentlessly fraught ever since they had jumped off the boat onto the wobbly pontoon and now, as he drove to the airport leaving his whole world behind, he knew the door was closing tight behind him.

'You know we never paid the hotel bill.'

'You're paying for it at the bar.'

Freeman nervously laughed at Jeneta's astuteness before she asked:

'Where are we going?'

'France. You're French now.'

'What does that mean?'

'It means you're complicated,' he chuckled.

Jeneta still had the passport in her hand and briefly flicked through it.

'A small book to tell me who I am, that's not complicated – it's stupid.'

Freeman laughed again.

'You're right. I was so stupid I had to have two!'

The late afternoon sun was low and harsh, forcing Freeman to pull the sun blind down so he could clearly focus on the road ahead and watch the gates of the airport come closer until he was pulling up in the small dirt car park outside departures. They left the guns in the glove compartment and entered the busy airport. He could see through to arrivals and the endless stream of families returning home, laden down with baggage.

Getting a ticket for the next flight out was easy, but he didn't dare risk France. What if the embassy staff had managed to walk away sober from the hotel and put out an alert for anyone arriving from this place? Better to fly elsewhere and enter France by road.

Having bought two first class tickets to Zurich, which he found fitting and amusing, they sat in the upmarket departure lounge nervously waiting for their plane. Freeman was acutely aware that he was still the wanted face for two high profile assassinations and wouldn't feel secure until touching down in Zurich. Jeneta was just nervous of flying in the sky. He had figured Jeneta's passport was safe as the ambassador now had Malo and wouldn't want to show his dirty shameful dealings of how things had transgressed. Maybe in the morning, Malo's body would be conveniently found, floating in the harbour by a member of the embassy staff. Freeman didn't dare that risk; best assume he was still a wanted man.

Zurich, 3rd September 1968

JENETA HAD GRIPPED his hand hard during take-off, her wet palm not easing tension until the ground was lost from view below the clouds.

'How can it be possible to be above the clouds? Can we follow the setting sun to the other side of midnight?'

Freeman had no answers to these questions as they watched the orange glow of sunset blaze the clouds below them to the west.

He fell asleep and dreamt of darkness while Jeneta hummed a lullaby, herself drifting off to talk with ghosts both old and new.

Waking to her damp grip as the plane bumped on the runway, he viewed the terminal building getting closer until they jerked to a stop outside its drab facade. It was late summer now and the early morning sky reluctant to let go the night. He sleepily looked out onto the grey light of a European dawn.

There was no issue going through customs, except he had to show what was in his carry bag, but this was Switzerland and even ten carry bags full of cash it wouldn't have raised a brow.

It was a few hundred miles to Lyon-Bron where he hoped his car would still be parked. From there, it would be a long drive on winding roads to get back to his Bayonne apartment.

Freeman had no idea if he should be going back to Bayonne, but it was somewhere he knew, somewhere safe and maybe Jaffa was still around to offer some solution to his empty stateless self.

He eventually found a taxi willing to drive them across the border for an outrageous sum and, after the driver had picked up his own passport, they sped off in the direction of Lake Geneva in the haze of the late summer morning.

Jeneta stared around at the new landscape from the back seat where she sat close to Freeman, as he puzzled at their predicament. Occasionally, she turned and smiled when something really caught her eye. Smiling back, he knew that behind every newfound feature would be the straight jacket of a dull European life. He wondered how either of them could ever make it back or find another way. He had managed well before because he had had the dream of home. Without that dream, he now imagined forever fishing the empty sea of an endless lonely shore.

He drifted in and out of sleep with the gentle movements of the car. He dreamt of ocean waves until Jeneta nudged him, pointing to the tranquil lake, it's soft light blue glistening with the sun.

Soon they were in France. Only when he had paid the driver off at Lyon-Bron did he feel safe and free from the madness of last week. Finally relaxing, he beamed a smile.

'Welcome to France.'

Seeing the Mustang, he was relieved he had taken the unwitting precaution that he may be coming back. The keys were still be hidden in the wheel arch.

They ate at the airport, a long lunch with little conversation. Jeneta had asked if they were taking another plane and was relieved when he said no, that they would drive the car with the top pulled down so they could feel the wind and maybe catch the scent of Africa afar. She had laughed, knowing his tease was aimed at himself as much as it was her.

He drove slowly back, the warm air softly rushing over them. He spoke about everything, from the moment he had found his murdered parents, to that fateful day fishing the mouth of the Ardour where he had met a Kali Jaffa (a meeting that had somehow been orchestrated long before he had ever fished the lonely Bayonne shore at dawn) and of all the crazy things that had happened until they had met in the hotel, and then of how he had really shot a president and of Ralph's demise.

It was a long story. He paused when he came to Mawji and she helped him with his confusion.

'He's like you, not wanting to see what he really is.'

'A Kali Jaffa?'

'No, the morning star or sparkle on an ocean wave.'

Freeman turned, glancing at her profile, wondering at her words before turning back to watch the endless road ahead. Not wanting to voice his thought, he held onto his breath, but soon exhaled, trying to lose the word in the sound of rushing air.

'Light.'

'And you the dark.'

He didn't like that one bit and said nothing, but she drove the point home.

'You are brothers now.'

'And you? What are you Jeneta?'

'Yours.'

'God damn it! Do I have a choice in any of this?'

'It's been your choice. Why, do you feel bad?' She giggled.

'I don't want to be like him, that's all,' Freeman complained, reflecting for a moment before carrying on:

'I'm wanted for two assassinations, nearly got killed a hundred times, my best friend's dead, I've lost my home and on top of that I'm cursed with some kind of hocus-pocus voodoo spell. I feel fine, but you tell what's fine about all of that?'

'You feel fine because it suits you.'

He knew she was right, it had suited him, it had been exciting, right and he had survived.

'Then why am I so bloody mixed up with it?'

'Because until you are transformed there can only be confusion.'

'Oh that's just great! All messed up until I change into some barking mad Kali Jaffa. What about you?'

'I'm Osu. There's nothing to transform.'

Freeman, laughing nervously at the absurdity of it all, put his foot down hard to race towards a devil he hoped would still be waiting in the green hills of the Pyrenees.

THE FLAMING SUN was low and dead in front, as they entered the outskirts of Bayonne. Jeneta had fallen asleep, her head flopping against Freeman's shoulder, rolling back and forth every time he shifted gear.

Even after the long drive open to the air, it was comfortably warm and he felt no chill. However, soon after leaving Lyon-Bron, Jeneta had put on the oilskin jacket, as she had only ever known the never changing tropic heat.

He woke her with a nudge and she looked straight into the setting sun, mumbling:

'Are we home?'

'I hope not.'

He laughed at himself as she looked around at the last of the season's tourists, relaxed, well fed and staring at the odd couple in their expensive open car. He voiced her thoughts before she had a chance:

'They think they've seen a ghost.'

'Do I look so strange?'

'A rare bird,' he quipped, remembering Jaffa's words.

A moment later, he drove through the arch into the courtyard, stopping in front of the faded Basque graffiti wall.

'I live upstairs.'

The shop was closed. He was pleased about that – explaining another woman to Eve, especially Jeneta, wasn't something he wanted to deal with right then. It could wait, or better still, he would never have to.

The oak door opened and the musty air of the dark lobby wafted out; Freeman felt he had broken the seal to an ancient tomb. They stepped inside and he slammed the door shut, waiting until their eyes adjusted to the dreary light. He viewed his fishing rod and gear stashed in the recess underneath the stairs, full of dust and cobwebs, and at the empty space where his bicycle had stood.

It all seemed such an age away.

In the apartment, he opened the windows on both sides to let the air blow gently through before going to the bathroom. He had a shower and a shave, the mirror reflecting him thin and gaunt with burning wild eyes. Disturbed by the image, he did what habit told him. Putting on a stylish shirt, he spruced up as best he could to give some semblance of being back and being him. He looked again. No longer recognising the man staring back, he knew he would have to seal the tomb back up again. Being lost had become a natural state for him.

Jeneta had knelt on the bed, leaning against the windowsill to look down the street with its pretty painted houses, until darkness took it all away. It was only then that Freeman came back into the room, knowing that his Bayonne days were bygone days and that he needed to hang on for whatever came up next. He hoped it would be soon.

Jeneta used the bathroom. When returning to the room, she saw Freeman take the original handgun Jaffa had given him from the drawer and place it in his jacket pocket. She asked if they were expecting trouble. He answered that that stuff was probably over but he dared not take the risk.

He handed her a shawl that Rebecca had left behind, for the night may have a chill. It was much more elegant than the oilskin, but before they had taken even a dozen steps outside the door, she smelt it and threw it to the ground, saying she wouldn't wear his ex girl's things. Freeman stopped to ponder sadly Rebecca's disregarded state but Jeneta pulled him on so he could take the lead to the cafés by the Nive.

It had started as a dull and uneventful evening. Having eaten, they were sitting in silence at an outside table, watching the passersby. In the cool night air, Jeneta shivered and Freeman absent-mindedly passed his jacket over. She wrapped it round her skinny frame and felt the heavy pocket. Pulling the gun, she placed it on the table. Panicking, Freeman grabbed it, placing it back from where it came and started to explain the rules of this civilised and most proper place.

She was French now, but he stopped himself from saying more. Then, half-laughing and half-complaining, he asked:

'What are we going to do?'

Only a soft and subtle breeze blew back and she softly spoke:

'You have to follow it.'

He tried to sense its message.

'To where? The wind forever changes direction.'

'Not the wind, the whisper. It whispers to you, not me.'

'But I can't hear a thing.'

'Not tonight, but maybe soon you will.'

'Did the ghosts tell you that too?'

'I'm Osu.'

'La Font.'

'La Freeman.'

She laughed mockingly and he laughed out of some slight panic that hid the truth.

THE CRASS OPULENCE of Biarritz lay to his left as he stood high up on the rocky crag by the old lighthouse, sweeping his eyes down and across the sandy beach to the Virgin's rock on the far side. The wind was blowing hard from the sea and had driven most tourists back into the tightly packed narrow streets of the main town for relief against flying sand and salty spray.

Listening to the powerful thuds of the surf crashing heavily down onto the wet sand, Freeman glanced over to the casino near the far end of the beach, remembering different days. Biarritz now left him empty and he no longer found any joy from the decadence of its shoreline. He missed the uncomplicated simplicity of home and, as he turned away from the picture-perfect view, felt the faded echoes of his longing heart rise up with every footstep to the car.

Their sojourn of the previous evening to the Nive had been short. Soon after the gun fiasco, they had headed back to the apartment to sleep like tired dogs until the noise of morning traffic and people chatting in the shop below became too much, forcing them to rise a little before midday. They had enjoyed their close entwined and lazy time in bed and, as he looked at Jeneta lying there, staring up and smiling at him, he knew there was never any going back again. Freeman was gone. Long live his new found self.

After going to the bank and checking that the cash had really been deposited, they had headed for Biarritz so Jeneta could buy some stylish clothes or rather clothes that Freeman felt would help her blend and mix, to keep the stares and curiosity to a minimum.

She had waited by the car as he went up to the lighthouse. He threw the khaki green shorts, now recognisable only as a ripped up faded rag, into the swirling surf as it crashed over the jagged rocks below. They were spent and useless, as he now had her by his side. By the time he had joined her by the Mustang, the empty pool in his heart was still and silent, the lonely echoes gone for good. He wanted to say something most profound, but couldn't. The sight of her all dressed up as a Biarritz doll made him burst out laughing. She laughed too, punching him on the arm hard, exclaiming:

'I can't live here!'

As Freeman fired up the engine and drove slowly through the narrow crowded streets, Jeneta took off her expensive fashionable dress and uncomfortable modern shoes and threw them out the window, much to the amusement of people strolling by. She replaced them with Honey's baggy slacks, the now grimy white shirt and tight canvas shoes, which had split and showed her toes.

Moments later, the rest of the recent-purchased clothing spewed out the car to litter the cobbled stone streets. Freeman chuckled, knowing he was heading into Bayonne town to let her loose to buy the things she liked, not what he thought she ought to wear. It was some time later, as he sat outside a café near the main open square, catching the pleasant rays of the afternoon sun, that she appeared with a bag loaded full of suitable Jeneta attire. She sat down opposite him, still wearing Honey's clothes. Her large golden-hooped earrings, which had been lost in the swamps, were now replaced, catching the sunlight, shining bright against her skin and afro hair.

There was nothing left to do and only one place left to go. She knew that too and understood when he said they should leave while the light was good so she could see the pretty landscape he had mentioned in the long tale he had told on the way back from Lyon-Bron.

Listening to the rush of air, the drive along the Nive to the crunchy gravel drive was slow and pleasant. It helped to wash away the memory of the last time he drove this way with

Ralph. For Jeneta it made his story real as they closed in on the inevitable conclusion.

Across the closed gate, they could see the movements of the swing lounger, half-hidden behind the foliage of the black cherry tree and heard the murmurs of a soft and quiet conversation. Close to the gate in the grassy garden stood the three cows staring straight at them, as if they had been waiting for Freeman and Jeneta to arrive.

The gate clanged shut behind them and, as they moved into the garden, the murmurs stopped and someone jumped off the swinging lounger, making Freeman urgently pull his gun and point it straight at the shape of a man reaching for his own handgun sitting on the wooden table.

It was Luk, but he stopped dead before he had had a chance to pick it up. Freeman was fast, not smiling and ruthlessly asked:

'Expecting someone?'

Luk shrugged as he had in that dark bar in Africa and sat back down to swing. Elsa was by his side.

Freeman put his gun away and asked again:

'Well?'

'It's never safe here being Basque and Jaffa said nothing of your return.'

'That's because you and I have no business since you shot Marcel Malo.'

'But he's been busy yet again.'

Luk indicated to the daily newspaper lying open on the table. Freeman saw a picture of a man called Marcel Malo who had been shot trying to escape the French secret service in the city of his homeland. He was from Algiers and had been a Legionnaire before hiring himself out to whoever had the funds. The article was short, as the assassination of a petty despot was of no concern to the outside world. Because Malo was French, the French had to show they had cleaned up this dirty and embarrassing mess.

'Never heard of him,' Freeman scoffed.

He looked at Elsa, but she was looking at Jeneta who threw Freeman a dirty glance as she asked:

'Is that her?'

'Jeneta meet Elsa. Elsa, this is Jeneta,' Freeman said, changing into English.

Jeneta sneered. Freeman, not wanting to explain to Elsa that he had told Jeneta everything, picked up Luk's gun so it was out of her reach, and handed it to him. Luk grabbed the gun as the lounger swung by, smiling as if he knew that Jeneta was probably capable of anything.

'So where is he?'

Luk shrugged and nonchalantly remarked:

'Who knows, sailing out the way they came to who knows where.'

Freeman remembered the Basques joking that Jaffa had sailed up the Nive, then he remembered their laughter about Luk's wife and he looked at Elsa again who was smiling for she saw Freeman's confusion written on his face.

'We live here now. They gave us the house so long as we look after the cows.'

Freeman quickly barked back at Elsa:

'Tell me where he went.'

'He sailed up the Ardour to where it meets the Nive, my friends told you that, and later kept the boat down at Saint Jean de Luz, right opposite where the café is. My guess is that he's sailed back out by now,' Luk answered.

Freeman's perplexed face told Luk to carry on and not tempt Freeman's temper.

'We loaded up the boat with arms. Jane's going to drop them off to...' Luk shrugged. '...somewhere. We don't know any more than you.' He paused, seeing Freeman confused, wanting for answers. 'How we didn't all get killed is a miracle and nothing less than sorcery, but he's gone for good now.'

'You've missed them Freeman. You always were a bit late with everything,' Elsa teased.

Luk briefly laughed, but it was short lived as Jeneta was suddenly on her, screaming and trying to strangle the life out of Elsa who fought back cursing racist slurs and, as Luk tried to intervene, they all fell off the swing in one big noisy clump. Freeman wanted to laugh but instead he let a shot fly out, as it was the easiest yet most unsubtle way to break it up.

Jeneta stopped her fight and Luk looked up at Freeman and then towards the gate with a worried frown.

'You're too dangerous to have around here, Jaffa's gone and with him all our forays overseas. We have our own campaign now.'

Jeneta stood up and Freeman knowingly nodded to Luk before promptly leaving the property, pulling Jeneta with him.

'I'm with you and don't have to be having any other girls...any in the past are past,' he stated firmly as they drove off into the late afternoon towards the main road.

'That's the deal,' remembering Rebecca's words.

'I can't live here.'

'Nor can I, it seems.'

Slowing to join the main road, he turned to look at Jeneta. She was laughing, making him feel dumb and idiotic.

'If you had listened to the breeze you would never have had to visit that place.'

'But I couldn't hear its whisper.'

'Hear it now.'

'Can you?'

'I know the breeze is speaking.'

Freeman listened, heard nothing except the rushing wind but knew exactly where to head. Jeneta laughed some more.

'Trust it. It is for you to follow, not me.'

They remained in silence until pulling up outside the quay-side café in Saint Jean de Luz where the café owner greeted Freeman with a wave, pointing to the sailboats anchored in the middle of the harbour.

Freeman led Jeneta along the pontoons, out to the farthest point. Near to where they stood sat a large expensive looking yacht, the type of boat that could weather the roughest seas.

Anchored ten yards out, the bow faced the harbour en-trance. As Freeman studied the starboard side, he saw Jane and Jaffa staring back at him.

Bewildered and lost for words, he turned to Jeneta. Before she could say a word, Jaffa spoke:

'Are you lost?'

'Completely,' Freeman parried back.

'I suggest a long cool beer with your feet up for a month or two before following the lure of a tantalising ocean breeze.'

'Is that where you're going?'

'A free man would know the answer to such a simple thing.'

'To where the poet's whisper mingles with the endless singing breeze?'

'Exactly Freeman, exactly.'

'Take me with you. I can't stay here.'

'You had enough to buy a boat and now you have enough to buy a brand new life. It's waiting for you, out there, where you cast your line far from the lonely shore of dawn.'

'I cast for home, but that's all ruined. Lost and gone for good.'

'But you were never catching it, merely wishing it to be there once again.'

'Why didn't you tell me you wanted The Black Shells?'

'People rarely do as they are asked and if they do, they aren't the type to shoot a president for some Kali Jaffa, mumbo jumbo voodoo spell.'

Freeman smirked at the similar words he had used himself.

'You needed to believe home was in your reach,' Jane added.

'It was and I had it back, except only ghosts live there now.'

'Be careful what you wish for, Freeman.'

Freeman heard the rattle of the anchor chain as Jane started the motor to get them to the harbour mouth. In a last moment of desperation, Freeman pleaded to Jaffa:

'Give me something. Even Mawji seemed to have some idea of where to go.'

'At the edge of the world, near where the dragons live and the sun wakes up, there's a land with a wild north coast. Fringed with desert and the green of crocodile infested swamps, you could buy a house, do some fishing, farm some cows and feel quite at home with your new found friend – and wait until the whisper pulls you out to sea one very dark and silent night again.'

The boat steered towards the harbour entrance and Freeman watched it meld with the sun setting over the Bay of Biscay. No one was looking back as Jeneta started whispering the strange words she had used on Mawji's boat.

'What's he done to me?'

'Saved you.'

Feeling the warmth of darkness fill his empty heart, he turned to see her gleaming eyes and mysterious wide smile. Turning again, he watched the fierce red glare giving up the day and heard the words he knew were true.

'Jaques La Jaffa, take me where the whisper meets the breeze.'

'We need to buy a boat first,' Freeman chuckled.

MEANWHILE, far away across a continent, Jaffa headed south along a deserted green clad shore as the sun dipped down over the horizon far to the starboard side. Honey sat on deck at the apex of the bow looking back at Mawji steering at the helm. She was wearing a dress and Mawji shouted out:

'Are you trying to get me overboard again?'

Honey laughed and boomed back over the noise of engine and rushing surf:

'What is it with you?'

As the last of the sun sparkled on the ocean waves, she added:

'It's Honey and gold all the way now.'

'Is that a threat?'

'A promise with every new and sun drenched breaking day.'

'Poetry! We're in for one hell of a ride!'

Thank you for reading!

If you enjoyed this, maybe you will like other books by Ben Gilbert:

The World Peace Journals – This is the true story of World Peace Trekking – a Nepalese Trekking Agency that the author owned and ran. It documents a Nepal not spoken or written about in other travel or adventure stories – not sparing the reader from harsh realities, corruption and madness; a sojourn into the Himalayas that succinctly captures the myths, history, geography and people in a way that shocks but also brilliantly entertains.

Mumbo Jumbo – A diverse collection of imaginative short stories and travel journals.

www.ingramcontent.com/pod-product-compliance
Lightning Source LLC
Chambersburg PA
CBHW030406180626
46812CB00005B/1950